STRANGERS'
KINGDOM

Brandon Barrows

Black Rose Writing | Texas

First printing

This is a work of fiction. Names, characters, businesses, places, events, and incidents are either the products of the author's imagination or used in a fictitious manner. Any resemblance to actual persons, living or dead, or actual events is purely coincidental.

ISBN: 978-1-68433-743-9
PUBLISHED BY BLACK ROSE WRITING
www.blackrosewriting.com

Printed in the United States of America
Suggested Retail Price (SRP) $19.95

Strangers' Kingdom is printed in Garamond

*As a planet-friendly publisher, Black Rose Writing does its best to eliminate unnecessary waste to reduce paper usage and energy costs, while never compromising the reading experience. As a result, the final word count vs. page count may not meet common expectations.

"Je me souviens." (I remember.)
–Provincial motto of Quebec.

• • •

For everyone who is doing the best they can.

The Northeast Kingdom is a three-county area in the northeastern corner of Vermont, bordering both New Hampshire to the east and Quebec to the north. One of the most rural regions in the state, it has nevertheless been a gateway between the United States and Canada for centuries.

Vermonters typically refer to it simply as "The Kingdom".

STRANGERS'
KINGDOM

PROLOGUE

May 1992

The tall bag of bones swung a vicious right that seemed to whistle in the stillness of the thin night air, scraping through the empty space between my chin and throat, just barely avoiding contact with flesh. Seemingly in the same motion, as if using the momentum from his swinging fist, he turned and dashed off into the dim recesses of the alley he'd been hanging around the mouth of – for hours, if Rosalie Stompanato was to be believed. I had no reason to doubt her.

"Police! Get back here!" Shouting was pointless, but I had to try. I gave chase to the already-vanished figure, plunging after him into the deeper darkness between two aging apartment houses. My fist, which I only then realized I was making, unclenched and I reached for the holster under my left shoulder, muttering, "God damn it."

It was pushing midnight and in just over nine hours, both Rosalie Stompanato and I were due in court for the attempted murder trial of her mid-level racketeer husband, Thomas "Tommy Stomper" Stompanato. Stompanato, loosely connected to the much larger Castella crime organization, had been on a lot of people's radars for years, for everything from small-time protection rackets to credit card scams and money laundering for bigger outfits. Major investigations by Albany city police, New York state police and even federal authorities produced charges and convictions against numerous Stompanato pawns, and even a couple of lieutenants, but Tommy Stomper himself somehow always remained clean enough to skate away. It took a domestic situation, a middle of the night, literal knock-down-drag-out in which he pulled Mrs. Stompanato out of their lavish home in suburban Malta and, according to witnesses and Rosalie herself, tried to remove her teeth with the aid of a conveniently placed curb. "Stomper" wasn't just a clever play on his family name.

When I got the tip about a disturbance at the Stompanato residence from a state-trooper friend, I couldn't help being just a bit grateful for this bit of rage-fueled stupidity. The man had been so clever for so long that it looked like he'd never fuck up, that we'd never find the crack that would pull open his operation and let us drag him out into the light. For Rosalie Stompanato, it was a nightmare, but a lot of us who were after her husband felt gratitude and guilt in equal measures. One woman's nightmare was a godsend for multiple agencies.

After the incident, Rosalie Stompanato moved out of her stylish home in nearby Malta to a small apartment in the area where she grew up, inside the city proper. Family and friends she knew there were long gone, but the return to a familiar place apparently brought a measure of comfort. It was understandable and it made both the county prosecutor's work in prepping her for the trial, and my department's in protecting her, that much easier. Despite the charges against him, not to mention his associations, Stompanato made bail and his organization worked on. With a trial looming over his head, but no date set, the mobster seemed to keep his nose relatively clean, knowing the state's attorney would be more than happy to tack additional charges onto the list he was already facing. That and time, as weeks became months, allowed Rosalie Stompanato to make a life for herself unmolested.

"At least the kids are already grown and out on their own," Rosalie told me once, in a private moment. "If this happened ten years ago…" She broke down without finishing, but I knew what she was thinking.

I kept in regular touch with her after that, partially because I felt she needed the support, but also hoping to pick up something that would further widen the chink in Tommy Stomper's armor. She seemed to be doing as well as could be expected. She was even starting to feel safe again, she told me – until the night before the trial finally began.

It was past eleven o'clock when I received the woman's call; I'd given her my home number and told her to call any time, for any reason. She noticed a figure, she said – a tall, gangly man she didn't remember ever seeing in the neighborhood before, who spent hours standing in the mouth of the alley directly across from her apartment.

"It's probably nothing," I told her, as much to convince myself. Tommy Stomper proved he wasn't stupid, but with so much riding on the events of the next day, maybe he was becoming desperate. "But I'm happy to check it out."

When I arrived on Rosalie's street, fifteen minutes after her call, I saw exactly who she was worried about and exactly why. He stood just outside the circle of light cast by a streetlamp, hanging around the mouth of an alley. I watched for a few minutes and he did nothing at all – not so much as light a cigarette, shuffle his feet or cough. He wasn't worried about being seen.

I exited the vehicle and approached.

Closer up, I could see he was a sickly thin young man, skin so pale it almost seemed to glow in the dimness. He wore a faded blue hooded sweatshirt that hung from him like laundry on a line and his hair was short, mussed and unwashed, making it look like blond barbed wire. I'd have bet his diet consisted largely of amphetamines.

The guy's eyes, watchful and wary, scanned me as I approached. I flashed my badge and said, "Evening." That was all it took. Those animal-alert eyes went wide and his fist swung out in an arc and then he was gone, rabbiting towards the nearest hole.

My feet pounded the pavement, echoing sharply in the narrow, trash-strewn space, all senses searching for signs of the danger I was rushing headlong into. Light beckoned from a short distance and after a moment, I burst out into the next street. Even the soft yellow glow of sodium lamps seemed brilliant after the pitch-dark of the alley and, as my eyes adjusted, I turned left then right, spotting a figure disappearing around the corner. I followed, telling myself I was being stupid, telling myself I should go back to Rosalie Stompanato's, make sure she was all right, call it in, ask for additional officers, all while my feet took me closer to where I saw that retreating form.

I turned the corner, saw a flash duck around yet another corner. At the mouth of the alley, I allowed myself an instant's rest before entering. Even from the street, it was clear this was a dead-end. There was nothing but darkness down this brick corridor – the alley was blocked up midway down.

I drew my weapon, fumbled in my coat pocket for my penlight, flicked it on, then aimed it and the weapon down the length of the alley, sweeping the narrow width of the space.

"C'mon out. There's nowhere left to go."

My heart pounded in my chest and there was a stitch in my side, but I felt good all the same. Stompanato's intimidation failed, and I caught his crony in the act. Witness tampering charges would be a bonus year or two on Stompanato's sentence.

There was a rustle behind a pile of discarded cardboard boxes. "Let's go," I commanded. "Now."

The figure rose like a scarecrow in a concrete field, arms lifted in a half-hearted pose of surrender. I flicked the flashlight's beam upwards; he shied away, blinded by the brilliance, his head turning and one arm flying up to protect his eyes. I shifted the light so I could hold both it and my weapon in my right hand then started forward, plucking a pair of handcuffs from my pocket. With my left hand, I reached for the man's wrist. Up close, I could see he was barely more than a kid.

"You're under arrest for disobeying a lawful command, resisting an officer and—"

I never got to finish.

The fist I'd narrowly avoided before thrust out again, catching me hard in the right shoulder, a wave of pain and shock jolting down the length of my arm. He was a lot stronger than his frailness suggested. He followed up with a two-handed push that sent me spinning off to one side, banging my other shoulder off of the rough stone wall of the alley, before rushing past, trying again to escape.

I threw out a hand, grabbing a fistful of his sweatshirt. It stopped him, but only long enough for him to half-turn and chop an open-handed blow down onto my elbow. Fresh pain skittered along my nerves, but I didn't let go, instead raising my right hand, only to discover it was empty. Somewhere in those chaotic two or three seconds, I dropped my gun.

I cursed and struggled for a better grip on the kid's clothing. He was thrashing wildly, yelling, "Let go! Let go!" his voice shrill and his mind going into panic mode. The decision between fight or flight was no longer his to make, but it seemed as if he was trying to choose both options simultaneously.

"Settle down! Cut it out, God damn it!" I snarled, freeing one hand to cuff him alongside the back of the neck, trying to startle him into a semblance of calm. "Nobody's going to hurt you, but you're digging yourself one hell of a hole!"

He ignored the words and continued to flail around. I tried to tackle him around the waist and ended up dragging both of us down to the filthy floor of the alley, where we rolled around for a few seconds, trading a punch a two. We were making enough noise that lights in the surrounding buildings came on. I hoped someone would have the sense to call 911, but even if they did, I knew nobody would arrive soon enough to help me get out of this. I was on my own.

Just as the thought flew through my head, the kid stopped moving. I allowed myself to hope he was coming to his senses at last. Then his hand shot out, straining to reach beyond my head, and when it came back into view, his fingers were wrapped around a chunk of brick the size of a small loaf of bread. He reared up, holding the thing above his head, prepared to end things between us. In the scant light of the nearly forgotten flashlight, his eyes looked huge and empty.

My own eyes flew all around, frantic, searching for a way out. The other man was straddling my chest and his knees kept me effectively pinned to the ground, but my arms were free and my fingers scrabbled across the rough, cold ground, searching for something, anything, to break this deadlock. They closed around something even colder, something metallic and familiar.

As the brick came down, my fist came up, and the explosion of noise and light only inches from my face all but knocked me senseless.

1

September 1993

I left state route 114, swinging the Taurus in a slow, lazy turn onto the grandly named route 114C-East Turnpike, towards Granton. I'd stopped even glancing at the map an hour or so earlier, having memorized the names of the turns I was looking for and deciding I barely even needed that. There simply weren't that many roads in this part of Vermont. I figured if I kept to the paved ones, I'd get where I wanted to be sooner or later.

I hoped it was sooner.

I shifted in the seat, trying to find a more comfortable position, one that would allow some feeling besides a dull ache in my backside. The drive was picturesque, but after over three hours behind the wheel, I was sick of it. You can only look at so many trees and little ponds and half-cleared fields and dilapidated barns and distant mountains before they all start to look alike.

I came up and over a small rise in the road and before I was all the way down the other side, I was in Granton, crawling along what I took to be the main drag. It looked like the downtown area you could find in any town of a certain size anywhere in America, and probably Canada. Cracked blacktop, divided by a faded white line, separated it along a north-south line, both sides of the street lined with angled parking spaces facing little storefronts that probably dated back to the 1940s or '50s. I passed a shoe-store, a drugstore that still sported a faded Rexall sign, a florist, and a place just called "Keith's" with no sign of what goods they sold or services they offered. If I stuck around, I'd have to poke my head in there, if only to satisfy my curiosity.

After three blocks, there was a four-way intersection and I pulled left, turning north onto Crescent Street. Directions I had told me to look for a "fancy brick building". I found it easily enough; it was hard to miss, being the single largest building I'd yet seen in town. A white sign with the black, stenciled words "TOWN CLERK - POLICE" across the lower part of the second story was just confirmation it was the right place. I crawled the car down to the end of the block and swung it into a metered parking space. I hopped out, locked the door, pumped a couple of quarters into the meter, and walked the half block back towards the police station.

The Granton PD's headquarters might have been "fancy" when it was built. Now it just seemed sad and out of place, hulking between its neighbors, a small office building on one side and what might have been an apartment house on the other. The place was three stories, made of weathered red brick and fronted by a set of white marble steps in which two darker paths had been worn by the passage of who knows how many feet – one on the left and one on the right. I wondered which was up and which was down. A brass plaque was affixed to the wall just off to the left of the entrance. It read "H.L. Lewis 1921".

As I stood on the sidewalk, looking the place over, a man of about seventy, wearing a navy-blue jumpsuit, heavy work boots and carrying a push-broom, came out of the wood-and-glass door at the top of the stairs. He took a single step down then stopped in mid-stride, his gaze fixed on me, his expression somewhere between wariness and interest. Whatever routine I interrupted must have been pretty ingrained.

I nodded in his direction, started up the stairs to meet him halfway. "Afternoon," I said.

"'M'elp ya?'"

Translated: *May I help you*? God bless that Vermont accent. Been a long time since I heard it anywhere outside of ancient memories. I wasn't sure if I loved it or hated it.

"No, I think I'm in the right place. Thanks, though."

"Yessuh." He gestured with the broom, as if granting me permission to pass. I stepped by him and headed inside.

The heavy front door let go with a muffled bang behind me as I looked around. The interior of the building was dim and close, lit only by a few recessed florescent lights overhead. I wondered what H.L. Lewis originally built this place for; it sure wasn't intended to house police or town offices. Not with this set-up.

A sign on the wall directly ahead read "Police" with an arrow pointing to the right. Another, below it, showed an arrow in the opposite direction and read

"Town Clerk". I hoped Lewis would at least be proud to find his building put to such good civic use.

I turned right and halfway down the hall was hit with the familiar smell of a police station, a result of the curious, not quite stale, not quite fresh, not quite dirty, but not quite clean quality the air in any police station takes on. It's a mixture of coffee, paper, disinfectant and humanity. It felt like being home. Maybe it would be.

Behind a pebbled-glass door, a small reception area waited, divided in the middle by a low wooden railing, forming a partition between the public space and the police bullpen. A long bench lined the wall to my left. There was a rack full of brochures to one side of it and a corkboard covered in notices hanging above it. Seated at a desk just on the other side of the railing was an angular, fiftyish woman with graying-black hair pulled into a loose up-do. She fiddled with a pencil in one hand and a book of crossword puzzles in the other. A nameplate on the edge of the desk read "Reception", like the place was a dentist's office or something.

Hell, maybe it doubled as one. It was a small town.

"Hi," I said, stepping up to the desk.

The woman looked up from her puzzle, turning surprisingly soft brown eyes on me, taking the edge off of her otherwise drab appearance. Her smile was the kind of utilitarian face-crease people used to dealing with the public develop. "Can I help you?"

"Luke Campbell. I have a two o'clock appointment with Chief Skillman." I glanced at the clock on the wall to the left of the reception desk. One-thirty-five. I made better time than I expected on the trip up from Albany. "I know I'm a little early, but I thought I'd stop by and check in, anyway."

"Oh!" she said, surprise turning the smile from professional to personal. "The New York detective!"

I tilted my head and gave her a small, answering smile. "I guess that's me." If you asked Manhattanites, Albany—the whole rest of the state, really—barely counted as New York, but the way she said it left me with the impression that it was better to agree than put a damper on her excitement.

The woman stood, thrust a hand over the desk to shake. It was my turn to be surprised as I took her hand and her greeting spilled out over lips moving so fast they were a blur. "I'm Jeannie Brown. Nice to meet you. Nice to have you here! I'll let the chief know you're a little early. I doubt he's doing anything important. Wait here just one moment." She turned and bustled away into the recesses of the building, leaving me wondering at the total about-face in her demeanor.

I stepped back, leaned to one side, trying to get a look into the corridor of gray-cloth-covered cubicle walls she disappeared down. That wasn't the welcome I was expecting. Truthfully, I wasn't quite sure what to expect, but it sure as hell wasn't that kind of enthusiasm. I'd forgotten what little changes could mean to small towns.

Left alone, my stomach took the opportunity to speak up. I wished I hadn't been early for this meeting, maybe took the time to find some place to get a bite beforehand. There was no chance to reconsider, though, to call for Jeannie and say I'd be back. Slow, heavy footsteps sounded outside in the hallway, followed swiftly by a shadow against the pebbled-glass. The door swung open and a living scarecrow walked in, wearing a uniform so dark blue it was nearly black. The gold badge on his left breast caught the overhead light at just the right angle to throw off a momentary glint that highlighted the word "CHIEF" embossed on it.

Chief Aaron Skillman needed no further introduction, so I offered my own. I stepped forward in the small space, hand outstretched. "Chief Skillman? Luke Campbell."

"Little early, ain't you?" he said, but took my hand and shook, anyway. His grasp was lighter than I'd have expected, almost delicate. His voice was a strong baritone and he was tall, at least six foot five, but rail-thin and the skin hung from his face as if he was ill for a long time and only recently recovered. But the black eyes, made tiny by his size and the folds of skin around them, shone with intelligence as he watched me intently, still grasping my hand.

Finally, he released it. I said, "Yes, sir. I was just telling your secretary—"

"Oh, chief!" Jeannie said, choosing that moment to reappear. "Thought you were back in your office. Mr. Campbell's here for—"

"I can see that," Skillman said, cutting off further explanation. He gestured with his head, while raising the wooden gate that, set off to one side of Jeannie's desk, blocked entrance to that area. "C'mon back, Campbell."

I lifted my shoulders a little in Jeannie's direction and she lifted her eyebrows in return—signaling my apology and her telling me she understood—as I followed the chief back into the depths of Granton's station. We passed six cubicles on the way, laid out boxcar style, three to the left and three to the right. Only two, one on each side, were occupied.

In the first was a very heavy-set man in a uniform that matched the chief's, save that, where the chief's hung on him like they were made for a much larger person, this man's was tight to the point of looking ready to burst. The man was having coffee and a sandwich while reading a newspaper. As we passed, he nodded in the chief's direction, ignoring me. In the other occupied cubicle, a youngish man, probably not yet twenty-five, sat pouring over a handwritten document of some sort, laboriously transcribing it to a more official-looking form using a typewriter to pick and peck out one key at a time. He paid no attention to either me or the chief.

Past the little cubbyholes, there were four doors at the end of the hallway, two to a side, each with its own pebbled-glass window and label, stenciled in gold paint. The doors on the left read "CHIEF" and "CRIMINAL INVESTIGATIONS". Those on the right were labeled "INTERROGATION A" and "INTERROGATION B".

Skillman opened the door to his office and stepped aside, gesturing for me to precede him. Moving through the door, the dense odors of must and cigarette smoke hit me like I'd walked into a wall. My nose twitched and I said a silent prayer I wouldn't sneeze my brains out and make a fool of myself.

Chief Skillman entered behind me, closed the door and moved to an ancient desk, covered in coffee stains and the sort of bumps and scuffs that give old furniture its character. It was heaped with documents and papers and folders of all sizes and shapes, many unlabeled, in piles of no obvious organizational scheme. Several filing cabinets stood against the rear wall, their tops likewise piled with paper detritus.

I wasn't sure how formal the chief intended this interview to be, so I stood where I was before the desk, waiting for him to make the next move. He took his time settling into a roll-chair, finding a comfortable position, before waving a hand in the direction of a thinly padded, straight-back, metal chair in front of the desk, the only other furniture in the room. "Sit down, Mr. Campbell."

I sat.

The chief pushed aside a few papers, came up with a packet of Camels, opened it, shook one out, stuck it between his lips. I didn't smoke, hated the things in fact, and already the smell of cigarettes that pervaded the room was making my chest feel tight. To my relief, though, the chief didn't light his cigarette, just rolled it back and forth across his lips a couple of times, before pressing it into the corner of his mouth.

He noticed me watching. "Trying to quit, but I don't feel right without one of these damned things hangin' from my lip," he offered. "Anyway, I'm not much for small talk, Mr. Campbell, so let me just ask you this: why do you still want to be in law enforcement?"

At least he wasn't wasting time dancing around the question. It was a fair one. I said so.

He nodded. "Most folks would probably run screaming."

I shrugged. "Guess I'm just not that bright."

"Well," he chuckled, "maybe just stubborn."

"Look," I said, "only two people were there that night and I'm the only one who's still walking around, but everybody's got an opinion, regardless of how much they know or don't know or think they know. And when it comes right down to it, the only opinions that matter were those of twenty-three of my peers who decided there wasn't enough evidence to indict. It was a good shoot. Internal affairs cleared me and the state's attorney himself said after the fact that he wouldn't have even tried to get an indictment if that kid hadn't turned out to be a state senator's junkie son, looking to score in the wrong neighborhood at the wrong time. But every day, I've had people telling me this, telling me that, about what I should have done, how it should have been handled, and it got to the point where I couldn't do my job, where the scandal was all anybody knew or cared about as far as I was concerned. And when it got that bad, the chief of detectives down in Albany suggested, *strongly* suggested, that it might be time to resign. So here I am."

I sat back, realized I'd been leaning forward against Chief Skillman's desk, a stance that probably came across as more aggressive than I intended. I took a breath, trying to calm the hammering against my sternum. I hadn't meant to say that much, to get as worked up as I had. It'd been a long time since I talked so much about what I went through and it just sort of spilled out. And that wasn't even half of it. I hadn't mentioned a word about Lina, my ex-wife.

Despite my outburst, Skillman didn't bat an eye. I guessed he already knew pretty much everything I told him. Calmly, he said, "That bad, huh?"

I bit the inside of my cheek and muttered, "That bad."

"And after all that, I'll ask you again: why do you still want to be a police officer?"

"Hell if I know. Maybe it's because it's what I studied in college and I'm still paying student loans. Maybe it's because it's all I've ever done for work."

"Where you from, originally?"

"Here," I said. "Vermont. I grew up in Starksboro."

"And how d'you end up in Albany?"

"I went to SUNY-Albany, studied criminal justice. Spent a couple years thinking I was going to be a lawyer."

"And why'd you stop thinking that?" Skillman rolled his cigarette over to the other corner of his mouth. It must have been soggy as hell, by now. I wondered if he'd swap it out for another soon.

"New York State Police came to campus recruiting. I never really thought about being a cop, but after talking to a couple of them, this one guy convinced me that there were already too many lawyers in the world, but you can never really have enough cops."

The chief nodded thoughtfully, as if that was something profound. "Could be he's right. So why aren't you with the staties, over in New York, if that's the case?"

"Couldn't pass the physical tests. I breezed through the written exams, managed all the practical ones, but I could never quite dead-lift that two-hundred-fifty pounds. I guess I didn't realize how much that really is until I had to try moving it. At any rate, the recruiter I worked with said he'd give me a good recommendation for any town or city department I cared to apply to. I was already in Albany, so…." I shrugged.

"I see." Skillman nodded. "That doesn't really answer my original question, though," he added.

"Guess not."

Skillman sat staring at me, waiting.

"Okay," I said, finally. "I guess… I guess maybe I'm just an idealist with a head full of crap like justice and fair-play and that sort of thing and—"

I cut myself off, started again. "No, damn it. Even that's not really it. You know what? The truth is I *like* being a cop and I'm damned good at it. I worked my butt off for four years to make detective and even harder for four more after that. I had the second-highest closure rate in Albany's major crimes division and I'm proud of it. I was a good cop and I got railroaded and god damn it, I'm not going to let it kill a career I love."

I was getting angry again, like I let myself become a few minutes earlier, like I promised myself I wouldn't get again. My cheeks burned, though whether in rage or shame, I wasn't sure.

Skillman smiled. "That's the truth, huh?"

"That's the truth," I snapped.

"Okay, then." He nodded, as if settling something with himself. "I'll start you at four-hundred a week – that's ten dollars an hour for forty hours, plus whatever overtime is required. Your official rank and title will be detective, because I haven't had one in about half a dozen years and I need someone who's trained in actual criminal investigations. Most of what we deal with is bar-brawls, domestic situations, DUIs, petty crimes. When we get something serious, we've been havin' to turn it over to the state police or the Essex County Sheriff's Department and frankly, it sticks in my craw, so if you're as good as you say you are, you'll be welcome."

Skillman began rummaging around in his desk drawers as he continued. "Now you'll have a title the rest of the fellas don't, but you'll wear the same uniform as everyone else and you'll spend at least a night a week doing road patrol, just like everybody else, myself included, has to. There's only eight of us here, including me and you, and this way nobody's gotta do it more than once a week unless they want to."

The chief found what he was looking for, lifted it out, tossed it onto the desk between us. It was a gold shield, identical to his own, except it lacked the embossed "CHIEF".

"Take that and let Jeannie know your measurements so she can dig up a uniform for you. First thing tomorrow, we'll get you a service weapon and see if cruiser number eight is road-worthy. Nobody's used it in a while, so it'll probably need gas, air in the tires and maybe a tune-up."

I sat back in the chair, a little stunned. "That's it? I'm hired, just like that?"

Skillman quirked an eyebrow. "Unless you don't want the job."

I shook my head. "No, no. I do, sir, and I'm grateful for the chance."

"But?" he asked. "I sense a 'but,' detective."

"After everything I just told you, after my… outburst, you want to hire me?"

The chief smiled. "Maybe I'm just an idealist, Campbell. Maybe I agree that you got railroaded. Maybe I can see that you *are* a good cop who likes his work, just like you said." He stood, reached across the desk to seal our agreement. We shook and he said, "Maybe, if I'm offering the job and you want it, the why doesn't matter one way or another, does it?"

I guessed maybe it didn't. I reached out and picked up the badge.

2

I turned the gold-colored shield over in my hands, relishing its smoothness against my fingertips, the weight of the thing in my palm. It felt right. It felt like home. It wasn't so long that I'd been away, but I hadn't realized how much I missed it until that moment.

"Well," the chief interrupted my thoughts, "square, then?"

"Yes, sir."

The older man nodded as he plucked the soggy remains of the unsmoked cigarette from his mouth. He jammed it into an ashtray, crushing it as if it was actually burning. He picked up the pack of Camels, then put it back down, apparently reconsidering. "Okay, then," he said, turning his attention back to me. "Let's go see your office."

He stood, pushing the rolling chair back with his hips as he did, then moved to the door and threw it open, again gesturing with one hand for me to precede him. I stood, slipping my new badge into the pocket of my coat.

We didn't go far. Out in the hallway, Chief Skillman opened the door marked "CRIMINAL INVESTIGATIONS" and stepped inside, leading the way for once. I followed him in as an overhead light flicked into life, giving the small room a soundtrack of loud, harsh buzzing from a pair of older-style florescent lights. Even so, the room was just a shade above dim, deep shadows hiding more of it than was visible – shadows cast by a veritable mountain of junk. Cardboard boxes, piles of manila folders, chairs—some obviously broken, some still serviceable—even a wheel-less bicycle frame were all crammed into the small room, cutting the floor space down to just enough room for the chief and me to stand among it all. Peeking out from under the piles of detritus I could see a desk near the room's far wall and filing cabinets lined the near wall, to my left. There may have been more along the right-side wall, but the junk was piled too deeply for me to tell.

"Damn it all," Skillman cursed. There was barely room for two adults in the cramped space, but he pushed past me, leaned out of the doorway and hollered, "Barnes! Get your ass in here!" The chief turned back towards the room, shaking his big head slowly, annoyance plain on his face. His eyes scanned the heaps and piles of boxes and folders and odds and ends, following the same course mine had. "What the hell?" he muttered, tapping the useless bicycle with the toe of his boot.

The heavy-set—fat, really—officer I saw earlier huffed up, uniform straining to contain his bulk. Seen close up, he was a little older than me, a little shorter, and he probably had eighty pounds on my one-eighty-five. His face was red and little beads of sweat stood out along his hairline, though whether from the short jog down the hallway or the tone of Skillman's voice, I wasn't sure. Maybe both.

With both Skillman and myself inside the room, there was no space for a third man, so he stood just outside the doorway and asked, "You yelled, chief?"

"I did," Skillman said calmly, waving a hand to indicate the room. "Ben, tell me what you see in here, will you?"

The redness drained from Barnes's face in an instant, replaced by a look of stricken pallor. "Ah… crap, boss. I'm sorry, I—"

"Tell me what you see." It was no longer a question.

Officer Barnes threw a glance my way, as if looking for help we both knew I couldn't provide. "Lotta junk."

Skillman nodded. "Right. Lotta junk. What else?"

Barnes was at a loss. The big man gave up, shrugging his broad shoulders, tugging one side of his shirt out of his pants. I hoped for his sake that Skillman didn't notice. Barnes looked like he didn't need any more strikes against him.

Skillman sighed. His voice was soft, almost fatherly, when he said, "A job left undone, Ben. You know how I feel about that kinda thing."

"I'll get right on it, chief."

"You do that." Skillman pushed out of the room, brushing past his officer, leaving the man with a gentle pat on the shoulder.

I didn't know what to make of it. Skillman did nothing overtly threatening, hadn't even gotten angry except for the initial quiet outburst, but Barnes looked like he might as well have been in front of a firing squad. I was sure Skillman had sides I hadn't seen—I'd only met the man forty minutes earlier, after all—

but Barnes's reaction seemed over the top. Maybe Skillman was prone to fits of anger. Maybe Barnes was a habitual offender already on thin ice. I just had no way of knowing, and that bothered me, but, with nothing else to do, I followed Skillman, avoiding looking at Barnes. I figured I'd let the guy keep a little of whatever dignity he had left.

The chief was headed in Jeannie's direction, back to the front of the little station. Over his shoulder he said, "Sorry you had to see that, Campbell. I asked that boy days ago to clear that place out for you."

The statement made it sound as if my taking the job was a given. Maybe in Skillman's mind it was. It made sense, I supposed; with my history, offers of jobs in law enforcement weren't exactly rolling in.

Passing back through the cubicle area, the young cop was nowhere in sight, though whatever typing he was working on still sat next to the typewriter, several sheets thick now. Another fresh form of some sort sat in the machine waiting to be filled out. I wondered if the Granton PD used computers at all.

We came to the front area. Jeannie turned her chair around when she heard us coming, crossword puzzle once again in hand. "So what's the word, chief?" She smiled faintly, looking from Skillman to me then back.

"He's in," Skillman said, jerking his head in my direction. Directly to me, he added, "Jeannie'll take care of you, detective. Get your paperwork and so forth sorted. After that, take the afternoon to get yourself situated and tomorrow, come see me first thing in the morning, eight o'clock sharp." He started back down the hall, then stopped, turned. "Don't forget measurements for his uniform, Jeannie."

"Oh, I won't, chief," she said, throwing me a wink.

I wasn't sure if I was supposed to laugh or not, so I just grinned, glad at least to be welcome.

•   •   •

Jeannie Brown surprised me. From the way she looked, you'd guess her to be no nonsense, humorless, all-business. The sort of person you'd want as the gatekeeper of a police station. Even one in such a rural setting must get a lot of cranks and hard-cases walking through its doors. And she *had* given me that impression in the first few seconds of our meeting, only to push it aside with a smile and some bright enthusiasm. I might have written it off as a momentary lapse, but now, as she helped me through the various forms that made my employment by the town of Granton official, she completely shattered it. As I filled out line after line, sheet after sheet, she kept up a near constant stream of bubbly conversation, giving me the low-down on the town and my new colleagues, excluding the chief, about whom she said very little.

"You'll like it here, Mr. Campbell. Granton's a nice little place." She craned her head to get a better look, upside down, at the document I was working on, filling out past employment history. "Nice place to raise a family," she added, going fishing.

I bit. "I'm not married."

Her smile returned, a little coy now. "Oh, really." I didn't get the feeling she was on the make, despite the way she said it. She wore no wedding ring, but she was at least twenty years older than me and from the look she was giving me, sizing me up, I pegged her as a matchmaker. The kind who lives vicariously through the couples they paired up. Always a bridesmaid, never a bride, and happy to have it that way.

"Tried it. Didn't take."

One eyebrow rose as she gave me another look, thoughtful this time. "Well, I won't pry. Maybe you'll tell me about it someday, Mr. Campbell."

"Call me Luke."

She liked that. She said so. "Short for Lucas?"

"No, just plain Luke. I'm named after some great-uncle I never met. About this part, here." I pointed to a line on the form, changing the subject. "Current address. I don't have one in town." I didn't really have one at all, aside from the fleabag motel back in Albany where I'd been sleeping the last few months and a P.O. box where I got mail. Practically everything I owned was in a pair of suitcases and a couple of cardboard boxes in the trunk of the Taurus. When I left New York that morning, I didn't know if I'd end up being offered this job but, in the back of my mind, I knew I'd probably never go back to Albany, either way.

"Well," Jeannie sat back in the chair, crossed her arms and looked towards the ceiling. "There's the Red Garden Hotel over on Dumont. I don't know what rooms run, but Helen Reddy runs the place and if you tell her you're Chief Skillman's new hire, I'm sure she'll give a good deal."

"Why would that matter to her?"

"Civic duty?" she posed it as a question. She shrugged. "Chief Skillman has done a lot for this town and everybody knows it."

The words were plain enough, and quite possibly true, but it seemed an odd thing to say. I let it slide, though.

"I'm sure Helen will take good care of you," Jeannie, adding nothing in the way of explanation.

I let that pass without comment, too. I wasn't in the mood to plumb the depths of this town's social structure at the moment. Not on an empty stomach, anyway.

"Thanks," I said. "I'll check it out." I pushed the last form across the desk into Jeannie's waiting hand, then asked, "Where's a good place to eat around here?" It was close to three o'clock and I hadn't eaten since a roadside diner somewhere back in New York that morning.

Absently, busy perusing the form, Jeannie answered, "Callaway's over on Main is decent and cheap. They do breakfast all day, too."

I stood. "Sounds good. We all done for now then?"

Jeannie looked up, a twinkle in her eye. "Not quite." She reached into a desk drawer, pulled out a measuring tape. "Don't forget I still need those measurements."

•　　•　　•

After pumping a few more quarters into the parking meter outside, I left the Taurus where it was and walked the four blocks south back to the intersection of Crescent and Main, taking the opportunity to stretch my legs and get a little more familiar with the town.

From what I saw on a map hanging in the tiny lobby of the dual-purpose police station/town clerk's building, Granton was laid out in a rough double-diamond shape, with Main Street, a.k.a. the 114C-East Turnpike, forming the east-west dividing line between the two halves, and Crescent Street bisecting it vertically. North along Crescent, five or six blocks past where I left the car, the ground sloped gently, but visibly, upwards and you'd end up in Pennemont Hills, one of Granton's two upper-class neighborhoods. South of town a few miles was Lake Maidenstone, and on its shores was the other one, appropriately called Lakeview.

The lake was important for more than just its scenery, though: an annual fishing derby sponsored by the town provided some tourist dollars every August. In the less tony parts of its shore were cabins, both private and for rent, and a small motel. With fall fast approaching, though, both cabins and motel would be pretty well abandoned by now, I supposed. Granton had around sixty-five-hundred year-round residents; during the months of July and August, it swelled to over nine-thousand with tourists and summer residents who owned lake homes. These tidbits about the town spilled from the firehose of information named Jeannie Brown. Maybe not important at the moment, but they were nice things to know if I was going to be living and working here.

I came to the intersection, turned left and headed east, walking past more little storefronts and neatly trimmed trees planted at regular intervals along the edge of the sidewalk. Nestled between a hair-salon and a dry-cleaner's was Callaway's Diner. An old-fashioned neon sign clung to the side of the building, overhanging the sidewalk. I pictured the hot-pink glow it must have thrown off after dark painting the sidewalk like something out of an old photograph and had a flash of nostalgia for a time I was too young to remember. Granton suddenly seemed like that kind of town.

I pulled open the door and, met by the ting-a-ling of an overhead bell and the comforting smells of grease and coffee, went inside. The place was narrow and nearly empty in this time between lunch and dinner. A dozen chrome and red-leather stools lined a counter along the right-hand side of the place and four booths nestled against the left. A burly, bearded guy wearing a blue-and-green-checked plaid shirt under Carhartt overalls sat at the near end of the counter, a plate of half-eaten pie and a nearly empty beer mug in front of him. Three stools down, an elderly man in a sweater-vest and chinos read a newspaper and sipped coffee. Otherwise, the place seemed empty.

I sat down at the last stool on the far end of the counter, the one closest to the kitchen. Through the service window, I could see a middle-aged man standing at a grill, smoking a cigarette and shuffling some minute-steaks across the sizzling-hot surface. The door next to the window, leading back into the kitchen, opened and a waitress stepped out.

"Can I help you, sir?" She had a heavy French accent, making it sound more like *Can ah 'elp you, sair?* but it was a perfect fit for this girl. Anything less exotic-sounding coming out of her mouth would have been a let-down. She was probably in her early twenties and tiny, no more than an inch over five feet. Her face, simultaneously angelic and waifish, was framed by a halo of frizzy, chin-length hair so blonde it was nearly white. She was trim, with a narrow waist and sweetly curved hips that even the drab light-pink and white nylon waitress uniform could do nothing to detract from. As exhausted and hungry as I was, she was so exquisite I forgot all about food and rest.

I must have looked like a fool, lost in such thoughts. She asked again if she could help me, if I wanted a menu. I mentally slapped myself back together, tried out a smile and said, "Sorry, been on the road all day. A little loopy. How about a sandwich?" I jutted my chin towards the kitchen-window. "Maybe some of that steak he's grilling up back there? Smells great."

She didn't smile back, only replied, "Certainly. With French fries okay?"

"Sure."

"Something to drink? Soda? Coffee?" She had already moved toward the area with the soda fountain and coffee machine, looking expectantly at me.

"Coffee sounds good."

She nodded, filled a cup, set it on a saucer, placed it in front of me. From beneath the counter, she took a little bowl full of individually packaged creamers and set it on the counter, too. "Your food will be right out," she said before turning and disappearing back into the kitchen without another glance in my direction. Her manner wasn't exactly cold, but it was hardly friendly, either, as if she was intentionally putting up a wall between herself and customers. I guessed with her looks, she didn't need to play nice to make decent tips.

I slumped a little on the stool, feeling a drain that had nothing to do with exertion or hunger. Only four months divorced, I had no desire to go chasing after women, but something about this girl lit a fire inside me like I hadn't felt in years. Maybe not ever. I wished she wore a name-tag so I could at least know who I'd be fantasizing about later on.

I noticed the old-timer a couple of stools down giving me the side-eye, trying to pretend he was still focused on his newspaper. I nodded in his direction. He swiveled his stool away from me. I wondered if I somehow offended him.

The waitress returned, swinging the door open with her lovely hip, causing it to rebound lightly against the opposite wall then narrowly miss her behind as she swished through. It was a practiced move that added some theatricality to the service, intentional or not. She set my sandwich in front of me, the fries still steaming. "Anything else, sir?"

"Can I ask," I began, "your accent. Quebecois?"

"Yes," was all she said.

I opened my mouth to follow-up, but was interrupted by a small voice from behind me. "Mama?"

The beautiful waitress swung out the waist-high door in the counter that separated server from patron and moved to the booth directly behind me. I hadn't realized it was occupied, but I could hear her lilting mezzo-soprano, pitched too low for words to carry, going back and forth with a childish voice. I shifted slightly to my left, pretending to reach for another napkin from the nearby holder, allowing me to see out of the corner of my eye that she was speaking with a little boy, about seven or eight years old. He was sitting in the back booth, surrounded by a pile of books and schoolwork. His head didn't top the seat-backs, hiding him from view from any place further down the diner's length. I turned back to my lunch, thinking the woman hadn't looked old enough to have a kid that age, but he called her "mama" and there was no mistaking the affection that radiated from her as she spoke in hushed tones to the boy.

The door of the diner opened with a jingle and the hushed conversation behind me ended. Mouth full of bread and steak, I turned to see a youngish man coming into the place. Despite a face that was probably only twenty-five, he looked weathered and worn-out, as if he used up his share of life-experiences early on. A red, hooded sweatshirt and dirty blue-jeans covered a tall, lanky frame. Something about him put me in mind of steel wire, like he'd bend but be difficult to break.

But that wasn't the reason he stood out.

It was the way he entered the place: quietly, almost furtively, as if trying to sneak in and, even with the distance between us, I could see his eyes flicking back and forth, taking in every inch of the place, scanning for danger. I knew that look. It was almost mandatory in ex-convicts, people used to watching their backs every minute of the day.

I kept my eye on the man as he sidled up to the counter. So did the burly guy at the opposite end and the waitress, who quickly moved to put the barrier of the counter back between herself and this newcomer.

The guy sat down on the stool next to the old-timer, one seat away from the man in the plaid shirt, whose eyes were now glued on his new neighbor. The waitress moved slowly in that direction, but clearly with reluctance.

"Coffee, please," the young man said. His voice was quiet, but hoarse, as if he yelled himself out somewhere along the line and wasn't yet recovered.

"Other places to get it," the bearded guy said. His voice was calm, but there was thinly veiled menace in it.

The newcomer ignored him, kept his eyes on the counter in front of him.

Wordlessly, the waitress carried the coffee pot and a mug towards where the young man sat. No cup and saucer for this guy. She set down the mug, readied to pour, but the burly man reached out to place his hand over top of it, shook his head. "Don't serve this fucker, Chloe."

Without looking at either of the two, she simply said, "It's my job. Please move your hand."

I sipped my own coffee, watching with naked interest.

The younger guy threw a quick look towards the man in the Carhartt overalls, then one towards the waitress – Chloe. "I wanted to—"

"*Fuck* what you wanted, Ecare," the bearded man sneered. "And fuck *you*." He reached over, grabbed his neighbor by the wrist and stood up, dragging the smaller man to his feet, as well. "Get the hell out of here and leave the lady alone."

I saw enough.

I left my stool, tried to insert myself between the two men before something serious broke out. I put one hand on the bigger man's left bicep, met his eyes. "Let's calm down. Let go of him and back away."

"Who the hell are you?" Anger flared in his eyes and the menace he barely contained before shifted targets, landing squarely on me. "You sticking up for this shit-prick?" His eyes scanned me, trying to decide if he could take me or not. He decided. "You his friend or something? One of his prison butt-buddies?"

They always go there. When they don't know a thing about you, bullies always go there. "I'm not anybody's friend, I'm not on anybody's side, so let's just—"

"You got that right, you ain't!" He finally did as I asked: he released the wrist of man he called Ecare, but only to free up that hand for a swing at me.

He was fast and it nearly landed, but I was watching for it. I felt the muscles bunch in his bicep just before he pulled away from me and knew he was going to do something stupid. I leaned to my right, letting his right cross sail through empty air just to one side of my head. Simultaneously, I reached out my own right hand, clamped it onto his left arm again and pulled him forward and down, away from the counter, away from Ecare, throwing him off-balance and sending him stumbling forward. I brought my knee up to meet him and gave him a thump in the belly. Not enough to down him, just enough to get his attention.

The wind flew out of the guy and for a second, I thought he might puke up his pie and beer, but to his credit, he righted himself, hopped back a few steps and brought his fists up in something akin to a boxer's stance. As the breath he exhaled reached me, I realized that the empty mug I saw hadn't been his first. Not by a long shot. His breath smell liked an old keg. He didn't seem drunk, but I'd seen men with BACs three times the legal limit who gave no outward signs of intoxication. I didn't know how many this guy had in him, but he held them pretty well. At least until something provoked him.

Whether drunk or sober, though, he seemed to have brawling experience and it was obvious he was feeling froggy. He leapt forward, swinging another right at me, even faster than before, all the weight and momentum of his moving body behind it. This time, he was quick enough that I wasn't able to move entirely out of the way and his fist glanced off the side of my jaw, sliding part of the way across my cheek before he pulled it back.

He may have had street- or bar-fighting experience and he was definitely a bruiser, but I had the advantage of formal training and I wasn't going to give him another chance like that.

The man cursed under his breath and sent another meaty right flying in my direction, holding his left up in a guard-stance. I ducked beneath it, came up under his guard and threw a rabbit punch into his Adam's apple. As he gagged and staggered a couple of steps backwards, I backed off. He began choking, his face bright red and spittle spewing from his lips.

"Done yet?" I asked. I didn't mean to antagonize him, but it just came out and that was the result.

He roared and charged forward through the narrow space of the restaurant. I faked to my right, pretending to aim towards his left, which I figured was his weak side as he clearly favored his right. He took the bait and moved to block. I slipped inside his guard again and chopped a stiffened hand down against the muscles between his neck and right shoulder; his right arm went suddenly limp, hanging at his side as if broken and the look of surprise on his face should have meant this thing was over.

It didn't.

Instead, he slammed his big head into me, going for my face but striking me in the solar plexus, knocking the breath from me, and pushing me back a couple steps. He tried to press the advantage, swinging his left fist down in a hammer blow that I twisted aside from. I swung my right up in the opposite direction, putting all my remaining strength into an upper-cut that connected beneath his jaw and sent him flying up an inch off of the ground. He came down to earth and fell backwards, collapsing to the floor, finally down and, at least temporarily, out.

"That was awesome! So awesome!" I looked behind me and saw that the boy had abandoned booth and homework to watch the brief fight. His eyes were ablaze and he was practically vibrating with excitement. Chloe, the waitress, came out from behind the counter and grabbed him around the shoulders, pulling him from the booth and ushering him hurriedly back into the kitchen. He kept looking over his shoulder, afraid of missing any more action, as she murmured something in his ear.

In the door they went and out came the middle-aged man I saw at the grill earlier, cigarette still clamped between his lips, grease-stained apron covering a little round belly. He looked at the body sprawled on the floor, to me, back to the burly guy, whose chest heaved up and down, still breathing heavily with exertion despite his unconsciousness. Several days' worth of salt and pepper beard growth sprawled patchily across the cook's cheeks as a look somewhere between horror and amusement danced in his eyes. "Well, god damn, son."

"Sorry," was all I said. I suddenly felt very self-conscious. Chloe peeked at me through the kitchen window and the old-timer at the counter stared with aloof disdain. During the brawl, the man called Ecare had taken the chance to make an escape. I wanted to ask him what the hell it was all about. I hoped I'd get the chance.

"Uh, if it helps," I dug in my pocket, came out with the badge Skillman gave me. "Luke Campbell. Just joined the Granton police. So that whole thing was official," I added lamely. As official as a fist-fight could get, anyway.

The cook pursed his lips, shook his head. "Well, officer, you sure as hell know how to make a first impression."

3

"Guess what's done is done," Callaway's cook said. He turned my way again, stuck out a hand. "Cal Callaway."

We shook.

"Not a nickname," Callaway offered without my asking. "My parents were just big on alliteration."

I nodded distractedly, watching the guy on the floor as he began to stir. "Call over to the station for me, will you? Tell them I've got a drunk and disorderly in custody."

Callaway looked at me askance. "That really necessary, officer? Lloyd's a half-decent guy, he just—"

"Took a swing at a cop and then kept at it when I didn't go down."

The other man looked at me a moment, something working itself out in his mind. I stared right back. Not aggressively, just letting him know I wouldn't back down.

Callaway made a decision, shrugged. "Your call." He went back into the kitchen, leaving me with the man he called Lloyd, now struggling to a sitting position.

Lloyd sat up slowly, then used one of the stools to lever himself up to his feet. It took him a moment and a couple of tries but he made it. I didn't offer him any help, just watched.

Once on his feet again, he wobbled a bit then gingerly sat on the stool he previously occupied. He rubbed at his bushy jaw, ran a hand over his arm, then slapped at it viciously, like he was trying to get the circulation moving again.

"It's not asleep. The nerves are pinched. You'll probably be fine tomorrow morning, but you better get a doctor to check you out just to be sure," I told him.

The guy's eyes flew up, tried to pin me in place. There was anger in them, but fear, too. I doubt he'd been handed his ass recently or often, and it seemed to earn me a measure of his respect.

I held up the gold-colored badge I was given less than an hour ago. "Glare all you want, as long as that's all you do. So far you're looking at charges of drunk and disorderly and assaulting an officer. Feel like adding anything else to the list?"

He thought about it, but not for long. He shook his big head back and forth. "I didn't know you were a cop."

"Doesn't matter. What's your name?"

"Lloyd Truman."

"You live in town, Lloyd?"

He nodded. "Yes, sir."

I glanced towards the kitchen window. Chloe was gone, but Callaway was watching us now, phone receiver pressed to his ear. He nodded, said something I couldn't make out, then disappeared from view. A moment later, he came back out through the kitchen door. "Domanski's comin' right over, Officer Campbell."

I hadn't met a Domanski yet, but any cop with cuffs for Truman and a cruiser to drag him back to the station was good enough for me. "Thanks."

Turning back towards Truman, I said, "While we wait, tell me what that was all about. What'd this Ecare guy do to you?"

Truman shot a look at Callaway, who held up his hands and backed away, shaking his head. "Keep me out of it."

Truman looked back my way. "You really don't know who Ecare is?"

"I'm new in town."

The big man snorted, shook his head. "Guess so." His mouth snapped shut and I knew I wouldn't get any more out of him.

It didn't matter at the moment. I was out of time, anyway. The door of the little restaurant flew open and in walked a tall, solidly built man in his mid-thirties in the deep-blue, nearly black, uniform of the Granton police. He had dark-blond hair, All-American-Boy features and sharp, clear eyes that instantaneously took in the scene.

He greeted Callaway then nodded in my direction, and said, "You must be Campbell."

"And you're Domanski."

Domanski's lips quirked in the faintest semblance of a smile. "We'll meet and greet in a bit." He turned towards Truman. "You been fightin' again, Lloyd?"

Lloyd Truman just nodded.

"Picked the wrong fella this time, huh?" Domanski continued.

Truman nodded again, a hint of chastisement in his manner.

Over his shoulder, Domanski addressed me. "You're pressing charges, huh?"

First day in town, first day as a member of the Granton police, I didn't really see any other option. It would make me at least one enemy, I imagined, but letting this kind of thing slide set a far worse precedent.

"Yep," I told Domanski.

The other cop nodded. "All right. Stand up, Lloyd."

Truman did as instructed. Domanski gave him a brief pat-down, pulled from Truman's pocket a battered-looking Swiss Army knife, slipped it into his own pocket, then slapped cuffs onto the captive man's wrists. Hands on Truman's shoulders, Domanski turned the larger man around, pointing him towards the door. "C'mon, let's go then." To me, he added, "Ride back with us?"

"Sure." It was only four blocks, but I was exhausted and sore. Lloyd Truman was a brawler, all right, and the way Domanski talked to him, it was clear he got plenty of practice. "Give me a second."

Digging into my wallet, I pulled out a ten and tossed it down onto the counter. "Sorry we had to meet this way," I said to Callaway, who was filling the unperturbed older guy's coffee mug.

Callaway shrugged. "It is what it is," he said, watching Domanski and Truman exit the place.

I looked towards the kitchen window, hoping to catch another glance of the girl, Chloe. No such luck. "Well," I said. "Thanks for lunch, anyway."

Outside, I slipped into the passenger seat of Domanski's cruiser. My first look at a Granton police vehicle didn't leave me with the best impression. An older Ford Crown Victoria, the thing was white and gray, trimmed with the same dark-blue color of their uniforms. It was drab and ugly and something about it screamed rural police. Screamed "hick town". Like Callaway said, though, "it is what it is."

"How do you like Granton?" Domanski asked without an ounce of sarcasm.

I worked up a grin I didn't feel. "Seems like a nice little town."

The other man laughed. "It really is." He jerked his head, indicating the man in the backseat. "Don't let the welcoming committee discourage you."

Truman said nothing in his own defense.

•   •   •

Less than three minutes later, we pulled into the parking lot behind the police station, nestled in between another cruiser and a battered old pickup truck that must have been someone's personal vehicle.

Domanski hopped out, popped Truman's door and helped him out of the car. "Step lively now, Lloyd. My shift's over at four."

"Sorry, Mason," Truman said. I almost believed he meant it.

We took a back door into the building and went down a flight of concrete steps, covered in thin, textured vinyl, into the bowels of the building. It emptied out into a long, dimly lit corridor that seemed to run the length of the building, branching at two places off into side-passages that were each secured with heavy, solid-looking doors with serious locking mechanisms.

Domanski marched Truman ahead of him, tossing over his shoulder, "Seen the holding cells yet?"

"First time."

"Well, they ain't much, but they're home. To some folks, anyway." He chuckled as he stopped at the first side-door, unlocked it with a key from the ring at his belt and nudged Truman through.

Inside, another officer, shorter than either Domanski or myself, but heavily muscled, sat at a steel and laminate desk, a game of solitaire laid out before him. He looked up at our arrival. "Hey, Domanski. Hey, Lloyd. Who's your friend?"

I spoke for myself: "Luke Campbell. Just joined the force today."

"Oh, the New York fella." Seemed everyone knew me already.

Domanski said, "Shane Stevens, Luke Campbell. Vice versa. Shane mans the holding cells four days a week."

"Gives me plenty of time to improve my game," Stevens said, waving a hand over his cards. He turned his attention towards Lloyd Truman. "What'd ya do this time, Lloyd?"

Truman's head twisted in my direction. "Took a swing at this one."

"More than that. He tried to take my head off. Charges are drunk and disorderly and assaulting an officer."

Stevens whistled. "If Skillman don't say different, you're probably headed over to Newport, Lloyd."

This whole back-and-forth was starting to bother me. Domanski knowing Lloyd Truman and greeting him casually back at Callaway's was one thing, but this just didn't seem right. This type of fraternizing would get someone in deep shit where I came from.

"Can we just get him processed, please?"

Stevens and Domanski shared a brief look, then Stevens stood up. "Sure, sure. Leave Mr. Truman to me." Now it was "Mr. Truman" rather than Lloyd.

"Thanks," was all I said.

Domanski headed back out into the hallway, then turned in the opposite direction from where we entered the building, giving me the dime tour along the way.

The Granton police department's cells were identical to any number of other small-town holding tanks across the country: dark, damp, buried in a basement that got very little light or air and with nothing to do but stare at the walls, counting the days until you were released. Only thirty days max, though, Domanski told me. Anything more than that, they got shipped to the nearest state prison, over in Newport. Most of those who spent time in these cells were sleeping off drunks or waiting to be transported elsewhere.

At the end of the long hallway that comprised the town jail, we headed up another flight of stairs, arriving at the end of the hallway I was first in a couple of hours before. A short walk took us back to the police station proper.

Jeannie was gone from her desk when we walked in. In her place was the young officer I saw typing away in a cubicle earlier. He was doing the same now, on Jeannie's typewriter. It looked like he was working on the same set of documents, too. He looked up as we entered. "Hey, Domanski."

"Hey, Loenfeld," Domanski returned. "You met Campbell yet?"

Loenfeld looked my way. "Seen 'im. Haven't actually met. You join up, then?"

"Yeah," I began, but got no more out as heavy footsteps thumped their way from deeper in the station. Chief Skillman appeared, gaunt and unsmiling.

"Detective Campbell. Can I see you in my office?"

"Sure, chief."

Domanski and Loenfeld looked at each other as I moved past them, but neither said anything.

I followed Skillman into his office. He sat behind his desk, his fingers tented in front of him, his gaze boring into me. "Some first day, huh?" He said.

Without being invited to, I sat, my head nodding. "The town always so lively?"

Skillman didn't chuckle at my half-joking question, didn't react at all. His voice flat, he said, "I need you to understand something here, Campbell: this is a small town and a small police force and we need to be a little flexible sometimes."

I *didn't* understand. That must have been clear to Skillman, because he launched into a further explanation. "I understand someone taking a swing at you your first afternoon in town is probably not the welcome you expected from Granton, and I don't think it's the one you deserve, but pulling official status into a little dust-up like that is not something that's going to fly if you're going to be working for me."

I was stunned and I couldn't hide it. I'm sure I looked as surprised as I felt. "There's some misunderstanding here. This wasn't—"

"I know Lloyd Truman likes a drink and likes to fight when he's had a few. We all know that about him. His poppa was the same exact way. Doubtless that's where he gets it from. But he's one of the 'characters' you're going to run into time and again working in this town as an officer of the law and personal enmity has no place in the relationship between you. Is that clear?"

"Absolutely, Chief. But that's not what happened here."

He held up a hand. "I heard the story from Callaway. I don't need to hear it again from you. I understand Lloyd was picking a fight and you stepped in, but there are better ways to handle the situation than tying up time and the town's resources. Now he's in a cell and Stevens'll have to book him in, photograph and fingerprint him, the whole nine yards. It's a waste of time for a little fist-fight in which there was no lasting harm."

He paused. "You don't claim he did you any real damage, do you?"

I shook my head, biting the inside of my cheek, not trusting myself to respond aloud. I couldn't believe what I was hearing.

"Good. Then you understand why bringing him in like you did was a waste of time and I won't have my officers wasting their time or my resources. Especially my brand-new detective, who's supposed to be solving *real* crimes. I'll tell Stevens you've reconsidered pressing charges. Lloyd can spend a night in the tank then we'll let him go home."

Blood rushed in my ears and something twisted in my guts. I couldn't believe what I was hearing. This sort of off-the-cuff law enforcement was not what I expected from Skillman, based on the impression he already gave me. He berated Barnes for forgetting to do a little cleaning, but now he was chewing me out for bringing in a belligerent drunk? The man's priorities were skewed as hell.

"At what point, sir," I ventured, trying to keep all emotion from my voice. "Can I charge and arrest someone? For future reference," I added.

Skillman sighed; his eyes, peeking out through the sagging flesh around them, looked exhausted. "When there is legitimate danger to life, limb or property, detective, you can arrest suspects to your heart's content."

"Fine. Thanks for the clarification." I stood. "Is that all, sir?"

"It is." He changed the subject: "You got a place in town to stay?"

"Going to get that squared away right now," I said, no longer certain I wanted to stay in Granton at all.

4

In just over two hours, I went from accepting a job and glad to have it, to no longer being certain I wanted anything to do with this damned town or its weirdly mercurial chief of police. What I was certain of, though, is that no matter what decision I made, I wasn't in any shape to make it right then and there. After half a day spent driving and then getting into an unexpected, and bruising, workout, I was dead on my feet exhausted. I needed a place to stay, at least for the night.

Jeanie Brown mentioned a hotel on Dumont Street, the Red Garden. I walked back through the station, hoping for a word with Domanski, but saw no sign of him. I said goodnight to Loenfeld, still manning the front desk, and left. In the lobby, I consulted the big, full-color map of town and found Dumont Street. From the map, it looked like it was a fair distance away from the station, but Granton was small enough that with a car, you could probably get just about anywhere in town in fifteen minutes or less.

I found the Taurus where I left it. The meter had run out, but there was no ticket on the wind-shield. I wondered if anybody even bothered checking these meters. I slid beneath the steering wheel, started the car up and headed south down Crescent Street. At the intersection with Main, I took a right, back the way I first came into town, and after two blocks west took another right onto Flowers Road, heading north again. After one more block, I took a left onto Dumont Street. The trip there from the station took maybe seven or eight minutes.

Dumont Street seemed to be what passed for Granton's professional district, lined with neat single and double-story buildings full of offices, many fronted by large signs visible from the street. These listed firms offering accounting and investment services, legal representation, real estate agencies and even an architect. Near the end of Dumont, on the corner of Dumont and the oddly named West Street—odd, since it ran north-south—was the Red Garden Hotel, nestled between an appliance store on the West Street side and a single-story office building, with a big "FOR LEASE" banner hung above its entrance, on Dumont Street. A narrow driveway separated the Red Garden from the office building and following it lead me to a parking lot that sprawled out at least a couple of acres and seemed designed to serve both the hotel and its neighbors. Unless the place was some sort of major hotspot during the tourist season, though, it seemed like overkill. The lot was about eighty percent empty.

I parked and went around the sidewalk abutting the driveway, back to the front of the building. A little wash of cool air spilled over me as I entered and while the weather wasn't particularly warm for a September day, the air-conditioning felt nice and woke me up somewhat. The lobby was larger than I expected, sparsely furnished with three clusters of three over-sized wingback chairs each, each cluster with a potted plant and a coffee table. It was clean and functional, but utilitarian. A commercial hotel, not a resort. Unlike most of the commercial hotels I'd been in, though, there didn't seem to be a restaurant, not even a coffee shop, on premises. The lobby had front and back entrances, from the street and the parking lot, respectively, a single elevator in the far corner and two or three other, unmarked doors, none of which seemed to offer even the basic amenities you'd expect. I chalked it up to the size of the town. Except for those supposed-fishermen every summer, Granton probably had few out of town visitors.

I crossed the space from door to registration area, my footsteps echoing on the tile floor. Though clean and brightly lit, there was nobody else around and it made the place feel just a bit eerie. A moment before I reached the desk, however, a woman came out of a side-door in the area enclosed by the long, waist-high platform. She smiled. "Hi, welcome to the Red Garden."

"Thanks," I said, returning her smile with a nod. She was a nice-looking woman, about forty, with auburn hair and pale-brown, almost tan, eyes. She wore a red suit-jacket with tiny black and white pin-stripes over a white blouse and a solid-color skirt that matched the red in her jacket. The jacket's pattern brought to mind the plaid Lloyd Truman wore, but only for a moment. Nothing else about this woman was anything less than feminine. She exuded a warm, inviting energy that was impossible to ignore. She was the perfect person to welcome a weary traveler.

She eyed me for a moment, the smile still on her lips, but curiosity in her eyes. I suppose the lack of luggage seemed off, but there was something else in her gaze besides.

"Checking in?" she asked.

I nodded. "Yes, please. I don't have a reservation."

She smiled again, just a smirk this time. "This time of a year? Not a problem. We're glad to have you."

"Thanks."

She laughed, a light, breezy sound. "That sounded weird, huh? It's not that guests aren't always welcome, it's just that we're getting into the slow season. We're glad for anyone walking through the doors."

There was a computer on the counter, its bulky monitor turned to one side, but she ignored this and instead pulled out a big, black, old-fashioned registration book from somewhere under the counter and flipped it open. "Hardly need this thing, but, records, you know? Suppose I should get with the times and learn how to use the computer. I let the kids who work for me fuss with it, but I make them jot everything down in here, too."

She looked up, looked me right in the eye; the smile still lingered. She slipped a blank registration card onto the desk between us and pushed it, and a pen, towards me. "Anyway, all on your own? Just you in the room?" I nodded. "How many nights will you be staying?"

I'd been watching her performance, fascinated despite myself, wondering if that's what it really was: a performance for my benefit—or at least customers in general—or just the way this woman was. After barely looking at a woman for months, the waitress, Chloe, stirred something inside me and reawakened my awareness. This woman, too, was hard to ignore.

But I wasn't here for that. Whatever I was feeling, I tamped it down, pushed it aside. The day made me vulnerable and I was well aware of that.

"I'm not sure," I said. "At least one night."

Then I remembered the other thing Jeannie told me. "I'm new to the town's police force, actually; Chief Skillman just hired me today. Jeannie Brown told me to mention the chief's name to the owner of this hotel and maybe there'd be some sort of discounted rate?" I posed it like a question, not wanting to seem pushy, like I was expecting special favors just because I knew a couple of names.

The woman in red's eyes lit up and she clapped her hands together, just once, like an excited kid. "Oh, really. Well," she stuck her hand across the partition between us. "I'm Helen Reddy. This is my place."

"Like the singer." I accepted the hand, shook, nodded, smiled, just friendly. "Luke Campbell. Nice to meet you."

"Just like, but not quite as rich or famous. So Jeannie sent you my way, huh?" Helen smiled again, something coy in it this time. "And here I thought she didn't like me. What am I doing with this thing?" She flopped the big register book closed with a muted *whoomf* sound and turned toward the wall behind her, pulling it open to swing out like a hidden door. Built into its center was a cabinet, cleverly constructed so it was nearly invisible when closed, and filled with keys on little pegs. With barely a glance inside, Reddy reached out and snagged a key then turned back to me. "Here we go. Room four-oh-six." She handed the key across, a sturdy bronze-colored thing on a rectangular leather fob marked "406" in faded gold, swiping the still-blank registration card off of the counter as she pulled her hand back. "It's a little suite – bedroom and a sitting room with kitchenette. Probably the best room in the place aside from mine."

"Thanks, I appreciate that, but—"

She waved a hand, dismissing the thought before I even finished. "Don't worry about the cost. Let's call it a hundred a week and you can stay until you get settled in town. You can hold off on paying until you get your first paycheck. Does that sound fair?"

I'd been paying eighty bucks a week for a flop-house residential hotel in Albany. That price gave me nothing but a tiny room and a bathroom down the hall. A hundred for what was basically a small apartment sounded far better than fair. It sounded like a chance to stretch my legs a little, try living like a human being again. And didn't being human again sound nice?

I smiled without having to force it. "Thank you, Ms. Reddy. That's very generous of you."

"It's missus, but don't let that bother you." She winked.

I didn't know what to say. Helen Reddy, as always, it seemed, had an answer. She laughed and tossed me another smile. "Missus but unattached, if you know what I mean." She paused, maybe waiting to see how I'd react. When I didn't in any particular way, she continued, "At rate, welcome to town, Mr. Campbell. We're glad to have you."

I got that impression loud and clear.

I thanked Mrs. Reddy again for her generosity and headed back to the parking lot to get some of my things from the Ford. I grabbed the larger of my two suitcases, the one with the bulk of what little clothing I currently owned, and hauled it inside. The lobby was once again empty; Helen Reddy was nowhere in sight. I said a silent thanks. Her friendliness was appreciated, but a little much at the moment. Even without coming out and saying it, she made it clear she was interested. Maybe it was me, maybe it was every unattached male who came through her hotel. I didn't know and I wasn't sure how I felt about the matter. The memory of an angelic face with a blonde halo floated across my mind's eye.

The hotel's only elevator was on the far side of the lobby from the front door, off to the left of the registration desk. I pressed the up arrow and the door opened immediately. Inside, I depressed the button for four, the top-most floor, wondering how many other guests the Red Garden had at the moment. I still hadn't seen anyone besides the owner-manager, Mrs. Reddy, and the parking lot out back was nearly empty. What vehicles there were out there could easily be employees of the appliance store next door.

The elevator dinged and the doors popped open, interrupting my thoughts. The fourth-floor hallway was long and brightly lit, white paint reflecting the light to make it seem even brighter. Lining either side of the hallway were sturdy-looking tan doors with brass plates denoting room numbers. Generic artwork adorned the walls, the kind you can find in any hotel hallway anywhere in North America and possibly beyond.

There were six rooms on either side of the hallway, twelve total on the floor. Four-oh-six was at the end of the corridor on the right-hand side, and had a little alcove separating the door from the hallway, the only room I saw with one. The door opened into a room maybe twelve by fourteen feet, longer than it was wide, the far wall comprised almost entirely of two broad windows looking out onto Dumont Street. There was a worn, but comfortable-looking couch fronting a coffee table and facing a television set bolted to a bulky stand. More hotel-bland artwork was mounted above both the couch and the television. Beneath one of the big windows was a small desk, complete with telephone, and a set of hotel stationary. Next to it were two chairs: a plain, wooden one facing the desk and a worn-out easy chair, its back to the windows, angled to face the rest of the room.

The area immediately to the left upon entering the room was the kitchenette. A short counter bore a toaster oven, with blond-wood cabinets above and a mini-fridge below. Along the wall was a tiny, two-burner stove and between it and the counter, a stainless steel sink. A door mid-way down the wall presumably led into the bedroom.

Everything looked to be a decade or more old, but seemed in good repair. Aside from the odd spot here and there on the carpet, everything was clean and there was no layer of dust on any of the flat surfaces, something you might expect to see in a small hotel during their off-season. It looked like a place I could call home, at least for the time being.

I went into the small bedroom and found a queen-sized mattress, covered in a somewhat faded red bedspread, bordered on either side by a nightstand, each with a lamp, one with a telephone and alarm clock. A small dresser stood to one side of a shallow closet, the door already open, showing a handful of hangers, dangling empty from the bar. Above the dresser was a large mirror, mounted to the wall, and on the side opposite of the closet was a door leading into the suite's bathroom. There was a small window above the bed; its curtain was half drawn, but I could see that it looked out onto West Street.

I dumped my suitcase on the bed, pulled it open and caught sight of myself in the mirror. I never considered myself a good-looking guy, my features were far too heavy and blunt for that, but I couldn't remember ever looking as rough as I did now. In the wan light of the fading day, coming through the half-open curtain, my skin seemed sallow and there were dark bags beneath my eyes. I shook my head, deciding Helen Reddy put on the same act for everybody. There was no reason to put it on solely for a guy who looked the way I did, no matter how it seemed.

I sighed with exhaustion and flopped down onto the bed. I was asleep in moments, my dreams haunted by visions of beautiful angels with white and pink wings and gaunt unsmiling scarecrows.

5

Knocking sounds woke me with a start. I opened my eyes in darkness, looked around in confusion, unable to remember where I was. It came back to me as my gaze fell on the alarm clock, its face glowing redly, the dim light like a beacon in the otherwise-black room. The clock read five-twenty-two a.m. I was asleep for a little over twelve hours, but it did nothing except leave me more tired.

The knocking came again, heavier this time and more insistent. I slid off the end of the bed, mussing the coverlet, twisted around and got to my feet. My back ached from sleeping in an unnatural position on a strange bed. Still groggy, I ran fingers through my hair as I walked gingerly through the unlit, still-unfamiliar room towards the front door, wondering who it could be. Who even knew I was here?

Light from the hallway seeped through the peephole, poking a thin, bright finger into the blackness of the room. It didn't do much more than lead me unerringly in that direction and I didn't bother checking through it before opening the door.

A man who looked about fifty, in the dark-blue uniform of the Granton police, stood in the hallway, fully kitted out with gun-belt and peaked cap, the first Granton officer I saw wearing one. "Campbell?" he asked without preamble.

"Yeah, Luke Campbell."

"Chad Moss." He stuck out his hand. We shook. "We got a body for you. Skillman wants his brand spankin' new detective on it."

That woke me up in a hurry. "Lead the way."

. . .

I still had my doubts about this town, about its police force, but as long as I was technically employed by the Granton PD, I couldn't very well say no – not if I ever wanted to work in law enforcement again anywhere else. I already had a reputation; I couldn't afford to be the guy who refused to do his job, too. For now, at least, Granton really was my last chance. Besides, professional curiosity and ethics wouldn't let me do any such thing even if I really wanted to.

Outside, we climbed into Moss's patrol car. He cranked the engine, flicked the headlights into life, and slid smoothly out of the Red Garden's parking lot onto Dumont, turning the car towards the east.

"Sorry to wake you," Moss said, after neither of us had spoken for a few minutes. "The hotel doesn't have a switchboard until six, so I was sent over to collect you."

"How'd you know where to find me?"

He flicked a little quirk of a grin. "You may be *the* detective, but the rest of us are still cops." He chuckled. "It's a small town. Only a couple places you could be staying. 'Sides, Loenfeld said he heard Jeannie recommend the place to you. I had to wake up Mrs. Reddy, too, but she gave me your room-number when I showed up."

"So it's just the two of us, then?"

"If there's anything to this thing, we'll have to radio the station and get somebody from the county medical examiner out, but for now, yeah."

We were back on Main Street by then, cruising through the bright-yellow pools cast by sodium-lamp streetlights, past the darkened windows of stores and other businesses still locked up tight for the night. The sky was turning a pre-dawn gray, but there were no signs of life in Granton yet. The start of most people's day was still a few hours away; only Callaway's Diner was lit up, but the place looked empty from the instant's look I got at it.

I turned from the street, looking over at Moss, one of only two members of Granton's police department I hadn't met the day before. I thought at first that he had a couple of decades on me, but with a better look, I put him closer to forty than fifty. He had a bulldog face, deeply lined around the mouth, and severely thinning hair that made him appear older than he probably was. He'd removed the cap before getting in the car and he had a habit of pushing his fingers through what hair he had left every few minutes. I guessed it was why he wore the hat to begin with.

I changed mental gears. "Tell me about the body."

"More like what's left of one," Moss replied.

"What's that mean?"

Moss met my gaze for a moment before turning back to the road. He answered: "'S'what Chief Skillman said when he called in, half an hour ago or so. Said he got a call about a body out off Little Dip Road. That's an old off-shoot of Peak Ridge Road, the main logging road east of town. Guess whoever called him said that the thing looked like it'd been out there a while. Chief told me we better get you on it before there was nothing left for you to sink your teeth into."

"Someone called Skillman about it? At home?"

"It happens, people call him direct 'stead of calling into the station." Moss shrugged. "He's been around a long time and he's in the book."

I supposed that made sense, but that didn't mean it sat well with me. This off-the-cuff police work wasn't at all to my liking, though I guessed even Skillman couldn't help it if someone called him personally instead of going through the proper channels.

"The chief say who called it in?"

"Nope, probably didn't give a name, anyway, though. Could be why they called the chief himself, come to think of it."

"Why's that?"

"Not much reason to be up that way, except maybe some out of season deer-hunting. Some poor sap probably stumbled on it, hauled ass out of there, figuring to pretend he never saw it, then got a case of conscience. Calls to the station are logged automatically by the phone system, but calls to the chief can still be anonymous, if you want 'em to be."

"And Skillman cares more about bodies than poaching. I guess I can understand that," I told him. "I'd still like to know who made that call, though, if we can find out."

"Why? Doesn't make any difference who found the thing, does it?"

"Let's just say that as far as I'm concerned, people who find dead bodies in out of the way places are always worth talking to."

·   ·   ·

We mostly rode in silence after that. Moss made a few attempts at small-talk and I answered, but didn't allow myself to get too engaged. My mind was elsewhere. The timing of this supposed body being discovered seemed a little pat. Chief Skillman wanted a real detective on his small-town police force because, he said, while murder cases were rare, he hated the fact that he wasn't equipped to handle them. Within hours of hiring me, his "real" detective, a body turns up. Coincidences like that didn't sit well with me.

Ten or twelve miles east of the town, we turned north onto Peak Ridge, a narrow, hard-packed dirt road that angled gently upwards into the hills. The road was hemmed in closely by dense stands of trees, a mix of small conifers and the occasional bigger, leafy tree, like an odd sugar maple. The foliage split the rising sun's light into patches and strips across the road as it filtered through the trees. The ride was bumpy; deep ruts from the passage of heavy vehicles clearly showed this road got a lot of use. A few times I had to hang on tightly to avoid knocking my head against the side of the car.

Moss chuckled. "Welcome to Vermont, detective."

"Welcome *back*, you mean." I grinned. "I was born and raised here."

That seemed to surprise him. "My mistake," was all he said, though.

We lapsed back into silence, save for the noise made by the cruiser on the rough road. A few minutes passed before Moss slowed the car and announced, "Here it is, Little Dip." He turned the cruiser onto a secondary road that was barely more than an animal trail, snaking upwards into the steeper hills. Still-visible indentations in the earth showed that trucks once passed through this way, but grass and scrub brush moved in long ago, reclaiming the road. It wasn't quite virgin woods, but it was doing its damnedest to get back to its natural state.

"How are we supposed to find this body out here?" I wanted to know.

"Supposedly," Moss said, gritting his teeth as we banged over a particularly bumpy patch, "it's just a little ways back of the old Ledford Logging Company camp. Skillman said we should look for a big rock shaped like a little barn."

I resisted the urge to snort my disdain. I hoped the chief wouldn't joke about a body, but this felt like a snipe hunt, a way to break in the new guy. If not for the fact that I doubted Skillman would waste Moss's time, too, I might have believed it. Not that it would have stopped me from investigating.

The once-road twisted and turned through the woods with the meandering casualness of a mountain stream, the angle of ascent growing noticeably steeper. Tough as it was, the police cruiser wasn't suited to this terrain. I thought of the pickup truck I saw in the station's parking lot and wished Moss was driving something four-wheel drive.

Then, with an almost startling suddenness, we popped over the top of the hill, leaving the road and the densely packed woods behind and coming out into a clearing. Moss pulled to a stop and we both climbed out. I swept my eyes across the area, taking it all in. The woods had been clear-cut, stumps pulled up and all, and while long grass and more scrub-brush had rushed in to fill the void, the area was still ringed by four tumble-down buildings and the rusted remains of a logging truck, half-disassembled and sitting on moss-patched cinderblocks.

"Ledford Logging's camp," Moss explained, walking around the front of the cruiser to stand beside me. "Folded up fifteen, sixteen years ago must be now."

"Huh. Any idea who owns it now?"

Moss pursed his lips, shook his head. "Not sure anybody does, actually. C'mon." He gestured towards the far side of the clearing, where the woods were thickest, creeping slowly but surely back into this little patch where man's presence lingered, then marched off in that direction. I followed, keeping an eye on our surroundings, feeling as though these dilapidated buildings could hide just about anything way back here in the hills. My fingers brushed against the new police badge in my coat pocket. It wasn't as comforting as a sidearm.

We pushed through the brush, angling upwards, Moss in the lead. I didn't know when it last rained in the area, but there was a thin layer of muck on the ground and an early morning wetness to the undergrowth that quickly soaked through the cuffs of my pant-legs and the low-cut dress shoes I'd been wearing for almost twenty-four hours. I was still in the tan suit, white shirt and light-blue tie I wore for my interview the day before. I suddenly, deeply, regretted not taking a minute to change clothes before leaving the hotel, but Moss hadn't said a thing about where we were going and it honestly never crossed my mind.

It was impossible to tell from the old logging camp how high this hill was, swathed in trees as it was, but it was clear that this was rough territory to be hiking around in unprepared. It also didn't help much that I hadn't gotten any regular exercise since my resignation from the Albany police force. After only a few minutes, I was huffing and puffing with exertion; sweat stood out in droplets on my face and I could feel my underarms getting damp.

Several steps and a couple of feet above me, Moss paused, looked down. "You okay, Campbell?" I looked for snark in the question, but found none; the other man seemed genuinely concerned.

"I'm fine." I shrugged out of my jacket, slung it over one arm. "Just a little out of shape, I guess."

"Those shoes aren't doin' you any favors, either." He pointed towards my feet. "Soles must be slipping out from under you every step."

He was right. The smooth leather soles were comfortable and perfect for walking around on sidewalks and black-top, but I'd have to buy something more suited for tromping through the woods. I may have been born in Vermont, as I kept reminding people, but it was a long time since I lived here.

Another three hundred feet brought us to the top of the ridge and I thanked god for some level ground. My heart was pounding in my chest and my legs were aching as if I'd run the whole way up.

Moss noticed and said, "You know, it might have been a heart-attack."

I gave him a questioning look.

"The body, might be somebody just had a heart-attack out here and nobody's found 'em 'til now. It's happened before. Somebody who isn't really in good enough shape for hunting or hiking or whatever comes out on their own and just keels over."

He had a point, one I hadn't even thought of. I said so.

"When you're as old as I am, you'll think of it."

I was tempted to ask how old that was, exactly, but let it go. There would be time to get to know each other if I stuck around Granton.

"Well, let's split up," I said. "And try to find this rock that looks like a barn."

Moss nodded and stalked off in one direction while I went another.

It didn't take long. I hadn't gone over five hundred feet before I spotted it: an economy car-sized lump of silvery-gray granite, shaped vaguely like the classic New England gambrel-roofed barn. It was covered in lichen and moss and nestled in a blanket of dead leaves, like Mother Nature had tucked it into bed. And sure enough, there was a body, leaning up against the side of the stone as if it just sat down to take a rest.

I approached slowly, squatted on my haunches, studying the thing. It was a man, though age was impossible to guess. Whoever called Skillman guessed right:

the body had been out here at least half a year, and the weather and wildlife hadn't been gentle. Filthy khaki pants, a lightly padded outdoor vest and what was once a black t-shirt with a logo I didn't recognize were holding the torso together, despite rips and tears where something had worried at the body. There were still shreds of flesh clinging to the head, though most of the face was gone. Up and down the thin arms and between scraps of hair, dirtied, sun-yellowed bone peeked out as if trying to escape from its dried out prison.

And smack in the middle of the forehead was a pencil-sized hole, like a small caliber bullet might make.

At least I could rule out heart-attack.

6

I stood up straight and let out a breath. At least the first couple pieces of the investigation were already in place: I found the body and determined that the death wasn't natural. I wasn't overly optimistic about the next steps, though. I already had a feeling that this was the kind of body that would give any cop headaches. At least it wouldn't be nightmares. This was one of the tamer crime scenes in my experience.

Cupping my hands around my mouth, I called for Moss. I stepped back from the body, taking a more detailed look at the immediate surroundings. I moved a good forty or fifty feet away, in the opposite direction I arrived from, trying to imagine walking through these woods and coming upon the body purely by chance. There was a slight chill in the air, but it carried with it the rich scents of the trees and the decaying leaves that carpeted the forest floor. Early morning birdsong formed an intermittent accompaniment to the sounds of my feet crunching across dry leaves and pine needles, and other natural detritus. It was a quiet, peaceful day out here in the hills and, other than the body itself, at first glance there wasn't really anything out of place. Even the body might not be startling if you saw it from a distance and didn't bother getting too close. From where I stood, parallel to the top of the small ridge, back to the deeper woods, it could well be someone who just sat down to take a rest – if you even noticed it at all.

I walked the area in a slow, wide circle around the barn-shaped rock, with the edge of the ridge as my western boundary, looking for evidence that anyone else had passed through this area lately. I still wanted to talk to the mystery someone who tipped off Chief Skillman. The carpet of dead leaves that covered the ground wouldn't leave footprints or much other sign of passage, but I still felt I had to look. A little south of the rock, not far from where I stopped to survey the area, something small and white caught my eye. I pulled my handkerchief from my back pocket, stooped and came up again with a soggy, half-smoked cigarette, just about ready to fall apart at my touch. It didn't look recent to me, but I wasn't sure how long something like this would last out in the woods. I closed my handkerchief over it, gently folded the fabric into a loose square and put it into the breast pocket of my shirt.

Maybe five minutes had passed since I called for Moss. I considered giving him another shout when he came hiking up the side of the slope to my left. "There you are," I said.

"Sorry, made a loop around the base of the hill. I heard you, but figured I'd be better off just finding you than shouting back. What's up?"

I really needed to get my radio, service weapon, and uniform as soon as possible.

I shook the frustration off and led Moss to the body. He let out a low whistle, then clucked his tongue. "At least we know it's not fresh."

"I already know more than that." I moved towards the body, squatted, jabbed a finger at the hole in the skull. "What's that look like to you?"

Moss's eyes focused on the spot I pointed out, then widened. He dug a pen out of his pocket, held the blunt end of it up against the hole. "A shot from a twenty-two, I'd say." He leaned back on his haunches and sighed. "Poor bastard."

We both stood. Moss said, "I'll get back to the car, radio it in. Probably be a couple hours before we can get the team from the county up here, though."

I nodded and said I understood, then added, "You got evidence bags in the car?"

"Of course."

"Good. I'm gonna do some poking, so call it in then bring some of those back for me, would you?"

Some men might have balked at being given direction by the new guy. Moss seemed glad to have someone take control of the situation. "Sure thing, detective," he said and stepped off the edge of the ridge, half-walking, half-sliding down the slope until he disappeared from view.

I walked back and forth in front of the big rock, trying to picture the scene, trying to get a feel for the victim, if that's what he was. The man wasn't dressed for hunting or hiking. What other reason was there to be out here, then?

One word sprang to mind: suicide.

I imagined someone hiking out here surrounded by nature's beauty, exhausted and depressed but trying to find some solace in the place. Maybe making a last-ditch effort to find a reason to keep struggling ahead. Then, finding none, overcome at last, sitting down, pulling out the weapon that he carried up here, just in case, and—

But if that was so, then where *was* the weapon? Was it possible that whoever found the body helped themselves to a morbid souvenir? It wouldn't have been the first time.

I approached the body and studied its position closely for a moment, then dismissed that idea. The bullet-hole was almost dead center in the middle of the forehead. It wasn't impossible to shoot yourself like that, but it would be extremely awkward to hold a weapon in such a way. Even if you did, the weak position of your wrist bent in such a fashion would probably result in the force of the shot knocking your hand back, flinging it violently away. Maybe even make you drop the weapon. This man's hands were at his sides, almost peacefully, as if he never even saw it coming.

No, suicide didn't seem likely.

An accident? That wasn't impossible, either. Maybe the first impression I got, that this man looked as if he simply sat down to take a rest, was more accurate than I imagined. He wasn't dressed for a hike in the woods, but an inexperienced outdoorsman might not have known that. My own clothes were a perfect example. Moss mentioned out of season hunting. Though not the most likely possibility, could it be that some hunter mistook this man, with his khaki, almost fawn-colored, pants, perhaps with bad light obscuring his shape, but not the light color, for a deer and made a fatal mistake?

I shook my head. It was almost an attractive theory, except for the wound being so small. Nobody hunted deer with a twenty-two. That was a gun for shooting squirrels or rabbits and it hardly seemed likely that someone would mistake a full-grown man for a squirrel.

That left just one real possibility.

Granton's new detective had a months-old murder on his hands.

• • •

I climbed up onto the barn-shaped rock for a better, elevated view of the area and, in my mind, laid it all out in a series of squares. I wish I thought to bring some string to make a physical search grid, but hindsight is twenty-twenty. It occurred to me then that I didn't know what the Granton officers' capabilities were regarding evidence collection. Not a lot of call for that in domestic situations or DUIs. The county sheriff's department would have crime-scene technicians at their disposal, but Skillman brought me in specifically because he didn't want to bring *them* in on these kinds of cases. I doubted either he or the sheriff's department would let me use their technicians and then keep the case for myself.

That meant that I would have to do most of the collection work myself, if not the processing. I had some experience, but not the proper tools or the training to do the job the way it ideally should be done. I was coming to realize that rural police work meant making do with what was at hand. Anything I found that required expert scrutiny I would have to send out to the state lab to be worked on. The situation also meant that I would need to keep a careful, watchful eye on any other local cops who assisted me. Moss seemed like he had a good head on his shoulders and, so far, he was willing enough to take direction. I didn't think I would have a problem with him, at least.

Carefully, I climbed down from my perch and got to work.

Half an hour later, as I was squatting near the base of the rock, poking through a thick pile of leaves with the aid of my pencil, turning damp leaves over individually to avoid contaminating any potential evidence, Moss came tromping back up the slope. Earlier, he seemed better equipped, both in body and footwear, to handle the hike, but after repeatedly climbing up and down the steep ridge, even he looked to be feeling it.

Sweaty, slightly red-faced, and breathing heavily, he announced, "County coroner's team is on its way. Won't be here before ten or so, though."

I flicked a glance at my watch, as I stood: it wasn't quite eight yet. We had already been out here ninety minutes. At least Moss's time was well-spent. I had nothing to show for mine.

Moss must have been reading my thoughts. "Any luck up here?"

I shook my head. "Not yet, but I've barely scratched the surface."

The other man crossed to where I stood, handing over a fistful of clear plastic evidence bags. "I got these, like you asked. What else?"

"Who's at the station this morning?"

"Loenfeld answered when I radioed over, but Jeannie should be in by now. The kid's probably headed home for some shut-eye. Domanski's supposed to be day-shift today and the chief'll probably be in any minute if he's not already. He's usually at his desk by eight at the latest. You thinkin' we need a third man out here?"

"No." I looked around at the area; the woods were thick and deep, but this area was relatively isolated, cut off from the rest of the forest by its elevation and the surrounding rock formations. I would have loved more hands, but it just didn't seem possible. Small as it was, Granton couldn't afford to have all three of its on-duty officers tied up, and I didn't expect, nor want, Chief Skillman to come out here. I didn't think I'd like the way he'd handle it. He hired me to deal with this kind of thing and I planned to do so my way.

"Not right now," I continued. "Let's see what the two of us can do while we wait for the medical examiner's folks."

"Good enough. Just point me in the right direction."

I asked Moss some questions, trying to get a feel for his skill-level with this sort of thing, then gave him a few pointers and assigned him an area to start on. With two people searching, I decided to try a different tactic: starting outward and working our way in. I'd already searched the area around the corpse as thoroughly as I was able and found nothing. I hadn't touched the body itself; I'd let the experts from the county coroner's office do that. I set Moss in an area about forty feet north of the barn-shaped rock, while I headed back to the spot where I found that cigarette. It might have been meaningless, but it was the only place I had to start.

We spent a painstaking hour going over the ground inch by inch. I kept an eye on Moss as best as I could, calling out occasionally, asking how he was doing. The answer was always "Nothing yet." It didn't answer my question, but I appreciated his focusing on the task, at least.

One thing the search yielded was confirmation, more or less, of the thoughts I already had. If this was a suicide, there would have been a gun and it was now certain there wasn't. It didn't mean someone else hadn't gotten to it first, but I had to hope that wasn't the case. If it was an accident or a murder, there would hopefully be a shell, but I didn't find any of those, either. Someone might have collected the shell, though, or, if the weapon was a revolver, there might not have been any to collect in the first place.

I stood on cramped and knotted leg muscles, my back complaining after the night's bad sleep and morning's hard work, and stretched like a cat, trying to draw each of my muscles out to their full length, pulling the kinks out of them one by one.

Moss saw the motion and gave me a questioning look. We were only about twenty feet apart by that point. "What's up?" he asked.

"Nothing." I licked my lips, then ran my tongue over my teeth, wishing I'd taken a moment to brush the fur from them before leaving the hotel. "Just needed to stretch."

"You didn't eat anything yet today, either, did you? Must be pretty darned hungry."

I hadn't even thought of it, but he was right. I suddenly realized how empty my stomach felt. It chose that moment to voice its complaint, the gurgling sound loud in the quiet of these woods. I tossed Moss a sheepish grin. "Thanks for reminding me."

"Be right back," Moss said, holding up a finger, as if pinning me in place. He paused, looking back over his shoulder. "A break's okay, right?"

"Sure. I could use one."

"Okay, be back, then."

Moss turned again towards the slope, disappearing from view in seconds. I leaned back against the bole of a massive red pine and slowly let myself sink to the ground, closing my eyes and releasing a deep sigh. I was right about this being the kind of body that gives cops headaches. Unless the county coroner found something, I didn't have much to go on or even a direction in which to look.

I opened my eyes and let them drift across the scene until they landed on the body, only a short distance away. Who was he? How was it that his life came to an end here? Was there someone out there looking for him? I would have to check missing person reports once I got back to the station. That wasn't a task I relished, either, but it was a potentially important source of information.

I closed my eyes again, trying to fit what little I knew together, trying to form some sort of plan for moving forward with an investigation that might well stretch on into the next few months. Maybe even years. It was like trying to put together a puzzle without having all the pieces or even knowing what the larger picture was supposed to look like.

I opened my eyes, not focused on anything, and my gaze dropped to a spot I'd probably seen a dozen times that morning and never noticed. A spot where the leaves and other forest scree were piled thick and high amidst the twisted gnarls of a sugar maple's exposed roots – and in a way that didn't look quite right. I heaved myself to my feet and moved closer, wondering how I missed it. The leaves, twigs, dried out pine needles and so forth were arranged in a jumble that couldn't possibly be natural; there was just no way that such an unrelated tangle of cast-off plant matter would come together on its own the way it had.

I got down on my knees, heedless of the damp and dirt soaking through my already-dirty pants, and examined the pile from multiple angles. I pulled the pencil out of my pocket, decided it wasn't up to the job and grabbed a nearby stick from under a more-natural accumulation of leaves and used it to flip the pile over, revealing a neat little collection of cigarette butts. And not just a few. There looked to be fifteen or twenty of them, as if someone sat on these roots and chain-smoked an entire pack. Sat smoking and waiting, or watching… or talking.

I leapt to my feet, careful not to disturb the pile, and aligned myself with it and the final resting spot of the mystery man Moss and I came to find. It was a straight line, perhaps a dozen or fifteen feet between the two points. An easy shot with a handgun.

My heart flipped in my chest and a chill crept across the back of my neck. It wasn't definitive evidence, but detective work is as much intuition as anything else. I had very little doubt that I was standing where a murderer once stood. I took the folded handkerchief from my pocket, opened it and took a hard look at the butt I collected, comparing it to the pile on the ground. Were they a match? I didn't know, didn't really know how to tell, in fact. These would definitely be going to the state lab. I transferred the first cigarette into an evidence bag and dropped it into my jacket pocket.

"Hey, Campbell!"

At the sound of my name, I turned to see Moss climbing back up to the top of the hill, a thermos in one hand and a large metal lunchbox in the other. He stopped by the moss-covered remains of a tree that had fallen at the edge of the ridgeline and set down his burdens. I crossed the space between us as he grinned and said, "What do you city guys call this? Brunch?" He opened the lunchbox, showing off three sandwiches wrapped in cellophane and an accompanying apple.

My stomach audibly grumbled at the sight. "I'll call it whatever you want if you'll share."

"Happy to." Moss grinned and we sat down on the log, the food between us. Moss poured me a capful of lukewarm coffee and handed over one of the sandwiches. "Peanut-butter and jelly. Hope that's okay."

"Thanks, Moss." It was just fine with me. A break now and then I would show Moss the cigarettes, get them into evidence bags. A clue and the prospect of food were beginning to change my outlook on the situation.

"Chad's fine," the older man said.

"Then thanks, Chad. And you can call me Luke."

Moss unwrapped a sandwich then bit into it with obvious relish. He chewed thoughtfully for a moment, swallowed, then said, "You know, I've been a cop for almost twelve years and this a first for me. This kind of, you know," he waved a hand, vaguely indicating the surrounding area.

"Well, you handed these things off to the sheriff's department before, right?"

Moss nodded, chewing. "Yeah, that's right. Or the state troopers. Not that we get a lot of murders out here, but it happens once in a while. Skillman hates having to call other departments in on something. Guess he thinks it makes him seem... weak? I dunno. Seems funny, though, huh? Chief Skillman hires you for just this sort of thing and then, *bam*! Very next day."

"Yeah," I said. "Funny."

Moss must have heard something in my tone. He seemed embarrassed. "No, not funny like that, but... I mean, it's... Well, and this is all a little... exciting isn't quite the right word, but—"

"I know what you mean," I said, saving him from further embarrassment.

The sun was rising higher in the sky, shining down on us through the canopy overhead, burning off the remaining dampness of the night and the chill of morning. It would turn out to be a gorgeous fall day, the kind that tourists from all over come to New England to experience, though maybe not this far off the beaten path.

Moss and I ate and chatted, mostly about past work experience and the town of Granton itself. He was a lifelong resident. Except for a two-year stint in the army right out of high-school, he'd never lived anywhere else and he had a wealth of anecdotes about the town and our colleagues. As we talked, the awkwardness between us, the distance that existed naturally between two strangers, was evaporating. Over Wonder Bread, peanut-butter, and cold coffee, it felt like were becoming friends.

For a little while, there was no mention of the man whose life ended not thirty feet from where we sat.

7

When we were finished eating, Moss announced, "Well, I better head back down to the cruiser. This thing," he tapped a finger against the radio he wore on his left shoulder, "is a little spotty way back up here. Don't wanna miss anything coming in."

I stood. "Guess you're right. I suppose the coroner's team will need someone to lead them up here, too."

Moss gathered up the remnants of our "brunch", stuffing the waste into his lunchbox, then asked, "You staying up here, detective?" He cast a look in the direction of the body. "Doubt *he's* goin' anywhere."

The man had a point, but all the same...

"Yeah, I'll stay a while. It'll give me a chance to think about this some more with everything fresh in my mind."

Somehow, it just didn't feel right to me, leaving someone who'd been abandoned out here for so long alone again, even knowing we would be back soon.

Moss shrugged, said, "Okay. See you soon then," and left.

•   •   •

"Late March or early April, I'd say at a glance." The deputy county coroner's tone was flat, without inflection, as disinterested as if I asked him what kind of car his neighbor drove, like he was speaking about something that didn't affect him in the slightest. Earl Cushman was medium height, medium build. His hair and clothes and complexion were all shades of gray. Only the blue, latex gloves he wore while giving the body a quick once-over lent him any color. He looked as if he was given the role of a medical examiner by some film director looking to play up a stereotype. I wondered if it was the case that men like him were attracted to the work or if the work made them like this. I supposed a degree of detachment was necessary to work with the dead, day in and day out. I supposed I should already know that. But I could never bring myself to be quite that aloof.

Cushman and two young men, one an employee of the coroner's office and one apparently a college student doing field work-study, arrived just before ten o'clock. One of his assistants took a couple of dozen photographs from every possible angle and then Cushman himself examined the body. He spent less than ten minutes taking measurements, making notes, occasionally making small sounds to himself as the facts he was accumulating churned through his mind. His actions were quick, precise and practiced. It clearly wasn't the first body he saw in the woods. Even when he noticed the bullet-wound in the man's forehead, he did nothing but scribble an additional line on the note-pad he carried. The man was thoroughly professional, I had to give him that.

Now, Cushman's pair of assistants were zipping the body into a shiny black bag as he continued his recitation of facts. "Something's clearly been at the body. Coyotes in these woods, you know. But it's not nearly as bad as it could have been, both in terms of predation and decomposition. I'd say it was still pretty cold out when this happened, probably even still some snow on the ground. With weather like that, the body wouldn't be frozen through, but it'd be cool enough that most bacteria wouldn't be active. That would slow decomposition enough to allow the tissue to dry out on its own without breaking down too much. Then, by the time the local bacteria was waking up for spring, there wasn't as much of a foothold for it."

"I see," was all I could say to that explanation. I was impressed by what Cushman deduced after just a few minutes with the body. Still, the impersonal manner in which he relayed the information made it a little hard for me to admire him. There just shouldn't be such a clear-cut divide between the living and the dead.

There was one thing I wanted to know, though: "Why do you think that the damage to the body is mostly confined to the face, though, Doctor Cushman?"

The thin, gray man flicked what might have been a smirk. The kind of smirk that the smartest kid in class aims at the dumb-dumb who asks the most obvious question during every lesson. "Some of the softest tissues in the body, Mr.

Campbell." He paused, then added, "Well, I'll know more after the autopsy. You'll have my office's report by the end of the week."

"Thank you, doctor," I said. We shook hands and separated, he to give some further instructions to his two-man team and me to join Moss, watching from near where we rested earlier.

"So what do you think, detective?" Moss asked. Either he wasn't used to the idea of calling me Luke yet or didn't think it appropriate in front of the others.

I fingered the bulging evidence bags I was carrying around, unwilling to let them leave my sight or even grasp, not wanting to break the evidentiary chain. "I think it's time to get back to town."

●　　●　　●

The cool dimness of the Granton police station felt strange, foreign even, after a morning of fresh air and sunlight. Every brick, every floorboard, seemed weighted with age and purpose it was only reluctantly bearing. The woods were older, but had a way of self-renewing that nothing man-made could ever hope to match.

Back up in the hills, Moss and I waited in the cruiser for Cushman's team to finish their work, then followed the white panel van—emblazoned with the livery of the Orleans County Sheriff's Department—down the precarious path of Little Dip Road and out onto the main logging road, heading back towards town. I asked Moss about the logo; Granton was in Essex County, I thought, and weren't these county officials, rather than sheriff's department personnel?

"Yeah, we're in Essex – smallest county in the state, though, right? Orleans, next county over, and Essex are a sort of joint district for a lot of things, these kinda services included. Not always convenient, those guys havin' to drive all over two counties, but it saves money for taxpayers, at least. The sheriff's department stuff is to make it more official or something, I guess."

I chalked it up to another aspect of rural police work.

Like the ride out, the ride back to town was mostly silent. I had a lot on my mind and Moss, after having been up all night on road patrol and then half of the day up in the woods, was about on his last legs. I offered to drive, in fact, but he declined. "Worked longer shifts than this before. I'll be fine," he said.

Once back in town, Moss dropped me off in front of the Red Garden for a shower and change of clothes before I went into the station to write up my report and decide on next steps. As I slid out of the patrol car, I thanked him for his help, let him know how much I appreciated all he'd done. That bulldog face folded into a tired smile. "Don't keep us in suspense, detective," he said, before throwing the car into gear and pulling away from the curb.

I went inside, through the tan-tiled lobby, my footsteps echoing to fill the cavernous space. A youngish woman with dishwater-blonde hair and a conservative, navy-blue blouse was on the telephone at the front-desk. She nodded as I went past her towards the elevator. Helen Reddy was nowhere in sight. As good as she was to me the day before, I was glad. I still wasn't sure what to make of her and I had no mental bandwidth to spare the question at the moment.

In my little suite, I stripped off the grimy remains of what had been my favorite suit, draping the jacket and pants across the back of the wooden desk-chair by the window. I would have to figure out where I could get dry-cleaning and laundry done in town. I slipped the evidence baggies full of soggy cigarette butts from the jacket's pockets, laid them out on the desk, along with the contents of my pants pockets, and took a long moment's look, wondering if there really was anything worth knowing in those filthy, cancerous things.

I hated cigarettes, hated smoking, and wanted to hate smokers, though I couldn't quite go that far. It was a disgusting habit, one that was literally asking for the sickness and pain it brought. Asking for a slow, lingering death. A death I saw twice: once a parent, once a grandparent. My mother saw it, too, when her father was sick, hooked up to oxygen machines, confined to bed because he didn't have the energy to move on his own, but even then, she only put her own habit aside long enough to bury him. Everyone makes their own choices and the rest of us don't need to understand them. But still, I wondered if she enjoyed those last few years before the habit caught up with her, too.

I slapped briskly at my stubbled cheeks, trying to knock the morbidity from my mind. Maybe being as detached as Cushman wasn't such a bad thing. I was sure he never had these kinds of thoughts.

I moved through the bedroom into the bathroom, finished stripping and ran the water as hot as I could stand it. I stood under the tiny, steaming bullets, letting them do their work, washing away the grime and sweat, letting the water carry it and thoughts of lonely deaths in the woods down the drain. For the moment, anyway. I already knew I would spend a lot of time on that subject for the foreseeable future.

I gave myself ten minutes to relax under the shower before stepping out, using a thick, rough hotel towel to dry myself. The coarse fabric left my skin pink and slightly raw, but I felt clean and refreshed. I felt better than I had in days, in fact.

I used the tail-end of the towel to wipe away steam from the mirror and gave myself a quick shave, scraping away the last remnants of the Luke Campbell I'd been when I walked into the room. When I was done, I examined my handiwork and decided that, for all that it took out of me after months of inactivity, getting back to work was good for me. Very good. I stared into the mirror and the man who looked back was more familiar than the one I'd been seeing lately. This was a man with a purpose.

I brushed my teeth, combed my hair, dressed in clothes pulled from my suitcase. I would have to unpack later on.

I collected the evidence bags I left on the room's desk, along with my keys, wallet, badge, and miscellaneous belongings and slipped out of the room, down to the parking lot and into my car. On my way through the lobby, the girl I saw at the reception desk was checking in an older gentleman. A guy a little younger than myself, in a suit that had seen better days, sat in one of the lobby armchairs, glancing through a newspaper. So I wasn't the only guest the Red Garden had, after all.

The drive to the police station only took a few minutes. This time, instead of parking on the street, I drove around back and parked in the same spot the beat-up old pickup truck from the afternoon before occupied. I wondered if maybe that was Moss's personal vehicle. Or possibly Loenfeld's.

And then I was inside the building, in a foreign-seeming place that I already knew I would spend a lot of time in. Maybe the rest of my working life. With that thought, I realized that before I even left the woods that morning, I'd decided to stay in Granton.

•　　•　　•

Jeannie Brown gave me a warm smile as I walked into the station proper. "Good morning, detective."

Was it still? It seemed impossible that it wasn't even noon yet. I resisted the urge to check my watch. "Morning, Jeannie. Chief Skillman in?"

"Always. Eight a.m. sharp every morning."

"Thanks," I said, slipping past her desk.

"Hold it." She put out her arm like a traffic cop, pinning me in place. "I just put a call through to him, so he'll be busy for a few minutes." The warmth I was already coming to associate with Jeannie disappeared, replaced by the all-business persona she put up when I first met her. "How did you make out yesterday? You getting settled in?"

It was funny; a likely murder, Granton's first of the year, at least, and probably for a lot longer than that, and she wanted to know about me.

"Fine. Thanks for the recommendation about the hotel. Mrs. Reddy gave me a good deal on a room. It seems like a nice little place."

Jeannie made an "mhmm" noise, then asked, "Glad to hear it. What do you think of her?"

"What do you mean?"

She smirked. "She's very friendly, isn't she?"

"Is that why you sent me there?"

She let out a throaty chuckle. "Good lord, no. I like you too much for that, Mr. Campbell."

"Just 'Luke' is fine. And what does that mean?"

"Luke," Jeannie looked me in the eye. "I sent you there because this town has three places to stay if you don't have a home of your own: the Red Garden, Monroe's Motel, which is as close to skid-row as it gets around here, and those cabins down by the lake, almost none of which would see anybody safely through the winter. They just weren't built to be lived in year-round. I sent you to the Garden because it's a nice place, like you said." She put a hand on my arm, wrapping her fingers around my elbow. "I'm sure it's tempting, but just trust me, okay? Helen Reddy isn't your type."

"Okay. I don't get where this is going."

Heavy footsteps scraped down the hallway behind Jeannie's desk. Chief Skillman appeared, towering and stone-faced, an unlit cigarette clamped dead center in the middle of his mouth. "Morning," he said, the cigarette rolling smoothly to one side, as if propelled by the word. "Detective Campbell," he motioned with two-fingers, curling them inwards towards his palm, "C'mon back."

"Sure." I disengaged myself from Jeannie's grasp, glad for the chance to escape that weirdness. Helen Reddy might be on the prowl, but Jeannie hardly seemed prudish enough to be worried about that sort of thing. I would wonder about it later.

Skillman led the way into the bowels of the station, bypassing his door and opening the one marked "CRIMINAL INVESTIGATIONS", the office he told me the day before would be mine. "All yours," he said, gesturing for me to enter.

I stepped into the room. Skillman followed, flicking the switch on the overhead lights, bringing them stuttering to life. The change in the place was remarkable. The lightbulbs had been replaced, giving the room a harsh, but clean, yellow-tinted light and by it, I could actually see this as a work-space, instead of a junk-heap. The piles of detritus—the chairs, the boxes, the useless, wheel-less bicycle—had all disappeared. Left behind was the desk, free of clutter, bare except for a telephone, a blotter, and pen-set, as well as the filing cabinets along the rear wall – and yes, a matching set along the wall that was hidden before. There was a small window behind that desk that had been completely obscured the day before. Two chairs went along with the desk, one behind it, one in front of it. A set of shelves that I hadn't noticed the day before took up part of the rear corner of the office, in the space where the two rows of filing cabinets intersected, and held camera equipment. In the opposite corner was a small, old-fashioned secretary's typing desk, complete with a typewriter that was probably thirty years old. It was within easy reach of the desk if I was to turn the chair to face it. The space was outdated, but looked like somewhere you could get some work done.

"Go ahead, detective. I said it's yours, didn't I?" Skillman added, after I had a moment to take it all in.

"Thank you, sir." I stepped completely into the office, moved to the nearest filing cabinet. The top drawer was stuffed full of file folders, and in each was a copy of a case report, some with other, accompanying documents. From what I saw, the reports seemed fairly well written up, though only some were typed; many were hand-written and the quality of penmanship varied wildly.

Skillman moved to the chair in front of the desk, sinking ponderously into it. "Newer files are in my office. Stuff from the last seven, eight years."

I turned so he wouldn't have to speak to my back, sliding the filing cabinet closed behind me. He wasn't facing me. He was already seated in the visitors' chair, so I moved behind the desk, and tried the rolling chair out for comfort, setting my evidence bags on the side of the battered wooden desk. The chair's padding was thin, but wasn't too bad – until I leaned back and nearly fell, the chair trying to dump me over backwards onto the hard-wood floor. I just barely caught myself, my flailing fingers gripping the edge of the desk.

Skillman surprised me with a chuckle. "Swap it with this one when I get up, why don't you?"

"Think I will," I said, righting myself.

"Anyway," Skillman continued, "Newer files are in my office. You can move 'em in here if you want or leave 'em where they are. Doesn't matter much to me. There's probably some open cases in the more recent files we've got, but they're still old enough that they probably aren't going to bother anybody, so let's worry about those once you've got a handle on your current situation." He locked eyes with me, raised an eyebrow. "And here's where you tell me about that."

I told him. The tip he received was correct, there was a body up in those woods, and it had been there a while.

"What's it look like?" he asked. "Loenfeld said you got the county medical boys out there."

I nodded. "Yeah, I did. It looks to me like murder."

"Why do you say that?" Skillman's lip twitched upwards, deforming the already-soggy cigarette.

I told him about the bullet-hole and the position of the body.

The cigarette drooped, wilting like a flower in the heat of summer. Skillman seemed to remember its existence and plucked it out, flicking it towards the wastebasket off to the side of the desk. "Could be murder, sure, but where it was found? I'd bet suicide. Some out of work logger goes up there, feeling blue, maybe liquored up, decides he can't stand the way his life has turned out and that this is as good a place as any to get off the train. Logging is a transitory sort of employment for a lot of these fellas and there's been a number of men over the years I've been doing this who've just disappeared. We never know if they've moved on or if they've gone out into the woods somewhere and just never came back out."

I shook my head slowly. "I don't think so. If it was suicide, there'd be a weapon and Moss and I searched that area as thoroughly as possible."

"But you weren't the first up there."

"I know. I thought of that. It's always a possibility somebody who wasn't actually involved with the death walked off with the weapon. Who'd you say called this tip in to you?"

Skillman's expression was unreadable. "I didn't. Couldn't. Never said."

"Man? Woman? You got caller ID at home?"

"Man. Nope."

"We could have the phone company pull the LUDs."

Skillman's brows knit; maybe the term was unfamiliar to him, but he understood what I meant from context. He shook his head. "Let's not go that far. I don't want anybody getting jammed up over doing their civic duty. It's their right if they want to stay anonymous. Like the staties' tip-line commercial on the TV says, 'We want your information, not your name.'"

"I'd really feel better about—"

"And what's that you've been luggin' around?" Skillman interrupted, pointing a long, bony finger at the evidence bags I'd temporarily forgotten about, intent as I was on the conversation.

I moved the two bags to the center of the desk, the smaller one holding the single cigarette butt and the larger one holding the pile's worth. "Hopefully evidence." I told him about how I found the butts at the scene, the position in relation to the body and the way someone tried to hide the larger pile.

Skillman cocked an eyebrow again as he reached out, grasped the larger bag. He hefted it in his huge palm, as if testing the weight, before setting it back down again. "You gonna make a case with *those*?"

I shrugged. "No way to tell. I'll send them off to the state lab once I get Dr. Cushman's autopsy report, see what they can tell me. Between these, the coroner's report, and whatever the victim had on his person, I should know more. I'm hoping he has ID, but a courier is supposed to bring whatever they find on him in before end of day."

The chief nodded, slapped his thighs lightly and stood. In the small room, he seemed to tower over the desk. "Well, sounds like you've got a plan for this thing. Let me know how it plays out or if you need anything."

I stood, too. "Actually, I do need a few things, chief."

"Oh?"

"I've got the badge, but I still need a service weapon, radio, and at least a couple of uniforms."

"Right, and you'll want the keys to a cruiser. I told you to take number eight, didn't I? The keys'll be with Jeannie. She's handling the order for your uniform, too, right? Okay. And tell Domanski to get you arranged regarding a weapon. He's got keys to the weapons lock-up. Good enough?"

"Yes, sir."

"All right then. Back to it, detective." He nodded and went out the door, closing it softly behind him.

I sank down into my chair, remembering not to lean too far back this time. My gaze fell on the two bags of cigarette butts sitting on the desk. Then it drifted towards the wastebasket.

8

There was nothing much to do with the problem at hand until I had more information. I sorted through the desk drawers, found a marker and notepad. I wrote the relevant time, date and place on the evidence bags, then jotted my thoughts and a rough timeline of the morning's events on a sheet of yellow, lined paper from the pad. I slipped the notepad and bags into the bottom drawer of the desk and left the office.

It was just about noon and I wanted to get a few things taken care of before the end of the day. Domanski was not in any of the cubicles that formed the hallway outside of my and Chief Skillman's offices. They were all empty, in fact. I went down to the front area where Jeannie was picking at a salad in a Tupperware dish, forking up pieces of leafy greens and dipping them into a tiny, plastic bowl filled with a creamy-looking orange goo. Her other hand casually flipped the pages of a magazine.

"You know where I could find Domanski, Jeannie?"

"Try the cells. He radioed in ten or fifteen minutes ago saying he was bringing a DUI in. I had to call Spillane's Garage to have the car towed."

I thanked her and headed out of the reception area, down the hallway towards the building's basement level.

Even at high noon, the holding cells were no less dark or gloomy. The long, cement-block hallway at the bottom of the stairs carried the faint echo of voices. I followed them to the area where I met Stevens the day before.

Domanski and Barnes were in conversation, Barnes seated at the desk Stevens occupied the day before, and Domanski leaning against the edge of it.

Domanski was saying, "—weaving all over the damned road. Went almost a mile before he even noticed I was on his ass. When he finally pulled over, I said, 'Dan, what do you think you're doin'?' and the damned fool says, 'Going to work, ossafur Domanski.'"

"'Ossafur?'" Barnes laughed.

"Yeah. Just like that. And so drunk he forgot Harger's fired him last month, I guess. Blew a point two-two on the breathalyzer. Least he didn't fight me any, but I felt bad putting the cuffs on him."

"Too bad. Nice guy, for a drunk. Well, that's his license for another year."

"Yeah, his license… but it's really too bad for Melissa and those kids having to put up with him."

Domanski noticed me standing there listening. He turned. "Morning, Campbell. Heard you got a big one."

"We'll see what it turns out to be. Skillman said you'd get me set up with a service weapon."

"Sure thing." He turned towards Barnes. "Finish up with Mr. Sarver for me?" It was 'Mr. Sarver' in front of me, I noticed, rather than 'Dan'. I was still an outsider, I supposed.

Barnes told Domanski no problem. Domanski said to me, "Come on this way," and headed back towards the hallway.

Before I followed, I said to Barnes, "Hey, thanks for getting that office cleaned out. I appreciate it. And," I hesitated, unsure what kind of ground I was treading, but added, "sorry for that ass-chewing you got."

Barnes lifted his broad shoulders in a lethargic shrug. "It happens." He didn't expand on that. I let it go.

"Well, thanks," I said and followed after Domanski.

The other man hadn't gone far. Out in the basement's single long hallway, he stood by the door nearest the stairs leading up into the first floor of the building. The door was unmarked, but was newer and had a more-solid look to it than the others, setting it apart. Domanski produced a key from a ring hanging on his belt, opened the door, and stepped inside.

The Granton police's armory wasn't impressive by the standards I was used to in my previous career, but seemed like overkill for an eight-man police department, one of whom I still hadn't even met by my count. One wall of the small room was taken up by a gun-rack that held a half-dozen shotguns and a pair of rifles. Next to it was a free-standing wire-mesh unit that supported four ballistic vests. Mounted on the wall to my left was the kind of display a home collector might have, loaded with a dozen side-arms, an even mix of revolvers and automatics – mostly thirty-eights for the revolvers and nine-millimeters for the autos. To the right was a work-bench with tools for cleaning, maintenance, and minor repairs.

I let out a low whistle. "You boys don't fool around out here, huh?"

Domanski shrugged. "Most of this has never been touched."

"Where'd it all come from? Seems a little excessive, if you don't mind my saying."

"Don't mind at all. It ain't mine." He chuckled. "It's just the sort of thing gets accumulated over the years, I guess. We get a budget from the town every year, and a supplement from the state, just like every other department in the area. All the money's gotta go somewhere. Next year, we're adding a new cruiser, I hear. Well," he waved a hand towards the wall of pistols, "take your pick. Let me know what you end up with and the serial number so I can register it to you internally."

I glanced at Domanski's harness, noticing the Glock nine-millimeter in his holster. Pretty standard, but not to my taste. If he was going to let me choose, I might as well see if I could find what I wanted.

Turning towards the rack of weapons, I looked them over carefully, took a few down, testing the balance and feel of them in my hand. I settled on a snub-nosed thirty-eight revolver, the classic "Police Special" that could be holstered at the hip or under the shoulder, but was small enough to fit in a pocket if necessary.

Domanski watched with feigned casualness, but I could sense his interest. "Like the old standbys, huh?"

"I guess I do," I said, slipping the pistol into the side pocket of my jacket. Nestled in its hiding place, the small weapon felt massive, as if the weight of the thing would be noticeable to anyone who laid eyes on me, but looking down at myself, there was hardly a difference. I lifted the gun from my pocket, handed it to Domanski. "This is the one, I think."

"You sure? Most of the boys carry nine mils these days. Me, included," he added, patting his own holstered weapon. He eyed the weapon in his hand, then looked up at me. "Not much stopping power to this thing."

"Yeah, I'm sure. If I'm lucky, I'll never have to worry about how much power it has." I was thinking back to a night not nearly long enough in the past. Not long enough to put behind me, at any rate.

The other man nodded, stepped to the work-bench and pulled from a drawer an official-looking ledger on a clipboard. He copied the weapon's make and serial number onto the paper, printed my name next to it, then handed it to me. I signed where indicated and he traded me the weapon for the clipboard.

"We got a spare harness upstairs," Domanski said. "I'll find it and a radio for you. Once you get a uniform, you'll be official, huh?"

"My next stop," I told him.

•   •   •

Jeannie Brown was way ahead of me.

As I walked back into the front area of the station, she said, "Detective Campbell! Perfect." She disappeared down the hallway, reappeared a moment later carrying a uniform covered in a clear-plastic bag, like it just came back from dry-cleaning. "Try that on," she told me. "Burkhart's just sent it over."

"Burkhart's?"

"Raymond Burkhart. The tailor over on main. I gave him your measurements, had him make alterations to this to fit you."

I took the hanger from Jeannie.

"Go ahead, try it on." She shooed me off in the direction of my office.

Between Jeannie's measuring and Burkhart's tailoring, they did good work. The uniform fit perfectly. Domanski was right. Wearing the outfit made my place in Granton seem official. There was no mirror in my office, but I knew what I looked like while wearing it: a cop.

Skillman asked why I wanted to stay in law enforcement. Why I wanted to keep being a cop. Wearing the uniform, the answer was clear to me: there was really nothing else I could be.

I let myself enjoy the moment.

9.

I let Jeannie ooh and ah over me in my new uniform for a few minutes. She asked about the fit, tried to inspect the areas the tailor adjusted. It was almost funny how much she seemed to enjoy herself. The old girl was a born flirt, though you would never know it when first meeting her. Even knowing she wasn't interested in me in that way, though, I wasn't terribly comfortable with all the attention. Still, she seemed like my best ally in town at the moment, so I let her go on a while. I had a feeling I would need at least one person on my side.

"Well," Jeannie said. "Now you're official."

"Almost. Skillman said you've got the keys to cruiser number eight for me."

She gave me a skeptical look. "Road patrol already? You had a pretty busy morning."

"No." I shook my head. "Just want to get more familiar with the town right now. But," I added, "eight is the cruiser Skillman's assigned me, so I better get used to it, too."

The older woman looked at me appraisingly, then held up a finger and disappeared down the hallway, as she had earlier. She returned a moment later, a set of car-keys dangling from her outstretched fingers. She pressed them into my hand, threw me a hard look and said, "Don't push yourself, detective. Okay?"

"I won't," I promised.

•   •   •

The department's motor-pool was a four-car garage on the opposite side of the parking lot from the station itself, a squat, red-brick building backed up against a stretch of woods. Nobody was around, but there was only one vehicle in the bay, so I assumed the dark-blue Crown Victoria was cruiser eight. The keys in my hand fit both the door and the ignition, validating my on-the-spot detective work.

The motor didn't want to turn over right away, but I got it going and pulled out of the garage, out of the parking lot, and away from the station, leaving behind its resident den mother and its strange, mercurial chief. Initially, I had no destination in mind, but maybe subconsciously I knew where I was going, because almost before I realized it, I turned left onto Main Street and was settling the police car into a parking space across from Callaway's Diner. I hadn't eaten lunch, so it was as good a destination as any, I decided.

It was only a little past twelve-thirty and Callaway's was busy. Before I even pulled open the glass and steel door, I could see the booths along the walls were packed. All but a couple of the stools at the counter were occupied, too. I was glad, in an abstract sort of way, to see the place was doing good business. A little small-town pride for the place I decided would be home. Home for the time being, anyway.

I settled onto one of the empty stools, the same stool the unflappable old man with the newspaper occupied the day before, and reached for one of the menus stuffed into a black, metal wrack on the counter. A voice to my left said, "Uh, hey there."

I looked to find Lloyd Truman, still in his blue-and-green-checked plaid shirt and dun-colored Carhartts, sitting on the next stool over. He was sporting a fresh bruise on his cheek. I didn't remember hitting him there.

"Remember me? From yesterday?" Truman added, unnecessarily.

My jaw throbbed, just for a moment, at the memory of the man's meaty hands slamming into it. Truman held out one of those hands now, but not in a fist; it was open, extended for a shake. A sign of truce.

"I just wanted to say sorry. I got a little sauce in me yesterday and then saw Ecare, that fucker— I mean, um… well, you know. I wanted to tell you I appreciate you dropping the charges and I'm sorry for what I did."

I stared at the other man a moment, giving him the critical eye. He seemed genuinely contrite, in a kid-caught-red-handed sort of way. I accepted the hand, shook it once. "Fine," I said, turning back to the menu. It really wasn't fine at all, but I had no say in the matter. Skillman made that clear.

"Can I maybe buy you lunch, officer?"

I turned back towards Truman. "You're really sorry, huh?"

"Yes, sir."

I hesitated, the noise of the busy restaurant swirling around us, forming a kind of curtain that cut the two of us off, obscuring our conversation from those around us. Ordinarily, I wouldn't be caught dead accepting any favors from a man I arrested not twenty-four hours earlier, but I had a lot of questions about Granton and Lloyd Truman seemed like he would have at least a few of the answers.

"Okay," I said.

Truman broke out in grin of relief, his teeth barely showing through the tangle of beard. "Great. No hard feelings, huh? Oh," he said, as if remembering, "we didn't really get introduced, did we? I'm Lloyd Truman. I work up at Whitehead Logging."

I knew. I didn't bother saying so. "Luke Campbell."

Chloe, the lovely waitress, came over at last, forestalling any further conversation between me and the man I still thought should be in a cell. She showed no flicker of recognition at seeing me. Despite everything that happened since arriving in town, though, she had never entirely left my thoughts. Seeing her again refreshed my first impressions of her and reinforced what I felt the day before. There was little time to ruminate on or explore those thoughts, though; she was all business as she took my order for a burger, done medium, fries, and a root-beer. Then she topped off Truman's coffee mug and disappeared again.

Truman let out a wistful sigh. "Somethin', ain't she?"

An understatement I could readily agree with. "Yeah."

"You know what, though?" Truman faltered for a second, as if arranging his thoughts. "I feel like... Well, it's like she's walkin' around asleep. And you kinda want to wake her up. You know what I mean?"

I knew exactly what he meant, but before I could say anything, a small voice cut in, "Hey, I know you!"

The stool swiveled, allowing me to get a look at the new, waist-high participant in the conversation. The boy who was doing homework in a back booth yesterday afternoon stood before me, backpack slung over one shoulder, eyes gleaming with excitement. "You're the guy who cleaned Mr. Truman's clock with those karate moves!" There was a slight French lilt to the boy's speech, heavier on certain words.

Lloyd Truman chuckled, deep in his throat. The boy seemed to notice him for the first time, but wasn't embarrassed at all by the faux pas. "Oh, you guys are friends now, huh?"

"Sure," Truman smiled. "That's how big boys do it sometimes. Knock each other around a little, then we can be pals."

The little boy's face scrunched up, puzzling over that idea. "There're guys at school who knock me around sometimes, but we aren't ever going to be friends. Hey," he said, his expression changing again, sliding into a semblance of the slick look he probably thought he was pulling off. "Could you teach me some of those moves you did, mister?"

I shook my head. "I don't think so. A long time ago, I was taught martial arts to help me with my job, but those moves can be dangerous. I wouldn't want you to hurt yourself or someone else fooling around with them."

The child's eyes, the same light blue as the eyes of woman who must be his mother, grew dark and his expression clouded over. "There's some people I'd *like* to hurt." The childish honesty, and the anger behind it, was a little disconcerting.

"Then I'm definitely not going to teach you any of that stuff." I changed the subject. "How come you aren't at school, son?"

"I don't like eating lunch at school," he said, letting his voice trail off. He added, "It's not that far away, so when mama's working, Mr. Callaway lets me eat in the kitchen if I stay out of the way."

Between those bits of information and what he said a moment ago, pieces fell into place. I remembered my own school days as a pudgy little kid who feared the playground, the lunchroom, and any other place without direct adult supervision. I gave the boy a quick, appraising glance. He was small for his age, slight, and as towheaded as his mother. I pegged him at seven or eight, but there were younger kids who would have outweighed him easily. I didn't know the exact circumstances the boy was living under, but my heart went out to him all the same.

The boy's mother returned then, carrying the plate with my meal. "Roland,"—Ro-*land*, she pronounced it, the French way—"don't bother the customers."

The boy opened his mouth to respond, but I beat him to it. "It's no bother, miss."

Lloyd Truman piped up, "This is Luke Campbell, Chloe. He's the new cop Chief Skillman hired yesterday."

The woman called Chloe showed no interest at all. She said only, "Hello." To her son, she said, "Roland, get back to school now, okay?"

Roland threw a glance my way, then looked at his mother and nodded. "Okay, mama." He turned to me again and said, "See you, mister!"

"Take care now, Roland. We'll talk again." The boy grinned, then turned towards the door. I watched him trot down the aisle, backpack bobbing along. A couple of customers were on their way out, too, and one of them held the door for the kid.

"Is there anything else I can get for you?" Chloe asked.

"No, I'm fine, thank you."

She nodded and left without another word, seeing to diners on the far side of the counter.

It had been some fifteen minutes since I entered the place, and the restaurant was beginning to empty out a little. The lunch rush in Granton didn't last long, it seemed, at least not at Callaway's.

"See what I mean?" Lloyd Truman asked, his voice seeming louder now that the place was a little quieter. "Like she's in a daze except where that boy's concerned."

"He's her son, right?"

"Yeah, he's hers all right. Only thing that girl's got."

"What do you mean?" I wanted to know.

The big man sighed, shook his head slowly. He took a sip of coffee and when he spoke again, there was genuine sympathy and compassion in his voice. I decided there was more to him than the bruiser I pegged him as when we first met. "Ain't really my story to tell. The whole town knows it, but…" He stopped himself, then changed tacks. "Hell, you probably got a file on it somewhere in your office, yeah?"

I sat up straighter. I was interested before. Now I was concerned. "Okay, now what does *that* mean?"

Truman blew a gust of air. His eyes flicked towards Chloe, coming back down the aisle behind the counter, a coffee pot in hand. He put his head near mine, his tone conspiratorial. "Finish your burger, okay? I'll tell you, but not here."

I wanted to know what the man had to say, but I was in no hurry, either. I half-expected that, for all the build-up he was giving it, the story wouldn't be anything I couldn't have guessed on my own. And I didn't want to rush through my meal, either; the burger wasn't only free, it was good, too.

When I was through, Truman took a last sip of his coffee, stood, slapped a twenty down on the counter between our dishes and said, with a wave in Chloe's direction, "For the both of us, okay? And keep the change." The girl nodded her head, but otherwise didn't react.

The big man clapped a hand on my shoulder in an overly familiar gesture and jutted his chin towards the door. I followed and, outside, took the lead, pointing towards where the cruiser was parked. "If you're worried about privacy," I said, "Let's talk in here." I climbed in behind the wheel.

After a moment's hesitation, Truman opened the passenger door and slid, in as well. "Heh, never been in the front of one of these things."

"I'll bet."

His eyebrow went up, but he didn't take the bait.

"Need a lift anywhere? We can talk on the way."

"Nah," Truman said. "You need gas, though." He waggled a thick finger at the dash. "You know where Spillane's is? The town's got an account there. It's where all the town vehicles fill up."

I didn't know. I said so. "How do you know where the town has accounts?" I asked.

One of Truman's shoulders lifted in a half-shrug. "'S'no secret and it's a small town. West, okay?" He pointed towards where Crescent and Main intersected a couple of blocks away.

I put the car into gear and moved away from the curb, pulling a u-turn and heading in that direction. "Okay, so... what's the story? What's the connection between Chloe and that guy, Ecare, that pissed you off so much? By the way," I said, remembering, "what's Chloe's full name?"

Lloyd sighed again. "Sad story. Real sad. And, well, first of all, her last name's DeJonge, though it *should* be Butler."

"That's gonna need some explanation, too."

Lloyd told me to turn left onto Crescent, heading south. Then: "I'll get there. Like I said, you probably got a file on it in your office somewhere, but basically the story is like this: seven, eight years ago, kid named Alan Butler—he was the star of the local high school's hockey team, handsome, popular, all-around-

American boy; you know the type—goes up to Quebec with some friends for a little fun. Lots of kids around here do it, have for years. The drinking age there is only eighteen, you know? Anyway, the Butler kid and some friends go up one night, and come back the next morning. Nothing out of the ordinary. Only Butler goes back the next weekend, alone. And keeps going back up, every weekend for what must be a couple months. His folks are getting worried. I mean, he's a senior in high school, he's already been accepted to UVM,"—I didn't need him to tell me that meant the University of Vermont—"but then, finally, one night he goes up and next morning comes back *with* something: a cute little number named Chloe DeJonge. You with me?"

"Uh huh." I pulled onto the concrete skirt of a filling station with a yellow and white sign that read SPILLANE'S. I put the cruiser off to one side, away from the pumps so I wouldn't block them, and shifted gears into park. "Keep going."

"Okay."

But Truman didn't, not right away.

He looked out of the window, craned his neck as if looking for something in the direction of the gas station's main building. Whether he saw it or not, I didn't know, but he said okay again and then: "So, kid Butler comes back with a new friend. He met her at some club or party or whatever that first night he and his friends went up and they got along real well, if you know what I mean." Truman waggled his pinky finger and grinned. "And the girl got pregnant, 'course they didn't know that for a while. But they're young, they're in love. Nothing else matters and they're going to make it work. Butler's parents are furious, of course. They think he's throwing his life away for some girl he doesn't even know – and Quebecois to boot. You know, a lot of folks around here have French-Canadian blood in 'em and most people are happy to take their money when they come down here, but that's about as far as it goes sometimes. The Butlers aren't any exception to that. So they're pissed, with good reason. But the kid and the girl say to hell with you, we'll make it work. He's gonna finish school, she's gonna get a job. They'll make it work and in the meantime, they're together as much as possible."

"Okay," I interrupted, "it's a classic love story. I get that. Where's the tragedy?"

Truman scowled, annoyed at his flow being broken. "I'm getting there." His face relaxed. "So, okay… these two lovebirds are making it work. Mom and pop

Butler aren't happy, but the kid is eighteen, he's an adult basically, and they know 'f they push any harder, they'll just drive him away. Here's where Nathan Ecare comes in."

A middle-aged guy in a gray, mechanic's jumpsuit came out of the gas station a few yards away. He looked hard at the police cruiser, but didn't come over. He scratched at his forehead before going back inside. I turned the two-way radio on, set the volume to just above its lowest setting, half-expecting to hear something come over it any moment.

"Chloe and the Butler kid are off doing whatever they were doing one night near the end of the school year, early spring. They've been together a few months at this point and the girl is starting to show the pregnancy. She's a tiny little thing, so it really shows, you know? She isn't going back up to Quebec much at all anymore, but staying with the Butlers most of the time. Whatever folks she's got back home don't seem to care, I guess, cuz it's like she's cut that place out of her life at that point. So the kids, they're out, doing whatever, coming back home to the Butlers', not having any clue what's going on a few miles away. And, I'm not a hundred percent sure myself, but long story short, Ecare's got himself into some trouble at the border and is tearin' down the backroads trying to outrun some staties. Either he turns a corner or the Butler kid does, doesn't matter, but the Firebird the Ecare boy drives slams right into Alan Butler's Volvo. Kills Alan instantly, bangs Chloe up something awful."

"Jesus."

"Yeah." Truman sighed. "Well, Ecare's in shit. Vehicular homicide plus trying to evade the cops, and whatever else they add besides. Something with drugs, if I heard it right. Pretty serious shit." He shrugged. "He was just a kid himself, same class as Alan Butler at the high school. His family's got the bucks, though, so he gets a fancy lawyer and ends up with something like six years in prison. Life ruined, of course. Was headed to Dartmouth that fall. Not that he didn't get what he deserved, I mean. But it don't seem like much when a family's lost their only son and that poor girl's lost the love of her life. Alan Butler's gone forever and Nathan Ecare is already out of prison. Every time I see that little bastard around town, I go a little red, I'll tell you."

I ignored that last part. I said "Jesus," again and added, "Miracle the baby wasn't hurt in the accident, at least."

"Yeah. Guess that's what the Butlers thought, too. They were… hmm. Not sure how to put it. The whole thing kind of drove 'em a little out of their head,

I guess. Not sure they're sane to this day, actually. Became real Bible-beaters, if you know what I mean."

"I can imagine. So... Chloe?"

"Butlers let her stay with 'em after she got out of the hospital. Just until she gave birth. Story gets a little fuzzy there. Depending on who you believe, either the Butlers wanted the girl to put the baby up for adoption or wanted to adopt the baby themselves. Either way, Chloe said no, she was keeping it."

"I don't blame her after what she went through. That kid is a tangible link to Alan Butler."

"Exactly. Well, Alan's folks didn't think much of that, I guess, so she was out of their house pretty soon. Don't know why she's stuck around as long as she has, though. I mean, what's to keep her here?"

I wondered the same thing. I said, "You seem to know a lot of details about this, Lloyd."

"Like I said, small town. Word gets around fast... especially something like that. I'm telling you officer—"

"It's detective, actually."

Truman didn't miss a beat. "I'm telling you, man, there are no secrets in Granton."

I didn't believe that for a second.

10

The car was silent for a moment. Truman and I sat, each of us with our own thoughts.

Finally, he said, "Well, Campbell, that's all I got to say. Guess I should be gettin' on now."

I nodded. "Sure. Thanks for the story. Let me gas up and then I'll give you a lift to wherever."

"No need." Truman unbuckled his seat-belt, unlatched the door. "Here's fine."

"You sure?" The area was hardly desolate, we were still in town, but there wasn't much on this stretch of road aside from the filling station, a few homes and a stretch of woods.

"John Spillane's a buddy. We'll shoot the shit a while."

"Okay, then." I reached across the space between us. Truman grasped my hand, shook. "I'll be seeing you, Mr. Truman. Stay out of trouble, will you?"

Truman threw me a lopsided grin, said goodbye, and slipped from the car, shutting the door behind him with a muted *thump*. He walked quickly to the gas station then disappeared inside.

I turned the engine over, crawled the car towards the row of pumps. I was hardly out of the vehicle when the jump-suited guy I saw earlier approached, long legs striding confidently across the concrete. He stopped a few feet away from where I stood, one of the gas pumps in my hand. The guy was about forty, with a head of thick, ginger hair fading to gray in little patches. His face was round, open, with no particular expression, but his eyes were intelligent and searching. His eyes seemed too small for the big face.

"Hey, there, officer. Fill 'er up for ya?" he asked.

"I can manage," I said, popping the gas tank open and fitting the nozzle in place. I pulled the stiff trigger and the sound of moving liquid began to churn. "You Spillane?"

"Yes, sir. John Spillane."

I shifted the pump to my left hand, stuck out my now-free right. "Luke Campbell. Just started on the Granton PD."

Spillane met my grip, shook once then released it. "Yeah, Lloyd was sayin'."

He was fast. *Warning people about me?* I wondered.

"What do you think of the place, so far?" Spillane asked.

"Seems nice. The town's got an account with you, I'm told."

"Yes, sir," Spillane nodded. "Gas, towing, parts, service. Whatever you need."

"Can I leave this rig with you for a tune-up? Drop it off later today? Chief Skillman assigned it to me and it needs a once or twice over. Had a bit of a time getting it to start."

He asked "Drop it here?" He sounded uncertain. "I usually send one of my guys up to your place for routine stuff."

"What's faster?"

Spillane hesitated. "Well… depends what it needs. I mean, your shop's got the basics, but if it needs anything more than that…"

"You got everything a vehicle could need here, I assume?"

"More or less, yeah. You talked to Skillman about this?" he asked.

There it was. Chief Skillman's long arm. "No," I said. "I'll square it. He said he wants me road-ready ASAP," I lied. I made a big deal of checking my watch. "It's nearly one-thirty now. Can I drop this thing off around four?"

Spillane thought for a second then nodded, slowly. "'S'long as it's cool with the chief."

The gas-pump popped, bucking slightly in my hand, signaling a full tank. "Great. Thanks a lot." I replaced the nozzle on its mount. "I need to sign anything for this?"

Spillane shook his head. "Nah."

"Then I'll see you later." I got back in the car and pulled out of Spillane's, heading back towards the center of town.

·　　·　　·

"Detective. My office."

I barely set foot in the station before Skillman's voice boomed out of the depths of the building. Jeannie cast a look in my direction, one that mixed curiosity with sympathy—the chief's tone was unmistakable—but she said nothing as I pushed aside the heavy wooden gate next to her desk and headed down the hall.

Skillman's door was open. He was already seated at his desk. A fresh, unlit cigarette dangled from the edge of his lip. He didn't look happy to see me. "Sit down," he ordered.

I sat, carefully arranging my face into its most neutral expression. "What's going on, Chief?"

"I just had a call from John Spillane."

No surprise there. I didn't bother pretending. "My cruiser needs a little work. Didn't want to start when I first tried it."

"I understand and I appreciate your being proactive, but *you* understand, Campbell, that there's a way of doing things around here. A way that works and has worked just fine for a long time." He held up a hand as if to forestall any argument I might make, though I'd kept my mouth shut.

"Campbell, you came here from what I assume to be a thoroughly modern department in a good-sized city and you want to make changes. I understand and appreciate that, too. It's why I hired you; we could sorely do with a little modernization. But whatever changes you want to make, let's keep to the field of investigation and let's run them by me beforehand. It'll be a lot better, a lot smoother and easier, if changes come from the top down. You tell me what you need, what you want to do, and if I agree, I'll make those changes. As far as administration, and anything involving funding and whatnot, you just leave that to me. Okay? You understand me?"

"Yes, sir." This type of power-play came as no surprise. At least he was being relatively pleasant about it.

"Okay. Now," he plucked the cigarette from his lip, made to toss it into his wastebasket, then seemed to change his mind and set it down on the rim of his ashtray instead. "One of John's boys will be along later on, so get that rig of yours into the garage for 'em." He shifted gears with no segue. "How's your investigation coming?"

There couldn't possibly be any changes in the little over two hours since we last talked about it. Skillman was sending me a message, putting me in my place: *Do your job, don't rock my boat.* I got the message loud and clear.

"Still waiting on the courier with the victim's effects, sir."

"Good enough, detective. On your way, then."

There was no mistaking that message, either.

Dismissed, I headed to my own office. I closed the door behind me, sat down in the unsteady chair behind the big, nearly empty desk. Frustration churned in my belly, but there was nothing I could do other than work through the problem before me.

I picked up the phone on the desk, made an educated guess and hit zero. There was a single ring, then Jeannie's voice answered, "Granton Police." I told her it was just me and asked if she could bring me whatever files we had on missing persons, going back, say, three years, or tell me how to find them myself, if that was easier. "Hold on, Luke," she replied and hung up with a *click*.

Maybe five minutes later, there was a knock on the door, followed immediately by Jeannie herself, wearing a wry look and carrying a thin manila folder. "I thought I better get the missing persons file from the chief's office for you."

No more needed to be said on that subject.

"Thanks, Jeannie, I appreciate it." I flipped open the folder. It contained a document with maybe a dozen pages, mostly consisting of a list of names and scant biographical information about each: age, sex, marital status, last known address, last date confirmed seen and so forth. It went back a lot more than three years; at a glance, I saw that some dates from the mid-seventies. This folder must have been Skillman's master list. I looked up at Jeannie. "There are individual files on each of these?"

"Should be. If they aren't in here," she pointed to the filing cabinets along the walls, "they'll be in the chief's files."

I nodded. "Okay. Thanks again, Jeannie."

She smiled, said, "'S'what I'm here for," and left the room.

I removed the paperclip holding the individual pages of the file together, spread them out across the desk before me, and took up my notepad and pen, ready to winnow the numbers down to something manageable.

It only took a few minutes to eliminate the vast majority of the list. There were just under a hundred people listed, far more than I expected, even with Skillman's statement to me about how every year a few loggers disappeared from town. The earliest was from nineteen-seventy-one and the most recent was from the spring of the current year.

Before seventy-one, I wondered, did nobody bother to keep track of who went missing or was it rather a matter of nobody caring? I was just a kid then, but I remembered the world being a lot different. Maybe there was a time when people figured if someone wanted to disappear, it was their own business. I knew from experience that many of those people were probably willing "ghosts" – folks who simply got sick of the life they were living and thought they would be happier if they just left it all behind. The majority of disappearances anywhere could be explained that way.

Whether my theory was true or not, those long-missing people weren't my concern just then, so I eliminated anyone reported missing before nineteen-ninety, since it was a nice, round number. I also eliminated all the women, not that there were too many, maybe twenty total. That done, the list was cut down considerably. I scanned the rows of data, jotting down names that fit my date-range and gender criteria and when I was done, fifteen minutes later, I had a dozen names to look into further.

Skillman said that the files in my office were all older, nothing newer than maybe seven or eight years ago. Probably the last time someone occupied this office, based on the amount of accumulated clutter I saw. I took the oldest name on my list, a Lester Froshet, last confirmed contact June of ninety, last known address one of the motels along the highway outside of town, and moved to the filing cabinets. They weren't exactly the tidiest I ever saw, but they weren't too bad, either. In a larger organization, these files would be assigned case numbers and sorted that way. In Granton, files seemed to be sorted by the name of either the victim or the perpetrator, if one was known, though the newer ones did have case numbers jotted down on the files, as well. It wasn't the best system, but I managed to find the appropriate drawer without too much effort. But there was no file on Froshet. I decided not to check another name from the list. It was the oldest and if it wasn't here, none of the others would be, either, I guessed.

I went back to the desk, scribbled a quick copy of the list on a fresh sheet of paper, arranged the documents from Skillman's file back in their original order and closed the folder. Back up the dusty, empty hallway, I stopped at Jeannie's desk, where she was on the phone. It didn't sound serious or like anything official. My presence didn't seem to bother or hurry her at all, either, but after a few moments, she said goodbye and hung up. She turned and, without preamble, asked, "Did you find what you needed?"

"Maybe." I paused, then added, "No idea, if I'm really honest." I set the manila folder down on the edge of her desk and placed the copy of my list on top of it. "Could you do me a favor and return that to wherever you found it?

And I'd like the files for each of these names. I checked, but none were in my cabinets," I fibbed. "Hopefully they're in Skillman's."

"Of course," she said. "Anything else?"

The door to the corridor opened, forestalling whatever I might have said. A middle-aged man entered. He was dressed in a blue polo shirt with a logo I didn't recognize on the left breast, khaki-colored slacks and a plain, blue baseball cap, a gray ponytail spilling out from beneath it, waggling back and forth as he moved. Cradled beneath his left arm, he was carrying a large, white, plastic envelope about the size of a grocery bag. The envelope bulged slightly at the base, as if the contents had all settled there. In his right hand, he carried a clipboard. His eyes slid over me without recognition, settling on Jeannie. "Hi, Jeannie. Got a package for a Luke Campbell."

"Good timing," I told him, lifting the wooden divider separating us. "I'm Campbell."

"Got ID?" he said.

I threw a glance at Jeannie, who gave me a kind of facial shrug in response. The guy picked up on it. "Sorry, bud, I know her, but I don't know you."

"No problem," I told him. "I get it." I dug out my wallet, showed him my New York driver's license. I hadn't thought about it before, but I supposed I would have to find time to get a Vermont ID.

The courier glanced at my license, double-checked the name on the package, nodded. "Next time, I'll know you," he said.

"Sure." I accepted the package from him. This close, I could see the logo on his shirt read "Priority Express" and there was a matching logo on a sticker affixed to the big, white envelope. The guy shoved his clipboard and a pen in my direction, too. I signed where he indicated.

He touched the brim of his cap, nodded, said, "Thanks, all," and was out the door.

I said to Jeannie, "Let me know on those files," and headed back to my office.

• • •

Still warmed up, the florescent lights buzzed back into life, throwing their glare over the ordered emptiness of my office. I moved to the desk, tore open the top of the envelope and slowly upended it, carefully dumping the contents out onto the broad, flat surface. In a few moments, I had arranged before me a small plethora of plastic bags and a type-written note from Dr. Cushman.

The note read: *Enclosed: all items found on John Doe's person, save for articles of clothing (vest, logo-printed t-shirt, trousers, undergarments, socks, Dockers shoes), contained within, labeled by type. Clothing held back for further testing. Autopsy report will follow at earliest opportunity. — Cushman*

There was a second page of the note, as well, containing a detailed inventory of the items. I sorted through the bags, holding each one up to get a look at the contents. A handful of coins in one; a set of keys in another. Other bags held a pink, plastic comb, missing one of the teeth; a ballpoint pen with a name and phone number printed on it; a tube of chap-stick; a badly stained handkerchief; an also badly stained scrap of paper that looked like it was a receipt of some sort. That was it. Just junk, the everyday ephemera we all accumulate and carry around with us. But no wallet, no ID. I supposed that would be too easy.

I pushed aside all the evidence baggies except for the ones containing the pen and the receipt. The information on the pen was probably useless; thousands, millions probably, of its type were given away every year by businesses of all stripes. Besides that, it was pretty badly faded and I couldn't make most of it out. I jotted down what I could read: *Reynard and Pearce – 802-555-X97X*. The full phone number would have been nice to have, but with a name I could probably find it. There was an additional line between the name and the number, probably an address or some sort of company motto, but it was only the suggestion of blue lines on the white plastic tube. I didn't matter much; the name and partial phone number should be easy enough to locate.

I hoped the receipt might be more helpful.

I set the pen's bag aside and lifted the receipt's. It was that very thin, fragile paper that comes out in narrow, vaguely printed strips from inexpensive cash registers just about everywhere. The writing on it was both faded from the cheapness of the printing and obscured by the water- and dirt-stains at least half a year, if Cushman's approximation was correct, of weather left on it. I opened the bag, removed the sales-slip, held it up to the light. It helped a little; I could make out the words *city* and *drug* near the top and a line-item that read *Coca-Cola – 6-pck* and another that might have said *magazine*. That told me something, anyway. The question was whether it would be useful. A definite location for the merchant or a time and date of purchase would be nice. Like a wallet containing ID, though, it was too much to hope for. I didn't know Granton well, but how many drugstores could it have? At least a few. And who could remember such a generic purchase off the top of their head after who knew how long? Nobody at all.

I let out a heavy breath and sank into the straight-backed chair in front of the desk. Well, this wasn't much, but it wasn't nothing at all, I supposed. Nothing at all was what I started with. Now I was maybe an inch or two beyond that.

The telephone rang, the sound very loud in the quiet office, jangling me to instant full alert. I leaned over the desk to pick it up. "Granton Police. Luke Campbell speaking."

"Campbell? The guy on the body, right?"

Who the hell...?

The voice answered the question before I could say it out loud. "This is Frank Lautner, editor of the *Granton Telegraph*. You got a minute to give me a quote on this thing?"

"Sure. How's this: how the hell do you know about it?" I paused for effect, then continued, "Wait, don't tell me. 'Small town.'"

Lautner chuckled. "You got it. Word travels fast, no matter what you do." I wondered who talked. It was either someone in this office or someone in the county coroner's. My bet was on the source being someone in the building with me.

"Especially if you broadcast it. Police scanners are pretty common around here, you know, Mr. Campbell," the reporter said. "Anything you don't want folks knowing about, I'd keep off the airwaves."

Of course, I thought and cursed myself for a fool as Lautner added, "So how about something for the readers?"

I shook my head, though he couldn't see it. "There's nothing to tell. How do you normally get official information?" I wanted to know, curious. "I don't suppose Skillman sends out press releases."

"Nah. I call him up and he gives me the low-down, but since you were hired for this kind of thing, I figured I'd call you directly. Glad to see the extension hasn't changed from when old Marc Whittington had it. That'll make it easier for us to get in touch."

Exactly what I wanted, I thought bitterly. "Listen," I said. "There's really nothing to tell right now, so can you do me a favor and keep a lid on things for a little while? A few days, anyway. I don't want people panicking or tromping all over the scene of the crime – if it *was* a crime," I added.

"We're a weekly, Mr. Campbell," Lautner said, a tinge of annoyance coming into his voice. "My cut-off day is Thursday for Saturday publication. It's Tuesday afternoon now. If I don't get this thing written up and filed by three p.m. Thursday, it won't make it in at all this week."

That would be fine by me.

"Can't you give me something? I'd rather not," he continued, "have to go over your head." The message there was clear. I wanted to grit my teeth, but held back. It felt as if everyone in Granton had a free pass to push me around by using the threat of Skillman.

"How about this," I began and told him about how the new officer in town, fresh from the "big city" of Albany, hired as Skillman's chief detective, got into a fist-fight with local Lloyd Truman his first day in town. I hated the idea, hated the thought of that sort of publicity, but it might be enough to put the man off. With a whiff of something like real news in his nostrils, I figured this Lautner wouldn't bite, but I didn't know how else to get rid of him. I knew too well that making enemies of the local newsmen was a bad idea.

"Well, I don't know," he said. "I was going to run something to that effect already, but I suppose I could beef it up a little. It *is* news. But," he continued, "you'll give me a head's up when there's something you can tell me about this case you're working?"

"Of course," I promised.

"Okay. Suppose it'll have to do." The man sounded glum, but resigned.

"Can you do me one more favor?"

Lautner laughed again, a little more the man he was when I first picked up the phone. "You don't ask for a hell of a lot, do you?"

"I try not to. Can you tell me if you know of a business around here called 'Reynard and Pearce?'"

"Oh, is that all? You could have found that in the phone book. They're the biggest law-firm in town."

Well, maybe John Doe's pockets held an answer or two, after all.

11

I thanked Lautner for the call and for his help. He said, "Sure thing. Give my regards to the chief, will you?" I told him I'd be sure to and hung up.

I sat a few moments, staring at the telephone, thinking about what Lautner told me and the list of names I compiled. A part of me wanted to hop into the cruiser and find the offices of Reynard and Pearce right that very moment. The detective in me wanted to know what the hell good that would do. What would I ask them? *"Any clients disappeared in the last few months? Do you recognize this pen?"* I almost laughed, but it wasn't really funny. It was only the first day, but there was so little to go on, I was beginning to get the idea that this really was one of those cases that wasn't going to go away any time soon. There was just too little to grasp.

A knock on the door interrupted my thoughts, followed almost instantly by Mason Domanski. He leaned into the open doorway, half-hidden by the frame, and reached out a hand in my direction. "Hey, hoss. Keys on ya?"

I was confused. My face must have shown it, because he added, "For your cruiser. Mikey Gibson's here. From Spillane's?"

"Ah, damn. I forgot all about that."

"No worries," Domanski grinned slyly. "We all know you're busy."

I stood, dug in my pocket, tossed the key, all on its lonesome on a slim, black ring, Domanski's way. He snatched it out of the air. "Won't even tell Skillman on you," he smirked.

I grunted, humorlessly. "Thanks, Domanski."

"You got it." He disappeared, the door closing behind him.

I sank back down into the desk chair. My eyes fell on the small pile of evidence Cushman sent over, at the list of names I wasn't sure would do me any good. I cast a glance at the clock, mounted on the wall above and to one side of the door. Quarter after three. I'd been working for more than ten hours, since Chad Moss knocked on my door at the Red Garden just before five that morning.

I was suddenly very, very tired.

•　　•　　•

It was three days later, Friday morning, that I walked into the station just after eight o'clock to find Loenfeld sitting at the front desk, stifling a yawn with the back of his hand.

"Long night?" I asked.

"You'll find out soon, enough," he quipped. "You're on road patrol Monday night, right?"

I nodded.

"Better spend some time getting to know the area, then," he suggested.

I told him that was a good idea, as if I hadn't already been doing just that, and moved to head further into the building.

"Hey, Campbell, before you go, got a message from the county coroner's for you."

I stopped, my hand on the heavy wooden gate. "Dr. Cushman?"

"Yeah." He picked up a slip of paper from the desk. "Called about half an hour ago, said he's finished with your John Doe. Guess they work early hours."

"Good news." I thanked Loenfeld, said I'd see him later and went back to my office. On the way past, I noticed that Skillman's door had light behind it. Jeannie said he was always at his desk by eight and from what I saw the last few days, it was true. What he did on a daily basis, however, was anybody's guess. After seeing so much of him my first twenty-four hours in Granton, I'd only seen him once or twice since.

In my own office, I flicked the light on, sat down at the desk, and dialed the number on the paper Domanski gave me. A woman answered. "Orleans County Coroner's office."

I told her who I was and who I was calling for. She put me on hold. Several minutes crawled by, then: "Cushman speaking."

"Dr. Cushman, it's Luke Campbell."

"I know," he said. Wasting no time, he went on, "I'll send over my typewritten report later this morning, Detective Campbell, but I called earlier because I thought you might want to hear more about what I found directly from me, so you can ask any questions you may have in real time."

"I can come over to your office, if you like," I offered.

"I don't think that's necessary. There's not a whole lot to see that would be valuable to you. Let me cut to the chase, though. The body is a white male, approximately five feet, nine inches, weighing approximately a hundred and fifty pounds. That's likely twenty to thirty pounds lighter than he was in life, due to loss of fluids and reduced body mass from animal predation. Age is somewhere between twenty-five and thirty years, based on bone density and jaw structure." He paused, whether for a breath or effect, I didn't know, then added, "Did you know the male jaw continues to grow for a time into the twenties? Sometimes as late as twenty-seven years old."

I told him I didn't. I asked if it mattered.

"It's sometimes helpful for establishing age. Speaking of the jaw, there was significant dental work done on this man. Several cavities filled and the removal of two bicuspids, almost certainly for orthodontic corrections. Braces, in other words. This was someone who probably came from a good family. Good enough to worry about cosmetic appearances and to have the money to do something about it. Anyway—"

He went on giving me details. The man seemed to have been in good health at time of death. There was a severe fracture of the left radius, long-healed. Cushman managed to take prints from several fingers, but didn't yet have any results back on those, and might never have any, depending on whether the individual was ever in a situation where his prints would be taken. Cushman expressed doubt about civil service print records, but said he'd sent a request for both criminal and military record-checks.

Finally: "And for the big question, the gunshot wound. It was, of course, the cause of death. There's no doubt about that." He threw out a brief flurry of medical terminology about the precise location in the skull where the bullet penetrated and the area of the brain that was damaged, most of which went over my head. He went on. "Whether it was suicidal, homicidal, or accidental, I can't definitively say, though, if pressed, I'd ruled out suicide. The angle on the entry wound is just a little too high for that."

"As if someone stood over him and fired down?" I asked.

"Possibly, but the angle, while high for someone shooting themselves, is also a little low for that. Unless the shooter was not a very tall person or was perhaps seated or kneeling. Clinically speaking, it's not like anything I've seen before. It could mean nothing, but I honestly can't say." His tone held the equivalent of a shrug. "I did, however, recover a badly mangled slug from the skull and I'll send it out to the state for a ballistics examination. Maybe you'll get lucky."

"Guess we can hope," I said, thinking the odds were unlikely. "And what do you have for an approximate date of death?"

"No better than my original estimation." I could picture him shaking his long, gray head. "Late March or early April. The cooling effect of the weather, then the effects of being exposed to same for so long, has done quite a job obscuring those details. Your best bet," Cushman offered, "is to track down dental records. A lot of money was put into this mouth and somewhere there's a dentist, and or an orthodontist, who profited nicely. Somebody will have records of it. All the information you'll need will be in my official report."

"Okay, doctor. Thanks a lot, for your efforts and your time."

"Glad to do it," he said, that tiny smile he showed me when we first met evident in his tone. The words and that image combined in a slightly disconcerting way. It really did take a special sort to do Cushman's job.

"Well," the doctor said. "Good luck to you, Campbell."

I thanked him sincerely because we both knew that I would need it.

•   •   •

After hanging up, I jotted some notes about what Cushman and I discussed on the notepad that I planned to devote solely to this body. I would type them up and add them, along with Cushman's report, to the official file later on. For the moment, my scribblings were mostly to keep track of my own thoughts.

I knew it would take time to make progress – time for Cushman's fingerprint record requests to be processed; to get his report to me with the possibly crucial information on the body's dentition; time to compile a list of dentists in the region and get those dental record requests in to them, then more time for those offices to get around to checking them. After spinning my wheels over the last few months, I wanted to make a big splash as soon as I got back on my feet. I wanted to close this case swiftly and neatly, to prove to Skillman and myself, that

I was still a top-notch cop. That this just wasn't that kind of case was becoming increasingly obvious.

A short, heavy knock rattled the pebbled glass of my door. I slid the notepad into my desk and said, "C'mon in."

Ben Barnes's pudgy face appeared in the gap between door and frame. "Got a call for you, Campbell. Stolen car reported over on Meddick's Place."

Granton's first murder in who knows when was an important case in a lot ways, and presumably to more people than just me, but that didn't mean the rest of the town's crime was going to take a powder while I solved it.

"Thanks. I'm on it," I said.

12

With the stolen car, at least, I got lucky.

Mrs. Brandy Roethes's tan, nineteen-eighty-four Mercury Grand Marquis disappeared right out of her own driveway sometime in the night. She wasn't exactly frantic when I arrived to take her statement, but she was upset. She was already forty minutes late for work at the local A&P and how long would it take to find her car? I gave her a ride over to the grocery store as she gave me the details on the vehicle: the make, model, year, color, plate-number. She had no idea what the VIN was offhand. She also gave me the crucial bit of info that she had lived alone since the passing of her husband from a massive coronary last summer, but that the keys to the car were gone when she woke up that morning. She had an adult son, but hadn't spoken to nor seen him in nearly two years.

"Is that helpful with your case, officer?" Mrs. Roethes asked.

"Very," I told her.

"I know you'll find my car, Officer Campbell." She smiled as if I'd given her the best compliment she had all year. It brightened her face considerably and you could see, behind the years and the cares and the wear they brought with them, that she was once a pretty woman. Then she asked, "Could you pick me up at four?"

I told her we'd see.

I called the "case" in to the station. Jeannie Brown was at the desk, in her role as dispatcher, receptionist and all-around office matron. "Try Addy's," she suggested.

I had no idea what that meant, and said so. I learned that "Addy's" was a junkyard west and south of town. If the car was stolen by joyriding teenagers,

Jeannie rationalized to me, somebody would have reported them tearing up the backroads and state highways by now. That no one had done so, seemed to indicate that it was a "real" theft. The only place in the area to get fast cash for something like a stolen car was Addison's Junkyard and Salvage. The owner had never been charged with anything, but enough parts from stolen vehicles turned up there over the years that Skillman kept an eye on the place.

When I rolled patrol cruiser eight into the hard-packed dirt parking lot of Addy's, nearly a mile down a private road indifferently paved with crushed gravel, the Grand Marquis was sitting out in plain sight, right in front of a tin shack sporting a faded, hand-painted sign reading "ADDISON'S". A distance behind the shack could be seen towers of rusting scrap, the rows of which seemed to stretch on for miles, some many times taller than seemed safe or prudent. I wondered how long it took for a pile of steel to rust itself together into something so solid.

I got out of the cruiser and went over to the car in question. The keys were still in the ignition. I sighed and shook my head. Somebody was doing time for possibly the stupidest crime I'd ever seen.

Inside the yard's office, a pot-bellied man of about fifty, in grease-stained overalls, stood at a card-table cum desk, jawing thickly into a flimsy-looking princess phone that was probably once white. His eyes caught mine as I walked in, but he showed no real interest. He took his time with his call, grunting single-syllable words occasionally and jotting something down on the top sheet of a receipt booklet with itemized columns. Taking an order for parts, I guessed.

I looked around as I waited. The walls of the place were thickly papered in old calendars, running towards swimsuit models and hot-rods, and ads for Penzoil and car-parts. A worn, but comfortable-looking office chair was pushed into the corner of the room, next to a filing cabinet doing double-duty as a coffee station. Unlabeled boxes, some leaking fluids onto the peeling linoleum floor, were everywhere, stacked as haphazardly as the mounds of scrap outside.

After a couple of minutes, the man I took to be Addison hung up, turned towards me and asked, "What can I do for you?"

I jutted my chin towards the door. "That Grand Marquis."

"You interested?"

"Very." He confirmed for me that he was Sloan Addison, third-generation owner of the yard, before I told him that the car's owner reported it stolen. He didn't bother putting on a surprised act. All he said was, "A fella comes in here with the keys and title and says he wants to sell the thing, who am I to question him?"

I had to keep my jaw from falling open. "He had the title?"

"Sure. It was in the glove-box."

I shook my head. People do the damnedest, and the dumbest, things.

Addison looked like a grease-ball, but he was calmly cooperative once all the facts were laid out. The car was sold to him, for three hundred bucks, less than two hours earlier by a Dylan Roethes, who duly filled out the paperwork for the sale and to transfer the title. Roethes. Things were getting clearer by the second.

"It didn't bother you that the title was in the name *Brandy* Roethes?"

Addison shrugged. I mentioned that it might bother the county prosecutor, who took a dim view of receiving stolen goods. Addison surprised me with a single laugh, sharp and raw like a half-feral dog's bark. "Yeah, okay. I'm cooperating, aren't I?"

He was at that and making the charge stick might have been troublesome. I decided I would run it by Skillman later on, since he was already aware of Addison's business proclivities. I called Spillane's, asking them to tow the car to the A&P in town and to have someone notify Brandy Roethes once it arrived. I considered trying to get Addison to do it himself, but I didn't think he would be *that* cooperative.

I found Dylan Roethes an hour and a half later, sitting in Brook Park, not far from Granton Elementary, drinking from a bottle wrapped in a brown paper bag. He was in his early twenties, sandy-haired, wearing a white, sleeveless undershirt, camouflage-patterned pants and heavy boots that looked military-grade. When I approached him, he looked up at my face, bleary-eyed, looked down at the harness and badge I was wearing, then calmly put his bottle down and raised his hands, a shit-eating grin on his lips. Addison and the kid were the most cooperative criminals I ever encountered.

The car was safely returned to Brandy Roethes, who was thankful, but seemed disappointed I wouldn't be giving her any more rides. Young Roethes, I learned, was AWOL from Fort Monmouth, down in New Jersey. His mother claimed she had no idea her boy had even joined the army, much less come home. Why he decided to steal and sell his mother's car, Dylan couldn't explain.

"It just seemed… like a good idea, I guess," was all he had to say for himself. Like so many television commentators, I worried for the future of our youth, but it was up to the county prosecutor's office to worry about the future of Dylan Roethes in particular.

•   •   •

The whole thing was wrapped up in just under three hours and it wasn't quite eleven-thirty when I deposited the Roethes kid with Shane Stevens in booking. I was thinking about getting some lunch as I walked into the station proper and found Jeannie Brown looking grave. She gave me no opportunity to ask why. "Need you to take a lost-child call, Luke. Came in just a couple of minutes ago. Moss and Pohlman are on the road today, but Moss is dealing with a domestic and Pohlman's way down south of the lake."

I had no more thoughts about my belly. "Of course. Who is it?"

"Roland DeJonge."

13

In just over a minute, I was again in the cruiser and heading in the direction I just came, back towards Brook Park. This time, I passed the park and turned down Park Road towards Granton Elementary. A short, plump, quietly pretty woman in a plain cornflower-blue, knee-length dress and a tall, rather dour-looking man in a utilitarian, charcoal suit were waiting in the parking lot for me. They introduced themselves as Mrs. Yeager and Principal Evans. They reminded me a little of an educational equivalent of Laurel and Hardy.

"Thank you for coming so quickly, officer," Evans began.

"Detective Luke Campbell." I offered my hand, shaking each of theirs in turn. "Please tell me everything you can."

Evans looked toward Yeager, who flushed slightly, a guilty look creeping over her features. "Go ahead, Carolyn," Evans prompted. "Please."

The woman nodded, firmed herself up. "I was on morning recess duty today. The younger kids, the first, second, and third graders, have recess from ten-fifty-five to eleven-twenty. It tires them out a little before lunch and makes that a bit less of an ordeal."

I nodded, made a noncommittal noise, just to show I was listening.

She continued: "They get their sillies out, use up some energy. We aren't a very big school, you understand, so one recess monitor is usually enough. But because we aren't very big, there aren't many kids who… I mean, the kids who stand out stand out even more. Roland"—she did not pronounce it the French way—"is one of those kids. He's a very nice boy, but the way he speaks, his family background, it makes him easy pickings and there's only so much we can do for him here to prevent that."

"I've met the boy. He mentioned something to that effect."

"So you understand," Evans cut in. "Well, Roland is in second grade, and there's a group of third-graders who like to use him as their main target. They're the oldest kids among the younger classes, so they get a little bit of a superiority complex around the younger children – especially Roland as he's different and so small." He sighed, hard, through his nose. "They push him around, a lot, and punishment is only an option if we see it, which we often don't."

"He mentioned something like that, too."

Evans glanced at Mrs. Yeager again, who took the cue. "Today, I don't know how it started, but I saw the end of a fight, and I was very surprised because it seemed like *Roland* was the one who was getting in most of the licks. He had one of the other boys down on the ground and was using some sort of karate chop on him, it looked like."

A pounding began at my temple.

"Well, I separated them. The other boy was crying and there was a big red welt on the side of his face and another forming on his throat. I sent Roland back to his classroom and told him to tell his teacher he was sent in early and that we'd be discussing this with Mr. Evans after school."

"And since it's only a little past noon, I'm guessing he never made it to the classroom," I ventured.

Prettily plain Mrs. Yeager's expression grew more worried, while stern-looking Principal Evans's grew more serious.

"Yes," the tall man said. "I've already had the vice-principal and a couple of teachers without morning classes search nearby. The park, a drugstore that carries candy, magazines, comic books. Places like that, where a kid might think to cool his head. We have a couple of walkie-talkies for emergency situations, and this seemed as good a use as any. So far, nothing, though."

"That was good thinking," I told him, my own thoughts on where I could search that they hadn't. I wished I knew the town better. "Don't alert the other children, obviously." Evans nodded. "Just go about your day as if everything's normal. The fight you can't keep quiet, the entire school probably already knows about it, so if anyone asks, expresses concern for the injured boy, and just tell them Roland is being taken care of and they'll see him in class on Monday. It won't help the poor kid's reputation much, I imagine, but better that than make the other kids worry."

Both the teacher and her boss told me they understood, though the look on Carolyn Yeager's face said it would be harder to comply than I might think. I understood how she felt, but there was no time to take it into consideration. The whole exchange with the pair of them took maybe five minutes, but every moment counted.

I gave them a last instruction: "Call the station ASAP if you hear anything or find Roland." I returned to my car, slid back beneath the wheel and cranked the engine to life.

I radioed into the station to give Jeannie an update. I asked if Moss or Pohlman, who I hadn't yet met, was available to help with the search yet.

Jeannie told me, "Pohlman is still involved in some sort of assault way at the south end of town, Luke, and Moss is on an domestic situation that sounded pretty bad."

Too many of them are, I thought.

"Okay. When either of them are freed up, give them the low-down, will you?"

I rang off and drove, my eyes on the road and the surrounding area, looking for any sign of Roland DeJonge or any place a kid might think to hide when he's having a bad day and just needs to get away. The whole time, my thoughts were on what the kid said to me in the diner, *"There're guys at school who knock me around sometimes",* and how he asked me to teach him the martial arts he saw me use. I wish I'd listened more to what he was really saying: *help me.*

I thought also of the beautiful, sadly blank face of his mother, Chloe. Had anyone told her what was going on with her son? At that very moment, it would do nothing but worry her, and the school wouldn't want it known any more widely than necessary that a child went missing under their watch, but she had a right to know. The boy was hers, after all. The only thing she had, if Lloyd Truman was to be believed.

I spent over an hour slowly trawling the streets of Granton, heading west from the school towards the area around the north end of the lake, then looping back around to the east through the less-populated stretches between the edge of town and where the real Northeast Kingdom forests began. There was no sign of the boy. Occasional calls to the station gave me little hope, even after Moss joined the search. Neither Moss nor the school officials seemed to think Roland could get very far on his own, but I thought back to when I was a child and the time I ran away.

I was almost ten years old when my younger brother was born. Ten years as an only child, in a reasonably prosperous family, the only recipient of my parents' love and attention. Then, overnight it seemed, there was no time for me. I didn't know how to handle it. Most of my friends had a brother or sister, or two, but those kids were all close to the same age and more like friends, part of the gang, than siblings. What was I supposed to do with a little baby brother who couldn't ride bikes or read comics or even play ball? A baby who took so much of my parents' time that it was like I just faded into the background of their lives? For my whole ten years, I was the center of my parents' world, at least so I thought. Then, suddenly, there was an outsider who came along and pushed me aside.

If I wasn't needed, I decided, I simply wouldn't stay and one night, after dinner, while my parents were occupied, I packed my backpack and left. I walked almost four miles, I was later told, through the gathering fall darkness, until I found a barn to sleep in. If I concentrated, I could still feel the comfortable scratchiness of the hay against my skin and the rich, earthy smells of animals sleeping only a few feet away. In the morning, though, I decided I didn't want to spend another night sleeping anywhere but a bed and headed home. I got home early enough that my parents never even realized I was gone until I told them. They hadn't known how neglected I felt, they said, and for a little while, it got better.

I smiled at the memory and realized my thinking of it was no coincidence. I'd passed several barns, belonging both to working and to abandoned farms, after leaving the limits of the town proper. I pulled off the road, pulled out the map of Granton I carried in the door's side-pocket, just in case I found myself lost in the little town's confines. I found the road nearest to Granton Elementary that led out of town, then put the car in gear and pulled a U-turn.

It didn't take long to make my way, via interconnecting backroads, to the imaginatively named East Road. There was a Christmas tree farm at the intersection of East and the unnamed side-road I came off of, acres of neatly aligned Douglas fir trees stretching off from the road towards the distant, deeper woods. There didn't seem to be anyone around, and it seemed an unlikely spot for Roland to be, so I turned the car left, and headed back towards town.

I didn't have long to travel. Three miles passed, putting me just about a mile and a half from the town itself, before I came across a huge, empty barn, looming at the side of the road. Unpainted, its wood silvered with age and splintered from weathering, the building leaned slightly backwards, as if keeping its distance from the road and the vehicles that zoomed by, wanting nothing to do with the world that had passed it by.

I got out of the cruiser, took a quick look around the area. It was plain that the barn hadn't seen use in years, but that didn't mean this wasn't someone's property. Thin woods and dense underbrush crept out from the not-too-distant hills, filling in the area between the road and the true forest. The area must have once been clear-cut, but now nature was slowly but surely reclaiming it, reaching out of the still-wild spaces, filling the distance between the barn and the woods with tall grasses and scraggly underbrush to surround the base of the structure. I walked around the rear of the barn and looked down the road a little piece. I could see no farmhouse nor any trailer replacement, as was common in a lot of areas when the home someone's great-grandfather built finally began to fall apart. There was no evidence of anyone's presence.

Lifting the flashlight from my harness, I slipped between the splintered remains of a horse door into the interior of the barn. It was close to two o'clock and the sun was still more or less directly overhead, but the interior was murky, the shapes of the tumble-down building and abandoned odds and ends casting long pools of darkness. Even if it was well-lit, though, it would have been clear that this wasn't the friendly, homey sort of place I once spent a night in. Instead of comfortable hay, there were patches of thin, scratchy-looking grass growing up from the packed earth, clusters of moss on the damp, rot-eaten support beams and, scattered throughout, piles of some animal's droppings.

"Roland!" I called, pronouncing the boy's name the way his mother had. There was no answer save a scurrying of tiny feet somewhere above my head. "Roland, are you in here? It's me, Luke Campbell."

Outside, a car roared past, going much faster than the posted limit.

I swung the flashlight around the place, shining it into the darkest corners, illuminating cobwebs and piles of rusted scrap and heaps of ancient, moldering hay. In one corner, farthest from the ruined door I came in through, was what remained of the ladder into the upper hayloft. At first glance, nothing seemed amiss, but a telltale trail of broken spider-webs showed someone had recently passed through it into the elevated area of the old barn.

I shined the flashlight towards the top of the ladder and said, "C'mon, Roland. I see you up there. Time to come out."

It was an informed bluff that paid off. There was a stirring up in the loft and a moment later, Roland's face appeared in the beam of light, squinting and blinking against its brilliance.

"C'mon down, son. It's time to go back. Everyone's worried about you."

His pale little face scrunched up tightly. "No, they aren't. Nobody cares. And I'm never going back!" He tried to make it sound tough, defiant, as if it didn't matter a bit to him one way or the other, but the pitch of his voice and tears in the corner of his eyes said differently.

I moved to the bottom of the ladder, held my arms up. "Here, I'll help you down. C'mon now."

The boy's pout persisted, grew a bit darker even, but after a moment's pause, he gave in, turned around and started down the ladder backwards. I replaced the flash on my harness and when the boy was halfway down, I grabbed him by the hips and set him on his feet next to me. Taking him by the hand, I turned and said, "Let's go home, Roland."

"I don't want to go home," he said in a near-whisper. Then, louder, "I wish I could go some place nobody knew about me or mom."

"I know," I told him as we ducked under the remains of one wall, stepping back out into the afternoon sunshine. "I heard what happened, but a crummy old barn and a bunch of field mice are no replacement for your home and your mother, are they?"

The little boy shook his head slowly, not wanting to admit it, but unable to deny it. There were tears in his eyes as I led him back to the car and buckled him into the front passenger seat. Once I settled in under the wheel, I asked him, "You want to tell me what happened at school?"

Roland shook his head, swiped the back of one hand across his eyes then stared angrily through the windshield, gaze fixed on some distant point. Usually, awe and curiosity at sitting in a real police car wins most kids over. Roland clearly wasn't most kids.

"I know there was a fight," I told him.

After a moment, the boy relented. "They call me bastard and Quebequeer every day," he began. "And they push me around if I try to ignore them." He sniffled, managing to make the sound seem angry. "And today, when Jeremy Waters started in on me, I just got so mad I let him have it with those karate moves you did." His hands clenched in his lap as he relived the experience in his mind.

"It's tough, Roland, I know – just you and your mom. But do you think hurting people will make it better? Or running away when that doesn't work out?"

Roland looked at me, all the hurt and anger and hatred he had inside of him fighting to get out. "If I go somewhere else, nobody will know anything about me and none of it'll matter."

And that was true to an extent. Between the trouble the boy was having and Chloe DeJonge's own woes, I wondered why Roland's mother *didn't* go someplace else. Back to wherever she lived before meeting the Butler boy or somewhere new entirely. Maybe she didn't realize how hard it was on her son. I asked Roland if he had talked about this with his mother.

His head bobbed. "I told her how bad it is. She says I have to learn to get along with the kids. She said that life is like a battle you can't ever win, but you just have to keep trying."

I didn't know that I agreed with that. I sure as hell didn't like a mother telling that to her little boy. "Maybe I can talk to her," I said, as I turned the engine over. "Maybe between the three of us, we can work something out."

Roland looked doubtful, as if he'd heard that before and didn't I know it wasn't any use? He turned away and fiddled with the automatic lock button on the door. "You can try, I guess," he said with no enthusiasm. He turned back towards me. "Do I have to go back to school?"

"No," I told him. "Not today." That seemed to perk the boy up a little, at least.

I called in to the station, told Jeannie that I was bringing Roland DeJonge back to town.

"Chief Skillman called Callaway's so Roland's mother knows what's going on. He told me she'll be waiting at home, Luke."

"Roger," I said, feeling a twinge of anger at the chief for making the woman sit and worry these last few hours. She had a right to know what was going on with her son, but I had hoped not to have to tell her until it was all over.

As we rode, I drew the boy out bit by bit, making small talk with him. Roland was obviously intelligent, but very angry. Too angry for such a small child. Based on answers he gave when I asked about his favorite subjects and his hobbies, it seemed as though he didn't really have much of a life outside of going to school and sitting at home, watching TV or reading. He wasn't allowed outside when his mother wasn't home and she was often working. When she was home, there were no friends, Roland said, to go and play with. Maybe it wasn't entirely fair, but part of the anger I felt towards Skillman redirected itself towards Chloe DeJonge and the way she sheltered the child.

Once in Granton proper, Roland directed me to a quiet street seven blocks away from Granton Elementary. Taking side-streets and shortcuts, it wouldn't have been a very long walk either to the park or to Main Street, where Callaway's Diner, Chloe's employer, was located. The DeJonge house was a small, yellow ranch, surrounded by a dozen nearly identical houses, each with a tiny strip of front-lawn, and a stub of a driveway. There was no garage and the driveway was taken up almost entirely by a gray and white, navy-blue trimmed Crown Victoria twin to mine, save that it lacked police livery and lights. The paint on the car's doors was just slightly off in tint from the rest of the vehicle – newer, I supposed, and used to paint over the Granton PD emblems. The car seemed to be in good shape; I wondered if Chloe bought it at auction. Out of curiosity, I would have to ask my colleagues about police auctions in town.

I parked on the street, in front of the house. I expected Roland to bound out of the car and head inside, but he seemed reluctant. When I exited the car first and opened his door for him, he slid out slowly, then surprised me by putting his hand in mine. I guessed that a fight and a couple of hours in a creepy old barn left him needing a bit more reassurance.

We weren't quite to the front door when it flew open and Chloe DeJonge, still in her waitress's uniform, burst out, racing down the three low, concrete stairs and falling to her knees, her arms going around Roland as if clinging to him for dear life. Any doubts I had about this woman having emotions went out the window.

"Roland! Roland!" She kissed his cheeks, his forehead, his lips, crushed him to her chest and rocked back and forth on her haunches, telling him over and over how scared she was, how glad she was to have him home. After a couple of minutes, she drew back, looked him in the eye and said, "You scared me to death. You can't ever do that again." Her nose was red and a little runny; her eyes were bloodshot. Her fine, platinum hair was in disarray and hung over her forehead like a wind-tossed curtain. For all that, she looked more alive, more beautiful, than I'd yet seen her. I would never wish the fear she experienced on anyone, but it seemed to have brought her to life and for that silver lining, at least, I was glad.

She wrapped her arms around her son again, hugging him so tightly I expected him to protest, but he kept silent until she released him. She looked at me as if just realizing I was there, and stood. "Thank you, Mr. Campbell. Thank you so much."

"I'm glad to help, Ms. DeJonge."

The woman looked down at the boy again. "Say thank you to Mr. Campbell and come inside now, Roland. I know you skipped lunch today and you must be very hungry."

Roland turned towards me and said, "Luke is hungry, too, mom. Can he stay?"

Chloe DeJonge's eyes met mine. I said, "That's very kind, Roland, but I should—"

"But you promised we'd talk. All of us!" the boy reminded me.

"Yes, I did say that, but it's up to your mom."

For a moment, there was something like fear in Chloe's eyes, but it passed, subsumed by the return of the mask she wore when I first met her in the diner. "If Roland wants us all to have lunch together, it's the least I can do to thank you."

"Thank you," I said, as Roland tugged at my hand, pulling me over the threshold into the house.

"You know," the boy said, "except for when the big TV broke down last year and a repairman came to try to fix it, and Mr. Williams, the landlord, I don't think mom's ever had a guest in the house before."

Chloe DeJonge's mask slipped for a moment, a mixture of embarrassment and anger flashing across her features. "That's not true at all, Roland," she said. "Hush now."

Roland said nothing else, only threw me a grin then made a face at his mother's back. Whether what the kid said about his mother never having guests was true, I had no doubt at all that I was Roland's first guest, at least.

14

The house's foyer opened up into a moderately sized living room, appointed in older, but decent quality furnishings that gave it a comfortable, if somewhat old-fashioned, feel. Roland mentioned a landlord, and I wondered whether Chloe rented the place furnished or had hunted up all these pieces at second-hand stores. In one corner of the room sat a console television, draped in a purple cloth that didn't quite hide the screen. On top of it sat a smaller, portable television, apparently taking over its larger cousin's functionality. I guessed that the repairman wasn't successful.

In the opposite corner of the room was a hi-fi system with mismatched speakers. A box of records and a smaller one of cassette tapes sat on the floor next to it. The walls were sparsely decorated with framed prints and lithographs of works of art that leaned towards pastoral scenes, interspersed with photos of Roland at various stages of his young life. There were no photos, I noticed, of Chloe nor of anyone else but Roland, for that matter.

"Please, make yourself comfortable," Chloe said, gesturing towards the doily-draped sofa, the piece of furniture nearest the television sets. "I'll get some lunch ready. Is grilled cheese all right?"

"That sounds great, thank you," I told her. She moved down a narrow hallway as I turned towards the sofa, but Roland caught my hand in his and said, "C'mon, Luke! Come see my room!"

I let the boy lead me down the same hallway Chloe disappeared down. We moved through a corridor lined with more framed art prints, past a kitchen dominated by a white, tiled-topped table and matching chairs, a closed door I guessed was a bathroom, and to the end of a hallway with three doors, one straight ahead and one on each side.

"That's the basement," Roland said, pointing at the door ahead of us. "I don't go down there much. This one's my room," he jabbed a finger at the door to our left. "And that's mom's." He pointed to the remaining doorway. "Come see!" He opened his bedroom doorway and pulled me inside.

The room was small, the twin bed taking up more than a third of the floor space, and a good deal of the remaining area was given over to shelving units stuffed with books, models of cars and jets, and some action figures. A large, plastic globe had a place of honor atop a small dresser, next to a fragile-looking table lamp made of clay. The room had a single window, under which the bed sat, and the white, plastic roll-style shade was drawn; stickers of Saturday morning cartoon characters were stuck all over the inside of the shade.

"Don't tell mom, okay? She'd get mad," Roland said, seeing that I noticed the shade. He moved to draw it up, letting in the afternoon light.

I smiled. "She won't hear it from me."

"What do you think?" Roland asked, guilelessly. I supposed to a friendless little boy, showing off his private sanctuary for the first time, my opinion must have mattered a great deal.

"I think you've got a lot of good reads here," I told him, running my fingers over the spines lined up on the nearest shelf. "What's your favorite book, Roland?"

"Treasure Island," he said without hesitation.

I wasn't at all surprised that he named the story of a boy who stows away on a pirate ship and has the adventure of a lifetime.

"Roland! Mr. Campbell!" Chloe DeJonge's voice came from down the hall, cutting off any more literary discussion. "Lunch is ready!"

We returned to the kitchen where Chloe had set out three bowls of tomato soup and a plate piled high with halved grilled cheese sandwiches. Her back was turned when I entered, following Roland, but when she turned and placed a glass of milk before the chair the boy was sliding into, she wore the expressionless mask I first saw at the diner. It was hard to believe this was the same woman who was full to bursting with so many competing emotions just a little while ago.

"Roland, wash your hands before we eat," she said. The boy rolled his eyes, but hopped down from the chair and moved to the kitchen sink all the same. "What would you like to drink, Mr. Campbell? I have water or milk or I could make some coffee."

"Water is fine, thank you."

She nodded, filled a glass from a pitcher in the refrigerator and set it down on the table. She filled a second for herself.

When all three of us were seated, Chloe took Roland's hand in hers, bowed her head and mumbled something in French.

Roland turned my way. Voice lowered, he explained, "We don't go to church, but mom still likes to say grace."

Chloe's cheeks reddened slightly, but she finished her prayer. Save Roland, probably not a soul knew that about her before that moment. I felt like a heel making the woman uncomfortable in her own home. "Go ahead, eat up," she said.

We ate. The food was simple, but good. The grilled cheese was perfectly crispy and buttery on the outside, melty and deliciously rubbery on the inside. The soup was sweet and tangy and creamy. For all Roland's eagerness that the three of us should sit down and talk, however, neither he nor either of us adults said much. I complimented Chloe on her cooking and she accepted the comment gracefully. That was about the extent of it. Despite the silence, though, it wasn't uncomfortable. Rather, it felt like something I'd been missing without even realizing it. I looked across the table at a beautiful, capable woman and a bright, handsome boy and allowed myself to imagine what it would be like to repeat this scene daily.

When the meal was finished, I pushed aside dreams of domesticity while Chloe began to clear the table. "Roland, why don't you go watch TV for a while?" she suggested. The boy glanced my way and I nodded almost imperceptibly. He flounced out of the room, happiness in each step, all of his earlier troubles forgotten.

I carried the dishes that Chloe hadn't over to the sink, where she was filling a basin with hot soapy water. Without asking or being told, I took up a nearby dish towel and within moments, the woman's deft, sure hands finished with the first soup bowl and handed it to me for drying.

We were halfway through the dishes when I finally said, "Do you know why Roland ran away today?"

The small woman, her hands immersed in the dishwater, shrugged. "Because there was a fight. I heard it from Chief Skillman and the school."

"Because the kids at school call him a bastard and some nasty words for French-Canadian and he says nobody can do much of anything to stop it."

She flinched as if afraid of being hit and I was sorry to see it, but I didn't know how to pull this punch. She composed herself and said, "Those are just words."

I placed the sandwich platter on the counter, laying it atop the towel. "They aren't just words. They're words that hurt him and when those don't hurt bad enough, there are kids that beat him up just because they're bored. Roland ran away because he's a little boy in pain and he wanted to try to find a place where he could start his life over again." I tried to catch her eye, shifting my head more into her line of sight, but she avoided my gaze. "Don't you think he's too young to have to feel like that?"

Chloe whirled, looking at me at last, anger shattering the mask she'd built for herself. "And what should I do about it? Why should you even care?"

"I don't know what you should do right off the top of my head, but I promised your son that I'd talk to you about it. It's not my business, but he asked me to speak with you and I take that seriously. It takes a lot of courage to ask for help, especially when you don't think you're going to get it."

She hung her head, leaned forward against the counter, trying, but not managing, to hide the tears I saw in her eyes. It was obvious Roland wasn't the only one hurting.

"Can I ask you a personal question?"

"Can I stop you?" There was a sneer in her voice.

"Why do you stay here? What keeps you in Granton?"

Her head whipped towards me. Her eyes were red-rimmed and crackling with subdued rage. Her glare took the place of words she couldn't seem to find.

"I know a little about your situation," I began. I held up my hands, pleading innocence. "I wasn't prying, I didn't do any investigating or anything like that, but I admit to being curious after the scene in Callaway's the other day. You can't blame me for that."

Her expression softened. "No, I suppose not."

"I was actually more curious about that guy Ecare, and your friend Mr. Truman told me the whole story."

"He's hardly a friend." She shook her head. "He's just one of the roughnecks around here who won't stop staring at me."

I couldn't really blame them, but I also couldn't say that to her. Regardless of why, it was pretty clear to me that there were people in Granton who cared about her, even if it was from afar, and would gladly help her if she would only let them.

"Well," I paused, feeling as if I was threading my way through a minefield. "I'm very sorry about what happened to Roland's father, but I don't see why it means you have to stick around here if it's doing nothing but causing pain. Are the boy's grandparents involved with his life?"

She shook her head again. "They haven't even seen him since he was a baby."

"Their choice or yours?"

Her emotions flared again, bright and fiery, bringing life to her features. I hated making her upset, but I admit that I appreciated the beauty the animation gave her. "Why do you think I stay here?" her voice was low, but furious. "Do you think I don't want Roland knowing where he came from? I could go anywhere if I chose, but I stay here because this is where he came from. Did you see my living room? Did you see any photos of Alan? We were to be married, we have a child together, but I don't have so much as a single picture of the two of us together. This place, this god-damned worthless little town, is the only connection between Roland and his father. Alan's mother and father want nothing to do with us. They blame me for what happened to him, as if I *asked* that miserable fool Nathan Ecare to crash his car into us." Her voice broke and she choked back a sob, forcing herself to silence. The vague sounds of the television from the other room were the only noises in the house for a few moments.

"I can understand that," I said at last. Her look in response was a challenge, but she didn't put it into words. "I'd like to spend some time with Roland, if it's okay with you. I don't mean to be patronizing, but I think maybe he needs somebody besides a mother in his life. He wouldn't come right out and say it, but I don't think he has any friends to speak of and he told me he spends most of his time reading or watching television. A change of pace wouldn't hurt. Either him or you."

Chloe DeJonge eyed me skeptically, but said, "What did you have in mind?"

"Tomorrow's my day off. Maybe we could all go for a hike, have a picnic out by the lake or in the woods or something, if you know a good spot."

She surprised me by bursting out laughing. Unlike her anger, she didn't hide it. It was a good sound, even if the words that followed it weren't. "You're asking me on a date. You're using my son to get to me. Oh, you had me going for a second. Nobody has tried *that* before."

I shook my head. "No, that's not it at all. Well, maybe a little. I'd like to know both of you better," I admitted. "But my primary concern right now is Roland. That boy needs something and I'm very sorry to say it, but I don't think you can give it to him."

Her expression was thoughtful. Her eyes narrowed and she seemed to be trying to see inside my head. Roland's face popped around the corner of the hallway. "What's so funny?"

Chloe looked over her shoulder, turning from me towards her son. "Roland," she said, "do you like Mr. Campbell?"

The question surprised me even more than her laughter had, but Roland took it in stride. "Sure, I do. He's my friend."

The boy's mother turned back towards me, a strange, contemplative look on her lovely features. "Why don't you pick us up at ten o'clock tomorrow morning, Mr. Campbell?"

Roland was unsure of exactly what was going on, but hearing that delighted him. He let out a little "yippee" of joy and beamed happily at the both of us. A few minutes later, I said my goodbyes, promised to see them in the morning, then got back in my car. The sound of beautiful, gusty feminine laughter was at war in my mind with that odd look Chloe DeJonge gave me.

15

It was nearly four-thirty when I returned to the station. I radioed ahead, letting Jeannie know that Roland was home safe and sound and that I was on my way in. I hadn't called in a meal-break or anything, so I'd been radio-silent for a good stretch by that time and expected a chewing out from somebody – either Jeannie for worrying her or Skillman for breaking his nebulous regulations. When we spoke, though, Jeannie was as business-like and detached as I ever heard her, simply acknowledging my update.

When I walked into the station itself, Jeannie smiled, said, "Good work today, Luke," and that was about it. She didn't ask for any details, but I offered them anyway and told her where I found Roland and how I hit on the idea. She was attentive, but unexcited. It was out of character.

"Something wrong?" I asked.

Jeannie half-shrugged. "I couldn't tell you, Luke. Well," she stood, gathering her purse from one of the desk drawers. "About time for me to be getting home to put supper on. Hal will be home soon and he likes his supper on the table when he walks in the door."

"Sure," I said. "Have a good weekend."

"You, too." She smiled. "Enjoy your day off."

I figured I better check in with Skillman before he went home, too. I hadn't spoken to him much in the last couple of days, but I knew Jeannie's reticence had something to do with him.

In the hallway, I passed Barnes, who grinned and congratulated me on finding the DeJonge kid, then squeezed his bulk past me and continued on his way. Moss was sitting in one of the cubicles, typing, filling out a report and chatting with a man unfamiliar to me. Like Moss and myself, he wore the uniform of a Granton police officer. He was about halfway between our ages, somewhere in the late thirties, I guessed, with close-cropped, sandy hair and a vaguely military bearing. When he spoke, his voice was barely a whisper, but Moss seemed to have no trouble hearing him.

I rapped my knuckles on the metal edge of the cubicle wall. Moss looked up at the sound, his lips curled into the ghost of a smile. "Hey, Luke. You met Pohlman yet?"

The third man turned in my direction, as well, nodding his head slightly and extending a hand. "Lee Pohlman. Heard a lot about you." His voice was pitched louder than when he was chatting with Moss, but not much. It carried just fine, though. There was power in this man. "Moss is a fan," he added with a wry smile.

Moss looked a little embarrassed, but grinned all the same.

Pohlman and I shook. "Luke Campbell. Good to meet you."

"You, too. We'll talk more sometime, I'm sure. Time for me to get going, though." Pohlman turned to Moss and said, "See you tomorrow."

"Sure."

Pohlman took his leave and Moss turned back to me.

"Seems like a nice guy," I said.

"He's a little stiff sometimes, but decent enough."

"Sure, I know the type." I changed gears. "How's it going? Heard you had a rough one today."

"Ahhh, you know." The words were half-sighed. "It was bad, but I almost hate this crap worse." His right hand made a short, back and forth swipe through the air, indicating the typewriter and the half-filled sheet of paper in it. "You become a cop so you can help people, maybe solve a mystery once in a while, all that good stuff, but every time you do anything you spend more time writing about what you've done than you did doing it."

"In triplicate."

He grunted what might have been a laugh. "Don't remind me." He stood up, bent backwards to stretch his lower back. "That kid doing okay?"

"Yeah," I nodded. "He'll be fine."

"Good to hear it. Sorry I couldn't help more."

"No worries." I told him about finding Roland, about how happy his mother was to have him back. I skipped the part about the conversation I had with her.

"Wish I could have seen that. Never seen that girl look anything but miserable. Eh, well… maybe that's not the right word."

"It's okay, I know what you mean. How was yours, aside from rough? Jeannie said it was pretty bad when I talked to her earlier."

"Mm." Moss glanced down at the report in front of him. "You know the De Rossos, by any chance?"

I told him I didn't.

"Didn't think so. You will, though, if you stick around Granton. Marcus is a mean son of bitch when he's sober and when he's drinking, he's like the god-damned devil himself. His wife, Tracy, is only a little better. Normally, they know enough to not both be drinking at the same time."

I held up a hand. "No need to say more. I've seen plenty of those. They in the tank?"

Moss shook his head, frustration creeping across his face. "No. No charges. Neighbors called it in, said it was like World War Three next door, but the De Rossos insist it was just an argument that got out of hand. Her with a shiner the size of the moon, him with a lip split straight down the middle and a bleeding ear I swear to God had a bite mark in it. The house a total wreck, both it *and* them reeking of booze. Neither of 'em wanted to press any charges, but you could tell they wanted to keep fighting it out. Hell, they probably did once I left, just kept it quiet enough so the neighbors didn't complain." He sighed. "I hate like hell seeing people do that."

"Can't save them from themselves."

"No. I guess you're right about that."

"I'll let you get back to it." I nodded at the typewriter. "I better check in with the chief."

"Sure, go ahead." Moss nodded, then as I walked away, stuck his head into the hallway and added, "Hey, if I don't see you before I leave, have a good one tomorrow. Your first day off since you got here, right? Better make it count."

I planned to.

•   •   •

Skillman's door was slightly ajar and the light was on inside. I knocked on the doorframe.

"Come," came the deep-throated response.

I walked in, slipped the door back into its nearly closed position and greeted the older man seated behind the desk. He had his customary unlit cigarette clamped in the corner of his mouth and a weary look in his eyes. I guessed he was getting ready to head home for the weekend himself.

"Detective Campbell," Skillman said. "Fine work today with the DeJonge boy."

"Thank you, sir."

"Something I can do for you?" he asked, cutting to the chase.

"No, sir, just wanted to check in, let you know that Roland DeJonge is safe at home, back with his mother."

"She upset? The mother."

"Very, but she'll be okay, I think."

"Glad to hear it. Want to have a talk with those fools over at the school on Monday, I think. Kids can't slip through the cracks like that again. When they're on school grounds, during school hours, they should be locked down tight. Well, within reason, you know?"

I told him I did. I didn't tell him that I didn't think it would do much good. Evans and his people were probably already going to be making changes. I supposed the chief putting a little fear of God into them wouldn't hurt, though.

"How you making out on that other matter?" Skillman said, changing gears.

"Spoke to Cushman this morning. We agree that dental records are the best bet at finding an ID on the victim."

"So it's murder then?" Skillman asked, picking up on my choice of words.

"I think it's most likely. Cushman couldn't swear to it, but he said suicide or accident seemed less probable than the alternative."

Skillman nodded slowly, chewing that over in his mind. "You've taken a real interest in that boy, and the woman, too, haven't you, Campbell?"

"I'm... sorry, sir?" I said, caught off guard by the non sequitur.

"You were out of radio contact for over an hour, son." He stood, his long, narrow body unfolding like something from a stop-motion film, seeming nearly to fill the space between floor and ceiling. He spat his soggy, unsmoked cigarette butt into the trashcan, took up his hat—a peaked cap, adorned with a special, octagonal badge identifying him as chief of police—and set it on his head. "I won't begrudge you your personal life. Lord knows more cops have met girlfriends and wives on the job than anywhere else, but watch yourself, okay?"

I was confused. Was I being warned out of concern? If so, concern over what? To what end? And if it wasn't concern, then what was it?

"I'm not sure I understand, sir."

"No, I expect you don't. Just take my advice, son. Anyway, have a nice weekend, Detective," Skillman said with a note of finality, before coming around from behind the desk and sliding past me, heading out the door.

Not for the first time, I wondered what was going through the chief's head and what I had gotten myself into in coming to Granton.

16

Lost in thought, I walked into the side entrance of the Red Garden Hotel and, in the confined space, nearly ran into a smallish, well-dressed older man, struggling with a suitcase almost as tall as he was with a second, smaller bag slung over his shoulder. The side entrance was on a slight incline and there was a single step between the end of the short corridor and the hotel lobby's inner door.

The man lost his battle and his balance at the same time, and his shoulder collided with my chest. As his head turned, he snapped, "Watch it!" then seemed to actually look at me. His eyes went wide. He stammered, "I, I'm sorry, officer, I didn't mean…" There was a touch of the south in his voice.

I smiled and, without a word, lifted the larger bag one-handed over the threshold, pushed open the door into the lobby with my other and set the case down next to the door before continuing on my way.

The lobby was fuller that I'd seen it in my five days in Granton. What must have been two dozen people, mostly older and many looking as well-heeled as the gentleman I already encountered, stood around in small clusters chatting. At the lobby desk, both of the day-shift employees I was familiar with—Carl and Wendy, so alike in bland looks and pleasant manner they have could been siblings—were busy checking folks in. Through the double, glass-and-steel doors that fronted the street, I could see a bus, the kind chartered for tour groups, idling as some stragglers exited the vehicle.

I headed towards the elevator, but bypassed it, not wanting to tie it up when there were so many "real" guests, and ducked into the stairwell beyond it. The smell of cigarette smoke hit me the moment I started the climb and, two flights up, I found the source. Helen Reddy sat on the edge of a landing, a cigarette in one hand, a package of Virginia Slims hanging loosely in the other. A neon-green lighter and a white, Styrofoam cup lay at her feet. She was wearing a gray pencil-skirt, her knees tucked together, and a slightly loose red blouse that hung from her like it had been arranged by a master artist; rather than hiding her curves, the voluminous material seemed instead to emphasize them. Even at rest, in an unguarded moment at the end of the day, she looked great. The whole scene seemed like something out of an ad campaign aimed at selling the sexy businesswoman look.

She looked down at me and quirked a smile. "Hi there, Mr. Campbell."

"Mrs. Reddy," I said with a nod, suppressing the urge to cough, trying to breathe shallowly as the cloying smoke tickled my nose. Even the woman's good looks couldn't make me forget my aversion to those damned cigarettes.

Helen Reddy stubbed the cigarette out against the rough, raised edge of a stair, then dropped the butt into her cup. Maybe she picked up on my distaste for it. "When you say it like that, 'Mrs. Reddy' sounds like an old lady's name. Can we make it just 'Helen'?" She scooted over a little on the landing, patted the spot next to her.

"Sure." Despite the noxious odor hanging in the air, I sat. If she wanted to chat, I felt I owed her that, at least. She was doing me a huge favor after all. "Call me Luke, then."

"How was your day, Luke?"

"Busy," I said, noncommittally. I was sure she would hear all about it by tomorrow, if she hadn't already. "Yours?"

"You came through the lobby, right?" She laughed. It was rich and throaty and gave me the same, nebulous feeling of sensuality I felt on first meeting her. "The day was winding down and then—boom! Chaos out of nowhere. No reservations, half of them with special requests. I needed to step away for a minute. These things," she raised the pack of cigarettes, a rueful look in her eye, "are a harsh mistress."

I ignored that. "Glad to see you're getting some business, though. I was feeling guilty for taking up a room you weren't getting full price for."

"Pshaw." She batted the idea out of the air with a wave of her hand. "Not that I'm not glad to see those folks down there. We'll get some leaf-peepers in a few weeks, but this group is a nice surprise. They'll fill up a chunk of rooms for at least one night. They're some sort of casino bus tour heading up to Montreal."

"Huh, it's not that much farther on. I'd think they'd just keep going."

Helen shrugged. "You'd think so, but I won't question it as long as they're paying."

"Good policy," I said, standing. "Well, guess I'll be—"

She caught my hand in hers. "Got any plans tonight, Luke?"

Beyond wanting to get out of my uniform and maybe have a beer, I hadn't even thought about it. Before the last few days, I hadn't realized how big a toll my months of inactivity had really taken on me, and it wasn't just not being able to climb steep hills first thing in the morning. Even the everyday back-and-forth, up-and-down, in-and-out of police work exhausted me. Most evenings, by the time I got home, all I wanted to do was go to sleep. I felt better than that for once, but the novelty was still so new, I hadn't put any thought into what to do with it.

"Not offhand," I said.

"Would you like to have dinner with me?"

I'd been eating meals on the run for the last five days, twice from Callaway's when I could manage it—though Chloe hadn't been working either time, to my disappointment—but mostly from convenience stores or the station breakroom's daily supply of pastries and bad coffee. The late lunch with the DeJonges was the first time I actually had a sit down meal in two days. Lunch with one beautiful woman and dinner with another on the same day was something a lot of guys probably dreamed about, but thoughts of Chloe and Roland and the plans we made for Saturday sprung to mind and I hesitated long enough that Helen Reddy noticed.

"It's okay, you don't have to," she said. "It was just a thought."

"I'm sorry," I offered, feeling like an ass. "It's just been a very long day and I don't think I'd be good company."

Helen smiled, but it wasn't the warm, casual smile I saw a moment ago or the coy, flirtatious one from when we first met. It was a professional smile, the one that all guests of the Red Garden Hotel got – so long as they paid.

"Totally. I get it. Just another one that girl's gotten to without even trying." She stood, picked up her cigarettes, lighter and foam cup. "Well, have a good evening, Mr. Campbell." She headed down the stairs without a backwards glance, leaving me alone with my thoughts.

. . .

A skinny fist swings out of the darkness.

A voice, distorted but recognizably mine, calls out. The words are jumbled, but I know what I mean. I wonder if anyone else does.

There's a sense of movement, of speed, of time passing, but the actions that should be associated with those senses are missing.

There's sudden pressure in my chest. A weight holds me down, holds me back, keeps me in check and helpless. I struggle. My hands flail and scrape. I claw at the dirt, searching for something that I'm no longer sure even exists.

A weird light gleams above me. It seems like the source should be plain to see, because it's so close, so strangely bright for being so small, but I can never quite make out where it's coming from or why it hurts so much.

Then an explosion of light and sound and pain and confusion erases everything.

Again and again and again and again.

•   •   •

The phantom sound rang loudly in my ears as I bolted upright in the darkness. Soaked with sweat, I threw off the thin, starchy hotel sheets and swung my legs around to sit on the edge of the mattress. I took deep breaths and after a few minutes, my racing heart slowed down to something approaching normal. It was a couple of months since I had memory-dreams of that night. The night I killed Harlan Brown, the nineteen-year-old son of state senator Elmore Brown. The night I shot a kid standing in the wrong alley. A kid up to no good, looking to score on the wrong street corner, but still more or less minding his own business until I came along. Harlan Brown probably wasn't even aware Rosalie Stompanato existed, but he still died because of a chain of events in her life. Her life and mine.

Internal affairs cleared me in the shooting. Brown had a record as long as my arm, including a history of violence, and tox screens showed he was high out of his mind when he died. Reluctant witness testimony and my own injuries backed up my story. Paranoia, fear, and violence plus wrong time and place was a deadly equation. IA ruled it a "justified shooting in self-defense". It's easy to put the words down in a report when you've viewed the situation from a distance of time and impartiality. It's harder to believe them when you're the one who pulled the trigger.

And regardless of the facts, those words were no armor against public opinion nor did they stop Harlan's father, and his supporters, from running a campaign to see me prosecuted for his son's death. Ultimately, it came to nothing – from a legal standpoint, anyway. The rest of the fall-out I've mentioned already. And, of course, I'll be carrying that night with me for the rest of my life.

Eventually, I learned to put it out of my waking mind, but the dreams wouldn't let go for a long time. Department-ordered therapy, mandatory after any officer-involved shooting, taught me that it was normal for traumatic experiences to replay themselves like that, but knowing that didn't much help me *feel* normal. Strange as some of my experiences in Granton were, being in that town was the only thing that really helped me start down the road back to where I wanted to be.

I hadn't dreamed of those events in months, but I hadn't really dreamed at all the last few days. I was simply too tired after my shifts ended to do anything but fall dead asleep, then wake up eight or nine hours later to start all over again. I felt different Friday night, though, more energized, though that wasn't quite the right word. I knew it had to do with the time I spent with Chloe and Roland and I suspected the return of my worst nightmare had something to do with the vague guilt I felt – guilt tied up in emotions I wasn't quite ready to start sorting through. The look that Helen Reddy gave me in the hotel's stairwell, and what she said about "that girl" drifted through my mind.

I glanced at the clock on the bedside table: it showed six-forty a.m. in red, glowing numbers.

I heaved myself to my feet and headed for the bathroom, turning the shower on as hot as the knob would go.

I had a little over three hours to kill before I could start figuring anything out.

17

The morning was warm, the light of the early autumn sun lending the world a crisp cleanness that seemed to enhance the shapes and colors of everything around me. There was an intermittent breeze that rustled the color changing leaves and made the day seem colder than it really was if it hit you just right, giving us a taste of what was to come. Whatever was left of the summer was fast running out and fall was making its presence felt at last.

The Taurus glided to a stop alongside the curb in front of the DeJonge home. As I climbed out of the car, a flash of movement across the street caught my eye, but when I looked, all I could see was a curtain dropping back into place. I allowed myself half of a smile. If what Roland told me about visitors was true, I supposed the neighbors must have been surprised to see strange cars in front of the house two days in a row. Of course, the police cruiser I was driving, and the uniform I was wearing, the day before told a different story than an old Ford sedan and khakis did.

An off-duty outfit appropriate for the occasion was actually harder to assemble than I counted on. Except for the suit that I arrived in town wearing and the uniform provided by the department, most of my clothing consisted of undergarments and casual wear. I couldn't wear the suit or uniform to a picnic, but a Red Sox t-shirt and jeans didn't seem appropriate, either. Not yet, anyway. Of course, Roland wouldn't care either way, I figured, but I wasn't entirely sure what message my clothing would send to Chloe. I would still have to tread carefully when dealing with her. I settled on a not-too-badly wrinkled pair of khakis, a navy blue polo shirt, the only polo I owned, and a lightweight, zip-up windbreaker. I vowed to myself that I would do laundry, and maybe some clothes-shopping, very soon. At least my uniform would be clean for Monday. I took the opportunity of a free morning to drop it off at the drycleaner's next to Callaway's Diner, and they promised that I could pick it up that afternoon.

I wasn't quite halfway from the curb to the DeJonge house when the curtain in the big picture window was pushed aside and Roland's smiling face beamed out at me. His hand flew back and forth frantically. I returned the wave and added a full-fledged smile. The front door opened just as I reached it. Roland trilled, "Hi, Luke!"

"Good morning, Roland," I said.

The boy threw the door open wide, adding, "C'mon in. Mom's almost ready."

I stepped over the threshold and Chloe herself chose that moment to appear on the other side of the living room.

"Hello, Mr. Campbell," she said. Her face hadn't yet assumed the protective mask she normally wore. What she *was* wearing were faded denims tight enough that they looked as if they might restrict her movement, but that showed off the curves of her hips and legs nicely. Her top was a red blouse that fitted her as if it was custom-tailored. Plain, sensible-looking off-white sneakers covered her feet. A wide hairband the same color as her blouse held her platinum hair back from her forehead and completed the outfit. She looked incredible; domestic and exotic and motherly and enticing all at once. I barely knew this girl, but I had already seen more sides to her than I would have guessed existed from our first meeting.

"Hi," I said, trying not to stare at the lovely woman. "All set?"

She held up a finger. "Almost. One moment, please. Roland," she said, turning her attention to the little boy. "Your shoes are already on? Good. Why don't you go outside and wait?" It was said gently, but was not a question. "Mr. Campbell and I will be out in a few minutes."

"Okay!" he agreed happily, snatching up a small backpack and trouping out the door, pulling it shut behind him.

Chloe DeJonge turned towards me. "Help me in the kitchen a moment, would you?"

"Sure." I followed her in that direction.

In the kitchen, the white-tiled table held an old-fashioned picnic basket, woven from dark-stained wicker. One of the basket's wide top flaps was open. It was tightly packed with wrapped sandwiches and small Tupperware containers, and a large clear bag containing paper plates, napkins, and plastic tableware. There looked to be enough food for five or six people.

"What can I help with?" I asked.

Ignoring me, Chloe moved to the refrigerator, took from it two large thermoses then opened the basket's second flap and placed them inside. She poked around inside the basket for a moment, seemingly taking inventory, then closed up both sides, pushed a wooden slat in place to lock it, and slid the basket across the table in my direction. She looked up finally and said, "You can carry this to your car, please."

I was a little put off by the display, but I reminded myself that this was something I would just have to work through. I made the offer, but she was running the show. It wasn't as if I didn't understand why she put up these barriers between herself and everyone else. If I wanted to spend time with Chloe DeJonge and her son, I would have to do it her way.

"Sure," I said again and reached for the basket. As my fingers closed around the basket's handle, however, her fingers closed around my wrist, surprising me.

"Mr. Campbell."

"Call me Luke." It was almost reflexive at that point, after repeating it to so many people the last few days.

"Mr. Campbell," the woman repeated. She made a point to avoid my gaze, looking somewhere at my navel, as if trying to stare through me. "Today is for Roland." She paused half a beat, then went on. "He spent practically all of last night talking about today, about the things he wanted the three of us to do, where he wanted to go. He was more excited than I think I have ever seen him before. And after seeing that, and after what you said to me yesterday, I thought very long and very hard and decided... that you were right." She looked up, meeting my gaze. There was something strange in her eyes, something at once pleading with and warning me. "But don't get any wrong ideas, please – this is for *Roland*. Do you understand me?"

I kept my eyes on hers, expecting her to break away at any second. She didn't. She simply stared back and waited for my response. I swallowed, then said, "Sure," for the third time that morning.

•   •   •

It was colder by the lake, the wind stronger, steadier and carrying with it a cool moisture that touched everything around it. But neither the breeze nor the temperature bothered Roland DeJonge. The little boy, all smiles and entreaties—"Hurry up, mom!" and "C'mon, Luke!"—skipped ahead of us, racing towards the picnic area along the southwestern shore of Lake Maidenstone.

It was getting on towards noon. After we were all loaded into my car, we drove south out of town, down the lake road, past shuttered cottages, some privately owned and some rentals, sporting lawn signs with the number of a rental agency, and, a bit farther on, Monroe's Motel.

I saw what Jeannie meant about the motel being Granton's answer to skid-row. A good third of the windows in the long, single-story building were boarded over, the roof was sagging in several places and the whole thing was covered in dead leaves from more years' accumulation than I could guess. It was once a sky, or maybe robin's egg, blue, but weather and neglect left the walls faded and peeling, bare gray wood showing through in spots. A couple of junker cars were parked out front. One, sitting directly on rims and beneath at least a season's worth of dried needles and leaves, looked as if it was a fixed installation. The other looked like it might run with a little elbow grease. Out by the road, there was a faintly lit neon sign reading "VACANCY" but most of the rooms looked to be permanently occupied, various little touches here and there showing long-term residence. A flowerbox hanging from one un-boarded window seemed an incongruously innocent touch in a place that otherwise screamed decay and squalor. As we cruised past at the posted thirty-five miles per hour, neither Chloe nor Roland gave it a glance. I tried to put it out of my mind, too.

Two or three miles beyond the dubious motel, Chloe directed me to a state-designated protected area just off the road, by the tail-end of the lake. Small enough that nobody bothered giving it a name, according to Chloe, there were still signs posted all over the tiny gravel parking lot warning that hunting, trapping, logging, and motorized vehicles were forbidden beyond that point, along with contact numbers for the state parks department in case any of the signage was unclear. There was a heavily rusted, black Chevy pickup in the lot, but other than that, there were no signs of anyone but us being in the area.

I parked the Taurus next to the Chevy and Roland practically leapt out of the vehicle. Chloe kept him in check with a stern, though, gentle warning. He looked to me for support, but I gave him nothing other than a quick facial shrug and a smile. He got the message.

Chloe pointed us toward a trail she said she knew well and we trucked into the woods, Roland ahead, the pretty woman and I walking side by side a short distance behind. As Roland capered and laughed, kicking leaves across the ground and knocking more from the trees with a stick, I said to Chloe, "So you come hiking out here? I didn't imagine you were the type, if you don't mind my saying so."

"No." She watched her son enjoying himself, happy and carefree, adoration clear in her features. "I don't mind and I don't hike. Not really. I do come out here, though. Sometimes, I just need to be alone with my thoughts."

"I understand. What about Roland, though? He's having a blast, but he doesn't seem familiar with the area."

Chloe shook her head. "I took him here sometimes, when he was still small enough to carry, but when I come here now, I come alone. Sometimes I come when he's at school, if I have the time on a day off of work. There's a neighbor woman across the street who sometimes will watch him, but I don't like to ask. Not very often."

I wondered if that was the twitching curtain I saw. I supposed it made sense.

We walked in relative silence for a while, except for Roland, who kept up a steady, excited chatter. He told us about things he read, things he saw on TV. He pointed out plants and birds he recognized from "A Guide to Outdoor New England" he borrowed from the library over the summer. It was a miracle he didn't scare all the birds off, he was so noisy, but he was happy, and that was what mattered.

After a little more than an hour wandering back and forth along the meandering trail, we came to a clearing in view of the lake. Picnic tables and little stand-up charcoal grills were dotted around, along with more signs reminding us that this was a protected area. Roland ran ahead of us to claim a table, though there wasn't any competition. Down on the lakeshore itself, at a distance of maybe two hundred yards, there was a lone figure skipping stones across the water – the owner of the Chevy, I imagined. Other than that, there wasn't a soul in sight.

I set the basket down on the table Roland picked out and looked towards the lake. The noon sun sparkled on the cold water, sending up dazzling, ever-moving reflections as the waves gently lapped the shore. "It's beautiful," I remarked.

Chloe nodded. "Have you been before?"

"No. My first time seeing it this close up."

The woman turned. There was a gentle, somehow sad, smile on her face. "You'll have to come again when it's warmer." It was hard not to notice she didn't say "we" would have to come. There was nothing I could do but let it go.

Chloe made swift work of unpacking the basket, setting out three places in paper and plastic, stacking the sandwiches in a neat pile and cracking open the tops of the Tupperware. She prepared potato, pasta, and fruit salads to go with chicken, roast beef, and baloney sandwiches, Roland's favorite, she confided with a hint of distaste. I chuckled. "He'll grow out of it."

Roland returned from wherever he scampered off to and the three of us sat and ate and chatted about inconsequential things. Roland, as per pattern, did most of the talking while Chloe or I responded as appropriate. What surprised me was that he kept bringing up subjects I would never have expected a kid to, commenting on political and news items he apparently read in the newspaper. He hadn't been kidding when he told me he spent most of his time reading and, apparently, his tastes ranged far and wide. He said, for example, that he was recently reading about the whaling industry and various groups' efforts to shut it down. Something he read in the newspaper sparked his interest and he went to the school library to read more. Now, he was happily giving his mother and me a lesson on the subject.

When I was able to get a word in edgewise, I asked, "Now I know there's no whales, but what kind of fish do you think are in the lake, Roland?"

"That's easy," he said, a little smugly. "There's three kinds of trout: brook, lake, and brown. Plus, salmon and—"

"There's four kinds," a soft, raspy voice cut in. "You forgot rainbow trout."

He had approached unnoticed, the sounds of his movement through green grass and dead leaves smothered by Roland's youthfully enthusiastic chatter: Nathan Ecare.

I stood, eyes on the other, smaller man. My gaze flicked towards the lake; the figure I saw along the shore was gone. No, not gone – he was right in front of me, less than ten feet from where we sat, wearing the same sweatshirt and jeans I saw him wearing that day in Callaway's Diner, but now with a denim jacket over the sweatshirt. It was coincidence he was there. There was no way it could be anything else. In movies, detectives say things like, "I don't believe in coincidence," but a real cop learns that there're more coincidences in the world than almost anything else. With so many people living, breathing and moving around on a planet as small as ours, you're as likely to cross paths with the last person you want to see as anyone else.

Chloe stood, too, and her eyes, glued on the newcomer, were filled with a rage that leads to things you can't take back. She may have been willing to serve the man coffee when she was being paid to, in a room full of potential witnesses, but outside of Callaway's, the woman felt free to let her true feelings show through. What I saw in those eyes was just short of murderous. Of all the faces I'd seen Chloe DeJonge wear, this was the only one I didn't care for at all. It honestly even frightened me a little.

Casually stepping into Chloe's line of sight, I said, "Mr. Ecare," keeping my voice even.

He glanced around me, towards the woman and the child. "I was just leaving." He swung to one side, giving the picnic table and our little group space.

I moved to intercept him and, as he passed, reached out to catch his elbow, gently, not wanting to alarm him. I failed in that; he leapt backwards as if he stepped on a snake and one hand flew up defensively. His reflexes were impressive – prison-honed, I knew. He wasn't a big man, average-sized at best, and skinny. He would need good reflexes and good instincts to survive inside.

"Hold on," I said, quietly, one palm up. "I'd actually like to talk to you – but not here, obviously."

I knew enough of the connection between Ecare and Chloe DeJonge to know that her rage was justified, but I'd collected information, put together pieces, for a living for so long, I couldn't help myself. I wanted to know more.

"I don't want trouble." His eyes flicked from my face to some point behind me. To Chloe, I guessed. Something flashed across his features, something that changed his mind, his train of thought. Quickly, softly, he said, "Keith's, the bar on Main Street. You know it?"

"I can find it."

"I'm in there most nights." He said nothing else, only turned away and, a moment later, disappeared into the woods.

I sat back down at the picnic table, my heart thrumming like I just ran down to the shore and back. The encounter was tense, the feeling between Ecare and Chloe so thick you could have almost reached out and grabbed a handful of it, but it ended about as peacefully and anticlimactically as I could have hoped.

After a moment, Chloe say down, too, closer to Roland this time, as if wanting to keep him within easy reach.

"Well—" I began, but didn't get a chance to finish before Chloe cut in. "What did you say to him?" she demanded.

"I asked him not to come back here. I didn't say why, didn't tell him you like to walk this area."

The lie came easily; it was out of my lips almost before I realized I was speaking. I knew why I did it, but not when I decided to.

Chloe looked at me hard, echoes of the anger she obviously felt towards Nathan Ecare reverberating in her eyes. Then she nodded, just once, and turned towards Roland, who hadn't said a word since Ecare horned in on his lecture on Maidenstone Lake's fish population. "Roland, why don't you and Mr. Campbell go play down by the lake for a little while? I feel a headache coming on and I think I need a few minutes alone."

Whatever Roland was thinking, he knew not to argue. "Okay." He slid off the picnic bench and headed towards the water. I only hesitated a moment before following.

18

Directly on the shore of the lake, the wind was stronger, coming along in a steady gust that left ripples in the water and a faint suggestion of dampness on my skin and hair. Roland seemed to take no notice, simply staring out across the water. On the far shore of the lake, to the northwest of where we stood, were a cluster of homes larger than any others I'd seen in Granton, many with small, private stretches of beach. Even from a distance of what must have been two or three miles, they seemed huge and elaborate. The homes of the town's true elite, I supposed.

"C'mon, Roland. Let's take a walk, give your mom a few minutes to herself."

The little boy turned away from the water slowly, as if breaking out of some in-depth train of thought, then slipped his hand into mine and led the way along the pebbly shoreline, heading north. We walked in silence for a few minutes, the only sounds waves lapping gently against the strip of rocky beach, intermittent bird-song from the woods far to our left, and the occasional, distant hum of traffic that carried across the water from somewhere to the north.

Ten minutes later, when we stopped, I crouched to scoop up a flat, rectangular chunk of slate and fling it out across the water, watching it skip half a dozen times before sinking with a muted *plip* beneath the surface of the lake.

"How about that?" I asked Roland. He smiled and said, "I've seen that on TV," as if it wasn't something he could just try himself.

"Pick out a rock," I told him. "Not too big, but not tiny, and as flat as you can find."

He squatted down, examined the scattered bits of stone around us and after a moment spotted one he liked the looks of. He straightened up, holding the stone and looking expectantly at me.

"Okay, now—" I came around behind him, positioned his arm out at his side and away from his body, so the stone was on the same plane as the surface of the water and all he needed to do was move his arm forward, directly from the elbow. "Throw that sucker!"

Roland's arm shot forward and the rock, released a fraction of a second too late from his grasp, went *plunk* into the few inches of water directly in front of us. His frown was less disappointed than confused. Before that balance could shift, I snatched up another rock, repositioned his arm and said, "Again, but this time, let it go just at the moment you feel that little snap in your wrist." He looked up and over his shoulder at me, confusion still evident, but then he nodded, positioned his feet and let fly. The throw still wasn't perfect, but the wide, flat stone hit the water and skipped once, twice, three times before sinking.

"Whooo!" Roland cried, elated. He turned to look at me, happiness gleaming from his features, then squatted, picked up another rock and threw it, too. This one skipped four times before sinking and Roland celebrated with an enthusiastic flinging of even more rocks, asking me each time if I saw that one. I praised the first few throws, watching him improve right before my eyes, wondering how many other simple childhood experiences this kid had missed out on.

"This your first time at the lake, Roland?" I asked.

He shook his head. "No. Well," he paused. "Not exactly. We came on a school trip last year when someone found a mating pair of American avocets." He turned to me and added, "That's a kind of rare bird." He hurled another rock towards the water, and continued, "It was in the marshes on the other side of the lake, but we didn't get real close and we weren't supposed to come down to the water."

"I see. Well, if you want to, maybe we could come back some time. Maybe do some fishing."

Roland's head tilted in thought and his brow furrowed as he searched for another good throwing stone. "I don't really like fish that much. You know what, though?"

I spotted a perfect stone, snatched it up and handed it to the boy. "What's that?"

"I'd like to go hunting maybe." Roland took aim at the huge target the lake presented then let his missile fly. "Maybe hunt deer up in the hills?" he posed it like a question. "A few months ago, Mr. Callaway had some venison that he let me try and it was so good! Did you ever have it? It's like steak, but... um..." His face scrunched up as he searched for the word.

I grinned at the eloquent, chatty boy's sudden loss for words. "I've had it."

"So you know, then," he said with a satisfied nod.

"I don't know if your mom would let you do something like that, though, Roland. I don't imagine she's too big on guns."

"Why not?" he asked. "She's got a gun."

That took me aback. "Really."

Roland nodded again. "Yeah, she goes shooting in the hills. I asked her to take me with her lots of times, but she always makes me stay with Mrs. Robinson when she goes."

"That's your neighbor."

"Uh huh," Roland said, wiping wet sand off of a rock that turned out to be too thick for skipping. "She lives across the street. Anyway, mama won't let me go out with her, but maybe she'd let me go with you since gun stuff is part of your job."

"Maybe," I said.

Roland spent a few more minutes skipping stones before exhausting the supply of suitable ammunition. He was about to go off hunting for more when I said, "Let's walk back and see how your mom is doing, okay?"

In his excitement, Roland seemed to have forgotten that we weren't alone at the lake. Reminded, he nodded, put down the stone he was examining and started back in the direction we came from. He didn't take my hand this time. Instead, he asked, "Why does mama hate that man, Mr. Ecare?"

What was obvious to adults oftentimes went right over a seven-year-old's head, but Roland was perceptive like no other kid his age and I'd been expecting the question since we left Chloe.

"I'm not sure if 'hate' is the right word, Roland," I lied, knowing hatred was exactly what I saw on Chloe's face. "But I think that's something you'll have to talk to your mom about."

The little boy nodded again and kept walking, his eyes turned towards his shoes.

When we returned to the picnic area, Chloe DeJonge was standing by one of the little, waist-high black-iron charcoal barbeques. She saw us and hurriedly shoved something into the grill, her free hand waving back and forth in front of her face. I couldn't smell the cigarette, but it was obvious what it was. The question was whether she was hiding it from me or from her son.

We crossed the remaining distance to the picnic table where our lunch still sat and Chloe met us. "How was your walk?" she asked Roland.

"Good," he said. "Can we have dessert now?"

Chloe forced a smile and lifted the lid of the basket, taking from it a square Tupperware container that turned out to hold half a dozen cupcakes. "Just one," she cautioned, offering it to Roland to take his pick. Once he had, she offered it to me, but I held up a hand and shook my head. "No, thanks," I told her and sat down, sliding onto the rough wooden bench.

Chloe selected a cupcake for herself and set it on a little paper plate. Roland, between bites of yellow cake and frosting, told her all about how he learned to skip rocks. I tuned out the conversation, but kept one eye on each of them and nodded where it seemed appropriate. I had other things to think about, information that I picked up in the most unlikely way, information that I wasn't sure meant anything but still couldn't put out of my head.

It was crazy. I kept telling myself that, but I couldn't stop thinking about guns, cigarettes, long walks in the woods, and the burning hatred on a pretty woman's face.

19

I was coming out of Parnell's Dry-Cleaning, freshly cleaned, plastic-wrapped uniform in hand when someone called out, "Hey, that you, Campbell?" I turned to see a man, hand upraised and grinning in my direction. He was somewhere in his mid-fifties, average height, little pot-belly riding just above his belt-buckle, but not hanging over it. Gray-haired and balding, making up for the deficit up top with three or four days' beard growth, he wore a dull brown suit, white shirt, and black shoes. No tie. He was no one I recognized.

"Can I help you?" I asked.

The older man stuck out his hand. "I've already done you a favor or two, so I sure as hell hope so. Frank Lautner." Bells rang. The editor of the local paper with whom I spoke on the phone, days earlier. "Good to meet you, at last, Campbell. You're a hard man to track down."

I shook his hand; his grasp was light, but firm. "Been pretty busy."

"So I heard. Nice work with that DeJonge kid. Damned shame the paper had already gone to print when it happened." I stiffened at the comment, said as if the matter was nothing but fodder for Lautner, but if the man noticed, he gave no sign. "Well, there's always the next one. That's the way the paper works, you know. You'll give me a quote?"

"I'm just glad Roland DeJonge is back where he belongs. It was nice meeting you, Mr. Lautner, but if you'll excuse me." I tried to move past him, using the uniform as a screen between us.

It didn't work. Lautner stepped lightly to one side, but turned and kept pace with me, walking at my elbow up the sidewalk. "Just Frank'll do. We're gonna be in contact a lot, so might as well hang up the formalities. Anyway, where you headed? Got time for a drink? On me — I'd like to hear more about the DeJonge thing for my write-up."

I stopped, looked at the smaller man. I tried to keep the irritation out of my voice, off of my face. I knew very well what the media could do to someone's reputation and career and the effect could only be magnified in a place as small as Granton. Lautner was right, though: he did me a favor once already. I supposed I owed him something, but I just wasn't in the mood. I was looking forward to today, to spending time with Roland and Chloe DeJonge, but after the incident with Nathan Ecare, something was lost that the three of us weren't able to reclaim.

"Mr. Lautner, Frank," I corrected myself before he could open his mouth again. "If you don't mind, I'd rather not talk about work. It's been a long week, a very busy first week in Granton for me, and this is my first day off since I've been here."

"After all those days off, though, you'd think a man would be rested up enough for a while, wouldn't you?" Something mischievous twinkled in the reporter's eye.

"What's that supposed to mean?" I asked, a tight little knot growing in my belly.

Lautner, loose shouldered, made an expansive gesture. "I get the Sunday editions from all the major newspapers in the region, Campbell. Think I wouldn't recognize your name? Even if I hadn't, I'd have done my digging on you right off the bat." He smiled, friendly but warning. "Trust me when I say that I've no interest in making unwarranted trouble for anyone, but I've got to have *something* to fill column inches. I'd really rather be your friend. I mean that. But friends help each other out, you know."

The tightness in my stomach bloomed into an anger that spread out through my chest. I sucked in a deep breath, trying to keep from making a fist. That was the very last thing I needed. "Let me check with Chief Skillman, see what the official line is, okay? You know him better than I do and you know that neither of us wants to step on his toes."

Lautner nodded. He didn't look happy, but he apparently recognized the sense in what I was saying. Skillman's power in this town really did run deep. "I guess that's fair enough." He met my gaze, suddenly grave. "Remember, though, detective, people will find out about what happened sooner or later. The question becomes when and how."

I nearly lost it. "Are you threatening me, Mr. Lautner?" It was difficult to keep my tone in check.

He shook his head, stepped back and threw up his hands. "No! No, not at all. I'm just saying it'll happen." He risked putting a hand on my upper arm, gave me a look that seemed honestly concerned. "Sorry if that came across wrong. I didn't mean— look, all you can do is make sure that this town needs you before it gets out why you're here. Make it so they don't care what happened before. You get me?"

Lautner was all over the map; I had no idea how to read him anymore. If it was a tactic, it was brilliant. I supposed it served him well in confusing and disarming interviewees, but I'd done my fair share of interrogations over the years.

"I get you," I said, gently shaking off Lautner's hand. "I'll give you a call on Monday, after I've talked to Skillman. Good enough?"

Lautner nodded. "Suppose it'll have to be. Be seeing you."

When I walked away this time, he didn't follow me.

•   •   •

Despite it being after five on a Saturday evening, Keith's Tavern—the sign painted on the wall of the tiny mudroom that fronted the place supplied the bar's full name—was nearly empty. The room was long and fairly wide, its walls paneled in dark wood, a bar with a dozen stools making up the left side of the room, six small booths taking up the right side, with seven or eight postage-stamp-sized tables in between. A pair of elderly men sat in the booth nearest the door, half-filled pint glasses and a game of cards laid on the table between them. A dark-haired woman somewhere in her thirties sat at the end of the bar, drawing circles in the moisture on its polished surface while ignoring whatever the guy in a trucker's cap and faded camo-patterned coat was trying to tell her. A sandy-haired kid who looked like he might *just* have turned twenty-one sat in the middle of the bar, nursing a shot of something dark-colored, and mumbling – to himself or the disinterested, shaggy-headed bartender, I couldn't tell. Off to the right of the door was a pinball machine with an "OUT OF ORDER" sign taped to its glass front, neighbor to a jukebox that was quietly pumping some slow-tempo country song out into the air. Generic art depicting hunting and fishing scenes, intermixed with license plates from every New England state, New York, even

Quebec and Ontario, covered the walls, except for a mirror and the shelves of stock behind the bar itself. It looked like any one of hundreds of bars you could find anywhere from Maine to Pennsylvania and probably beyond.

I stepped up to the bar, ordered a shot of rye and a beer chaser. As the bartender was drawing off the beer from a tap beneath the counter, I looked up and saw *him* in the mirror. Nathan Ecare, still wearing the denim jacket over a hoodie, sat in the booth farthest from the door, hunched forward against the table, low enough that his head didn't top the divider between the booths. I put a five on the counter, told the bartender to keep the change, earning me a nod of gratitude, and headed back to where Ecare was seated.

Closer up, I could see why he was hunched in his seat: he was reading, elbows supporting him against the scarred surface of the table. A worn paperback titled *A Sound of Distant Drums* was clutched in both hands. A war epic, I guessed, from the badly painted cover depicting explosions over a foxhole.

Cover aside, though, it must have been good because Ecare didn't look up, even after I cleared my throat to get his attention. Not until I said his name, did he turn. "Oh... hey," was his reaction, all forced casualness. I was sure he knew I was there the moment I approached. You don't last long in prison being unaware of your surroundings.

"You mind?" I asked and slid into the booth across from him without waiting for an answer.

He closed the book, sticking a damp bar napkin in it to mark his place. "I told you I'd be here, didn't I?" It was a fair point. "So...?" He let the question hang, unfinished.

I wasn't sure myself. I wanted to know more, but about what, I couldn't articulate. I knew how Ecare's life and Chloe DeJonge's first intersected, I knew the results of that encounter, but something was missing. There was far more going on in Granton than met the eye and I was sure I'd only seen the smallest signs of whatever was really happening. I thought of Skillman's constant caginess; of a long-decayed body in the woods turning up my first day on Granton's police force; of the scattered, seemingly useless bits of evidence that reflected against other things I learned, things that shouldn't possibly have been connected in any way.

I tossed back the shot of rye, blew air then said, "I want to hear it all."

Ecare pulled his nearly empty pint glass from the far side of the table, drained it, set it aside then looked at me, long and hard. The same process I thought I saw back at the lake began to play itself out across his features again and, for a moment, I was sure he would decide something different than he had before, maybe that this whole thing was a mistake.

Instead, he started talking.

20

Nathan Ecare's foot pressed harder on the pedal, bringing the speedometer up to eighty. His whole life was spent going up and down these back roads. Even in the middle of the night, even with the red flashing lights somewhere in the distance behind him, he wasn't worried.

The curves grew tighter. He cut them, each time sliding into the middle of the soupy mess mud-season made of the dirt road. And each time the tires caught just before skidding off the opposite side, allowing him to bring the Firebird back to the center of the road. He whooped with laughter; his friends joined in. Nineteen years old and immortal.

Headlights appeared in the rear-view mirror, bright yellow beams stabbing through the darkness, splashing off the rear end of the muscle car, limning three figures against its darkened interior. Red lights and a shrieking siren followed nearly instantly, so close they seemed to be coming from inside of Ecare's car.

"Shit!" Ecare spat. "Where the hell did he—"

"Bastard cut his lights, snuck up on us," one of his friends offered.

"Who gives a fuck how he did it? Punch it! Let's go!" the other said.

"I can't!" Something seized in Ecare's chest. He threw a look over his shoulder, past his friends, towards the state police cruiser coming right up on his ass. This was fun for the first few minutes, when he thought he could safely get away. Like something out of a movie. A story he could impress people with. He was sure he could lose them, to disappear into the night and forget the whole thing. It never occurred to him that the state police might be smarter than he was. Now he knew escape was as impossible as going back in time and forgetting this whole god-damned deal. All he could think was *Get rid of the dope, say you just got scared.* Resisting arrest or whatever the fuck they would charge him with was a hell of a lot better than being nabbed for dope-running.

Sweat, cold and sour, sprung from his forehead and the palms of his hands. The leather-wrapped steering wheel that had always fit his hands like it was made just for him was suddenly slippery and awkward.

And so was the road.

"Well fucking do *something!*"

Ecare bit his lip, said nothing.

They came down from Sherbrooke, crossing the border from Quebec at Canaan. A run Nathan Ecare made half a dozen times in the last four months. The money went up, the horse came down, both tucked into the special compartment rigged under the Firebird's rear-right wheel-well. Each trip, he brought a friend or two, a rotating group of guys, mostly, and girls a couple times. Nobody ever made the trip twice in a row except Nathan. There was nothing suspicious about teenagers going up to Canada, where the drinking age was still eighteen, for a little fun. Nothing suspicious and no problems coming back from any of those trips. No inspections, no side-eyed looks from the border agents, nothing but a brief "Anything to declare?" and a "Welcome home." It got so the guys at the checkpoint knew him and expected to see him once or twice a month. The agents practically waved him through at this point. Why not? He was a local boy, with the face and the manners and the accent to prove it. Besides, even with his father three years in the ground, Ecare was still an important name in the Northeast Kingdom.

This time, though, Dan Molony, the agent usually on the gate during the weekday evening shift, wasn't alone. The Firebird rolled slowly up to the low-slung, rust-red, arched metal gates and icy fingers slipped around Ecare's heart, gripping tightly. On the other side of the border, next to the pole flying the American and Vermont state flags, a pair of state police cars sat idling. In one of the cruisers sat a trooper, hand to chin, leaning on the wheel, watching the interaction between Molony, standing just outside of his customary booth, and a second, campaign-hatted trooper.

Ecare rolled to a stop a dozen feet from the barrier, but didn't cut the engine. Molony and the nearest trooper turned at the vehicle's arrival. The trooper's eyes met Ecare's. The young man found he couldn't breathe.

"Hey!" one of the other boys, the one seated in the backseat, snapped. Ecare didn't respond. His friend flicked the back of his ear, hard. "I said 'hey!'"

"Knock it off." Ecare grit his teeth and shifted uncomfortably in his seat. "What's wrong?"

"Nothing," Ecare snapped.

"Then just be cool."

Molony said something to the trooper, who nodded his assent. The border agent climbed back into his booth, waved the Firebird forward and Nathan rolled slowly towards the gate, stopping a foot or two from it.

Molony leaned from the booth's window. "Evening, Nate."

"Hi, Mr. Molony." The boy strained to keep his voice neutral, calm, natural.

"Back early tonight, huh?"

Ecare's eyes slid across the clock on the dashboard. Just after ten. "Not too early. Got a big day tomorrow."

"That right? Well, let's go through the motions. Anything to declare?"

"No, sir." Ecare's eyes flashed from the border patrol agent towards the state trooper, still standing by the booth, watching the interaction.

"Good enough." Molony leaned back into the booth, pulled the lever that swung the gate-arm upwards. "Welcome home, fellas."

"Thanks." Ecare put the car into gear and crept forward, minutely conscious of the policeman's continued scrutiny. The rear bumper of the car just cleared the gate when the trooper stepped out in front of it, hand up in a "stop" motion.

"Sir, I'm going to have to ask you to turn off the ignition and step out of the vehicle for a moment."

"Wh-why?" the boy stammered.

The trooper stepped forward, up to the window of the Firebird. "Turn off the ignition and step out of the car, please."

Ecare's heart dropped into his belly. He suddenly, desperately wanted a cigarette. Without conscious thought, his foot stomped down onto the gas pedal, hard enough to hurt.

The Firebird's big, eight-cylinder engine roared like a beast, suddenly and unexpectedly loosed from captivity. The car leapt forward, pressing all three boys back into their seats. The trooper jumped backwards, barely missed being tagged by the nose of the car as Ecare whipped it towards route 114, heading south. The second cop, the one who remained in his cruiser, lost no time in giving chase.

"God damn it, Ecare! You're crazy!" his friend cried, laughing. "They know your name, man!"

That was ten minutes ago and, for miles, since leaving route 114, trying to lose the cop on unpaved backroads, the mud was deep, but manageable. No sane driver would go this fast down these roads during mud-season even under the noon-time sun, much less the middle of the night. Ecare had no choice. Sturdy as the Firebird was, the rutted, muddy road felt like it was shaking the damned thing apart.

There were two sets of headlights, two sets of red flashing beacons, in the rearview mirror now. He knew it was hopeless. He didn't reflect on the actions that led him here. He glanced out of the side window at the darkness, at the densely packed trees rushing past as the headlights briefly splashed against them. He wanted nothing more than to disappear, to turn the car off the road into those woods and just cease to be until the world returned to a more familiar state.

Something went *spang* and ricocheted off the undercarriage of the car. Fear tightened its grip, making it hard to breathe. He was acutely aware of his own throat and the growing lump in it. Were they shooting at him? No, that was stupid. It was nearly impossible to hit a moving car with any accuracy on a nice smooth road in broad daylight. In the darkness, on this rutted, sloppy mess, there was no point trying. But he couldn't get the idea out of his head.

He turned, looked at his friend in the passenger seat. The other boy's eyes were tightly closed and his hands, balled into fists, were pressed against the side of his head, as if he could simply shut out what was happening all around him. Ecare threw another glance over his shoulder, at the lights growing close behind him. He could see, just barely, the outline of the trooper behind the wheel. No hands raised. That meant no gun.

He relaxed just a little, turned back to face the road, satisfied that at least nobody was trying to shoot him. There was an intersection coming up, another side road that would take him back towards 114. Maybe it was time to get off these backroads and onto pavement again. The road began to slope slightly downwards. As dirt roads in rural Vermont went, it was a good road, but it wasn't made for anywhere near the speeds the Firebird was traveling and now he really could feel the car rattling apart at the seams, bouncing and jostling and coming down hard with each bump and dip. Worse, the momentum of the downward descent, slight as it was, was taking over. He felt himself losing control of the vehicle.

Sweat poured down his face, forcing him to blink rapidly to keep it from his eyes. His knuckles were fish-belly white as he gripped the steering wheel. The intersection was just around the next bend. He would take it, get back to 114, and find some place, anyplace at all, to stop just long enough to toss the dope, then head back up the road towards the border. He would turn himself in to Molony. The guy seemed decent enough; maybe he would even go to bat for Ecare. It was a thin hope, but it was all Ecare had.

The Firebird turned the corner and the road started to flatten out again. The intersection was just ahead. Ecare's foot caressed the brake, bleeding off a fraction of speed, just enough to turn the corner. He twisted the steering wheel to the left, felt the rear end go into a skid, but not too bad – he managed half a dozen worse ones just tonight. The Firebird turned into it sharply, sliding through the mud, realigned itself with the road, and crashed head-on with an oncoming Volvo wagon that seemed to appear out of thin air.

The impact was like nothing Ecare ever felt before. The seat-belt across his shoulder and lap was like a blade straining to cut him in two, competing with the steering wheel that slammed into his chest, the two trying to see which could do the most damage. His forehead careened off the side window with a sickening cracking sound and some part of his mind wondered if it was the window or his skull that broke.

The Firebird came to a stop and darkness, deeper than the night outside, closed in. The last thing Nathan Ecare remembered were words that seemed out of order and senseless.

"… On your own, man."

•   •   •

September 1993

"That's all I'm gonna say," Ecare finished. His breathing was heavy, sweat dotted his forehead and his hands shook noticeably. Ecare clasped his hands together tightly, then slipped them beneath the table where I couldn't see.

I leaned back into the thin padding of the booth, sipped from my beer. He clearly said a lot more than he planned to. Once he started, the words just poured out of him like water from a broken dam. I wondered if it was the first time he told anyone what really happened that night – from his perspective, anyway. I wondered why he chose me. Maybe because I was the first person who asked. I couldn't know and I doubted he would tell me. He said he was done talking and I was inclined to believe him. Not that it would stop me asking.

I looked across the table at the other man, but he avoided my gaze. He seemed embarrassed. It was understandable; he told me something extremely personal. He also told me something I didn't know before.

"What happened to your friends?" I asked.

Ecare shrugged. "Fuck if I know."

"You never see them around town or anything?" Gears churned in my brain, the way they must have in Ecare's before he decided to tell me about that night.

"Man, I—" He choked, started coughing. When he was done, there were tears in the corners of his eyes. "I don't even know *who* they are."

"I don't understand."

Ecare looked me in the eye, tapped at the left side of his head then brushed away a greasy fistful of hair. There was a thick, jagged scar, maybe four inches long, standing out whitely amidst dark, unwashed hair. "I cracked my head so fuckin' hard on that window I didn't wake up for eleven days and when I did…" He shrugged.

"I don't believe it."

"Yeah, my fucking lawyer didn't, either."

Names popped to mind. "Reynard or Pearce?"

Ecare shook his head. "Neither. Some hot-shit guy up from Boston, but Mr. Reynard got him here, so I guess it's all the same. Mr. Reynard was friends with my dad and he… he was pretty good to me about everything when it happened. Better than I deserved."

The look he gave me was a challenge. "Anyway, it's the truth, no matter what you or anyone else believes. The doctors said it was possible. They don't really know how the brain works, I guess, and anything's possible when you started knocking out pieces of it. I really don't know who was with me and when the cops caught up, it was just me in the car. Molony and the troopers knew there were other guys in the car, but they never saw their faces and I can't remember who they were. I remember every god-damned thing about that night, but the faces, the names, they're just…" He flopped his shoulders in a frustrated shrug. "Gone."

"If you did remember, would you have given them up?"

"In a fucking heartbeat," Ecare sneered. "Whoever it was took off with the fucking dope, left me holding the bag. The *empty* bag," he added. "That put me in real good with—"

He caught himself, clammed up instantly. His face reddened. "Anyway, I'm done."

"With who?" I pressed.

"I'm *done*," he said again. "I've said all I want to, okay? It's all over, it's done. I did my time."

"And it's all behind you?"

Ecare sneered again. "Screw off. Why do you even care?"

"What happened to the drugs, Nate?"

Ecare slid out of the booth, grabbed his book off the table and shoved it into the inside pocket of his jacket, then dug in his pants pocket, pulled out three rumpled dollar bills and tossed them on the table. I pushed them back in his direction. "I'll get it, save your money."

"Don't do me any favors," he spat. "I don't know why I told you all that shit. I don't know why I even told you I'd be here. I don't know why I fuckin' talked to you at the lake in the first place. *Fuck*," he added. "This place is ruined for me now." He stormed off, weaving around vacant tables.

The bartender raised a questioning eyebrow, then shook his head and began to polish a glass, apparently deciding to mind his own business.

If only we all had that luxury.

21

Sunday began mercifully quietly.

I went to bed early on Saturday night, leaving Keith's Tavern around six-thirty, skipping dinner in favor of going straight "home" to the Red Garden to relax. I tried reading a brick of a James Michener novel I bought months earlier and never cracked, but ended up asleep before eight o'clock. I must have needed the rest because I slept late. Very late – I didn't roll out of bed until half-past ten. I showered, shaved and dressed, then ate a late breakfast at a café on Eustace Street, a couple of blocks west of the hotel, recommended by Wendy at the front desk. The eggs benedict were watery, but the coffee was good. Maybe I would ask Carl for a recommendation next time.

Early afternoon was spent in a laundromat on the other end of Dumont Street, nestled behind a sort of pseudo-strip-mall that housed three storefront offices facing the street with the laundromat and a photo-developers' shop out back of the building. The place was busy, it being Sunday afternoon, and the murmur and bustle of machinery and people was soothing. I had only been back to police work for a week, but it was a week that could rightfully be called eventful, so it was nice to lose myself in something so mundane.

Around three o'clock, though, I was bored mindless. I washed, dried and folded every piece of clothing I owned aside from my good suit, my uniform, and what I was wearing, and had no idea what to do with myself for the rest of the afternoon. I spent too much time idle in the last few months. I didn't want to fall back into that trap. I went into the station.

When I walked through the door of the station proper, Mason Domanski sat behind the desk that Jeannie Brown or Loenfeld usually occupied. He set down the newspaper he was browsing, cocked a grin and said, "Look at you, go-getter. Bored, huh?"

"Out of my mind. Here by yourself?"

Domanski nodded. "Except Shane down in holding. It's Barnes's day on road-patrol, otherwise it'd be him sittin' here on a weekend. He hates wedgin' his big ass into the cruiser, but fair's fair, right?"

I ignored that. "Didn't know you ever worked the dispatch desk." From what I saw and knew of Domanski's abilities, it seemed like a waste.

"Swapped with Loenfeld. He's doin' my road patrol tonight, so I can go to a thing my kid's got goin' on without havin' to duck out early. She does dance class," he added as an explanation.

"Also didn't know you had a kid."

He smiled. "Lily, eleven going on twenty-one, and got me wrapped around her finger."

"And you wouldn't have it any other way."

Domanski shrugged, his grin still plastered in place. "Guilty."

"Well." I lifted the wooden gate and slipped through. "Gonna catch up on some paperwork. I'll be in my office if you need something from me."

The Granton police station was hardly bustling during the week, but on a Sunday afternoon, it seemed almost eerily quiet. There was an abandoned feeling to the place. Even after speaking with Domanski, even knowing I wasn't actually alone, walking past the little cubicles the officers used without seeing a single one occupied, then passing Chief Skillman's door without seeing a light on inside, left me feeling as if I was the only one in the entire building. It was hard to shake the idea that I was cut off from the rest of the world. No matter the day or time, the station house on Western Avenue in Albany was always crowded, loud, busy. The dim, empty space of the Granton station served as a reminder of just how far I was from the life I left behind.

I slipped into my office, flicked on the light. There was a small pile of half-finished paperwork on my desk that needed attending, but what caught my attention was the large, manila envelope sitting on top of it. It was addressed to "Detective Luke Campbell, Granton Police," but it hadn't come through the mail. I opened it and found a three-page ballistics report on the slug pulled from my John Doe. Cushman must have received it sooner than expected.

I scanned the pages. Much of the information was meaningless to me and since no weapon was found to compare to the spent round Cushman pulled from the body, I wasn't entirely sure what good any of this would do in the investigation. Once a suspect was identified, a weapon might be found, but until then, this was all information I expected to do nothing more with than stick in a file folder and forget about, waiting for the time when—if—it was needed.

Dutifully, I scanned the pages, not really taking much of it in, until I reached a section near the end of the report and saw: *"Probable match to Smith & Wesson model 651 .22 caliber 'kit gun,' serial number BDAXXXX".* The line was circled and beneath it, added in a cramped scrawl, were the words *"This weapon is supposed to be in your department's custody."* The initials "E.C. M.E." followed. Earl Cushman, medical examiner.

Something electric shot through my nerves, dissipating any sense of boredom or lethargy the last few waking hours left me with. I was suddenly glad that there was nobody else around. I wanted no interruptions as I thought this through.

If Cushman's note was correct, the gun that killed my John Doe was in the department's possession, according to state records. I knew he thoroughly checked; he didn't seem like the kind of person to make such a mistake. I hadn't seen the station's evidence locker; there was no reason for me to yet. I thought about the weapons lock-up Domanski showed me, about the small army's worth of pistols the department had collected over the years. I didn't see any .22s, but I had to wonder, was there a murder weapon hiding among them? Something that was picked up in another case? Departments across the country used confiscated materials like cars and cash, but I never heard of any that used firearms captured during arrests. It just didn't make sense. There would be no standardization of arms, ammunition, or practice and the previous history of the weapons often tainted them beyond redemption.

That left taking this weapon in as evidence.

Cushman estimated that the body was out in the woods since late winter or early spring, though, so it couldn't have been in the department's custody for long. No, I realized, that wasn't necessarily true, but the alternative was a possibility I wasn't yet ready to consider. Not unless it became necessary.

I walked out to the front of the station. Domanski was still seated at the front desk, now sipping coffee and listening to a portable radio quietly spewing sports stats. The dispatch radio's static hum competed with it to create background noise. "Hey, Domanski."

The other man twisted in his seat, simultaneously turning down the portable radio to a barely audible whisper. "What's up?"

"You got keys to the evidence locker?"

"Sure. Skillman hasn't given you a set?" He reached down to his belt, pulled up the big key-ring he wore and separated a single key from it after a moment's search. "You know where it is? Across the hall from the armory." He stood. "Here, I'll show you. What're you looking for?"

I reached out for the key. "No, it's cool. You can't leave the radio, anyway."

"Yeah, you're right. Damn." He dropped the key into my palm then looked ruefully at the piece of softly humming machinery that kept the police force functioning. "Forgot why I was here for a second. I hate riding the desk."

"Don't we all. I'll bring this back shortly." Before he had a chance to say anything else, I was through the door to the main hallway, shutting it behind me.

•   •   •   •

The evidence locker was easy to find. Domanski had nothing to worry about on that front. I unlocked the door, flicked on the interior light and found myself in a room maybe twelve feet wide by twenty-five feet long, cement-floored, the walls lined with metal shelving units stacked floor to ceiling with cardboard boxes, some labeled, many not.

I had no idea where to look, but I knew what I was looking for and that there was nothing to do but start sifting through boxes. I spent over an hour searching, rifling through odds and ends that may or may not have been important at one time, easily dismissing most of the boxes' contents at a single glance. When I finally returned Domanski's key to him, I knew what I only suspected before: the only thing I cared about being in that room was not there to be found. That left me with possibilities I didn't care for at all.

22

The remainder of that day was hardly as peaceful or restful as it began. I tried to focus on my original purpose for being at the station, but reports on DUIs and petty thefts hardly seemed worth the effort compared to the possibilities running through my head. Before long, their weight crushed any other concerns and I gave up the effort as useless. Domanski was not at the front-desk when I left the station, but I didn't give it much thought.

It was after five o'clock and it was almost six hours since I last ate, so I drove the few blocks down to Main Street and found a place to park near Callaway's. Chloe wasn't working and the place was pretty busy, so I took a stool at the counter and ate a cheeseburger with only the company of my thoughts. As I paid my check, Cal Callaway caught my eye through the window back into the kitchen and gave me a nod and a little wink. I wondered what Chloe, or more likely Roland, told him of me. He seemed to be the closest thing to family the DeJonges had in Granton and my impression of him so far was fairly good. In a half-realized sort of way, I hoped he felt the same about me, though I couldn't have said what it really mattered. I didn't even know where I stood with Chloe yet; what did it matter what her pseudo-father figure thought?

I didn't know. Just that it mattered.

I went home to my room in the nicest hotel in a rural town in northeastern Vermont and thought about that and a lot of other things until sleep once again came early to claim me.

· · ·

I shouldn't have been in my office on Monday morning, but I was. I had my first night road-patrol coming up. Every Monday would be my turn to patrol the town and surrounding roads from six p.m. until four a.m. and I wasn't expected to be in for almost ten hours. But at eight a.m., I'd been there for almost forty minutes, pushing myself to finish some of the necessary busywork I abandoned the day before and waiting until I could call Earl Cushman to discuss the note he wrote me regarding the missing weapon. I tried his office the moment I got behind my desk, but was told the doctor wouldn't be in until later.

I was giving the write-up on the Roethes auto-theft report a once over when a short, sharp knock sounded on the glass of my door. "C'mon in," I said without looking up.

The door opened and Barnes stuck his head in the doorway. "What're you doing here, Campbell? Trying to make the rest of us look bad?"

I laughed, but not for the reason Barnes probably thought. "No, just catching up some. You know how it is."

"Yeah, I know, but *you* better catch up on some sleep. You're on road patrol tonight, right?"

I nodded. He said, "Then take my advice and get some rest. Sittin' in that car for seven or eight hours takes a lot more out of you than you'd think."

I looked Barnes up and down, at the paunch that hung low over his belt and the thick, fleshy jowls covered in a couple of days' stubble. He didn't seem like a bad guy, but he wasn't my idea of a cop, either. I was pretty confident that I could take more strain that he could, sitting or otherwise.

"Thanks," was all I said, though. "I'll get out of here before long. I just want to get some things done before I'm too far behind."

Barnes shrugged heavy shoulders, said, "Suit yourself," and disappeared, closing the door behind him.

I set aside the Roethes report and picked up the telephone again. Earl Cushman himself answered after three rings. "Dr. Cushman," I told him. "It's Detective Luke Campbell, over in Granton."

"Well, you've got good timing, detective," he said in his dourly dignified tone. "I just stepped through the door and heard the phone. In fact, here comes Anita. It's all right," he said, his voice slightly muffled. "It was for me, anyway. Yes, thank you. Now," he returned his attention to me, "I take it you received the forensics report on the round I recovered?"

"Yes." I told him, in as few words as possible, that there was no sign of that weapon in the station.

"Troubling," was his response.

"It's more than that, doctor, it's—"

"I know where your thoughts are going, Campbell," Cushman cut in. "Let me see what I can find out. My resources are hardly expansive, but I do, perhaps, have access to a few more than you." In a slow, carefully modulated tone, he continued, "Please believe me when I say I'm as disturbed by the possibility you're thinking of as you must be." He added, his voice returned to its more familiar tone, "I'll be in touch if I learn anything. Goodbye, detective."

"Thank you, doctor." I hung up the phone then stared at it for a few minutes, my thoughts doing a slow churn, grinding up what little I knew and trying to piece it together in a way that made more sense. Cushman wasn't the unfeeling, gray-clad robot he first appeared. I was grateful for that and, though I wasn't entirely certain what good he could do at this point, I was grateful for any help I could get. I already knew I would need it.

• • •

Around mid-morning, I went down to Callaway's again. The place hadn't yet filled up for lunch and when I passed through the glass-and-steel doors, Chloe was standing behind the counter, silently polishing its scarred Formica surface with a rag.

"Hi, there. This seat taken?" I asked as I slid onto the stool directly in front of her.

She looked up and almost smiled before catching herself and putting a semblance of her professional mask in place. "Sit anywhere you like, Mr. Campbell."

"Thanks. I already have. Could I trouble you for some coffee and maybe one of those?" I pointed at the glass-covered display of breakfast pastries halfway down the counter. She served the coffee, placing the steaming brew in front of me, then moved away, selected a pastry, deposited it on a plate and slid it down the counter in my direction. "Thank you," I told her.

She leaned on her side of the counter, her breasts straining beneath the pink cotton of her uniform. "I should be thanking you," she said softly, just the barest hint of a smile in her eyes. "Roland is so happy, he's been walking on air."

That made me smile. "I'm glad to hear it. When can we do it again?"

Chloe started, as if suddenly aware of our proximity, then straightened up. The hint of amusement disappeared and, once again, her face revealed nothing. "My son asked the same thing and I'll tell you what I told him: we'll see."

It was a place to start. I sipped coffee through a smile as she hurried away to serve someone else, hating to see her go, but enjoying the sight all the same. I tried not to think about the rage I saw in her eyes down by the lake or what it might mean.

· · · ·

At six that evening, my first night of road-patrol started and for the first several hours, it was as quiet as could be hoped for. When I checked in at the station, Loenfeld was just coming on for his shift as the dispatch officer and gave me a few tips on places to watch for speeders and what local residents I could likely expect to pick up now and again on DUIs. I appreciated the advice, especially as I didn't know the roads outside of the town proper too well yet, and was glad to have areas to focus on.

The town itself wasn't much of a problem. Except for a few bars and restaurants, after seven o'clock they practically rolled up the sidewalks, it was so quiet. Outside of town, though, was a different story, especially on the stretch of state highway that crossed through the outskirts of town and ran all the way up to the Canadian border. There were several roadside bars and taverns out there and a lot of DUIs and speeders were picked up either coming or going. Every other hour, I headed out that way, checking the western approach to Granton and, until midnight, it was clear of anything but the lightest traffic.

I was just about to come off one of the little side-roads that fed route 114, the intersection with its BB-pocked stop sign just ahead, when my headlights caught something dead in the middle of the road. The night was so peaceful, I started to relax a little and in my surprise, I stomped on the brake, bringing the cruiser to a skidding halt in the loose-packed dirt. I flicked the high-beams on, with no idea what to expect, and saw before me a big, fat 'possum, hunched down and leering at me through the windshield, her mouth open and hissing. Behind her, clinging tightly to her rear, were three miniatures. Mama and babies looked as surprised as I was. I rolled down the window, waved a hand. "After you, ma'am."

If she appreciated the kindness, I'll never know. Just at that moment, a vehicle barreled past the end of the road, heading south, back towards town. He must have been doing seventy-five. If I hadn't stopped for the 'possum family, that car might well have broadsided me as I turned onto the main road. I threw the car in gear, edged around the angry, cowering animals and cut out after the speeder, flicking on my red lights.

The road was nearly flat and fairly straight in that stretch and I caught up to the taillights ahead of me easily, flashing my roof-top lights, but the driver made no motion to pull over, still cruising along at twice the speed-limit. When I cut in with the siren, two quick whoops to get his attention, he finally acknowledged me – by pushing his speed up to almost ninety and temporarily leaving me in his dust.

I swore softly and flicked on the radio, calling in to Loenfeld on dispatch. He acknowledged, asked, "You need a hand, Campbell?" his voice sounding eager at the possibility of getting out from behind the desk. But, unless there was an emergency, that was a no go and I told him so.

I crept up onto the other car's rear-end, lights and siren screaming over my head, and opened up the public address system. "Pull the vehicle over to the side of the road!"

By the light of my high-beams, I saw two figures outlined in the car ahead of me and the one driving decided to get cute. His brake lights lit for a moment and I backed up, giving him room to slow down and comply with my order, but when I did, instead of stopping, he turned sharply, the rear-end of his car sliding dangerously close to the edge of a ditch as he ducked into a side-road called Moose Kill Run. He punched it up to eighty and disappeared out of sight.

I was angry, but not worried. Moose Kill was one of the roads I already explored and I knew it was a dead-end, going back a few miles into the woods and then abruptly ending at the top of a small hill with a clearing just big enough to turn around in if you ended up there by mistake. I was curious when I discovered that and a quick look showed me that the drop at the end of that road was at least forty feet deep and very steep. You could get up or down it on foot with some effort, but there was no place for a vehicle to go. With the road dead-ending and only a couple of houses tucked back in the trees, away from the road, there was little chance of anyone else being out at that time of night, so if this little punk wanted a race, I would give him one.

I cut the siren as I screeched to a stop, backed up, and turned onto Moose Kill, stomping the gas pedal, making the cruiser's big engine roar and bringing it up to over ninety. Within seconds the road started to climb and I lost a little speed, but still took the first curve at better than eighty. It occurred to me all of a sudden why this situation felt so familiar and I thought of Nathan Ecare and the story he told me.

I thought, too, of Chloe DeJonge. Anger and shame washed over me and I gentled the brakes, bringing my speed down to under sixty. If there was no danger of my quarry escaping, there was no reason to act foolishly. There was plenty of that in the world already.

I came around another corner and a landmark I recognized, a huge oak split down the center by a long-ago lightning strike. It sparked my memory: the end of the road was coming up soon. I realized, too, that the taillights I was chasing were gone. I slowed the car further, down to less than twenty miles an hour, and crawled towards the end of the road, eyes scanning all directions for the other vehicle. There was nowhere for it to go and, if he was local, the driver had to know that as well as I did.

Lights flared in the darkness, stabbing out of the night and blinding me for an instant, before an engine roared and the vehicle I was searching for found me. I could see it clearly for a moment and dimly it registered that the thing was only a rusted out Ford LTD that shouldn't have been able to haul like it did. Then instinct took over and I swung the car around to block the road, bracing myself while putting my full weight on the brakes.

The LTD tried to swing past my front-end, but the driver misjudged the amount of space he had and clipped the nose of the cruiser, spinning my vehicle around with an ear-splitting shriek of metal on metal and rubber on gravel. It came to rest facing back the way I came from, the headlights spotlighting the LTD as it tilted halfway off of the road, resting against a convenient tree. Its rear, passenger-side wheel turned uselessly inches off of the ground.

Adrenaline and anger surged as what Nathan Ecare had told me, my own imagination, and what just happened got mixed up in my head. I thought of what the stupid stunt a thrill-seeking Ecare pulled cost a woman and boy I was coming to care for. I thought about what might have just happened on a backroad in the ass-end of a town nobody who didn't live there ever even heard of. My heart beat so hard that the pounding in my chest actually hurt.

Driven by anger and instinct, I stomped out of the patrol car, weapon drawn, and jerked open the driver's door. "Out! Get out of there before I snap you in two!"

In the glare of the cruiser's headlights, the man behind the wheel looked pale and scared and young. His hair was slicked back in a greaser-type style that hadn't been popular in decades and he wore a leather jacket that he probably thought made him seem tough. With a gun pointed at him and no way to escape, though, he looked like what he was as he climbed out of the car: a scared kid who screwed up and knew it.

The passenger may have been tougher or maybe just more scared than the driver, because he exited, too, but he wasn't done trying to get away. He hopped out of his door, stumbled into the brush alongside the road and would have run if I hadn't fired a shot into the air, freezing him in his tracks. It was against all protocol, but I was beyond the point of caring.

"Turn around, put your hands up and get over here or the next one won't miss," I growled so fiercely I almost believed I would do it. The would-be runner turned and even in the darkness, I recognized him. Dylan Roethes. My already stirred-up blood began to boil. "What the hell are you even doing outside of a cell?"

He started back out of the brush, hands raised at chest height, but he was grinning. "Anything I want. I'm a free man. My mom didn't press charges once she got the car back. I had to give back what was left of Addison's dough, but..." He shrugged. "Guess I'll be spending tonight back there, huh?" He made a big production out of a yawn. "Oh, well, a bed's a bed. Jail's as good a place to sleep as any."

"Get over here." I was so angry that the tone of my own voice scared me. Roethes's friend picked up on it and turned even whiter in the glare of the cruiser's high-beams. Roethes didn't take the hint; he came, but he was smirking the entire way. I holstered the pistol as he approached and, when he was in arm's reach, lashed out, the baton on my left hip leaving its sheath and swinging up faster than the kid's eyes could follow, tapping him on the side of the jaw. Not hard, just enough to get his attention. Still, he cried out, staggering backwards, pressing the back of his hand to his face. "What the fuck?" he shrieked.

"Over here. In front of me." He complied. Some semblance of whatever military training he had before ditching his responsibilities must have kicked in because the way he stood vaguely resembled parade stance. I had his attention now.

"Let's try that again, Roethes. What are you doing outside of a jail cell? You were caught dead to rights and my understanding is you're AWOL on top of that. Why are you cruising back roads with this asshole, pulling stunts likely to get someone killed?"

His eyes darted around, from me to his friend, back again. There was no help, no escape, in either avenue. "I, uh…"

I lifted the baton, fully prepared to use it again. I wished the rage would fade. The feeling was like riding a bomb, falling from a great height, knowing it would explode eventually, knowing someone was going to be hurt by it and that it would take me along, either way.

Roethes looked into my eyes and apparently didn't like what he saw because he lowered his gaze immediately. He tried again. "Chief Skillman came down, said there was no harm done if the car was back where it belonged. A-and if I gave the money back."

"Skillman himself said this."

The boy nodded hard, almost frantically. His bluster, his wise-talk was gone and in its place was a scared kid, like his friend, whose name I still didn't know. Only the friend got it right from the start; he was smart enough to be afraid. There were big consequences coming for these two, no matter what Skillman let them get away with in the past.

I stared Roethes down, seeing in him another would-be Nathan Ecare. Instead of feeling grateful I could bring this to a close with nobody hurt, though, the simmering anger inside me grew stronger, threatened to boil over.

I raised the baton. Roethes shrank back, screamed, "Don't!" his voice high and shrill.

"Why not?" I asked, forcing calmness into my voice.

"Y-you're a cop." He said, as if that answered anything.

"You fellas could have killed me, or yourselves, with this stunt you pulled. That ever occur to you?" Probably it hadn't. Probably these two morons never for a moment considered the value of a life, not even their own.

I sighed, very tired, very sick of this conversation.

I put the baton back on my belt and reached for the handcuffs clipped behind my back. "Put your hands out. You first," I jutted my chin at Roethes.

I handcuffed the pair and shoved them into the back of my cruiser. The front-end was banged up pretty good, but it would get me where I needed to be. There was a state police barracks in Newport, twenty miles up the state highway. I wasn't taking any chances with these two spending a night in the Granton holding cells and then being put back on the street on some whim of Skillman's. I would swear out a complaint against them with the state troopers and let them deal with it. I wished then that I hadn't called into Loenfeld that I was after a speeder, but there was nothing to do but deal with the fallout later on.

As I pulled the cruiser around, headed back towards the main road, Roethes's friend called out, "Hey, what about my car? Someone might steal it's just sitting out here with the keys in it."

"I hope they do," I said. "Maybe Addy's will give them a good price for it, huh, Roethes?"

There was no response from the backseat.

23

"Detective. Wanna see you in my office. Right now."

If Chief Skillman ever had a friendly word for anyone, I hadn't yet heard it, but his tone seemed always to be especially frosty when addressing me. I couldn't blame him this time; my actions the night before were meant to provoke him, in a way.

After taking Roethes and his friend, a kid named Tom Whipple, to the state police barracks I swore out a complaint citing reckless endangerment, failure to yield, ignoring a lawful command, and half a dozen traffic violations. The state trooper at the desk gave me the side-eye, but agreed to take the boys into custody. For a little while, I felt good about it. Now came the fall-out.

Jeannie looked at me with sympathy. I asked her about ideas for fun things to do in the area the next time Roland, Chloe, and I could get together, which I planned to do, suspicions be damned, when Skillman appeared. All Jeannie said now was, "Better get going, Luke." Skillman was already disappearing down the narrow hallway leading deeper into the station. I moved to follow.

The door to Skillman's office was open and the man himself stood behind his desk, towering over it, casting a long spindly shadow that brought to mind a dead, lonesome tree out in the woods somewhere. An unlit cigarette was clamped in the corner of his mouth. That brought to mind a dead man, all by his lonesome out in the woods, sightless eyes staring at a mound of cigarette butts.

"Sit down, Luke," Skillman commanded, sinking into his own chair. It was the first time the chief used my given name. I didn't know if I liked it.

I sat. I cut to the chase. "Is this about the Roethes and Whipple boys?"

Skillman waved a hand. "You handled it the way you saw fit. Not how I'd have done it, but it's done, and they're out of our hair. Let the staties deal with them."

I expected anger, a dressing down, maybe even being fired for undermining the chief's authority, for making a decision I knew he wouldn't agree with. His casual dismissal of the whole thing was out of character. Skillman was a strange man, mercurial in his actions, but always keeping his thoughts to himself and silently pursuing his own policies. Maybe he recognized that nobody ever knew what he was thinking and that he couldn't fault any of us for that. I didn't really believe it, but it was a possibility.

"Now," the chief continued, leaning forward on his desk. "What's going on with that John Doe of yours?"

I had no progress in identifying the body. Skillman must have known that, but I told him, anyway.

"I see," he said. "Got any leads?"

Was I being tested? I supposed, whether the suspicions I harbored were true or not, I was. This was the exact job Skillman hired me for, after all.

"There are a couple," I said, wary, not willing to lie, but not willing to lay my cards on the table, either. "Dr. Cushman sent me a few preliminary reports and when I last spoke with him, he told me he's going to engage some state-level resources he has access to. Old crimes like this, though, sir," Skillman's eyebrow crawled upwards as I spoke, "they don't break easily, if at all. I'll keep at it, but I don't expect anything like a swift resolution."

"No," Skillman drawled. "I suppose not." The cigarette slid from one corner of his mouth to the other as a speculative look passed across the older man's face. Finally, he said, "Keep me informed. That's all."

Dismissed, I stood and headed to my own office, reflecting again on Skillman's strange aloofness.

• • •

Days later, I was sitting with the list of missing persons I made the day my John Doe was discovered, trying to form a plan of action as to how to further whittle it down without actually investigating each and every name's disappearance. It was starting to look as if there might not be any good angles. I sent out the information on the dental impressions taken from the body some time ago. It took a while, but I finally heard back from most of the dentists in the region. The answer was the same from each of them: those teeth did not belong to a patient of theirs. Sending the records on to the Veterans Administration, as well, got the same response. On the off chance of a federal record, I had Cushman run the imprints by the FBI, but I wasn't holding my breath for any sort of luck there, either. It occurred to me that I could try to get my hands on the dental records of each of the missing persons and have Dr. Cushman do a comparison to those from the body, but that would mean tracking down and getting the permission of a family member of each of the names on my list and then starting the process all over again. Who knew how long that would take?

It was frustrating. I had a body, a probable homicide, and I even had an idea of the weapon the man was killed with, but without an identity, there was no real place to start. It was a mirror-image parallel to the situation Nathan Ecare, if he was to believed, described, except that he knew exactly what happened, he simply didn't know who was involved.

At least, that was his claim. If it was true, though, he was still better off than I was; he knew Granton and had lived here all his life. I was an outsider, working with fragments I could scarcely even recognize. Without knowing how they fit together, what did I really have? Closing this case seemed as remote a possibility as walking back into the Western Avenue station house in Albany and being offered my old job back.

Even if that happened, though, I wasn't sure that I would accept. I had been in Granton a little under three weeks, but I was really starting to like the place. Anonymous bodies aside, there was a simplicity to the town that I found refreshing, a peaceful placidity that I didn't know I was missing. More than that, most of the people I met around town were friendly and pleasant, and I had good co-workers with whom I felt I was starting to make real connections – Chief Skillman notwithstanding.

I still wondered about the man. Most days he was holed up in his office, door closed, and aside from the times he called me in to speak with him, I rarely saw him. Not in the office, anyway. Strangely, I had seen him not once, but twice, on my night-time road-patrols. Both times, I was cruising one of the pitch-black backroads just outside of town when his white and gray cruiser slid from a parking space alongside the road and accompanied me for a distance—once behind me, once ahead—without any acknowledgement that he was aware of my presence. We both had radios in our cars, of course, but I was reluctant to make the first move and he showed no inclination to do so, either. I wondered if he was devoting his time to patrolling the activities of backroad lovers' lanes or if he had some other motive for those late-night drives. The man was simply inscrutable.

A rapid knocking rattled the glass in my office door and then, as if summoned by my thoughts, Aaron Skillman stuck his head inside. "Someone's found a body, detective."

"Another skeleton in the woods?"

Skillman smiled, but so slightly it barely tugged at his gaunt cheeks. "No, an actual body, this time. Some kids found it alongside Braun's River, a little ways up from the park."

I slid the missing persons list back into my desk and stood, adjusting my harness to more comfortably ride my hips. "I'll get right out there."

"I'll ride along." That surprised me, as did most anything Skillman said or did, I supposed. I must have either let it show on my face or simply taken too long to respond, as the chief turned and gestured. "C'mon now, Campbell. Only so many hours in the day."

I only nodded and followed. There was no use arguing. Skillman would do as he liked. He was the boss, after all.

Outside of the station, we climbed into Skillman's quasi-marked cruiser. It was identical to the vehicles the rest of us drove, a white and gray Crown Victoria with blue trim, but it had no police livery on the doors and no rooftop lights, only a detachable dash-top one. Skillman seemed to have no personal vehicle as it was the only thing I ever saw him drive. One of the perks of his job, I supposed.

The chief turned the engine over, shifted into gear and angled the car towards the street. "We're going to pick up a third for our little jaunt. That a problem?"

It wouldn't have mattered if it was, I guessed, so I only asked, "Who's that, sir?"

"Frank Lautner."

The editor of the local newspaper. Why in hell would Skillman bring him to a crime scene?

"I know what you're thinking, detective, but I have my reasons," Skillman said. "You may have a history of antagonism with the press"—I grit my teeth at that—"but Frank's a good man to have on your side and he's pretty insightful sometimes. Besides," he turned and winked at me. "He'll find out shortly, anyway, and letting him in on the ground floor wins us brownie points."

I didn't understand and only half-cared. I was growing sick of trying to understand the way Skillman conducted police business. As long as nothing interfered in the investigation, I had no choice but to let him have his way.

In the center of Granton, Skillman parked in front of the *Granton Telegraph's* offices, a small storefront with the name ornately stenciled in gold on the big front window. He left me sitting in the idling car while he went inside to call on Lautner. A moment later, the two men exited and climbed into the cruiser, Skillman back behind the wheel and Lautner in the rear. Lautner unslung a small leather bag from his shoulder and lay it on the seat beside him.

"Thanks for the rescue, Chief," Lautner said, buckling his seatbelt. "I'll happily chase news any day of the week instead of delinquent advertising accounts. How you doing, Detective Campbell?" he asked with no segue.

I didn't bother looking back. "Fine, thanks."

"I don't think the young man likes having me here, chief." The grin in Lautner's voice was plain.

Skillman chuckled. "He'll get used to it. He's a little set in his ways is all." Skillman tossed another wink at me.

The chief drove towards Brook Park, turned onto Park Road and then north onto a narrow dirt road that I probably would have dismissed as nothing more than someone's lengthy driveway. Up the old road we went, maybe half a mile, until a wash-out made it impossible for the car to proceed any further. We exited the cruiser and tramped further north on foot, following the east bank of Braun's River. Lautner complained about the muddiness, which I got a secret kick out of.

We went maybe another hundred and fifty yards up the river before Skillman stopped us and said, "I think it should be around here somewhere. Fits with what the boy who called it in described."

We weren't that far from town, really, but it was pretty well deserted, with no sign of recent passage other than ours. There were also no obvious landmarks to go by, at least that I could see, so I wondered how Skillman knew this was the place. The kids who supposedly found this body must have given him very good directions.

I looked around and nothing jumped out at me. The faint path of the dirt road was still visible, though even fainter here than back where we left the car.

It had all the hallmarks of an old logging road, probably one of the earliest in Granton's history, judging by its proximity to the town proper.

I went along a little further north on my own and saw a spot where the ground, instead of sloping down to the river, hung out over it a short distance. I edged over towards it and saw a little gully where the water had eaten away at the earth, carving out a chunk that looked as if a giant came along and took a bite from it. A huge maple had grown here, but at some point, the weakened bank beneath it collapsed, causing the tree to plunge over the edge. Incredibly, I realized, standing on the ledge, it not only still lived, but continued to grow and now formed a natural bridge over this part of the river, with some of its roots embedded in the bank and others twisting into the air, reaching for the sky and forming strange shapes as they sought out the sunlight.

I was so enthralled by the sight that I almost didn't notice the body, hanging by the neck from the maple, suspended halfway across the river, its toes dangling in the swiftly flowing current. Someone hanged himself from this conveniently secluded bridge.

I called to the others and pointed down into the narrow ravine. Skillman studied the body, faintly swaying on the end of the rope, pushed along by the momentum of the water across its toes and swinging back again with the man's own weight. "Suicide," Skillman said, matter-of-factly.

"Looks like suicide, yeah," Lautner agreed, digging into his shoulder bag. He produced a small camera and continued, "Found himself a good, out of the way place where he wouldn't bother anybody or be stopped."

"You know, a lot of murderers like privacy, too." I was irritated by the snap judgment of these two supposedly insightful men.

Skillman and Lautner shared a look, then Lautner moved closer to the edge, inching out onto the trunk of the tree and staring down at the hanging man. I noticed, watching Lautner, that the trunk of the tree appeared scuffed, with scarred bark and several small, broken branches, as if many feet passed across it over the years. It formed a natural bridge, so it made perfect sense, but it also meant that it probably wasn't a secret to anyone who spent much time in the woods around Granton.

Lautner reached the middle of the trunk and stared at the dangling body for a long minute. The man's neck was broken by his fall from the trunk and his head hung limply to one side, his face turned at an angle down towards the near bank.

"My god," Lautner said. "I think it's Greg Moran." He turned his face back towards where Skillman and I stood on the embankment. Lautner looked as if he felt ill.

"A friend of yours?" I asked.

Lautner shook his head slowly. "Friend of my daughter's. They dated off and on through high school. I liked him. He was a good kid. Had an interest in journalism, at least at one point. He actually interned with me at the paper one summer, and I invited him back the next, but he never followed up. After the kids graduated, Katie went off to college down in Mass and Greg went off somewhere, too. I forget where, but that was the last I heard of him, I guess. Don't see his folks more than once in a blue moon. Had no idea he was back in town."

Lautner carefully made his way back to solid ground, a glum, lost look on his face. "I knew that kid most of his life. What the hell could drive him to this?" He let the hand holding his camera trail at his waist, forgotten. If they keep at it long enough, eventually a cop or a reporter is going to find someone they know either dead or involved in something unpleasant. Maybe both. Frank Lautner was discovering that death wasn't so appealing or abstract when that was the case.

"Let's take some photos." I turned. "Chief?" I let the other man fill in the rest of the question for himself.

Skillman nodded. "I'll head back, get on the horn and get the coroner's boys down here. Sit tight."

"May I?" I held out a hand towards Lautner. He handed the camera over without a word then went to sit on a rock a little distance away from the river's edge.

I climbed down into the little gully, having to drop the last foot or two as it was nearly vertical from where the tree was. From up above, the bed of the river looked clean, clear, and shallow, but the silty bottom turned out to be both muckier and deeper than expected once I stirred it up with my passage. I still needed to get some good work-boots, I realized, as I felt the cold water seep into my shoes.

I backed up a distance from the hanging man, took a couple of long shots of the body, then moved back in close and took a few more photos from every angle that I could. The body of Greg Moran swayed back and forth gently, the motion almost peaceful, as if it was just another part of nature. It was calm and serene, but also eerie, standing there in the little river bed, ferns growing around me, birds singing, staring at the body of a dead man.

Shaking the thought from my head, I aimed the camera down at the ground, at the embankment, at the underside of the tree, snapping pictures off each time. After a few minutes, Lautner's head and shoulders appeared over the earthy ledge above me. "What are you looking for?"

"I don't know," I admitted. "Just looking around. Seeing what fits or if there's anything that doesn't." If this was a suicide, I would hope for a note of some sort, though that isn't always the case. And even if there was a note, it didn't have to be with the body. I would need to find out where Moran was calling home these days.

I ducked under the tree-trunk and moved a little distance away, up the river, feet squishing in the cold, wet silt. I spotted something that didn't belong: the burned down stub of a cigarette, laying just at the edge of the river, the white paper stained yellow where river water probably caused the leftover tobacco to leak and run. I bent down, scooped it up in my handkerchief and tucked it into the breast pocket of my uniform. It may have meant nothing. Moran might well have smoked a last cigarette, tossed it into the river, then climbed up onto the tree trunk and stepped off to his death. In fact, that was quite likely what had happened, but I couldn't ignore finding cigarettes at the site of another man's death. This made two bodies in less than three weeks in a town that averaged a suspicious death every other year from what I saw in the case files. I knew that the John Doe was most certainly not a suicide and I seriously doubted Greg Moran was, either.

I walked back to Moran's body. Hands on hips, I looked the situation over then turned towards Lautner, still watching from his perch above me. "What now?" he asked.

I shrugged. It might be hours until Dr. Cushman and his team arrived and there was really nothing more I could do.

"Get the body down," Chief Skillman answered, surprising both me and, Lautner, who startled and turned, looking over his shoulder. Skillman appeared a moment later, customary unlit cigarette dead center in the middle of his mouth, looking down at me from where Lautner stood. The cigarette was pushed to the side of his mouth as he continued. "I just talked to Cushman. He'll be here soon as, but I described the situation to him and he doesn't want to risk that boy's body ending up in the river."

I eyed the body and the rope. I wasn't thrilled with the idea of moving Moran without the medical examiner's team present, but I could see the point Skillman was making. The weight on that broken neck was already a strain.

"Okay," I said. "Let's cut that rope and lower him down, then. Hauling him up probably wouldn't be pleasant."

Skillman nodded. "Right." Knees bent, he clambered out onto the trunk of the tree, took a folding knife from a pouch on his belt and said, "Get ready, detective." He began sawing at the rope fastened around the thick tree.

Part of me reeling in disgust, I wrapped my arms around Greg Moran's waist and waited. A moment turned into a minute, the susurrus of Skillman's blade working on the tough rope drifting down to my ears, and then with a faint snapping sound, the rope came apart. The body dropped, becoming a dead weight in my arms and I struggled, first to keep my balance, then to move it to the side of the river where I could lay it down gently, away from the water.

Heaving for breath, I straightened up and glanced in Skillman's direction. The older man gave me a thumbs up. "Good job, detective. Nothing more to do but wait."

I nodded, pretending I was too winded to answer, and turned back towards Moran's body. I hadn't looked very closely at his face before then, strange as it may sound, considering how I inspected the rest of him and the area. Not many people really know how to act around a corpse, though, and I was no exception. Now I saw not a body, but a good-looking young man, somewhere in his mid- to late twenties. His half-open eyes still retained something that seemed as if it might be life. Though of course that was impossible, nothing but a trick of the light, it disturbed me.

The skin on the man's face was pale and puffy from the blood settling in the extremities. I guessed he hadn't been dead very long at all. A couple of days, at most. One thing was sure at a glance: the noose was expertly tied, which is harder to do than it seems. If he hanged himself, Moran hadn't taken any chances on slowly strangling. The noose worked as intended and he would have died the moment he hit the end of the rope.

Lautner appeared above me, still wearing a sickened expression. He braced himself and scrambled down the incline to join me. "What the hell happened to you, Greg? Why would you do this?" He turned to me. "He always seemed like such a happy kid."

"He's not a kid, anymore. You knew him, what? Seven, eight years ago, I'm guessing?"

Lautner nodded. "Something like that."

I knelt next to Moran, picked up his left wrist and pointed down at his hand. "You knew never him as a man, and I'm guessing he's had at least some recent unhappiness in his life. See that?"

Squinting, Lautner leaned forward to look at the narrow band of pale skin across Moran's ring finger. "He wore a ring." He stepped back, his head swiveling. "It didn't fall off or anything?"

"No," I said. "I doubt it. He left town years ago, you didn't know he was back, so he probably hasn't been back for long. It's your business to know what's going on this town, right?" Lautner nodded cautiously. I went on. "Then I'd say he went through a very recent divorce and came back to familiar ground to get himself adjusted."

"That makes sense," Lautner agreed, throwing a glance up the bank towards where Skillman sat. The old cop stared off into the distance, apparently oblivious to our conversation, though I was certain he was listening.

Lautner's eyes turned back to Moran. He sighed. "Damn it, Greg... Hey, you see this?" He knelt, brushed back a lock of Moran's hair. Just beyond the hairline, above Moran's left temple, was a large bruise. Even with the discoloration of death, it stood out sharply.

"No." I hunkered down and had a closer look. The skin was purple-blue and split at one edge of the bruise. It looked like Moran had been hit with something quite heavy and irregularly shaped. "That's a hell of a mark."

A shadow fell across the body. From above, Skillman's voice said, "Probably hit his head on one of those branches," he waggled a finger towards the tree trunk bridge, "jumping off of it."

I didn't think so. Not for a second. This was no glancing, accidental bruise, but something nasty and intentional. "Maybe. We'll know for sure once Dr. Cushman has a chance to examine him."

"I don't see how it could be anything but suicide," Lautner said. "Who could kill someone by hanging him? There're no lynch mobs around here. And why kill Greg, anyway?"

I had to admit, once again, that I didn't know.

"Luke is paid to be suspicious, Frank." Skillman took the cigarette from his mouth, split it in two with his fingers and then tossed the individual halves in different directions. If there was a significance to the gesture, it was lost on me. When he was done, he turned his gaze my way and said, "If it is a murder, detective, then all you've got to do is find a motive and a suspect. It looks pretty cut and dry what the murder weapon was." There seemed to be a challenge in his tone.

"At least it's a place to start." I wasn't afraid to take that challenge on.

I found a comfortable-looking rock and sat down to wait for Cushman and his team.

24

Shortly after we cut the body down, Lautner asked Skillman to take him back to his office. Skillman asked if I would be okay alone. I told them to go ahead. I was by myself with Moran for a little over an hour before Chad Moss showed up, tromping along the path. "Skillman sent me out here to keep you company." I told Moss it wasn't necessary, but I appreciated it, anyway.

Before Moss's arrival, I made another pass around the area, scanning for evidence, but found nothing. Some living company wasn't a bad thing. We shot the breeze for a while and then Earl Cushman and his two-man crew arrived. The three county men spent a little over an hour examining the body and the scene then packed Greg Moran's remains up for transport to the county morgue. Before he climbed into the van emblazoned with the Orleans County Sheriff's Department livery, I took Cushman aside and asked him what he thought: suicide or murder?

The thin, gray man shrugged his narrow shoulders and said, "Honestly, I couldn't say yet, Detective Campbell. I understand your suspicions—believe me, I share them; I've yet to see a hanging suicide this perfectly accomplished—but aside from the bruise you pointed out, there's nothing that explicitly contradicts the suicide theory. And even that bruise *could* have occurred the way you said Chief Skillman believes. Extremely unlikely, but not impossible."

"Okay, that's about what I figured. Thanks, doctor."

Cushman flashed a ghost of a smile. "It's what I'm here for. I'll contact you as soon as there's something to tell."

Moss and I hiked down the old logging road to his cruiser and headed back to more familiar parts of Granton. When we reached the end of Park Road, I asked him, "Know Greg Moran's parents?"

"Not personally." Moss shook his head. "Guess I'd know 'em by sight."

"Know where they live?'

"Sure… you want to go right now, though?"

"Someone's got to tell them and I'd like to speak with them besides."

Moss shrugged and turned the wheel hand-over-hand, making a U-turn in the middle of the street. "You're the detective."

"That's what people keep telling me," I said.

· · ·

The house, on a cul-de-sac at the end of Eaton Street, was small and neat. It was old, probably dating back to the boom period just after the Second World War, and while the porch had seen better days and the garage needed a coat of paint, it looked as if it was well-cared for over the years.

Moss asked, "You want me to go with, Luke?"

"Not unless you want to." I stepped out of the cruiser and leaned back in for Moss's answer. "I'd rather not," he admitted. "I don't do well with, uh… you know." I told him not to worry about it and moved up the short, narrow walkway towards the house.

I stepped onto the porch, the boards creaking beneath my feet. A gray-striped cat appeared from somewhere, looked me over and decided I was okay because it began to rub up against my shin. I gave it a pat on the head and then rang the doorbell. The sound echoed hollowly inside the house and after a moment, a shadow appeared on the other side of the prismed glass set in the door. The cat scampered away as the door cracked open and a woman appeared in the space between door and frame. Her hair was short and chestnut brown, framing a ruddy, plump-cheeked face that might have been anywhere from forty-five to sixty. There were laugh-lines around the mouth and the corners of her eyes, but the look she gave me was far from happy. In fact, she looked as if she expected to see someone like me.

"Can I help you, officer?"

"Mrs. Moran?"

She confirmed her identity with a "yes" and a nod, then added, "Are you here about my husband?"

So she expected me, or at least some sort of official visitor, but not for the reasons I thought. I would have to touch on that, but first things first. "No. It's about your son, actually."

Mrs. Moran nodded again, then stepped back and swung the door open wider. "Please, come in. Will your friend," she gestured towards the cruiser where Moss sat, looking straight ahead, trying to look inconspicuous and failing miserably, "be joining us?"

"Just me," I told her and stepped inside. Her head bobbed as she shut the door behind me. I got my first good look at the woman. She was comfortably plump, dressed in black slacks and a grey sweater; the lack of colors were somehow fitting, despite the rosiness of her cheeks. I hadn't even told her about her son yet, but it seemed as if she was already in mourning.

Mrs. Moran led me to a living room that was neat and tidy, but smelled of disuse, as if the windows were sealed up long ago and no fresh air could find its way in. A fine layer of dust coated everything, aside from indentations on the old-fashioned, mohair-covered sofa that fronted a big, console television across the narrow space. I gathered the Morans didn't entertain guests often. That seemed to be a running theme in Granton.

"Won't you sit down, officer?" Mrs. Moran offered, gesturing towards the sofa.

I realized I hadn't introduced myself and supplied, "Luke Campbell," before reaching out and shaking the woman's hand.

"Please make yourself comfortable, Mr. Campbell." She gestured again and I took a seat. She asked, "Can I get you anything to drink?"

"No, thank you. Please," I motioned, "join me, Mrs. Moran." The formality was already getting uncomfortable and it was silly to be offering the woman a seat on her own furniture, but I felt as if I needed to or else she would simply hover where she stood, nervous and fidgeting.

"You can call me Edie." She sat, folded her knees together primly and turned just enough so she could face me without it being awkward. "Okay. I'm ready," she said.

Everyone is different, everyone who senses what is coming prepares in a different way. I sensed that this woman wanted it like pulling off a Band-Aid: fast and painful, but over and done with.

"Edie, I'm sorry to say that your son, Greg, is deceased."

Edie Moran nodded, her lower lip finding its way between her teeth. She breathed a deep lungful in through her nose and a moment later it seeped out through her teeth, making a hissing noise that sounded like pure pain. "You're sure? It's Greg?"

"Yes. One of the people first on site knows your son pretty well. He gave us a positive ID." And the convenience of that wasn't lost on me. It was something to keep in the back of my mind.

"How did it happen?" She turned her gaze towards me and for a second, I wanted to lie to her, to tell her it was peaceful and painless and that her son didn't suffer.

Of course, I couldn't do that. I did the next best thing. "We've only just begun our investigation and I need to ask you some questions."

"Yes, of course." She stood, took a step, turned and sat back down. "I'm sorry. This— this isn't the conversation I expected to have. I thought you were here about Heath."

"That's your husband?"

She nodded.

"Why would you think that? Is Heath in some sort of trouble?"

Mrs. Moran opened her mouth, snapped it shut again, shaking her head in helpless frustration. "I don't know. He's been— since he retired last year, he's been…" The rest was smothered by a half-choked sob.

I reached out and put a consoling hand on her shoulder. "It's all right. Take your time. I could get you a glass of water or a tissue or—"

Edie shook her head, swiped the back of her hand across her eyes and visibly composed herself. "No, no. Thank you, Mr. Campbell. I'm fine now. I'm sorry that you had to see that."

"Not at all. Take all the time you need, it's perfectly understandable."

"I'm fine now." She looked me in the eye and I could see the strength of will she was putting into making that statement true. She needed it to be true very badly.

"Okay. Let's start from the beginning. Tell me about Heath and why you thought he was in trouble." The elder Moran wasn't the reason I came, but I had a feeling it was important.

"Heath retired last year from the phone company. He drove me nuts for the first few months. I told him he needed a hobby or a new job. Eventually, he found a hobby he liked: making beer here at home. 'Home-brewing', they call it.

And he started getting a little too fond of his own hobby, if you understand what I mean."

I nodded, made a noncommittal noise. I knew exactly what she meant, but who was I to judge?

"He's an adult and he can make his own decisions, but that doesn't mean I have to like it. We fought about it. A lot. It got so we were either fighting or not speaking at all. And then Greg came home."

I sat up a little straighter on the sofa. The story was getting where I needed it to be faster than I expected. "Okay, Greg came back to Granton."

Mrs. Moran pursed her lips in thought, trying to think of how to phrase what she wanted to say. "Greg got married very young; he wasn't even finished with college. After he met Shelly and they got married, we hardly saw or even heard from him. I guess the marriage went bad pretty quickly. They stuck it out for another few years and then she wanted a divorce and that's really all I know about it until Greg came home. He needed a chance to get himself back together and Heath and I were more than happy to have him. It gave us something to focus on besides ourselves. That was three weeks ago, and the first week was like a dream; we were like a family again and I was so happy. Heath even stopped drinking so much. For a while, anyway. Of course it didn't last. I know it's a kind of sickness, but..." Her shoulders flopped up and down in a gesture of helplessness. "Heath and Greg fought, about that and after a few days about *everything*, it seemed. It was sad, like Greg was the father and Heath the out of control boy. Heath has always been very... self-contained. I guess the freedom of being retired made him feel like he needed to sow his oats a little and Greg wanted the chance to do the same, back here at home, see his old friends and so on. Most of Greg's friends were gone, and the one he mentioned wasn't anyone his father thought he should be hanging around with."

"And who was that?"

"Nathan Ecare."

I shouldn't have been surprised. It was a small town and from what I knew, Ecare and Moran were around the same age. Wheels began to turn in my head.

"I see," I said.

Edie Moran nodded, slowly. "I don't know if they ever even met up, just that Greg mentioned his name and Heath flew off the handle. Heath was already a little drunk, even though it was only lunch-time, and he got so *angry*. There's nobody in this town who doesn't know what Ecare did and there's really nobody who wants him here, except maybe his mother, I suppose. I almost don't blame Heath, but Greg is an adult. He can choose his own friends." She had slipped back into using the present tense when speaking of her son. I didn't correct her.

She sighed mightily. "Greg tried to leave the room, to step out of the argument, and Heath got right in his face, saying as long as he was under this roof, Greg would live by his rules. I think he forgot all about the last ten years; he was speaking as if Greg was still a sixteen-year-old boy and not a grown man. Well, Greg said, 'You're drunk, dad,' and pushed him aside, trying to get Heath out of the way so he could leave the room. Heath followed him. I was afraid of what might happen. I don't know why they were so angry at each other, I just don't know what happened between them to make things like that, but they left and the next thing I knew, I heard a crash and more yelling—a different kind of yelling, like pain, not anger—"

The words were rushing out of her now, faster and faster, nearly manic as she purged all the things she kept bottled up inside herself. She was scarcely taking pauses to breathe, she was trying to get the words out so quickly.

"There was more yelling and I rushed out into the garage and there they were, standing, staring at each other with such *fury* on their faces. Greg was holding his head and there was a little blood trickling out from beneath his fingers and his father's beer-making things were scattered all over the floor and Heath's face was beet-red and I thought he was going to explode. I mean that literally: I thought his head might just pop off. And they were staring at each other and then something just broke and Greg said, 'See you later, mom,' and he walked out to the driveway, got into his car, and left."

Greg Moran's car. That was another piece of the puzzle. It certainly wasn't out in the woods with his body.

I waited and when Edie didn't continue, I prompted, "And Heath?"

She shook her head. "He said, 'I'm going out for a while,' and just walked away up the street. This was all two days ago. I haven't heard from either of them since."

"I see." My mind was churning, trying to put together pieces. I didn't know how they fit into the larger picture, but Edie Moran answered some questions about her son, at least. I was far from done, though. "Mrs. Moran, can I ask why you thought I was here about Heath and not Greg?"

"Greg can take care of himself. He's only been back three weeks. Before that, he hadn't lived here in almost seven years. But Heath…" She made a sound in her throat. "We haven't been apart for more than an eight-hour work-day in almost thirty years. And even then, he called me on his lunchbreak. I couldn't imagine not hearing from him for two whole days before all of," her hands fluttered in the air, "this."

"I know this is hard," I told her. "And I'm very sorry." I stood. "I'll see if we can find Heath, Edie. I'll want to talk to you some more about Greg later on, but for now, I think I've taken up enough of your time. Is there anything I can do before I go? Maybe someone I can call for you?"

The woman shook her head. Her mouth was clamped tightly shut, her face was turning a sickly color, and there was a pinched look around her eyes. I opened the floodgates and she released a little pressure, but now she was trying to put it all back inside. I felt for her. I really did. There was only so much I could do, though.

"I'm really very sorry, Mrs. Moran," I told her again. "I'll be in touch soon."

I left the room, then the house. As I closed the door behind me, I thought I heard muffled sobbing, though I wasn't sure.

I slid back into the passenger seat of the waiting cruiser. Moss looked at me and said, "That bad, huh?"

I just nodded.

25

I told Moss about Heath Moran's being gone for the last two days and an abbreviated version of the story about the blow-up between father and son.

Moss asked, "You think Greg would kill himself over something like that?"

"No. I didn't know him, but it doesn't seem likely."

"Yeah. I mean…" He hesitated. "Jesus, what a mess."

I radioed into the station, giving Jeannie the rundown on Heath Moran's disappearance. "Any ideas on where to look?" I asked.

"Hold on, Luke. The chief wants to speak with you."

The line went silent a moment and then: "Campbell? Skillman here." Even through the crackle of the radio connection, the man's voice lost none of its power. "Don't worry about Heath Moran. I've got some ideas and I'll handle it myself. You just keep on with those bodies."

Moss glanced over. I shrugged. There was no way to know what Skillman had in mind, but there was also no use going against him now. He would have his way and maybe it was better that he did. He knew Granton, after all, and its people knew him. I knew that if anyone could find the elder Moran, it was Skillman.

"Understood, sir."

Moss halted the cruiser at a stop-sign. "What now, Luke?"

"Back to the station, so I can pick up my own cruiser. You heard Skillman and I've got some ideas I want to follow up on."

"Hope it pans out." Moss pulled right at the intersection, headed back towards the center of Granton.

I turned towards the window, watching the town pass by. "Fingers crossed."

•   •   •

The Ecare family home was in Pennemont Hills, one of Granton's upper-class developments. Crowning the top of the hill overlooking town, the house stood by itself in the middle of a well-manicured lot of about two acres. It looked like old money, with a low, wrought-iron fence surrounding the lawn and tall, lantern-topped stone posts at the end of the driveway. There were two stories, with false balconies off the second-floor windows, and a huge picture window dominating the front of the first floor. The house must have commanded a breathtaking view of the lake on a clear day. The winter heating costs associated with all of those windows would probably eat up most of my paycheck. It was hard to reconcile the idea of the Nathan Ecare I met growing up in a home like this.

I rang the doorbell. The woman who answered was a blonde somewhere around fifty, still trim and shapely, though the tightness around her eyes and mouth spoke of the battle she waged to keep herself looking youthful. Makeup helped, but couldn't hide that it was a war she was slowly losing. She wore a dark-red sweater, khaki slacks, and gray house-shoes, fuzzy with age and use.

"Mrs. Ecare?"

"Yes." Her eyes went up and down the length of me, taking in the uniform. "Can I help you?"

"My name is Luke Campbell. I'm with the Granton PD."

"I can see that." She glanced past me, seeming to scan the surrounding area, then stepped aside, gesturing with her free hand. "Please, come in."

"Thank you." I guessed the invitation was less out of hospitality and more a desire to keep the neighbors from gossiping. That was fine with me, either way.

I stepped inside. She closed the door behind me and led the way into an enormous living room, the room that big window fronted. I was right, the view was magnificent. There was a fieldstone fireplace that took up most of the wall opposite the window. At least that would help with the heating costs.

"Would you like some coffee, Mr. Campbell? I was just about to have some myself."

I turned. "If it's no trouble."

"None at all." The woman smiled graciously. In the somewhat dimmer light inside the house, many of the signs of aging were hidden. Here, Mrs. Ecare could have passed for forty. "I'll be right back."

She disappeared, leaving me to my own devices. There was a long, comfortable-looking sofa in a subdued shade of red on one side of the room, the side with the doorway we passed through. On the opposite wall was a built-in bookshelf, though only half of the shelves held books. The rest were occupied by various small pieces of art- and craftwork, of varying quality. Some of it looked expensive. Some of it looked amateurish.

Mrs. Ecare returned, carrying a silver serving tray bearing two tiny ceramic cups, a miniscule bowl of sugar, and cream in a pitcher that matched the tray. "It's the maid's day off, so this is my own handiwork. If it's too weak or too strong, don't be polite, just say so and I'll try again." She smiled tightly and set the tray down on the table by the sofa.

"I'm sure it'll be fine, thank you."

We settled ourselves on the couch, arranged so we could face one another. Balancing the tiny cup in the palm of my hand, I felt fairly ridiculous.

"Now, Mr. Campbell, what did you need to speak with me about?" Her tone was light, but the tension was clear on her face. I knew a little about her life, through what I learned of her son, and I knew she must be reliving some unpleasant memories having me here.

"In a way, Mrs. Ecare, it's about your son, Nathan."

"Please, call me Corinne." A muscle pulsed in her throat as she set her cup down on the table. "Is Nathan in trouble?" The "again" was left unsaid, but was clearly implied.

"No. And I'm not here to cause either you or him any problems. I'm conducting an investigation into the death of one of Nathan's friends – Greg Moran."

Real surprise peeked through her patrician mask, her mouth forming a little "o". "Greg Moran? That's terrible. How did it happen? Are you allowed to say?"

"That's what I'm looking into. His body was only found this morning." I didn't want to say too much, but since Lautner was on the scene, Greg Moran's death was probably already known around town.

"Terrible," she said again. "Was it here? In Granton, I mean. I didn't know he was in town. The boys were such good friends but I think Greg went to college out state after they finished high school. I don't know if they were still in touch."

"So I've heard. About them being good friends, I mean. Greg recently returned to the area, but I'd like to speak with Nathan about him. Is he home?"

"Oh." She shook her head. "Nathan doesn't live here. He hasn't since all of that..." She hesitated in a theatrical sort of way. "Unpleasantness of a few years ago."

"He doesn't?"

"No. He chooses to live in that hovel, Monroe's. Down by the lake?" Her distaste was plain.

"I'm familiar with it."

Corinne sighed with the weight of the world. "There's no need for him to. He's perfectly welcome here. Or he could rent an apartment somewhere in town, if he wanted. The allowance I give him is plenty to live on."

I was beginning to understand why Ecare didn't want to live with his mother. I could guess what their relationship was like.

"May I ask you some questions, then?"

"Certainly, though I don't know if I can help." She picked up her tiny coffee cup and took a tiny, delicate sip.

I put my own cup down. "Greg and Nathan hung around together quite a bit?"

She nodded.

Puzzle pieces had tumbled around in my head for weeks. I decided to take a plunge. "I know Nathan made frequent trips across the border his last few months of high school. Did Greg ever go up with him?"

"I'm sure I don't know." There was an edge to her voice that wasn't there a moment before. "What does that have to do with the poor boy's death?"

"I don't know," I confessed. "I spoke with Greg's mother earlier, and she led me to believe that Nathan was important in Greg's life." It was only partially an exaggeration, if the friendship was really what sparked that last fight between Greg and Heath Moran.

"Well, they were friends... but that was years ago."

Weren't they "such good friends" just a few minutes earlier?

Changing tacks, I asked, "Do you know why Nathan made such frequent trips up into Canada back in school, Corinne? Did he ever talk about those trips at all? Mention any friends he went up with or maybe new friends he met across the border?"

"I don't know. I don't think so. We lived separate lives, even back then. When Nathan's father, my husband Paul, passed away we each dealt with it in our own way. Paul left enough money that neither of us will ever have to worry, but…" She shrugged narrow shoulders. "Since then, I've tried my hand at a lot of little things to fill the time." She gestured towards the handicrafts on the bookshelf. Looked like I was right about that much. "And I suppose Nathan has, too."

"I see." I picked up my coffee cup and sipped the last of the cooling coffee from it. Still holding the ridiculous little thing in my palm, I asked, "One last question: can you think of any other friends of Nathan's who might also have been close with Greg?"

Mrs. Ecare shook her head. "Not offhand. Oh, there was one boy, but…" She turned away, picking up her coffee cup, leaving the thought unfinished.

"But what, Mrs. Ecare?"

A sour look passed across her face, making her look more her age than anything else had. "It's so distasteful to even admit that Nathan was friends with him. His parents were nice people. Down on their luck, but—"

"A name, please, Mrs. Ecare? That's all I need, not the social commentary."

She shot me a nasty look, but it disappeared quickly. "Marcus De Rosso. I'm sure you can find anything you need to know about him in your police files."

The name De Rosso rang a bell, though I couldn't immediately place it. If there was anything to the woman's comment, though, I was sure one of the guys down at the station could fill me in.

I stood, offered my hand to the woman. "Mrs. Ecare, thank you very much for your time and for your assistance."

She grasped my hand delicately and gave me a smile that was only skin-deep. I asked her questions she didn't like and now she didn't like me. I didn't really care. "Of course, Mr. Campbell. I'm always glad to help, if I can."

As long as I wasn't asking questions about her son, that might even have been true.

26

I needed time to think. I had too many parts that looked like they should fit together, but weren't cooperating when I tried to assemble them.

I rolled the cruiser slowly down the hill towards the center of town, going by the station without giving it a glance. I was still on duty for a couple more hours but I didn't want to just sit in my office and stew. I knew that would get me nowhere. What I really wanted was to see Chloe, but that wouldn't get me anywhere at the moment, either. There were too many questions that needed answers. I promised myself that I would make time for her and Roland soon.

It was a little after three o'clock. I hit the intersection of Crescent and Main and turned right, towards the western edge of town, with no destination in mind. Just as I started to climb the hill out of Granton proper, the radio crackled to life.

"Disturbance out at Ozzy's Hideaway. Sounds like a pretty good ruckus. Worse brawl than the usual, anyway, from what the caller says," Skillman's static-laced voice said. It was very odd to hear Skillman over the radio and this was the second time today.

A moment passed before Moss, back out on day-patrol, responded. "Moss here, chief. I'm still at that accident I called in a bit ago – the ants-in-the-pants out of towner who took Raceway Road's name literally."

I picked up the handset and chimed in, "Campbell here. I'm already headed in that direction. I'll take it."

"Understood," Skillman said.

"Be along quick as I can," Moss added.

I gave the engine a goose and put on the lights and sirens. I learned in my early days on the Albany force that just the sound of police sirens was enough to break up a lot of disturbances. Odds were that at least some people involved had reasons not to want to be noticed by folks in uniform.

Ozzy's was a bar four or five miles southwest of town, popular with the local roughneck crowd. Though I hadn't been myself, someone from the Granton PD was out there at least once a week, I was told.

It was only a few minutes before I turned off of 114C and down the side-road that Ozzy's had all to itself. The building was a brown-stained cedar-shake structure that looked like it was once a house, the only real difference being the addition of neon beer signs. There were a few cars and half a dozen motorcycles in the parking lot, but there wasn't a soul around, at least not outside. For a place supposedly in the midst of a major disturbance, it was bizarrely quiet. I let myself hope that the sirens alone did the job and everyone was settled back down to their day-drinking.

I flicked the siren off, leaving the lights flashing, then exited the cruiser. I loosened my baton as I walked towards the entrance, wishing I had the pepper spray the Albany force started using just before I left. I only saw it used once, but it was impressively effective. If there was still a fight going on inside Ozzy's, it would do me a lot more good than the baton in controlling multiple people.

I opened the door and nearly tripped over a bearded, leather-jacketed six-footer, sprawled across the entryway. He wasn't alone, either; nearby was another man, in an identical jacket, propped against the wall, eyes closed, his breath bubbling through a broken, bloodied nose.

There were seven or eight other men scattered around the room, most of them taking cover behind postage-stamp-sized tables and the accompanying chairs that were turned over or pushed aside. Four of them wore leather jackets.

None of them seemed to notice me. Their attention was focused on the man standing in the center of the room. He was maybe five foot six, but he was damned near that wide, too, with a bull neck and arms as thick around as most men's thighs. There was a broken bottle clutched in one huge fist and he whipped it back and forth in front of him like a knife-fighter. His chest heaved as he breathed noisily, competing with a television commercial emanating from a set mounted over the bar, the only other sound in the room. The man's face was mashed to a pulp, one eye swollen shut, but there was a savage grin on his lips. It was clear he went through a hell of a fight, loved every moment of it, and still wanted more.

"C'mon, you biker pussies!" he shrieked in a voice higher than I would have expected, his glare bouncing from one face to another as he moved in a tight little circle around the center of the room, trying to keep the whole place in his field of view. "You little leather fairies started it, so don't tell me you're done already!"

"Just go home, De Rosso, *please*," someone pleaded from behind the safety of the bar.

De Rosso. That name again. Matching a face to the name, I realized where I heard it before Corinne Ecare mentioned it to me: the domestic Moss dealt with a couple of weeks ago that he described as brutal. Both of the De Rossos like to get drunk and fight, Moss said, but the husband was the worse of the two. The man before me fit perfectly with the image I formed at the time, right down to the tiny notch missing from the bull-necked little man's left ear.

I stepped out of the entryway and raised my voice. "Okay, De Rosso, that's enough."

The man whirled on his heel to face me. There was a gleam in his good eye as the corner of his lip jerked upwards in something that was neither grin nor sneer. "Well, hey now!" He jutted his chin at the nearest biker. "Looks like you boys can get on out of here. I got a new friend to pal around with."

If he was drunk, I would never have been able to tell from the way he moved or spoke. All his voice carried was a sense of malicious amusement.

"Put the bottle down and put your hands behind your head."

De Rosso bared his teeth at me. "Come and take it."

"Watch out!" one of the leather-clad men called. "He's hell with that damned thing!"

I drew the baton from my harness and held it low, in line with my right leg, ready to swing up and out or across as needed. There were still fifteen feet between the two of us, but I wasn't taking any chances with a man who terrorized half a dozen bikers all on his own.

"Last warning," I said.

De Rosso grinned and shouted, "Catch!"

His hand whipped forward and then something exploded just above my left eye, sending bright lights shooting through my vision. Somehow, I started across the room to my right, my legs moving with no direction from my brain. There was a table and a couple of chairs in the way, but even those didn't hamper whatever impulse was carrying me forward and I tumbled across the table, coming to a landing on the hard, pine-planked floor. I lay there in a nimbus of colored lights and dizzying pain.

Crazy laughter came from somewhere over my head, drilling into my half-numbed brain the message that De Rosso was on the move, but with a lot more focus than my stumbling.

A shadow fell across me and I rolled to the side, swinging the baton upwards in a shallow arc that went wide of any target, trying to brush away the mental fuzziness from the blow. With the awkward position I was in, there wasn't enough power behind that first swing to do any damage even if it did connect with anything and I never got a chance for a second. It was wrenched from my grasp and an instant later, I heard the sound of it clattering off of some hard surface.

I pulled my legs up underneath me and rose groggily to my feet, putting my back against a support-beam.

De Rosso stood a few feet away, smiling radiantly. "C'mon! C'mon! Make it good now!" He rushed forward, swinging those meaty fists like hammers.

I got my arms up, but they were heavy as lead and I only barely managed to take the first blow on my forearms. The second blow bounced off of my forehead where, I realized then, De Rosso had hit me with the thrown bottle, knocking the back of my skull against the support-beam. A new galaxy of stars formed behind my eyes, but I pushed off the beam, propelling myself forward to slam the heel of a hand into De Rosso's solar plexus before he could back out of my reach. His breath exploded from his lungs, spraying my face with stale beer spittle, but giving me a chance to slip aside and out of his grasp.

Like an amateur, I lost the baton and now I didn't even know where it was. My hand fell to the .38 at my hip. I almost drew it, but I knew it wouldn't stop De Rosso unless I killed him. I had to put him down with my fists or keep him occupied until Moss arrived. I almost wished I let Moss take the call, after all, and instantly felt ashamed for the fleeting thought.

De Rosso lunged at me again, but hadn't yet recovered his breath. If he had, he would probably have floored me with the haymaker he threw. Instead, I had just enough leeway to duck aside and slam a right into his jaw that numbed my arm all the way to the elbow. It was like punching a brick wall. He just blinked and made a huffing noise.

De Rosso threw another wide swing from the hips, trying to put all of his considerable power behind it, but it was slow enough that I could duck inside his guard and give him a quick right-left to the solar plexus. The breath *whooshed* out of him again and he leaned forward slightly. I chopped out a stiffened hand towards the nerve point between his shoulder and neck, the same blow I used to put Lloyd Truman in his place my first day in Granton, but through luck or skill, De Rosso twisted his torso and took it harmlessly on the point of his shoulder. He grinned evilly at me and struck out with a left that took me high on the right side of my chest, knocked me back, and spun me almost all the way around.

The fight carried us into a corner of the tavern, with De Rosso between me and the rest of the room. There was nowhere for me to go. Over De Rosso's shoulder, I caught sight of what must have been the bartender peeking up from behind the bar. One way or another, my baton had made its way to the top of the bar.

"The baton!" I yelled at the man, desperate for any way to end this short of shooting De Rosso.

De Rosso threw a look over his shoulder. "Naughty, naughty, Ozzy!"

It was only an instant's diversion, but it was all I had. I put all my weight behind a short charge and grappled De Rosso around the waist, dragging the both of us to the floor. He felt like solid steel beneath my body. I knew I couldn't hold him for more than a few seconds and there was no more thought or skill in the way I fought, only a desire to end this while staying intact myself. I slammed an elbow into De Rosso's nose, feeling a sickening crunch, then scrambled to my feet and towards the bar.

My fingers closed around the baton just as there was a yank on my harness that jerked me backwards. I stumbled, but kept my footing, used the momentum to turn on my heel like a dancer and bring the heavy wooden stick up and then down across the crown of De Rosso's skull with a savage *crack!*

I expected him to drop. Instead, he backed off three or four feet, grinned lopsidedly and dove in again, trying to tackle me around the middle the way I did him a moment earlier. He got his paws on me, but I was prepared and as we fell, I brought the baton down again, this time across the back of his skull, no longer caring how hard I hit him, no longer caring in that moment whether I killed him or not. He was a monster and all I wanted was to put him down.

We slammed into the floor and he continued to struggle. I laid the baton across his head again, lifted it for a fourth blow and realized that the third time finally did it. A spasm went through his body, then he was dead weight on top of me, unconscious at last.

I pushed De Rosso off and slowly got to my feet. My legs wobbled like I ran all the way from New York and my hands wouldn't stop shaking. I wanted a drink, a cold compress, about a thousand aspirin, and a very long nap. Most of all, I wanted to make sure Marcus De Rosso was secured. I clapped handcuffs around his wrists and, with the help of one of the bikers, dragged him out to the cruiser and locked him into the steel-mesh-encased backseat.

When I re-entered Ozzy's, the bartender finally came out from his sanctuary and now stood looking at the ruins of his tavern.

"Thanks for your help," I told him, not caring if he was insulted.

"Hey, I pay taxes so you guys can deal with the De Rossos of the world." He shook his head sadly. "He ain't *too* bad a guy when he's sober, but he's a raving fucking lunatic when he drinks."

"Then don't serve him!" I snapped.

"I *don't*." Anger radiated from the man. "Nobody around here with an ounce of brains does. He was drunk when he wandered in and fighting almost as soon as he did. Lord knows where he came from." His expression changed and he gave me a speculative look. "What the hell were you thinkin', coming all on your lonesome? Last time De Rosso was in here, it took three of your guys to bring him down. I said it was De Rosso when I called in," he added, almost defensively.

"Guess that part of it was overlooked by the dispatcher."

Or maybe omitted.

27

I washed the blood from my head and hands in the men's room and inspected the wound De Rosso's bottle left. It was about two inches long. I wasn't sure how deep it was, but I was pretty certain I would need stitches. I held a paper-towel to it, hoping there was a first-aid kit behind the bar.

When I came out of the restroom, Chad Moss stood at the end of the bar, talking with Ozzy. His face paled when he saw me. "Jesus, Luke!"

He crossed half the distance between us. I leaned against the bar, feeling again every blow De Rosso landed. There wasn't an inch of me that didn't hurt. I wasn't alone in that, either. The two downed bikers were huddled at a table in the far corner, their friends surrounding them like worried like mother hens. I didn't know if they were locals, but I hoped there would be no attempts at retribution.

"I got here as soon as I could." He threw a glance at Ozzy, then asked, "How did you manage De Rosso all by yourself, Luke?"

"It wasn't easy. I seriously thought about shooting him."

Neither one of us laughed.

Moss looked uncomfortable. He hitched at his harness. "I had a look in the cruiser when I showed up. I damned near shit a brick. If I'd known it was De Rosso doing the brawling..."

I waved away the implied apology. "Don't worry about it. Neither one of us knew." Someone did, though, if what Ozzy the bartender said was true and I had no reason to doubt him.

"How's De Rosso doing out there, anyway?"

Moss shrugged. "Out cold. Your work or sleeping it off?"

"Probably a bit of both." I turned to Ozzy. "You're pressing charges, I assume?"

"*Hell*, yes! Lock 'im up, throw away the key. If I never see that guy again, it'll be too soon."

"Sounds good to me." I nodded at Moss. "I'll get De Rosso back to the station. Get statements from the guys he laid out," I gestured to the bikers, "and then follow me back."

Moss was unsure. "You don't want to wait? You might need help getting De Rosso into a cell."

The cuts and bruises covering my body throbbed. My head rang like Christmas bells. I decided to wait.

•   •   •

As it turned out, I did need help, but not because De Rosso was still in a fighting mood.

I borrowed an adhesive bandage and antiseptic from Ozzy for my head and swollen knuckles while Moss took the bikers' statements. All six were eagerly cooperative. I gathered they thought they were tough guys until they met Marcus De Rosso. Now, they wanted to make sure he was safely locked away.

When I returned to the cruiser, De Rosso was sound asleep and sawing logs. Despite the bruises and the broken nose the peaceful look on his face made him seem almost child-like. It was a far cry from the man who singlehandedly waged a war of terror only a few minutes ago. Moss, too, had a look in the back. His face told me his thoughts were much the same as mine.

At the station, Moss helped me drag De Rosso from the cruiser and down to the cells. Barnes was on duty down there. The heavy-set man's eyes bugged out when he saw our prisoner and he practically leapt from his seat to get a cell open. Between the three of us, we got him down onto the narrow bunk. De Rosso remained asleep the whole time, thankfully.

"You better get a doctor in here," I told Barnes.

"Sure." Barnes's head bobbed up and down as he went to make the call.

Fifteen minutes later, an older man in a sky-blue suit twenty years out style, carrying a black Gladstone bag, arrived, escorted from the front-desk by Loenfeld. "Dr. Frame, Campbell," Loenfeld said by way of introductions.

The doctor made no attempt at small-talk. He simply entered the cell, performed a quick examination of De Rosso and said, scowling, "Bruises and that nose aside, he's just drunk. That's pretty much his natural state, isn't it?"

"Maybe," I conceded, "but we knocked each other around pretty good and I had to lay the baton across De Rosso's head a few times before he went down."

"*You* knocked him around?" He gave me an appraising look. "Well, you and a lot of others, too, over the last few years. Never done him any harm so far that I know of. The man's some sort of medical anomaly." He looked at Moss. "I can see this one's new, Officer Moss. You tell him about the De Rossos and Marcus in particular?"

"Yeah." Moss seemed faintly embarrassed.

"Well," He looked back at me, "De Rosso will be fine. I predict he'll wake up in about ten or twelve hours, bright-eyed and bushy-tailed and as good as new, except for the nose, which I'll set in a minute or two. Now you, on the other hand." He latched onto one of my wrists with surprising strength, lifted my hand up and cast a critical eye on it. "You need to soak these in some ice-water to get the swelling down or they'll be useless before long. And let me take a look at this." He pushed me down into a nearby chair, peeled the bandage off of my forehead, muttered something about stitches, and set to work.

A few minutes later, Frame had put five stitches in my head and swabbed me all over with anti-septic. Moss disappeared somewhere, probably to give Skillman a rundown on De Rosso, and Barnes retreated to the desk by the door, leaving the doctor and myself more or less alone.

When he was done with me, Frame set De Rosso's nose and then began to repack his bag. With his back to me, he said, "Keep that wound clean and, in about a week, stop by my office over on Chadwick and I'll take the stitches out. As for the rest of those bumps and bruises, take a long, hot shower and get some sleep. You need rest and a chance to heal." He turned to me. "You're tough, Mr. Campbell, but I presume you aren't trying to kill yourself. Not like that one." He thrust his chin towards where De Rosso snored.

"Kill himself?"

"Well, what else would you call it? I don't know why he does it, but he drinks himself into a stupor and starts these god-damned fights against insane odds. Trying to get someone to punch his ticket, I suppose. I'd guess he wants to die but can't bring himself to do it. Sad as hell." He shook his head, though it seemed more a gesture of disgust than pity.

"Why would he want to kill himself?" I asked.

"How would I know? Guilt, depression, repressed trauma. Could be anything. I'm not a psychiatrist, but also I'm not a fool and I can see what's right in front of me." Frame snapped his bag closed then leveled a finger at me. "Soak those hands in cold water. Soak that body in hot water. Then plenty of sleep. Hear me?"

"Yes, sir."

"Okay, then." Frame turned and marched towards the exit.

• • •

After the day's events, I wanted to see Chloe and Roland more than ever, but I was in no shape.

After I dictated a brief report to Loenfeld, who volunteered to write it up after seeing the state of my hands, I signed off duty and headed back to the Red Garden. The lobby was empty except for Helen Reddy, who gave me a brief, professional smile of acknowledgement as I passed the desk. Things were strained between us since that day in the stairwell. She wasn't wrong, though; "that girl" got under my skin and I already admitted it to myself. I needed to think about finding a more permanent place to call home very soon.

In my room, I took a long, hot shower, then sat on the couch, soaking alternate hands in a bowl of ice-water as I drank beer and tried to pay attention to a rerun of a mystery show about an old woman who solved crimes in rural Maine. It started out with a mysterious body and in less than an hour everything was wrapped up nicely. I fell asleep envying that amateur detective.

In the morning, my knuckles were red and swollen, but not as badly as I feared or expected. My head, however, ached as if someone was using it for a gong. I dressed, wincing at bruises and pains, then made my way back to the station. I entered via the rear door and headed directly to the holding area. Shane Stevens was on duty and we exchanged good mornings before I strode down the block towards where I left Marcus De Rosso the day before.

He was seated on the edge of his bunk, looking sober and clean and bright-eyed. "Good morning, officer," he said.

"Remember me, De Rosso?"

He shook his head. "No, I never remember a thing the day after, but from the looks of you," he tried out a small smile, "you're the one who brought me in. Hope I wasn't any trouble."

His speech was crisp and polite and with the alcohol out of his system, he almost seemed like a different person. Almost, except that there was still a hint of that malicious amusement from the day before gleaming in his eyes.

"My trouble with you is all over, so don't worry about it."

"Am I being charged?" he asked.

"Sure. There's four people who've sworn out complaints against you, including me. You're looking at a couple of years, at least."

De Rosso shrugged. "Bound to happen sooner or later."

"You're taking this awfully well."

He grinned at me. "What would be the point of hollering and carrying on about it?"

"You tell me. What got you started yesterday?"

He frowned then stood from the bunk and moved over to the bars of the cell. "Why do I need a reason to drink? Never needed one before."

"Maybe, but I've got a feeling you had one this time. Maybe something like an old friend passing on?"

"You mean Greg Moran." It wasn't a question.

"Wanna tell me about Greg?"

"What's there to tell? We were friends when we were kids. He moved away and I didn't see him for years."

"You sure about that?"

He gave me a long, neutral look. Finally, he said, "I couldn't even tell you the last time I talked to Greg."

"Talking isn't exactly the same thing as seeing, is it?"

"Don't play word games with me. What's Greg Moran got to do with this, anyway? I tell you, I just like drinking. It's a hobby, you know? Like some people hunt and some people play golf. Or chase little French girls." The way he smirked was somehow lewd.

It didn't exactly startle me, the way De Rosso probably hoped, but I took the bait, anyway. "And what do you know about French girls?"

"Oh, nothing much. Just that maybe someone's finally found a way to thaw out the local wildlife. That girl's a sweet piece, all right, but she's been locked down tight since Alan Butler."

"You knew Alan Butler?"

"Sure," he nodded. "We were in the same class in school."

"Along with Greg Moran and Nathan Ecare."

"Sure. Only one high-school in town."

I threw a look down the cellblock towards Stevens. He was engrossed in riffling some papers on his desk, but I was sure he was listening. I turned back to De Rosso and, lowering my voice, said, "All four of you friends?"

"With Butler?" De Rosso recoiled a little, a look of disdain on his face. "Not hardly. He was a straight-laced little schoolboy 'til he met that girl and wasn't much different afterwards. Sure, I was envious; every guy in class was. Hell, in the whole town, probably. But that's about as far as it went. We were never friends. The other two, they were okay. We ran around a little together. Us and another guy or two. What the hell does any of this have to do with anything, anyway?"

I blew air and shook my head, as if I was disappointed the other man wasn't catching on. "Moran's dead."

"Yeah... and?"

"And I don't think he killed himself. Do you?"

De Rosso opened his mouth to say something then snapped it shut. He opened it again, closed it. Staring at a point somewhere over my shoulder, he said, "I want to talk to a lawyer. If I'm under charges, you got to give me a phone call and I want to talk to a lawyer."

I frowned. "You sure that's how you want to handle this, Marcus?"

"Get me a god-damned lawyer!" he screamed, showing something of the monster I battled in Ozzy's Tavern.

Stevens appeared at my elbow, a look of concern on his face. "Hey, what's going on?"

"Nothing. Just Mr. De Rosso making more bad decisions."

I turned on my heel and left the two of them to their own devices.

28

I hiked upstairs to the main floor. Each step felt like it was three feet tall. My body was dragging and it wasn't just the bumps and bruises. I needed to speak to Skillman, but I really didn't want to.

It was almost twenty-four hours since the chief claimed the job of finding Heath Moran. I needed to know where that stood. It was getting so I really didn't trust Skillman, but I figured that was still something he could handle best. The man seemed to have the town in the palm of his hand.

I knew, too, that he would have something to say about Marcus De Rosso. In fact, I was surprised that he hadn't tracked me down himself yet. What he thought of the way I handled it didn't really matter. What did was whether he knew it was De Rosso out at Ozzy's or not. That was critical information I should have had going in. With the man's history, with his well-known rage that bordered on the murderous, purposely withholding his identity seemed almost tantamount to attempted murder. Not quite, but almost.

Jeannie was at her customary spot behind the reception desk, pecking out something on her typewriter. The dispatch radio hummed softly. The sound of the radio and the *clickety-clack* of the typewriter should have been soothing, but I barely heard them over the thoughts churning in my head.

"Morning, Jeannie," I said, closing the station's door behind me. I crossed the room, lifted the heavy wooden gate and stepped behind the railing.

Jeannie gave me a smile with nothing behind it and said, "Good morning, Luke." There was a fractional moment of hesitation before she added, *sotto voce,* "I'm so sorry about yesterday. Hal had a doctor's appointment and he's a big baby about going alone, so I took the afternoon off. The chief said he didn't mind handling the radio and, I guess—"

I held up a hand: full stop, please. "It's fine, Jeannie. No harm done." I smiled. "Not much damage anyone can do to this mug."

The look she gave me was lop-sided as she reached out and batted my hip with the back of her hand. "Don't talk like that. I know of a few people who like that mug." The look disappeared. "You better go see the chief."

"Already on my way." I turned down the hall.

Skillman's door was closed, as it always seemed to be. I knocked lightly.

"Come." The response was immediate.

I entered. Skillman perched on the edge of his desk, telephone in hand, his boney legs stretched out before him. The blind that usually covered the window behind the desk was open for once and the early morning light streaming through it made his shadow seem as if it could fill the entire room were he to just stand up. The customary cigarette was missing from the corner of his mouth. I think it was the first time I ever saw him without it.

Skillman held up a finger, so I waited by the door for him to finish his call. He wasn't saying much, beyond the occasional "yes," or "sure," and once, "all right," but someone seemed to be giving him quite a speech about something. Finally, after maybe two minutes, he said, "Well, that sounds like it's about covered. Thanks a lot."

Skillman replaced the phone in its cradle without looking behind him and said, "What can I do for you this morning, detective?"

"Good morning, chief," I began. "Wanted to check in regarding De Rosso and a couple of other things."

Skillman grunted and threw up his hands. "De Rosso! Maniac." He shook his head. "Just glad he didn't kill anyone. You're okay, I see."

"I've been better." I held up my own hands so he could see my swollen knuckles. "But I'll live, though I'm sure there's a couple folks out there disappointed to hear it."

Skillman's face was blank. "Is that right?"

"We all make enemies, one way or another. I wanted to ask, though—"

Skillman slid off of the edge of his desk, moved behind it and lowered himself to his chair, gesturing me to the visitor's seat.

"Thanks." I sat, grateful to take the weight off my battered limbs. "I wanted to ask you, though, since you put the call out. Did you know it was De Rosso out there? The bartender at Ozzy's told me he mentioned De Rosso specifically."

Skillman's eyebrow lifted. "I'm sure he told you that, detective, but the first I heard of it was when Moss radioed to say you were bringing De Rosso in. Believe me, had I known it was him, I'd have pulled Moss off that smash-up to back you up and come along myself, too, for good measure. That man's nobody to dick around with."

"Why would Ozzy tell me differently, then? It doesn't make any sense."

Skillman shrugged. "Cover his bases, cover his ass, whatever you wanna call it. Hell, I don't know how these people think sometimes. If I did, I'd have this town crime-free in a week."

There really was nothing to say to that. If Skillman was lying, he was lying. He took the call and if he said Ozzy didn't him about De Rosso, there was nothing I could do to prove otherwise. If Ozzy was lying, trying to cover himself as Skillman suggested, there was still nothing I could do. I almost regretted bringing it up, but I still felt like it had to be addressed.

"Guess so," I said finally. "Any luck with Heath Moran?"

"As a matter fact…" Skillman leaned back in his chair, placing his hands behind his head. "That call was about just that. Moran should be home in an hour or two."

"Just like that?" I couldn't hide my skepticism.

"Sure. The man's a drunk, though of a different breed than De Rosso, thank the Lord. Wasn't too hard to get the word out to all the bars, saloons, taverns and so on in the area. Somebody had to know where he was. All I had to do was wait." Skillman's grin was sly, like a fox who successfully pilfered the henhouse. "Found Greg Moran's car, too. Dear old dad has been driving it, I guess."

I sat forward in the chair. "So where has he been?"

"Over in Saint J." Meaning St. Johnsbury, the seat of Caledonia County, to the southeast. It was the largest town in the region. "Couple of town cops over there found the car and backtracked to Heath. A Caledonia sheriff's deputy who owes me a favor is driving both back here."

I didn't like it. It could be true, but it was too neat. How did Moran get his son's car? What made him stay away from home for so long, when he never had before? I didn't bother voicing these concerns to Skillman. He would have brought them up himself if he was at all bothered by them and I knew him well enough to know that unless he asked the questions, he didn't want to be told anything.

I stood. "That's some good news, at least. I'll have to head over there this afternoon and see if I can have a talk with him about his son."

Skillman looked me up and down and said, "No need to rush yourself. You had a hell of a time yesterday. Feel free to take the day, get your wind back."

"I appreciate that, sir, but I'd rather keep working. Staying still will just make me stiffen up. Besides, I really want to see if I can close out this Moran file before too much longer."

"Well…" Skillman clicked his tongue. "Suit yourself. Let me know if you need anything."

"I will," I told him, with no intention of doing any such thing.

•   •   •

The Moran house was still small and neat, as it was the first time I visited, but now there was a pall hanging over it. Nothing was overtly different, except for the addition of a slightly rusty, maroon Toyota in the driveway, but it was clear something was changed since the day before. Heath Moran's homecoming was not a happy one.

I rang the doorbell. Edie Moran answered before the chime finished ringing out. The quiet anxiety in her eyes disappeared when she saw who her visitor was, replaced by worry and open-mouthed shock. "Officer Campbell! How did you get those horrible bruises?"

"Line of duty, ma'am. May I come in?"

"Of course. Please." She stepped back and I stepped inside. When she closed the door behind me, she asked, "Have you learned anything more about Greg's… about…" Her features closed off. She was trying to hold herself in again.

"That's what I'm here about. I'd like to speak with your husband. He's come home, I'm told."

Her head went up and down. "Yes. In the kitchen." She bustled away. I followed.

The kitchen was as neat and spare and as out of date as the rest of the house. A thin-faced man of about sixty with a sharply receding hairline and heavy glasses sat at a Formica-topped chrome table facing the kitchen door. His eyes were red-rimmed and empty. There was a cup of coffee and a still-folded newspaper on the table in front of him. Neither looked to have been touched.

"Dear," Edie Moran began. "This is Officer Campbell. I talked to him yesterday about Greg and he'd like to speak with you now." She looked questioningly at me. I nodded and she backed out of the room, looking grateful for the escape.

"Mr. Moran." I approached the table. The other man didn't even look up. "I'm very sorry for your loss." I pulled the chair opposite Moran out from the table. He made no objection, so I sat. "I know this is a difficult time, but I have some questions I need to ask you."

"What the hell good can you do him now?" The voice was like rusty hinges on a forgotten door.

"I don't know." I sensed that honesty would get me farther than sympathy with this man. "But I don't believe your son killed himself. If that's true, I want to bring whoever is responsible for this to justice."

"Justice." He snorted then finally looked me in the eye. There was as much rage in his eyes as there was sorrow in his wife's. "What does that even mean?"

"Let me ask you some questions and maybe, if the answers help me figure some things out, I'll be able to tell you that."

Moran's gaze fell to the surface of the table. When his eyes met mine again, there was still anger there, but something else, too. I thought, maybe, that it was a sliver of hope. "You're serious, aren't you?"

"Tell me about the last time you saw your son."

The other man shifted uncomfortably in his chair, but he didn't hold back. "We had an argument. A fight, really. We said some nasty things to each other. Some stuff got thrown around."

"What was the fight about?"

He cupped his hands around the coffee mug, but didn't lift it. "You already know, don't you? Edie must have told you."

"I want you to tell me."

Moran sighed. "Ecare was what started it."

"Nathan Ecare."

He nodded. "Yeah. It seems stupid now. Maybe you wouldn't understand, but—"

"Try me."

"The boys were friends all through school. Real good buddies. Greg had as many friends as any other kid, but he and the Ecare kid were close in a way that I never really liked. Those two and another kid, Joey Chadwick. Chadwick was okay. A little dim, but not a bad boy. That other one, though. I couldn't put my finger on it, but Ecare…" He shook his head. "It sounds terrible to say this about a kid, but I knew, I *knew* from about the time that kid was ten years old – how do I describe it?"

He looked me straight in the eye. "That kid was a douchebag who was gonna screw up his life beyond all repair and probably take whoever was nearby down with him. Nothing I could ever put my finger on. He was polite, albeit in an Eddie Haskell sort of way, did okay in school, from a good family, lots of money. Maybe that was the problem. I don't know. And I don't know why I knew it, but I was right, wasn't I?"

I had to concede that point.

Moran went on. "But you can't tell a kid not to hang around his best friend. He'd find a way, no matter what I said, and besides, Edie always told me it was just in my head."

"Well… I understand all of that, Mr. Moran. Let's get to the last time you saw Greg."

Moran put his head in his hands, elbows on the polished top of the table. He stayed in that position for maybe five heartbeats. When he spoke again, his voice was softer. "I'm getting there. Greg was gone for a long time. You know that, right? Anyway, he was away from this podunk long enough I thought he'd have it all out of his system. What Ecare did, even if it was an accident, was horrible. But if there was one bright side, it was that whatever he was up to that night, Greg wasn't part of it for once, and it finally got Ecare out of my son's life. For good, I thought. It upset the hell out of Greg. I mean, the whole damned town was upset, but it hit Greg hard. Alan Butler was a nice boy and it was terrible what happened. But the bright side was Greg was free from Ecare's influence."

The older man groaned then looked up. "I know, all of this makes me sound pretty rotten. I don't care. Butler wasn't my kid. Ecare's not my kid. Greg is. *Was*," he corrected himself.

I let him go. Like Ecare that night in Keith's, it didn't seem like he needed any prodding after getting started.

"So Greg has been in town a couple of weeks, trying to get his life back together after a bad divorce. It was nice having him. We did a little work around the house. God knows, there's enough to keep us busy, and I thought it was good for him – for both of us. Then, a few days ago, Greg says one night, 'Dad, you ever have to say you're sorry when you know it won't mean a thing?' I asked him what he meant and he told me to forget it."

Moran shrugged one shoulder. "I thought he was talking about the divorce or something. That last day, I asked him early in the morning if he'd mind helping me slap some paint on the front of the house. He told me he couldn't, he had plans. I asked, you know, just casually, what those plans were. He got a little twitchy and told me it was no big deal. But I know my son, and I just had another one of those feelings. So I pressed him, and he started to get angry, but finally he said he needed to find Nathan Ecare because he had something he needed to tell him."

"That started the fight."

Moran shook his head. "Not right away. It was… it was me pushing, I guess. I mean, I got angry, too. Greg was back home, trying to rebuild this life ripped apart by a bad marriage and a worse divorce, and he wants to dredge up one of the worst parts of his past and—"

It hit me then, and I think maybe it hit Moran, too, though in a different way. Something in the room, something between us shifted, and he noticed.

He looked at me, eyes narrowed. "What? What did I say?"

"Nothing. Go on, please."

"You know something I don't. Don't play games with me." It was nearly a growl.

I gave Moran a hard look. The cop look. "I don't know anything yet, Mr. Moran. If I find something, you'll know it, too, I promise you that."

He didn't like it, but he had no choice but accept it. It made me a little sick with myself to play this type of game, as he called it. It was the same game Aaron Skillman kept playing with me, but it was necessary. Maybe I understood Skillman a little better in that moment.

"Let's skip the fight itself," I said. "I think I know all I need to about that. How did you get your son's car? And why didn't you come home?"

Moran stood, pushing the chair back hard with his hips. He began to pace the tiny kitchen. After a few moments' thought, he stopped, sat back down and said, "I took a walk, just like I told Edie. I was gone, I don't know, two, three hours. I sobered up, but I was still angry. At Greg for even thinking of bringing that little bastard Ecare back into his life and at myself for how stupidly I handled it. I was walking down the street, back to the house, and Greg's car was parked by the curb, a few doors up, in front of the Littlefields'. I thought maybe he changed his mind about seeing Ecare, but I couldn't figure why he'd leave the car there and not at our place. Then I noticed his keys were in it, which was strange, too. And it's foolish, but that made me angry all over again. Probably nobody's going to steal a rattletrap like that, but you never know. I thought I'd teach him a lesson, so I took it. I just cruised. I found myself on 114. I stopped at some dive, had a few drinks. Ran into a friend, we went to another bar, then another. I don't know where the time went. I don't think I've ever been quite that drunk before. I just... I don't know. It's just a blur. I don't remember heading to Saint J., but I guess we did cuz it's where the cops found me. When they told me—"

Abruptly, his voice broke and he turned away, trying to stifle a sobbing noise.

I stood. "Thank you, Mr. Moran. I'd like the name of your friend and a number where I can reach them, but other than that, I think we're done for now."

He looked at me. His red-rimmed eyes were wet now. "Yeah, sure." He gave me a name and a number. I jotted them down on my notepad. Then he said, "You really think Greg was... Jesus, it's hard to even say it. Murdered."

"Unfortunately, I do."

Moran swallowed, his Adam's apple bobbing up and down. "Then tell me the truth: is any of this helpful? I mean, at all?"

"I think so. All I can do is collect the pieces and hope they come together. I promise you, though, I'm trying."

The older man stood, leaned over the table, his hand extended. I shook it. He said, "If you need anything..."

I nodded. "I'll let you know."

Unlike with Skillman, this time, I meant it, but I hoped that when I next spoke with the Morans, I would have answers instead of questions.

29

Moran gave me more than he realized and far more than I ever hoped. Edie Moran said her son left in his car, yet a couple of hours later, it was still in the neighborhood. Greg Moran needed to find Ecare and talk to him about something important. Whatever it was, it seemed like it became a matter of life and death for Greg. The thought was melodramatic as hell, but still true. Finally, Moran told me something else that I hoped would solve a problem I'd wrestled with for weeks: the name of the third musketeer in Ecare's clique, this Joey Chadwick.

I sat in the cruiser for a moment, thinking, then got back out and walked up the street, checking the names on mailboxes. Three doors up from the Morans, I found one marked "Littlefield".

Knocking brought an elderly, tidily dressed man to the door. I introduced myself and explained what I wanted: had he seen the maroon Toyota parked in front of his house three days ago, around this time?

"No, sir, I didn't. Myra, that's my wife, and I were out of town most of the week. Her sister's birthday, down in Connecticut. Whole family went, almost fifty of us," he added, pride in his voice.

"Well, thank you very much for your time."

So much for that. I hoped I had better luck with the other pieces Moran dropped in my lap.

I returned to the station and made a beeline for my office. I made some phone calls.

Heath Moran's friend corroborated the man's story, the parts he was privy to, enough to satisfy me that Moran told me the truth. I didn't really doubt him, but I wasn't cutting any corners.

Earl Cushman was not in his office, but I left a message with an assistant, asking that they please check dental records for a Joseph Chadwick against those of our body. I was crossing my fingers as I hung up the phone.

My fingers were crossed, but it was more than just a hunch. I felt like the pieces of the puzzle were finally coming together. Despite my battered body, I actually felt good. I was certain that I was making progress in an investigation that stymied me almost from the moment I set foot in Granton. There was still a way to go, but if I was right about that body in the woods being Joseph Chadwick, it was a huge step in the right direction.

I pulled out the file I created on missing persons in Granton. Chadwick wasn't a name I recognized when Heath Moran mentioned it, but that didn't mean much. I didn't take the time to memorize the list. It wouldn't have mattered if I did, though – his name wasn't on it. If the body really was Chadwick, nobody reported him missing, and that could mean a lot of things.

I hit zero on the desk phone. When Jeannie picked up I asked, "Is Loenfeld around, Jeannie?" Loenfeld was the youngest officer on the force. If he was local, he would be about the right age to have gone to school with Ecare and his cohorts. Maybe he could tell me something about Chadwick.

"He's on patrol today," Jeannie told me. "Something you need him for?"

"Yes. When he radios in for his meal break, let me know, will you?"

• • •

An hour later, I was sitting across from Matt Loenfeld in a booth at Crispy's Chicken, a quasi-fast-food place on the road south of town. It was the first time the two of us were one-on-one and the younger officer didn't seem entirely comfortable.

"Sorry if I'm putting you out, Loenfeld," I told him, as I spread a paper napkin across my lap.

"No, it's fine. This just seems a little out of the blue, offering to buy me lunch," he said, his eyes on the small mountain of crispy golden wings piled on his paper plate. "I mean, we've barely said two words to each other."

"I know. Sorry about that, too. I hope to get to know everybody, but it's been pretty busy since I started this job."

"I'll say." Loenfeld barked a laugh. "You're really piling up the bodies, detective." He looked up, met my eyes and flushed. "That was pretty stupid, wasn't it?"

I didn't argue. I took a bite of my chicken. It was good – crispy and tangy outside, juicy inside. I swallowed, wiped my mouth. "Anyway, I'm hoping you can help me with some background information. You're local, right?"

"Sure," Loenfeld nodded. "Grew up right here in Granton. Lived here all my life except for during college, and I didn't go very far even then."

We chatted about Granton, what it was like when Loenfeld was a kid, versus now. Then I got to the point. "So did you know Greg Moran and his crowd when you were in school?"

"Not really," he said around his soda straw. He put the cup down, picked up a couple of French fries and dragged them through ketchup. "I was in tenth grade when they were seniors. I mean, I knew who Greg Moran was, and Nathan Ecare, and those guys, but we weren't friends." He popped the fries into his mouth.

"Marcus De Rosso one of those guys?"

"Yeah."

"What was he like?"

Loenfeld shook his head. "Not like he is now, I'll tell you that. Damned if I know what happened to him. He was a jock, like Ecare and Moran, maybe kind of a dick, but you know how popular kids are. Nothing to make you guess how he'd turn out."

That was interesting, but I filed it away for now.

"How about Joey Chadwick?" I asked.

Straw in mouth again, Loenfeld's head bobbed. "Yeah. I knew him a little. Played Junior League baseball with him one year when I was in middle-school. He was kinda small for his age, I guess, so he was playing with us instead of the Senior League. Quiet kid. A little slow, I think, but nice enough. Took directions from the coach as well as anyone." One eyebrow went up. "Why do you wanna know about him?"

"Not sure yet, but if it pans out, I'll tell you." Everyone in Granton would probably know before long, if I was right. "You know if he's still in the area?"

Loenfeld shook his head. "Couldn't say. His dad passed a couple years ago. I know cuz I saw the obituary in the paper. And I think his mom was already gone by the time I knew him. I know he was always real good friends with Greg

Moran and Nathan Ecare. He was really attached to those two. Almost like a puppy or something, but they seemed to treat him okay, and I don't think he really had any other friends. None I ever saw, anyway. I'd guess he took what happened with Ecare pretty hard." He shrugged. "I don't know what he could be doing for work, but family's what keeps most people in the area and far as I know, his dad was all he had. With his dad gone, Moran out of state, and Ecare locked up until just recently, there was probably no reason for him to stick around town. But like I said, I didn't know him too well, so take all this with a big grain of salt."

"Sure."

"You really can't tell me what this is about? I mean, I get why you'd want to know about De Rosso after the other day. But why Chadwick? I assume it's tied in with Greg Moran, but that was suicide, wasn't it? Seemed pretty cut and dry from what I heard."

I shook my head. "Sorry. It's an ongoing investigation, that's all I can say for now."

"Well, you're the detective. Guess poking and prodding is what Skillman hired you for, huh?"

"Someone's gotta do it," I agreed.

It needed doing, all right, only I wasn't entirely sure it was what Skillman wanted.

•   •   •

Loenfeld didn't tell me much, but he added a few more details to the picture. A quick trip back to the station gave me a couple more. There was no file on Joseph Chadwick, meaning if he was ever in legal trouble, it hadn't been local, but I was able to find his address in the phonebook. Jeannie also had a message from Dr. Cushman for me, but all it said was he received mine about Chadwick and would get on it as soon as possible.

The Chadwick family home wasn't hard to find, but only because I knew where I was going. It was off the beaten path, to say the least. 114 took me west out of town, then I turned north onto a side-road, then east onto another offshoot that took me into the foothills. I realized I was actually only a little further north than the Pennemont Hills subdivision and that some of those lofty houses must look down onto the woods surrounding the less-impressive homes where the Chadwicks lived. There was simply no way to reach this area directly from the northern side of Granton unless you could fly.

The Chadwick house was a story and a half, weathered-gray box that seemed as if it was trying to lose itself in the woods that surrounded it. Its only admission that anyone lived there was a mailbox that stood by the road, stuffed almost to overflowing with mail. A brief glimpse showed a lot of bills and a note, taped to the inside of the box's front flap, from the postal-carrier saying further service was suspended until someone cleaned this mess up.

I tromped across the un-mowed lawn, the grass as high as my knees, to the house. My suspicions about the body in the woods being Chadwick grew firmer with each step. The front door was locked, but it took less than a minute to find the key hidden over the door behind a loose piece of wooden siding. Inside, the place smelled of disuse and dust, and the unmistakable odor of a mouse-infestation, but was fairly neat otherwise. There was no electricity when I tried the lights in the hallway, but I supposed it was shut off months ago, based on all the outstanding bills in the mailbox.

Off of the front hallway was a small den with a pair of easy chairs and a writing desk. Inside the desk was more mail, opened and better organized than the pile in the box outside. Almost all of it proved to be bills, as well as a bank statement showing a few thousand dollars in a checking account, under the joint names of Joseph Chadwick and Martin Chadwick, who I presumed to be the father. The rest of the room was taken up by shelves of books and a small, portable radio sitting on the window ledge. Dust covered everything, more than even an absence of several months could account for.

I put the documents back where I found them and walked through the rest of the house, taking in the sense of the place. A living room was furnished similarly to the den, save the addition of a couch and a television in place of the radio. The small kitchen was neat, but reeked of mouse urine. There were little piles of droppings on both the table and the counters. Upstairs, there were two bedrooms, but only one bed was made and from the thick covering of dust, it hadn't been slept in for a very long time.

From what I knew, Joey grew up here, just him and his father, and continued to live here after finishing school. Both Heath Moran and Loenfeld said he seemed slow, so maybe it made sense for him to remain here even after reaching adulthood. It must have been comfortable, knowing the same home his entire life. Comfortable, but lonely, especially after Martin Chadwick passed, leaving

Joey all alone in the world without even the friends he once relied on. It made a sad sort of sense for that sort of life to end with a solitary death in the woods, if you took it all at face value.

I was convinced that the body Moss and I found in the woods outside of town was Chadwick. Dr. Cushman's comparison of dental records would be the iron-clad confirmation I needed and I was pretty sure I would get it before too long. I already knew the how and I believed I finally had the who, now I just needed the why. From an outside perspective, Joey Chadwick might have good reasons for suicide, if there ever was such a thing, only I knew he hadn't just walked up into the woods and shot himself. Someone might have wanted it to look that way, but there were too many mistakes. The scenario just broke down too quickly once you started poking at it. Add to that the disturbing element of the gun, one that was supposed to be in police custody, and it took on another sinister layer. But why Joey Chadwick who, from what little I knew of him, was harmless?

Only I knew that, too, didn't I? It had to come down to Ecare. Joey Chadwick and Greg Moran, both dead, both deaths superficially resembling suicide, linked by their friendship with Nathan Ecare, the perpetrator of the greatest tragedy in Granton's living memory.

I walked through the house, thinking about the story Nathan Ecare told me, particularly the two friends he couldn't remember, and how they left him that night, badly injured and probably terrified, to hang for the crime all three participated in. It was too far-fetched that he couldn't remember who he was with when all the other details were etched so clearly in his mind.

What would be the point of lying about it, though?

When he was going through the legal process, he could have traded their names for some sort of reduced sentence. Ecare didn't strike me as the self-sacrificing sort.

Revenge? It was possible, but again, Ecare just didn't strike me as the type. Eight years ago, he was a thrill-seeking kid. Even now, after surviving years behind bars, he was more scared and aimless than anything else. Ecare waiting, biding his time, then getting retribution wasn't impossible, but I sensed the hand of someone more detached, and far more ruthless, at work.

I let out a sound of frustration as I exited the Chadwick house, locking the door behind me and replacing the key in its hidey-hole. I was excited to fill in some blanks, to get some answers, but the more I thought about it, the more questions I had.

I became aware of a dull ache behind my right temple. I took a deep breath, filling my lungs with the clean, sweet-smelling air. I grew used to the smells and the staleness of the Chadwick house after a few minutes, but I didn't notice just how bad it was until I was away from it again. It was affecting my mood and my thought process. Outside again, I began to feel better, and I told myself to cheer up. I quite likely cleared a major hurdle today. There was still plenty of work to do, but for now, I deserved a break.

30

At the station, I added some notes to my personal files on both the body in the woods and Greg Moran, detailing what I did that day, what I was told and what I discovered for myself, along with a few lines of inquiry I wanted to think more on. Afterwards, I did a little paperwork that I'd been ignoring for too long and checked out for the day. It was just past four o'clock.

The conversation with Loenfeld put a bug in my ear that had nothing to do with any of my investigations. It was days since I last saw Chloe or Roland, but off and on, I'd been thinking about what I said to Chloe that afternoon, standing in her kitchen, about how Roland needed someone other than just a mother in his life.

I hadn't really spent all that much time with either woman or boy, but already I felt a sort of protectiveness about both of them, particularly Roland. Maybe it was because Chloe showed so much strength in living her life the way she did, after what she went through, that made me feel like I didn't have to worry too much about her, but Roland was another story. It was clear as day that the boy was suffering and I wanted to help, if I could.

I found a small sporting goods store in town. The eager young clerk was only too happy to sell me what I was looking for; I got the feeling it had been a slow day for him. Out on the street, I saw a payphone at the corner and wondered if I should call the DeJonge home or simply show up. I knew Chloe might be angry if I showed up without warning. If I called first, though, she might tell me I couldn't visit at all. I decided the former was the safer bet. Better to beg forgiveness than ask permission.

Soon, I pulled the Taurus to a stop in front of Chloe and Roland's house. I saw the twitch of curtains across the street and allowed myself a smirk. I was driving my personal vehicle, but was still in uniform so I supposed Mrs. Robinson would have more fodder for the gossip mill. It didn't bother me at all.

I moved up the walkway, rang the doorbell. After a moment, there were muffled footsteps, then the door opened. Chloe's cool blue eyes looked out through the gap at me. For an instant, I thought I saw something like pleasant surprise in them. Her voice was controlled, however, when she said, "Mr. Campbell. What happened to your face?"

I almost forgot about the bruises and cuts De Rosso gave me. Only now, when Chloe DeJonge mentioned them, did they pulse with a dull ache. I brushed it off, though, saying, "Hi. Nothing to worry about, I'm fine." I changed gears. "I'm sorry to drop in like this." I gestured with the heavy, opaque plastic bag I carried. "But I have something I'd like to share with Roland, if that's okay."

Chloe regarded me for a moment, then turned slightly and called, "Roland, you have a guest."

"Me?" The boy's thin voice came from somewhere close by. Probably camped out in front of the television in the front room.

He appeared in the doorway and the look that lit up his face when he saw me was the kind that I imagine parents live for.

Lina, my ex-wife, and I never really talked much about having kids, though I suppose we both sort of figured we would get around to it eventually. By the time things started going badly for me in Albany, we were married for nearly six years and the topic hadn't come up in quite a while. Kids were a moot point then. Lina stuck by me for a time, but after months of hell, all she wanted from our marriage was out.

The happiness on Roland's face, though, made me deeply regret not having kids of my own, as early as possible. Maybe it was for the best, looking back on the path my life took, but I was still sorry that only now, when I was already past thirty and single again, was I able to see that expression of pure, childish joy.

"Hi, Luke!" the boy trilled. Unlike his mother, he made no comment on the condition of my face.

I smiled. "Hi, Roland." To his mother I asked, "Can Roland come outside and play?"

Chloe raised an eyebrow, then something tugged at the corner of her mouth. She turned away before I could see the smile that threatened to break out. "Roland, show Mr. Campbell the backyard."

Roland burst out of the doorway, already running towards the corner of the house. "C'mon, Luke!"

I followed at a more sedate pace, not trying to hide my own smile.

The yard was a small, fenced-in space of patchy grass, moss and in a few places, bare earth where nothing grew. On either side were yards that were more or less the same, save for a barbeque grill and tiny patio in the yard to the left and a small shed in the yard to the right. At the rear of the yard, just beyond the fence, a thin strip of woods separated this street from homes on the next street over. As it was early October, a good deal of the foliage had already turned and dropped, giving either side a fairly clear view of the neighboring homes through the woods.

"It's not much," Roland said, an apology in his voice, "but here it is."

"It's perfect." I opened the bag. Roland hadn't asked me why I came, hadn't asked his mother why she ordered us to the yard, but he watched me intently, wonder in his eyes. I drew from the bag first one baseball glove, kid-sized, then another for myself and, finally, a shining-white baseball.

The little boy's mouth hung open and he looked from the gloves and ball to me and back again. Finally he said, "Baseball... but I don't know how to play."

"Lucky for you," I told him, fitting my glove onto my hand, ignoring the pinch to my bruised knuckles, and flexing it back and forth rapidly, trying to get the stiffness out, "I'm a good teacher."

I helped Roland on with the glove, showed him how to manipulate it to catch and hold the ball and how to flex it back and forth to break in the leather. He was serious, almost solemn, as he listened and practiced manipulating the glove. As I talked, I did the same with my own and the heady smell of the tanned hide brought back pleasant childhood memories. I hoped Roland could look back on this day with the same happy nostalgia.

"Now, let's try a little catch, huh?"

Roland's brows knit. "I don't know..." He cast a look towards the house.

"It's easy. You remember how to skip stones?"

Roland nodded rapidly.

"You can do that, you can do this."

"Okay!" he said, nodding once more for emphasis.

The kid was a quick learner. Within ten minutes, he was comfortable throwing the ball to me and with the easy, underhanded lobs I gave him, he could catch the ball three times out of five. We weren't that far apart, maybe only twelve feet, but it was a start.

And once he started, Roland looked like he never wanted to stop. He was a little clumsy, but his excitement and happiness overwhelmed any such minor concerns. Even with the coolness of an October afternoon, beads of sweat dotted his brow and he was breathing a little more heavily than usual, redness coloring his pale cheeks, pulled back in a fixed smile. It was the joy of pure, physical exertion and the pleasure of learning new skills.

Throwing the ball, catching Roland's return throws, watching him grow surer and more confident with each pass, I was happier than I could remember being in years. I even felt what must have been something like fatherly pride. This was a kid with more potential than most and it would be a privilege to watch him grow and develop.

Once Roland got the hang of things, we settled into an easy rhythm of back and forth, back and forth. The soft slapping sound of the ball in our gloves, the chattering of afternoon birdsong, and the occasional passing car off in the distance formed pleasant background noise to our simple game. We didn't talk much at first, other than my giving Roland instructions or pointers and his asking me occasional questions, but now, we had a chance to chat.

"So what do you think, Roland?"

The boy beamed. "I never knew sports could be this fun."

"Well," I smiled back, "there's a reason so many people like them."

"I suppose."

"How's school going?"

Roland's smile dimmed. He held the ball for a moment longer than usual, considering his answer. Finally, he lobbed it back and said, "It's all right."

"Anybody been bothering you?"

Throw. Catch.

He shook his head. "Not much. The teachers watch the bigger boys better than they used to."

Throw. Catch.

"I'm glad to hear it."

We chatted a little more about school, what his class was learning, what Roland was reading recently. Then I asked, "How has your mom been?"

I threw the ball. Roland caught and held it. "She's good." His smile grew wide again, showing tiny, white teeth, gapped where he recently lost one of his canines. "We talk about you sometimes."

"Oh, yeah?"

The boy nodded and came closer. "I'm not supposed to say, but I think she likes you," he stage-whispered.

I grinned. "Well, I like the both of you a lot, too."

Roland's cheeks flushed with fresh pleasure.

The back door of the house opened. "Roland," Chloe called. "It's getting dark. Time to come inside."

I glanced at my watch. Somehow, it was already past five-thirty.

Roland looked from his mother, standing in the doorway, to me. "She's the boss," I told him.

He looked disappointed, but didn't argue. With unfamiliar effort and a look of longing, he pulled off the baseball glove and made to hand it to me. I put up my palm. "That's yours, Roland. The ball, too."

"Really?"

"Of course. I'll keep this one, though, for next time." I gestured with my still-gloved hand.

"Thanks, Luke!" he cried, his happiness returned.

"See you later, Luke!" Roland dashed to the door, waved frantically, then slipped inside the house under Chloe's watchful eye.

I approached the door, but stopped several steps from it. "Thanks for letting Roland play catch. I had fun."

"Not half so much as he did, I think." Her voice was soft, pitched only for my ears when she added, "Thank you, Mr. Campbell. You are very good to him. He's been very happy since we met you."

"It's not one-sided, Chloe. I enjoy spending time with Roland. And with you, if you'll let me."

Chloe favored me with a rare smile, and stepped back, opening the door wider. "I think that would be fine. I already counted on for you dinner. Please."

She gestured and I entered. When I arrived, she was wearing her waitress's uniform, but she'd changed while Roland and I were outside. Now she wore gray slacks and a loose-fitting, maroon blouse, her platinum hair pulled back and held in place with a length of white ribbon. She looked effortlessly lovely and younger than I knew she was.

I'd been forcing myself not to think about the fact that Chloe DeJonge was one of the people on the short-list for a series of brutal crimes in this sleepy little town. The idea of a beautiful woman, bent on revenge for the death of the man she loved, the father of her child, wandering the lonely spaces of the woods, practicing with a gun until she had the skill to make up for the power she lacked, the skill that would enable her to overpower Ecare and his cohorts… it might sound plausible in the abstract, but just then didn't seem possible. It was Hollywood gold, but not the stuff of reality.

I hadn't seen Ecare in some time, but he was still walking around free as far as I knew. Joey Chadwick was shot—if that body from the hills *was* Joey Chadwick, as I was convinced—but Greg Moran was hanged. Gun or no, nobody would cooperate so far as hanging themselves for someone else's vengeance and Chloe couldn't have the strength to drop a grown man from that makeshift gallows. No, she may have motive, but the opportunity and means for those crimes just didn't match up.

Police work means asking a lot of unpleasant questions, though, and I wanted to cross Chloe DeJonge off the list of suspects permanently. I needed to inspect Chloe's gun. Not an easy subject to broach.

"I have some steaks marinating," she said. "I'll put them on the broiler soon. Come in and relax, Mr. Campbell."

"I wish you'd call me Luke."

Chloe regarded me and for a moment, I thought she would refuse, but instead she said, "Very well, Luke."

We stood at the edge of the kitchen. On the nearby counter, the meat sat in a shallow glass pan, covered in a dark liquid.

"Is there anything I can do to help?" I asked.

"I don't think so, I'm—"

"Mom! Look! I knew I had it!" Roland cried, racing in from the living room, a book in hand, to collide with the woman just as she was turning towards the sound of his voice. The impact knocked Roland reeling backwards the way he came, the book flying from his fingers, as Chloe stumbled towards me. I caught her, my hands on her shoulders. She relaxed against me for just an instant, then jerked away as if she touched red-hot iron, panic flaring in her eyes. Color rushed into her cheeks and her hand flew to her face.

"It's okay."

"It's just…" She didn't finish the thought, instead turning to Roland, as if she just remembered her son. "Roland! Are you all right?"

The boy leaned against the wall near the entrance to the kitchen, watching the two of us. There was something on his face that I didn't recognize. "Sorry, mama. I know I'm not supposed to run in the house…" He hung his head.

Chloe looked sternly at him a moment, but said, "Never mind that. Wash up and set the table, please."

"But I wanted to show you this book about baseball players that—"

"Now, please, Roland."

"Yes, mama." The boy set the book down on a corner of the counter and moved to the sink to wash his hands.

"I think you might have a new obsession on your hands," I half-whispered to Chloe.

"Well, it's always something." She turned away. "I better get the broiler started."

I tried again to offer my help, but Chloe declined and sent me into the living room to wait while she prepared our meal. I took a seat on the edge of the old sofa, my eyes moving across the room. Small and cozy and comfortable, it was a mark of Chloe DeJonge's strength that she could make a home like this for herself and her child. I was very attracted to the woman, but more than that, I admired her. I knew that this was a woman no one would ever truly defeat.

Chloe came into the living room, an apron tied around her waist, making her look lovely and domestic in a way that sent pulses of pleasant weakness through my chest. "Mr. Cam— Luke, dinner is ready." I was glad; my mouth was watering from the smell of the meat.

I followed her back to the kitchen. We sat down. Chloe and Roland linked hands and bowed their heads. While his mother's eyes were closed, Roland's hand snaked across the table and found mine, adding me to their ritual. I gave his fingers a little squeeze. Eyes still closed, listening to his mother say grace in soft, liquid French, he smiled.

When they were through, Chloe served each of us a steak, charred black outside, pink and dripping inside, with baked potatoes, and mixed cauliflower and broccoli. As the three of us ate, Roland chattered away, as he did at our lakeside lunch, but this time about baseball, telling us every little thing he knew. I was right, this was going to turn into a new obsession. His mother and I exchanged amused glances, each of us responding to the boy when appropriate.

Halfway through the meal, Roland said, "You should play with us next time, mom. I bet you could throw the ball really good and hard and far."

"Oh?" she asked, amusement in her voice. "Why is that?"

"You're so good with that gun, you hardly ever miss the cans, you said. I bet throwing the ball is just the same."

Chloe DeJonge's fork halted mid-way to her mouth, a bit of cauliflower quivering at its tip. She calmly put the fork down and said, "Roland, no gun talk, please. It's uncouth."

"But, mama, you said so yourself—"

"You're a good shot?" I asked her, looking across the table. Though I hated to take advantage, this was my opening.

Composed again, Chloe met my gaze and said, "Yes. I am. I'm a single woman, living alone with a small boy. Sometimes, I work late at night or very early in the morning and I thought it would be a good idea to be able to protect myself and my son."

"Protect yourself, yeah." I hesitated just an instant then took the plunge. "You ever take it with you when you go on those walks in the woods that you mentioned, when we were out at the lake?"

"Sometimes," she said, spearing a bite of meat on the tines of her fork.

The image of a skull with a tiny hole in its head, staring blindly out at the lonesome woods, came to mind.

"I'd like to see it, if I could."

Roland hopped out of his chair. "I'll get it! I know where mama keeps it—"

"Roland!" Chloe cried, more forcefully than anything I ever heard her say before. "Sit down and eat your dinner. You know that you are never, *ever* to touch the gun."

Roland withered under the barrage. Chloe stared him down a moment longer then turned her gaze back to me, icy cool again. "Why do you want to see it, Mr. Campbell? It's nothing special, just a little target pistol."

Now I was Mr. Campbell again.

"Curiosity," I lied. "Roland's talked about it before, and I'm a bit of a gun buff myself." I wish I could have told her the truth: that I wanted to clear her of any suspicion, that she was the only person I knew of who had a motive to kill Nathan Ecare's two closest friends. I wanted to tell her that I was praying the gun she owned wasn't a Smith & Wesson 651.

"Maybe another time," she said, setting her fork down on the rim of her plate. "Have you had enough to eat?"

"Sure, thank you. You're a wonderful cook," I told her, accepting the rebuff for now.

"Thank you." There was no smile on her face and her tone was almost as neutral as when I first met her in Calloway's Diner. It was as if we were back to square one, except for the two men whose deaths now hung over our heads.

31

The night was long and lonely.

There was an awkwardness between Chloe DeJonge and myself after the gun exchange. Roland was too excited about his new passion to notice, but it hung heavily in the air, weighting each of the few words his mother and I spoke to each other. We finished dinner and, after helping clean up the dishes and promising Roland we would play ball again very soon, I took my leave. There were three middle-aged couples, who appeared to be a group, checking into the Red Garden when I walked through the lobby, keeping Wendy busy. I guessed Helen Reddy's long-awaited leaf-peeper season was beginning.

After a shower and a beer, I lay in bed, staring into the darkness. It was still early, not eight yet. I was tired from the day, tired from playing catch with Roland, which used muscles I didn't ordinarily, and wanted to relax, but I wasn't ready for sleep. Lonely bones and the misery in Edie Moran's eyes kept my mind churning.

I spent hours going over what I knew or could reasonably assume.

Eight years ago, Nathan Ecare, along with two friends, went to up to Quebec, intending to smuggle heroin back across the border, an operation Ecare successfully pulled off at least several times before. This time, for whatever reason, there were state troopers present at the checkpoint and he panicked, trying to elude them. In all likelihood, the troopers weren't even there for him, but I understood a scared kid's impulse to run. All too well, in fact.

In the course of his attempted escape, Ecare cracked up his car, colliding with Alan Butler's Volvo, killing the other boy and leaving his pregnant fiancée, Chloe DeJonge, on her own. Ecare's two friends abandoned him, choosing to save their own hides. Ecare didn't mention it, but presumably, those friends made off with the drugs, as well, since so far as I could tell, Ecare wasn't charged with any narcotics offenses. After dickering with the state's attorney's office, he was sentenced to seventy-five months in prison, instead of the upwards of fifteen years a charge of vehicular manslaughter could carry, not to mention the various other crimes he was guilty of, all stemming from his escape attempt.

Ecare claimed he couldn't remember who was with him in the car. That story was as suspect to me as it must have been to the cops and the prosecutors of eight years ago, but none of us were neurologists and there was no doubt that Ecare received a serious head-injury. Maybe it was possible. I'm sure Ecare's lawyers found an expert or two willing to swear that it was.

Regardless, that left the question of who was in the car with Nathan Ecare that night. Who shared his guilt?

Ecare's best friends were Greg Moran and Joey Chadwick. Marcus De Rosso was also one of his buddies. Ecare was a popular kid and was certain to have other friends, but everything I learned pointed to those three being the closest. I would bet my last dollar that two of those three were his missing cohorts.

Ecare knew his life better than I did. If he wasn't lying about the memory loss, he probably came to these same conclusions already. Chloe DeJonge had every reason for wanting revenge, but so did Nathan Ecare.

Except that didn't add up, either. Motive, yes, but opportunity?

Joey Chadwick disappeared. Even without confirmation of the body in the woods being Chadwick, that much was certain after visiting his home, and my instinct told me my John Doe was Joey. If Cushman's analysis was correct, however, and I had no reason to doubt him, that body was in the woods for a minimum of six months. Nathan Ecare was only released from prison in July. There was no way he could have been responsible. Add to that the disturbing detail Earl Cushman gave me, that the gun used to kill the man in the woods was supposed to be in the custody of the Granton PD. I looked for that gun. It was nowhere to be found and asking around the station about that specific gun would only tip my hand if someone here was responsible.

And then there was Greg Moran, dead in a way that suggested suicide, but wasn't quite right. Putting aside his parents' doubts, the mysterious movements of Moran's car bugged the hell out of me. Moran drives off in the car, then his father finds it a couple of hours later nearly home. And where was Greg Moran during that time? Was he already in the woods, just north of town? Was he maybe already dead by then? If not, how did he get from where the car was left to that makeshift gallows? I was sure he hadn't returned the car and then walked all the way out there.

There was also what he told his father, about having to say he was sorry to someone and knowing it was pointless. Under the circumstances, who else could that person have been but Ecare?

There was an unseen hand at work here. Nathan Ecare didn't come up with the heroin smuggling scheme on his own. I knew that with absolute certainty. He was working for someone and that person's influence might well still be in play. If I could find the thread that led to it, I could unravel this whole thing.

I stared into nothing, thoughts swirling, trying to fit pieces into a pattern that was becoming clearer but remained stubbornly just out of focus, like a faulty Polaroid photo that won't quite develop.

It all revolved around Nathan Ecare. There was no getting around that. It was the only thing about this mess that was plain. I needed to talk to Ecare again. He told me a lot already, but not everything. I had to make him spill whatever he was holding back. Maybe he really didn't know the whole picture, but I was certain he knew more than I did. He spent a lot more time living with this hanging over his head than I had. I had to believe he wanted it all to be over and done just as much as I did, if not more.

I let out a sigh as I rolled over. The red-glowing numerals on the bedside clock blinked as they flashed over to twelve o'clock. It was the beginning of another day in Granton.

•   •   •

There was a commotion at the station when I pulled into the parking lot a little less than eight hours later. An ambulance, sirens wailing, roared out of the lot an instant after I pulled the Taurus out of its way. Through the windshield, the young woman at the wheel looked grim-faced. Whatever happened must have been ugly.

Mason Domanski, Shane Stevens, and Lee Pohlman were clustered around the stairs down to the lower levels of the building. A broad-shouldered, slim-hipped man in the green slacks, khaki shirt, and campaign hat of a state trooper stood with them, pencil and notepad in hand.

"What's going on?" I asked.

The trooper turned at the sound of my voice. Domanski looked past the other man's shoulder, saying, "Here comes Campbell, our detective."

The trooper faced me. "Some trouble in your jail."

"What kind?" The words were bad enough, but I didn't like the ominous way he said it.

"De Rosso," Stevens put in. "He, uh—"

"Tried to off himself," Pohlman finished. Stevens threw the taller man a bleak look. Pohlman shrugged and said, "No point sugarcoating it."

The trooper extended a hand towards me and said, "Detective Campbell? Trooper Edwards." We shook. He continued, "Man you brought in the other day, Marcus De Rosso – looks like he tried to hang himself."

My brows furrowed and I shook my head in confusion. "How? That cell was practically bare."

"Let's not do this out here," Edwards parried. He gestured towards the stairwell. The five us tromped down into the building and reconvened in the jail. Stevens moved to sit down in his accustomed placed behind the desk, then hesitated and decided instead to remain standing.

Edwards cast a glance around the area, his gaze finally landing on the opened door of the cell Marcus De Rosso once occupied. There was no one else in any of the other cells, currently. The single open door gave it a deserted feeling that, combined with what happened here, lent it a sense of eeriness.

"Marcus De Rosso," Trooper Edwards said, "Hanged himself from the bars of his cell, using a strip of plastic cut from the binding of the cell's mattress. He looped it around the bars and around his neck. Officer Pohlman," he nodded towards Lee, then glanced down at the pad in his hand, "tells me he was on jail-duty overnight. Just after seven a.m., he went to relieve himself, ran into Officer Stevens," his eyes flicked towards Shane, "who was coming on duty shortly. The two of them chatted for several minutes before Pohlman went to use the facilities. Then Pohlman and Stevens came down here and found De Rosso unconscious, hanging by the throat in a sitting position up against the bars."

I had to ask. "Was he—?"

"Dead?" Edwards shook his head. "Stevens and Pohlman," he nodded towards the two of them, Stevens standing behind the desk, Pohlman leaning against the front, "radioed Officer Domanski, who called for medical assistance, then the two of them administered CPR for nearly fifteen minutes until EMTs arrived. The ambulance service's dispatcher called my barracks and I arrived about three minutes after the EMTs. De Rosso isn't dead, but my understanding is he's critical. Now we need to know how this happened."

Edwards was very businesslike about the whole thing. Some people might have been impressed by his efficiency, but I have a hard time with cops who forget that they're dealing with human beings. I didn't know the man, and maybe I wasn't seeing his best, maybe he wasn't always like this, but the detachment bothered me.

"I see. First question is how did he get the mattress apart? Those things are pretty damned sturdy. You'd need a blade of some sort. I assume nothing like that was found?"

Edwards shook his head. "No." He turned towards Stevens and Pohlman. "Any thoughts on that, gentlemen?"

Stevens and Pohlman shared a worried look. Pohlman shook his head. "No, sir. No clue. He was going out to Newport later today for processing on multiple charges." He shook his head again, more slowly. "I'm pretty sure there was a pocket knife in his belongings, but we didn't give him his stuff back, so…" He held up his hands. "I got no idea."

There was a tightness in my chest and something fluttered in my jaw. Chadwick, Moran, De Rosso. Two dead, a third at death's door. Ecare was the connection. Ecare and someone else, whose arm proved to have a very long reach. Ugly thoughts rampaged through my mind.

Edwards was about to say something, but I beat him to the punch. "Is the chief here yet?"

"Don't think so," Domanski drawled. "He'd come stompin' down those steps pretty quick if he were. Jesus, I hate to be the one to tell him about this."

Pohlman suddenly looked ill.

"Okay. Domanski, get upstairs and get back on the desk 'til Jeannie's in. We've still got a police force to run." I turned towards the state trooper. "Unless you need him for anything else?"

Edwards's head shook almost imperceptibly. "Not at the moment."

Domanski bristled visibly at my taking control, but he tamped it down. He shrugged. "Sure. Chief'll be in soon. Guess I'll have to give him the low-down."

"Please do. I'll want to speak to him as soon as," Edwards said. "You can leave the details to me, if you'd prefer." His head swiveled and he said, "Officers Stevens and Pohlman, I think we're done for the moment, too. You're free to go about your day, but please be available." Stevens sat down at the desk and

Pohlman, still looking a touch green, nodded, muttered something unintelligible and made for the doorway.

Edwards turned to me and gestured. I followed him out into the hallway. Pohlman had already disappeared, probably to the locker room to get ready to go home for the day. I didn't envy the dreams he was likely to have once he turned in.

Sotto voce Edwards said, "You look like you've got something you want to tell me, Campbell."

"De Rosso was a fighter, strong as hell, with a head like a boulder." I pointed at my face. "He damned near killed me. A doctor told me De Rosso is probably suicidal, after a fashion, but that he'd never do it himself."

"You've got ideas on that then."

I nodded. "I've got ideas."

Edwards grimaced just slightly. "That's too evasive for my liking. Spill it."

I almost smiled. Edwards was starting to seem a little more human now. I wasn't sure what changed, but it suited him better than the law-enforcement robot act.

"I will as soon as I know for sure," I told him. "There's a lot going on this town, and De Rosso's tied up in it. I don't know how he got the mattress apart, I don't know how it got around his neck, but I just don't think he tried to kill himself. This was a desperate act, but it wasn't De Rosso's."

"Whose, then?"

I shook my head. "I can't say. Not yet." I held up a hand. "Not because I won't, but because I really *can't*. I just don't know for sure yet."

"You said you've got ideas," Edwards pressed. "I'll gladly be a sounding board."

"I appreciate it, but frankly, I've been dealing with this since the moment I set foot in Granton and it would just take too long to explain it all right now. I promise, I'll keep you in the loop, though. I'm pretty sure I'll need some outside help before too long."

Edwards looked at me, long and hard. It was clear he didn't like what he was hearing, but what could he do? I hadn't been here during the attack on De Rosso, as I was thinking of it, and I told him I didn't know anything for certain. There was nothing to hold me for, even if he wanted to, and I had the feeling he was willing to at least give me a chance on this, out of professional courtesy if nothing else.

"All right, Campbell. I admit you're in a better position than I am." He reached into his shirt pocket and produced a business card. Handing it to me, he added, "Call me as soon as you know something solid. If I'm not at my desk, if I'm out on the road, I mean, have the barracks patch you through to my cruiser."

"I will. Thanks."

"I'm a pretty good judge of character, Campbell. I think this bothers you more than any of the rest of us. Hell, maybe more than De Rosso himself. That's why I'm giving you this chance. Just don't make me regret it."

"I won't," I promised, hoping I could keep my word.

32

I felt like I had almost all of it. The pattern was as clear as I could ever make it on my own. I needed help and not what Edwards could offer me. There was only one person on the entire planet who could provide me with what I needed. Maybe Marcus De Rosso could have, but he was in a coma, possibly dying. I had to find Nathan Ecare, and fast before he wound up a faux suicide, too.

I swung the cruiser out of the parking lot, headed down Crescent, took a right at the intersection with Main and a moment later turned south towards the lake road. It wasn't quite eight-thirty in the morning, but the town was awake, the traffic heavy with morning commuters. The closer I got to the lake, though, the thinner traffic became until it disappeared almost entirely. With the summer tourist season over, this part of the town was all but abandoned, aside from the occupants of Monroe's and a few scattered private homes.

I pulled into the gravel lot of the long, ramshackle motel less than ten minutes after leaving the station. Morning sunlight fought its way through the cluster of pines that surrounded the building, giving it a dappled effect that helped to hide the smallest fraction of its dilapidation, giving me an idea of what it might have looked like during its heyday. It took a lot of imagination to picture, but it must have once been someone's pride and joy.

I parked the cruiser at the far end of the lot, next to the cinderblock addition labeled "Office". The lights inside the office were off, but that was fine. I didn't want to scare anyone off, and the fewer who saw my arrival, the better. I was pretty sure that Ecare wasn't the only Monroe resident who had a history with law-enforcement. That's not prejudice speaking, just experience.

I recognized Ecare's truck, parked halfway down the building, just this side of the junker car that was nothing more than a receptacle for pine-needles. I walked down the cracked sidewalk and knocked on the door. My knuckles made a hollow, muted sound against the heavy, but weathered wood, as if its core was rotting. There was no answer and after a few moments, I was afraid that I was too late. I tried again, calling "Nathan Ecare!"

Motion in my peripheral vision caught my attention. I turned to see a door, two rooms down, pushed open a crack then slammed quickly shut again. Someone other than Ecare noted my arrival and didn't seem too thrilled with it.

"Ecare," I said again, louder this time, the side of my fist thumping against the door. "It's Luke Campbell. I need to speak with you. It's an emergency."

There was a sound close to the other side of the door, a muffled noise of someone moving stealthily. I glanced up and startled for a second at the eye staring at me through the door's peephole. I realized Ecare must have been at the door for at least a few moments, watching and listening.

"Ecare. Open up, please."

The door opened a fraction. Ecare's face, puffed with sleep, his eyes faintly bloodshot, peered out. "What the hell do you want? You know what time it is?"

"I need to talk to you, and I want the whole story this time." I put my shoulder against the door, shoving it open and forcing Ecare backwards into the room. He stumbled, but recovered quickly. I gave the room a quick once-over. I expected it to be as down at heels and dirty as the motel's exterior, but Ecare's room was surprisingly neat. Not clean, exactly, but there was no clutter, no piles of clothing or takeout boxes, no stacks of empty beer cans. There were a pair of single beds—one made, one tangled from use—a low-slung dresser, supporting a cracked mirror and a small television set, and a single thread-bare armchair. Directly across the room from the entrance was a narrow doorway leading into a bathroom. A second doorway, off to its left, must have been the closet.

I turned back to Ecare. He was dressed only in a pair of boxer shorts. His body was even thinner than I guessed when I first saw him. He was so scrawny and pale that it was hard to believe he was once a star athlete. I tried to imagine him young and carefree, smiling and happy. I couldn't. Right now, his face was a mask of seething fury, but that wasn't the only reason.

He got himself under control as I watched. He opened his mouth to say something. I cut him off. "Sit down. This'll be as long as you make it, but I'm going to get the answers I need."

"You can't do this," he said, but it was resigned. We both knew he couldn't make me leave. He flopped down onto the edge of the unmade bed and sighed. "What do you want from me?"

I stayed in the doorway, not wanting to crowd him any more than I already was. It was unfair of me to trap him, but I was out of options and Ecare was almost certainly out of time. Whether he knew it or not, I was sure he was in danger.

"Marcus De Rosso."

Ecare's right cheek crept upwards in an expression half sneer, half confusion. "What about him?"

"Someone tried to kill him this morning."

"What?" The defiance disappeared, leaving in its place nothing but bewilderment and maybe a little fear. He shook his head. "What's that got to do with me?"

"You know exactly what it has to do with you." I pulled the armchair out of the corner, turning it to face Ecare. I sat, putting myself on the other man's level. "You may not remember who was with you that night, but you've figured it out. I did and I've only been in this town about a month. You've lived here your whole life and you know both Granton and yourself a lot better than I do. You went away for a long time, but now you're back and all of your friends are dying. Joey Chadwick. Greg Moran. Both of them gone. Now Marcus De Rosso. It's just you left."

Ecare's head was tilted down, but his eyes swiveled up towards me. "Screw you." There was no animosity in the words. There didn't seem to be anything at all in them. Ecare was shutting down right before my eyes.

"Listen, I've been thinking about this a lot. I've got a pretty good idea what's going on, but as long as it's just in my head, there's not much I can do about it. Whether you believe it or not, you're in danger. I want to help you."

Ecare's expression twisted into another half-sneer.

I ignored it and continued. "Believe it or don't, but it's the truth. But you know how the law works well enough to know that I need *something* to go on, something I can stick this whole mess together with and make it come out right. I need your help, Nathan. *You've* got the key to this thing. I just need you to share it with me. There's nobody else who can."

Ecare's jaw set and he stared past me, but I knew he wasn't seeing anything in this room. For long moments, we were quiet. There was no noise but the sound of our breathing. There were no sounds outside of this tiny space to penetrate its walls. Either Ecare's neighbors weren't in or they were the silent types. It was still for so long that the room seemed to close in around us.

Mrs. Ecare told me she didn't understand why her son chose to live in Monroe's. I was sure she hadn't ever set foot in this place. If she had, I think she would have understood perfectly. Nathan Ecare spent over six years in a cell. He may have been free to come and go as he pleased, but this run-down room was just as much a prison. It must have felt far more like home than that huge, airy house on the hill. He served out the state's punishment, but he was still punishing himself.

"How…" he began, then faltered. He cleared his throat and said, a little louder, "Is Marcus dead?"

I shook my head. "No. He's in bad shape, but I think we got to him in time."

Ecare looked up and met my eyes for the first time since he opened the door. "Did he say anything?"

There were a dozen answers to that question that popped into my head. I needed Ecare's help. He was on the edge. The right answer would push him over and maybe I could finally put all the various partial answers together into something whole. But the wrong answer would slam the door on his mind and forever seal away the secrets he spent so long carrying around inside of himself.

"He told me to find you."

Ecare nodded then looked down at the filthy shag rug covering the floor. A tiny sound reached my ears and it took me a second to realize that he was crying, softly and nearly silently. I let him have the time he needed.

It was two or three minutes before he looked up again. He swiped at his eyes with the backs of his heads. "I wasn't lying. Back then or now. I really *don't* remember who was with me, but…" He cleared his throat, trying to compose himself. "What you said, about me figuring it out? Yeah… I did. A long time ago. I mean, I don't know for sure, but it makes sense. When I woke up in the hospital, after the cops told me what happened and what was going to happen next… I kinda… I was in shock, but it didn't last too long. I tried to remember then and I couldn't, but I spent weeks in a bed, handcuffed to the damned thing cuz I was under arrest, but they couldn't put me in jail, and I had nothing to do but think. After a while, I could have visitors, and my mom came, and my lawyer and a few of my dad's friends and—" He swallowed hard; for a second, I thought he'd cry again. "And Joey. You said… Joey's dead?" There was a note in his voice, telling me he hoped it wasn't true.

"For a while, yeah. I'm sorry." I still needed Cushman's confirmation, but there was no longer any doubt in my mind.

Ecare nodded, his head bouncing up and down as if that made perfect sense. He took a deep, sharp breath. "He was a good kid, but he wasn't cut out for much. I wish I coulda hung around with him a little more." He wiped the back of his hand across his eyes again. "Joey came to visit as much as they'd let him. He was there more than my mom or my lawyer, actually. But when they moved me out of the hospital to the prison over in Newport, while I was waiting on the trial, that was pretty much the end of it. The kid didn't drive and, well…" He shrugged. "But Joey was the only one. No Greg, no Marcus, none of the other guys. I got a letter from my hockey coach, Coach Giles, saying he was sorry I wouldn't be able to play at UVM, that he hoped I'd go pro one day." He barked bitter laughter. "As if that shit mattered."

He was rambling now. I let him go. The floodgates were open, like they were that night in Keith's. He told me more that night than he meant to, I was sure of it. Maybe now it would be the same. As long as he told me what I needed to hear, I didn't mind listening to the rest of it. I was sure he needed someone to listen.

Ecare told me a lot more. He went off on tangents, about the prison, about the corrections system, about his family – especially his mother, whom he seemed to both love and disdain. He gave me a rundown on the nine months he spent in Newport while his lawyer and the assistant state's attorney's office went back and forth. They wanted him to roll over on whoever he was running the drugs for; like I had, they realized immediately he wasn't in the drug business for himself.

"That was like asking me to cut my own fucking throat, you know?"

This is what I was waiting for. "Then, maybe. Now, it's the only thing that'll save your life."

It was the first thing I said in probably ten minutes. Ecare startled as if he forgot I was there. Maybe he had. He stared at me, as if I was some sort of specimen on a glass plate he was trying to identify. Then he shook his head slowly. "No… I can't. I mean…"

I wanted to grab his shoulders and shake some sense into him. I didn't. It would just shut him down. I had to make him understand I was trying to save his life.

"Maybe that was true all those years ago. Look at me." He hesitated, but did finally meet my gaze. "Nathan, you've lived under this for a long time. I get it. But you went through hell and you're still here. It can't be any worse and when it's all over, it'll finally be *over*. I'll do anything I can to make it as easy and safe for you as possible. I give you my word on that. I just want to see justice done. For Joey, for Greg Moran, for Marcus De Rosso. For you, for Alan Butler, for Chloe DeJonge and her little boy. I was there that day, at Calloway's, remember? That was the first time I ever set foot in Granton and I saw you screw up your courage and talk to Chloe. You wanted to apologize, right? That took a lot of guts. You've got it in you to do any god-damned thing you put your mind to. You just have to trust me on this."

Ecare bit his bottom lip and his eyes began to fill with tears again. In a tiny voice he said, "I felt s-so god-damned bad for that girl and for Alan and—" He choked back another sob. "I never wanted to hurt anybody. I didn't want to fucking *kill* anybody. I was just scared." He started to weep openly, big, fat tears rolling down his cheeks, dropping off his chin to land on his lap or the dirty carpet underfoot.

Somehow, I found the right words, the right pathway through all the defenses he built up for himself over the years since the night that changed literally everything about his life. Now, it was all broken down and he was naked and scared and alone. No longer the lean, prison-hardened man who killed someone else and paid the price, but the terrified, guilt-ridden boy he was so long ago – the boy he kept hidden and protected inside the shell of his experiences.

"I just wanted to have a little adventure, a little, you know, fun, and make some cash on the side." Ecare brushed aside tears. "You know, I was gonna tell him? After that night, I was going to tell him I was done. It wasn't really much fun anymore. The excitement wore off. I guess it was too easy or whatever. I just wanted to be done and go back to being a kid. All I wanted was a little excitement and he made me a murderer. I mean, I guess it was my own fault, but it never would have happened if he hadn't asked me to begin with and I, I—"

He started to cry again, huge wracking sobs that shook his entire body. I wanted to hug him, to comfort him, to protect him. He did a terrible thing, it was true, but he served his time and he was punishing himself more than the state ever could. Everyone in this town seemed to hate Nathan Ecare for what happened, but nobody could hate him as much as he hated himself.

And I hated to keep pushing him, but it needed to be done.

I moved from the chair and squatted on my heels, putting myself in Ecare's space. "Who, Nathan? Who got you into this? Who have you been protecting?"

He met my gaze. There was pain and fear and guilt and something else in his eyes. Despite everything he went through over the last few years of his young life and everything he let loose in the last half an hour, it looked a little like hope.

And when he opened his mouth again, I finally had what I needed.

33

Jeannie Brown was seated behind her desk when I entered the station. She looked up from her typing and smiled sadly at me. The tragedy in the lower floor of the building seemed to have cast a shadow over her normal good cheer. Or maybe it was just the culmination of all the sorrow Granton experienced over the last few weeks. "Good morning, Luke."

"Morning, Jeannie. Is the chief in his office?" It was almost ten o'clock. Despite Aaron Skillman's strangeness, he had a certain set of patterns that he didn't deviate from if he could help it at all. If he wasn't in his office, I didn't know where he could be.

"He should be. He was already here when I got in. You heard what happened this morning, Luke?" Jeannie seemed to want to talk about De Rosso. I did, too, but not with her.

"Yes, I've already been in once this morning, Jeannie. I'm sorry. I'm hip-deep in something now." I lifted the wooden divider and stepped through. "We'll talk later." She nodded and went back to her work.

There was no light on in Skillman's office. I knocked on the door, anyway. A moment passed before he answered. "Come."

I opened the door, slipped inside. The chief was hunched over his desk, staring at its scarred surface. There were the usual scattering of papers, but he seemed not to be looking at anything in particular. The customary unlit cigarette was missing from the corner of his mouth. The blinds were drawn, covering the big window, as usual, but there were no lights on. Enough light forced its way through the Venetian blinds to see and navigate by, but the room was gloomy. Gloomier than the lack of light could account for by itself.

"Chief," I said.

Skillman looked up. Even in the low light, he seemed paler than usual, his skin looser, his eyes dimmer. He looked ill enough to be in a hospital. I hadn't seen him in a couple of days, and the change was disturbing. "Yes, Luke? You need something?"

His voice was barely above a murmur. I thought that I didn't like Aaron Skillman, that I had no positive feelings towards this weird, mercurial old man who ran the police force like his own personal fiefdom, telling no one the rules he wanted us to follow until we broke one of them, and then changing his mind at the drop of a hat. Looking at him now, though, I felt a surge of pity well up inside of me. Aaron Skillman was not a well man. That much was plainly obvious.

"I came to tell you that I've solved the murder of that body in the woods."

Skillman smiled so faintly it might have been my imagination. "Is that right?"

"Yes, sir. Also the murder of Greg Moran and the attempted murder of Marcus De Rosso."

Skillman stared at me and as he did, some semblance of the life and intelligence I knew lay within him flickered across his face. He jutted a chin towards his visitor's chair. "Sit down. Tell me about it."

I pulled out the chair. I sat.

Neither of us spoke for a long minute. "Well?" Skillman finally asked.

"You want to me to start from the beginning or jump straight to the point?"

Skillman shook his head slowly, that faint little smile growing just a bit wider. "How about this: who's your suspect, detective?"

"You."

The smile disappeared. Skillman tried to pin me in place with that stare of his, but the power it once held was gone. "That's quite a claim. Can you prove it?"

"At this very moment? To the satisfaction of a jury? No." I shook my head. "I could prove it, if you force me to, but it would be a long process and you've already done a good job of getting rid of most of the witnesses against you. But you don't really want me to prove a case, do you? That's never what you were after when you hired me."

Skillman pushed back from his desk a little and settled deeper into his chair. It was an illusion, though; I knew he was sinker deeper into himself. "Really? Well, why don't you tell me about this remarkable theory of yours then, detective?"

"You've been chief of police in Granton for, what? More than twenty-five years."

"Almost twenty-seven," Skillman supplied.

"And in that time, you've kept this place as clean as any town could hope to be. There're gang problems starting to pop up in little bubbles across the state, seed groups started by major gangs in New York, Massachusetts, Quebec, using Vermont as a corridor to run drugs to and from the border. Along the way, drug use is running rampant, especially close up to the border, where it's so easy to get it in and out. And yet Granton, so close to Canada that teenagers can come and go as freely as going to the mall in a bigger town, hasn't suffered any of the problems that many other nearby towns have. Why? Because you're the major supplier in the area."

"Am I?" Skillman's voice was flat, completely neutral.

"Yes. I don't know how you first got into it, but I know why: you saw what was going on, probably sometime back in the early eighties, and decided you couldn't stop it, but you could control it. People were going to get the stuff one way or another, but you could steer it away from Granton itself, and make sure that the people around here who got it were well-vetted, under the thumb of the local law if they got out of hand. They didn't know it was you, but they knew someone powerful was behind it and so they kept their noses relatively clean. Figuratively speaking, of course."

"Go on," Skillman said.

I shifted, a little uncomfortable at the way the chief remained so calm. I had him. I knew I had him and he knew it, too. I figured a lot of this out on my drive back to the station, but once Nathan Ecare gave me Skillman, naming the chief as the one who put him up to his amateur drug-running, it all seemed to fit. That Skillman didn't deny it didn't bother me. No, it was that he remained so eerily calm. It wasn't the calm of resignation, of a man caught who knew there was no way out. It was the calm of a man who felt nothing could touch him, that it didn't matter who knew his crimes.

He was still staring at me. I cleared my throat. I went on. "So Granton went on pretty much the way it probably has for decades, relatively untouched by modern problems. Until Nathan Ecare's last run for you. I don't know why you chose him as your transporter, it doesn't matter, but he made a mess of that final trip, accidentally killing the Butler kid, drawing attention to himself – and worse, maybe to you. Plus, of course, your merchandise disappeared. That probably pissed you off, I bet. You knew Ecare didn't go up alone, and yet he was the only one at the scene. Whoever was with him disappeared, along with the heroin.

"Ecare was pretty badly injured. In a coma for a while, I understand. And when he came out of it, he claimed he didn't remember a lot of the details of what happened. Somehow, through luck or maybe your influence, nothing ever came out about the drugs. I guess you could have chalked it up to cost of business and written it off, except someone stole from you and that couldn't be left to stand. Ecare is terrified of you, he wouldn't have told anyone who he was bringing in the drugs for, but that didn't mean nobody could figure it out. You had to make an example of whoever it was.

"I don't know why you waited so long. I don't know what kind of cop you really are, but I feel like you could have figured it out somewhere along the way in the last eight-plus years. One way or another, though, you started with Joey Chadwick. Maybe he told you what you needed to know, maybe not, but you couldn't do much until Ecare got back to town. And then Greg Moran came back, too, by coincidence. Not much else it could be. He was pretty eager to get out of Granton from what his folks told me. He probably only came back because he figured it was safe, because he thought if there were no repercussions after so long, there never would be. How am I doing?"

Skillman's eyes darkened. I got the feeling he was picturing it all his mind, reliving it, maybe going over each step of the last few years, trying to figure out the mistakes he made, trying to decide what he could have done differently. Or maybe that was all in my imagination.

He didn't say anything, so I continued.

"Greg Moran was there that night, in that car. We both know that now, though maybe you didn't until just recently. And Moran felt guilty. He told his father as much. He also told Heath Moran that he was going to apologize to Nathan Ecare. Not in so many words, but it was pretty clear once you know more about the situation. So, you killed him, trying to make it look like a suicide, the same way you tried to make Joey Chadwick's death look like one. You did a better job with Moran than with Chadwick, by the way. Come to that, I'm still not sure why you drew my attention to Chadwick's body. Another couple of years and that body probably would have wasted away to virtually nothing, and you'd be safe and sound on that front. Using a gun that should have been safely locked up in the evidence locker in the basement was foolish. Or maybe that was part of your plan?"

I gave him a chance to answer, but he didn't accommodate me. I went on. "Well, maybe if I never saw Chadwick's body, never been alerted by that too-obvious set-up, I might have accepted Greg Moran's 'suicide' at face-value. Some details of Moran's death didn't add up, but enough fit that if I wasn't looking for the out of the ordinary, it might have passed muster."

Still, Skillman said nothing. His eyes were focused on me, but they were deep and empty. I had no idea what he was thinking.

"And that brings me to Marcus De Rosso. Did you hope he'd kill me when you sent me out to Ozzy's place alone?"

At last, I got a reaction from Skillman. "I hired you to help keep the peace in this town, Luke. If you couldn't, it was best I find out. No, I didn't want you to die, but if you couldn't handle a drunken roughneck, I wanted to know. If it soothes your annoyance at all, you're the only man I've ever heard of who took Marcus De Rosso by himself."

"That's something, I suppose."

We stared at each other. Gears churned in Aaron Skillman's head. I could see him calculating, planning. That I pulled him out of his shell told me I was getting to him – or walking into whatever he had planned for me.

"Well," I began again. "You had Moran out of the way and I had De Rosso locked up. You must have known getting rid of him while he was in custody was irrational, that it would lead right to you, but I suppose you felt you didn't have any more chances. Once he was locked away, as Ecare had been, he'd be out of your reach for a while. You waited long enough already, you couldn't wait anymore. Maybe you wanted to be caught, I don't know, but you handled all of this about as badly as I can imagine. Tell me the god's honest truth, chief: did you want me to catch you? Is that why you hired me?"

Aaron Skillman stood, once more unfolding like a narrow shadow from an old horror movie. I stood myself and backed up, putting space between us. Skillman smirked. "Scared of the old man, huh?"

"Just wary," I countered.

Skillman nodded. "Good." He gestured to himself, holding his hands flat and brushing them down his front without actually touching his body. "What do you see, Luke?" He didn't wait for me to answer. "A sick, old man. Been fighting the cancer off and on for a couple years but now, I'm dying."

When I first met Aaron Skillman, I had the impression of a long illness from which he only recently recovered. The way his skin hung from his huge frame, the deep set of his eyes that held intelligence and cunning, but also untold weariness. I was half right, at least.

Skillman sat back down and gestured for me to do the same. "God-damned cigarettes. I grew up, you hardly ever saw anyone without one in their mouth unless they were eating or sleeping. And they knew, guess we all knew, really, what it led to, but you never think it's gonna be you."

He sighed. "You got a lot of it right, Luke. I hired you to catch me. I want to set you straight, though: I never did a damned thing for myself. All of this, the narcotics, and the rest, was for the sake of this town. You were right on the money when you said I thought I could control it. And for a long time, I did. It worked pretty damned well. I've been a cop for forty-one years, since nine days after I got home from Korea, and I've learned a whole hell of a lot about people and how they work. You got to get in front of them sometimes and steer them in the right direction. As police, we're supposed to pick up the pieces afterwards and hope that's good enough, but god damn it, we both know it isn't."

Skillman took a deep breath and his eyes took on that look again, the one that I knew meant he wasn't seeing me anymore. But he kept talking. "Ecare wanted some action, some excitement. His father was a good friend of mine and sometimes a business partner. He ran herd on the local dealers who worked for me. Nathan doesn't know that and I don't expect it to leave this room. It won't do anybody any good to know it now and it'd just make him think less of a man who was a pretty good fella.

"At any rate, when I heard it kicked around town that Ecare wanted to sow a little wild oats, I felt like I could steer him the same way I was steering this whole thing. It worked for a while. Instead of using the stuff, as he might have, he was hauling it and making a little money. It was a bad decision. A moment of insanity on my part. That's why I never went after Nathan himself. His friends were another matter, though."

He came back to himself and the look in his eye when it met mine was chilling.

"Luke, it took me a long time to find out who all was involved. Joey Chadwick gave me the pieces I finally needed. And I want you to know…" Something else came into Skillman's face and he broke eye contact. "I never set out to kill that boy. Joey never hurt a soul, but he was hurting himself. Somehow, some way, that poor dim kid blamed himself for what happened to his friends. He wasn't there that night, I got that out of him, but he felt like he should have been. Thought if he was, none of it would have happened, and his friend Nate would still be walking around free. The pain and sorrow in that boy, the fact he didn't have a damned soul in the world to share it with, broke my heart. But when he started squawking, when I realized that with what he knew anybody, even a poor fool like Joey, could put two and two together and come up with four, I decided I had no real choice. I put a bullet between his eyes, sure, but it was as much about relieving that kid of his misery as anything else." He shook his head. "They shoot horses, Luke. They shoot horses."

I didn't respond to that. Whether Skillman believed what he said or not, he admitted a murder to me. His reasons didn't matter one damned bit.

"Did Chadwick tell you Greg Moran and Marcus De Rosso were the ones with Ecare?"

Skillman nodded. "More or less. He knew about Moran for sure. De Rosso was a guess of mine. Moran coming back to town was coincidence, like you said, but I still ended up having to wait a while. I confronted De Rosso, told him I'd square it if he helped me fix Moran. He didn't like the idea, but..." He shrugged.

"De Rosso was the guiltiest one, wasn't he? That's what made him change so much. I've heard he was a nice kid."

"That's true," Skillman admitted. "I think that, and fear of prison, is the only reason he helped me."

"Helped you?" I prompted.

Skillman chuckled. "You think an old man, dying of cancer, could get that boy up onto that tree?"

"I guess not."

Skillman said, "De Rosso was the one who took the drugs. Used 'em, sold 'em, flushed 'em down the john. I don't know, don't care, never asked. But he took them from the car and between that and what happened to Ecare and to Alan Butler, it twisted him. He was plain mean by the time the change was done, and getting him to meet Moran and help me fix up the 'suicide' was easier than it should have been." Skillman inhaled deeply through his nose. "Something's wrong with all of us."

"Yeah." It was an understatement. We both knew it. It deserved no commentary. "And what about today?"

Skillman looked up, regret plain in his face now. "Since that night, De Rosso never could resist a drink. Suppose it never occurred to him there'd be anything but liquor in the cup. Once he was passed out, it was simple enough to string him up the way the fellas found him."

"You know, for a while there, you made it seem like Chloe DeJonge was behind all of this. She's the only one who has an obvious reason for hating Ecare and his buddies."

"Sure," Skillman said. "I can see how you'd think that, but it was never my intention to steer you that way, and if you got too far along that path, I would have stopped you. I was never out to hurt anyone." The irony of that statement, after he admitted killing two people and trying to kill a third, was apparently lost on him.

I stood. "I suppose the only thing left then is why. I half-understand your wanting to control the drug trade, but the rest? And why put me onto your own trail?" I was very bothered and I didn't care if Skillman saw. Skillman put so much pressure on me to solve the mystery of that lonesome body in the woods, knowing all the time it was his own handiwork.

Aaron Skillman smiled and there was something like affection in it. It disturbed me more than I can say. "This town needs you, Luke. No matter what happens, I'll be gone before too long, but Granton still needs someone who'll keep it going, keep it a safe and happy place to live. Maybe you don't agree with my methods, but I don't think you can disagree with my results. Until just a few weeks ago, with a few exceptions, this was about the best damned place in the world as far as I'm concerned. And a lot of other people would agree, I'll bet."

The chief shook his head and leaned back in his chair. "The boys I've got, they're good, run of the mill cops, most of them. Good men who do their jobs – but they don't have it in them. Domanski could maybe be a decent chief, but I think it'd burn him out. He doesn't have the problem-solving skills you need and it would frustrate him. The rest?" He threw up his hands. "You need brains, and compassion, both for the victims and the guilty. Nobody's all bad, Luke, and I think you see that more than anyone."

"So this was all…" I was aghast, amazed, stunned. "This was all some sort of elaborate *job interview*?"

"Call it that, if you like. I'm just tying up loose ends."

I shook my head, my mouth open in disbelief. "Even if that was so, you can't guarantee I'd replace you as chief of the department. The town council will make that decision, I imagine. And even if they chose me, what if I don't want the job?"

"Do you?" Skillman asked.

"I don't know."

"At least you're honest, Luke. I saw that when we first spoke, and I had a feeling in my gut when I read about you last year. You'll make a good chief."

"You've been planning this for that long?"

Skillman shrugged. "Here and there, bits and pieces, maybe." He looked at me, very seriously, almost solemnly. "So, what do you want to do now, Detective Campbell?"

"I don't really have a choice, do I?" I loosened the holster of my gun with one hand and pulled the handcuffs from my harness with the other. "Aaron Skillman, you're under arrest for the murders of Joseph Chadwick and Greg Moran and the attempted murder of Marcus De Rosso."

Skillman smiled broadly, for the first time since I knew him. "Good man, Luke. You take care of this town for me, will you? And especially Chloe DeJonge. She and that boy of hers need you, probably more than anyone else ever has."

The chief reached into the top drawer of his desk, drew something out. It was a small revolver. It looked like a Smith & Wesson 651.

Adrenaline shot into my veins, my heart skipped a beat. I drew my own gun from the holster and leveled it at the chief. "Put it down."

Skillman just smiled all the broader. "You'll find my confession in the bottom drawer, detective. Murders, drugs, names, places and all that. "

Then he lifted the little pistol, put it to his head, and fired.

EPILOGUE

I knocked on the door to the DeJonge house.

Chloe's face appeared around the edge of the curtain in the big picture window for a moment, just long enough for me to register the confusion and surprise on her face.

It was well after six in the evening and it was almost completely dark. A chill wind was blowing, carrying with it the promise of an autumn storm, one that would drench the town and maybe tear some more of Helen Reddy's precious foliage from the trees. I hoped her guests were able to get a good look at them today.

The scene at the Granton police station, throughout the entire town office building, in fact, was utter chaos for hours. I stood stunned, completely unable to move, after seeing Aaron Skillman end his own life, until Chad Moss, Mason Domanski, and Jeannie Brown came crashing into the office a minute after it happened. I remember a cacophony of screams and questions and crying. I think the crying was as much mine as Jeannie's. Death was no stranger to me. I once even killed with my own hand, but I was never before as truly close to it as I was in that office. Maybe that was Skillman's final lesson to me. Maybe it was just his own selfish way of avoiding the otherwise inevitable pain of illness and the price of his actions.

I don't know how it happened, but I found myself sitting in my own office with the phone in my hand. I called Trooper Edwards. He was at his desk. I tried to tell him what happened, but got only some of it out before he told me to stay exactly where I was, he would be in Granton as soon as humanly possible.

After he arrived, it was hour after hour of questions and answers and telling my story over and over and over again. Somewhere along the line, Earl Cushman showed up, though there really wasn't any need for a medical examiner. There was no doubt as to how Aaron Skillman died. After Cushman gave the body a cursory examination, he took a moment to tell me that I was correct, our John Doe was Joey Chadwick. I didn't need outside confirmation anymore, but I thanked him, anyway.

When everything was finally settled, as much as it could be for the time being, I left the station. I felt shakier and most disturbed than I had since the night in Albany when I shot a teenager who tried to crush my skull with a piece of brick while struggling with withdrawal and his own inner demons. Maybe I should have gone back to the Red Garden and straight to bed, but I couldn't imagine going home to an empty hotel room. There was only one place on Earth I wanted to be.

Chloe opened the door. She was wearing ratty denims and a man's button-up shirt that looked like it saw more than its fair share of use. I wondered if it belonged to Alan Butler. I don't know what she saw when she looked at me, but whatever it was must have disturbed something deep inside of her, unlocked something she kept hidden and stashed away for a very long time. The expression on her face was open and honest. It was concern for me.

"Luke! What's wrong? What's happened?"

I took her in my arms, surprising myself as much as I did her. But she didn't resist and when I tried to kiss her, she let me. Maybe she knew how much I needed the contact, the affirmation of life. Maybe she needed it just as much. She was stiff for a moment, but then she relaxed against me, and finally kissed me back and wrapped her arms around my neck.

I don't know how long the moment lasted, but I know what brought us out of it. "Ooooh!" came the thin, boyish voice. It was a jeer, but a good-natured one.

I turned, keeping my arms tightly wrapped around Chloe. Pressed against my body, she was warm and soft and everything I imagined the moment I first saw her. It seemed inconceivable that she could ever have been anything else.

Roland stood in the hallway leading to the kitchen, his face bright red, but plastered with a huge grin. "I knew you liked Luke, mama!"

A flush of pink stained Chloe's cheeks, too, and her body grew warmer. She tried to disengage herself from me. I let her squirm a little, then released her. "Luke! Have your lost your mind?" she asked.

"No. I've come to my senses. Chloe, I don't care how long it takes to make you believe it, but I love you and I love Roland and it took something awful to make me realize just how much I do. Maybe we haven't known each other all that long, but now that I know just how much you mean to me, I can't imagine spending my life with anyone but the two of you. Will you please give me a chance to show you how much you both mean to me?"

Chloe was flustered almost to panic, caught between indecision and change, between the pattern of life that she knew she could make work and the possibility of something else that might be better or might simply lead nowhere at all.

But she never got the chance to make that decision. It was Roland who took charge.

He came up between us, grasped each of our hands, bringing all three of us together and said, "Mama, you don't have to hide it anymore. If you like someone, you just have to tell them. It's a lot better once you do." He turned to me, gap-toothed smile lighting up his face. "Right, Luke?"

There were tears in my eyes for the second time that day, but for an entirely different reason. After all the scheming and misery I encountered in my life, Roland's innocence and honesty were tonic for the soul. "Right, Roland."

Chloe looked at each of us, then down at our joined hands, then back to me. She smiled, and it was like nothing I ever saw before. There was still a little trepidation there, but no longer any coldness or aloofness, only warmth and hope. "Dinner will be in a little while, Luke. Can you and Roland please set the table?"

"Nothing would make me happier."

They were the truest words I've ever said.

END

About the Author

Brandon Barrows is the award-nominated author of the novels *This Rough Old World* and *Burn Me Out* as well as over fifty published stories, selected of which have been collected into the books *THE ALTAR IN THE HILLS* and *THE CASTLE-TOWN TRAGEDY*. He is also the writer of nearly one-hundred individual comic book issues. He is an active member of the Private Eye Writers of America and the International Thriller Writers.

Note from the Author

Word-of-mouth is crucial for any author to succeed. If you enjoyed *Strangers' Kingdom*, please leave a review online—anywhere you are able. Even if it's just a sentence or two. It would make all the difference and would be very much appreciated.

Thanks!
Brandon Barrows

Thank you so much for reading one of **Brandon Barrows'** novels. If you enjoyed the experience, please check out our recommended title for your next great read!

Burn Me Out by Brandon Barrows

"Hard-edged and pulsing with life... pulls you in and nails you. An excellent read." **–Rusty Barnes, author of the** *Killer from the Hills* series